At the Sharpe End

At the Sharpe End

Hugh Ashton

ISBN-10: 1-91-260559-7
ISBN-13: 978-1-912605-59-0

j-views (expanded) Edition, 2018

www.AtTheSharpeEnd.com

j-views Publishing, 26 Lombard St, Lichfield, UK WS13 6DR
publish@ j-views.biz
http://www.j-views.biz
https://HughAshtonBooks.com

Book design and cover by j-views
Set in Warnock Pro 11pt, headings and titles in Skia

"*An intriguing trawl through the murky interface* where industrial espionage, high finance and plain criminality meet in the Far East, with global implications—a Sharpe twist on the genre." Ann Tierney, Managing Editor, Searching Finance (London)

"*Ashton did an amazing job* of making characters who should have been unlikable likable and then throwing them back into the despicable category. He manages to do this with multiple characters and he did so with real skill."

"*As an American who has spent time in Tokyo*, I am particularly intrigued by Ashton's depiction of ex-pats' life in Tokyo. The unromantic detail brings realism to the story, which deepens the reader's involvement in the story. The characters in the novel become familiar, and stay with the reader long after finishing the book. At The Sharpe End *is definitely in the "page-turner" category of novels. This is a book that readers will find difficult to put down, and they will feel satisfied at the end."* B. K. Thomas (USA)

"*First, Ashton knows Tokyo, knows the Japanese* (he's married to one), knows his way around in the financial world, and knows computer systems. ... Second, the main characters are well drawn and believable .... Third, and this is important, the secondary characters, both good and bad, the ones who supply the mystery and thrills (this is a thriller, after all) are so good that you hope to meet them in a sequel—the high-tech genius, his evil wife, her shady father, the Japanese cops and agents, and of course the British intelligence agents, who are becoming a welcome Ashton trademark. And finally, the book comes to a rousing, satisfactory conclusion."

"*The interests and challenges in this story* make me feel like I've been living in it for four days. I love it."

HUGH ASHTON WAS BORN IN THE UK IN 1956. After graduating from the University of Cambridge, he worked in a variety of jobs, including security guard, publisher's assistant, and running an independent record label, before coming to rest in the field of information technology.

A long-standing interest in Japan led him to emigrate to that country in 1988, where remained until 2016; writing instruction manuals for a variety of consumer products, assisting with IT-related projects at banks and financial institutions, and researching and writing industry reports on the Japanese and Asian financial industries. Some of the knowledge he gained in these fields forms the background for *At the Sharpe End*.

He is the author of many volumes of Sherlock Holmes short stories and two Sherlock Holmes novellas, which gained approval from the Conan Doyle Estate Ltd., as well as a book of short stories about the senior generation in Japan (*Tales of Old Japanese*), alternative historical novels and historical science fiction.

Hugh currently lives with his wife Yoshiko in the UK Midlands cathedral city of Lichfield, where he is working on future novels and stories.

Dedication

To the people of Japan, who were my hosts for over a quarter of a century, and who have displayed almost unbelievable courage and determination in the face of the most devastating natural disasters.

Foreword by Robert Whiting

ROBERT WHITING is a Tokyo resident, and the author of the bestselling *Tokyo Underworld: The Fast Times and Hard Life of an American Gangster in Japan*

THE PLOT OF THIS entertaining novel involves, among other things, North Korean yakuza in Japan, a subject with which I am familiar, and one that has a long colourful history dating all the way back to the post-war occupation of Japan when they first began dealing narcotics for the Pyongyang government .

The North Korean yakuza had their origins in the more than 2 million Koreans found themselves in Japan at the end of World War II, almost all of them having migrated during the years 1910-1945, when Korea was a colony of Japan, with many of them brought in as forced labour. With the Allied victory, the majority of these immigrants repatriated back to their homes in the South. But an estimated 650,000, either unable or unwilling to leave, remained where they were, granted special status by Occupation authorities, which gave them immunity from arrest and prosecution by Japanese law enforcement authorities. With Tokyo and other urban centres having been reduced to ashes by Allied bombing, many young Korean men turned to the underworld to survive. They formed gangs, ran gambling dens and protection rackets, and put their girl friends to work in bars and nightclubs that catered to the American GIs, giving them access to PX goods which they sold on Japan's burgeoning black markets, the only real economy in the country. However, they found themselves fighting constant battles over turf with pure-blooded Japanese gangs who resented the interlopers' incursion into their traditionally held territory.

Their struggle to survive became ever more difficult in 1948, when the northern and southern parts of the Korean Peninsula declared independence, putting an end to the old political entity of Chosun, as the undivided peninsula had been known as a province under Japanese rule. The south adopted the name The Republic of Korea and allied itself with the United States, while the north called itself the Democratic People's Republic of Korea and allied itself with its Communist neighbours China and Russia. Since over half the Koreans remaining in Japan had relatives in the North, they were naturally sympathetic to the DPRK, which put them at odds with fellow Korean migrants who had relatives in the South. Political conflict erupted, with both groups staging violent protests, and Korean yakuza gangs found themselves caught up in the battle and pitted against each other along party lines, so to speak.

Among the more active gang leaders was pro-ROK Machii Hisayuuki, leader of the powerful Tokyo-based ethnic Korean Tosei-kai. Machii, born in Seoul and raised in Tokyo, was strongly anti-Communist and worked with American intelligence agents from GHQ to suppress leftist strikes and eliminate the Communist North Korean operatives in Japan who had organized them.

At the same time, yakuza with North Korean ties, high-ranking members of the Kobe-based Yamaguchi-gumi among them, began the import and sale of heroin manufactured by DPRK generals in a Pyongyang factory. The heroin, 99% pure, and refined from raw opium grown in domestic poppy fields, was produced under the brand name of "Red Lion." North Korean fishing boats would transport the drugs, packed in aluminium tubes weighing one kilogram each, to coastal Japanese waters, where, in the dead of night, they were off-loaded to waiting yakuza vessels. Pyongyang's goal was two-fold: first to earn money to fund the operations of the Communist party in Japan and, second, to turn all the American GIs in the Occupation forces into heroin addicts so that they would be unable to fight alongside South Korean forces in the coming war with the North (which would erupt in 1950).

The Communist movement in Japan was eventually suppressed, with the added cooperation and help of General Douglas MacArthur who purged many of their top leaders. Conservative politicians managed to rule Japan for most of the next six decades, with the aid of yakuza who helped put down leftist protests, and the CIA which helped fund their operations under the aegis of the Liberal Democratic Party. And although Pyongyang's dream of an American army populated by heroin junkies never came to fruition, as agents from the Occupation's Counter Intelligence Corps and the Canon Agency intercepted many a shipment leading up to and during the Korean War (which ended in stalemate in 1953), pro-North Korean gangs maintained their ties to the motherland. North Korea went on to supply the Yamaguchi-gumi and other yakuza gangs with narcotics, (as well as handguns), during the latter part of the 20th century.

Foreword by Robert Whiting

Many yakuza including former Yamaguchi-gumi bigwig Takayama Kiyoshimi, still have relatives in the North.

Among the yakuza gangs of today, of which an estimated 30% are Zainichi Korean (including those of both pro-South and pro-North variety), the Tokyo-based Kyokuto-kai, with over 1,000 members, is said to be the principal facilitator of North Korean narcotics today, with the drug of choice being not heroin but crystal meth, courtesy of the Kim Il-sung, Kim Jong-il and Kim Jun-un regimes respectively. They may go by names like Kaneda or Kanemoto, as evidenced by arrests of gang members reported on the TV news, but you can be rest assured the real name is Kim.

AT THE SHARPE END author Hugh Ashton presents a fictional but accurate glimpse into the modern version of this underworld, set in present-day Tokyo, that is replete with modern-day North Korean yakuza, Pyongyang defectors, foreign and domestic intelligence operatives (of both the corrupt and honest variety), crack MPD detectives and a cast of gaijin characters who are refreshingly atypical. They are all wrapped up in a gripping tale of industrial espionage and global finance that is thoroughly convincing, and, at the same time, eye-opening.

Ashton's powers of observation where details of daily life in Japan are concerned are impressive, as are his descriptive abilities, storytelling skills and knowledge of the Tokyo underworld and the police who investigate it. I am certain you will like this book as much as I did.

Preface by the Author

WRITING FICTION SET IN JAPAN poses a challenge to the author. For those living in Japan, descriptions of everyday things and actions may sometimes seem superfluous, and serve only to hold back the story, but for those outside Japan, the things we take for granted here may need some explanation (for example, when entering a Japanese house, one removes one's shoes—a habit that becomes automatic after a while, but may need explanation, or at least a mention, for non-Japan dwellers).

Kenneth Sharpe's world is not that of the mysterious East, where esoteric Oriental wisdom is imparted to crass Westerners through subtle mystic practices—his Japan is centred on modern Tokyo—a world of foreigners who have made their home in an alien and sometimes bewildering society, often in definitely non-exotic surroundings, scratching a living from this vibrant city. With all the talk of depression and business downturns, Tokyo continues to be an exciting source of opportunities and adventure, even after my 22 years of life here, and hence I'm really happy to present my view of it. Though it doesn't romanticise the city or the country, it is not self-consciously a "mean streets" locale—Sharpe's Tokyo is pretty similar to mine, and if the streets seem mean to him at times, but not all the time, they do to me, too.

Though some place names and events exist in real life, they exist only to give authenticity to the story and the characters in this book, who are fictional and exist only in my imagination.

As well as thanks to my wife Yoshiko, who has provided loving support, I would like to express my gratitude to those people with whom I've had the pleasure of working and meeting in my 22 years in Japan. Special thanks are due to Mark Thomas, John Talbot, Eric Bossieux, as well as Cindy Mullins of 4M Associates, for constant encouragement and support (and helpful criticism), and Mark Schreiber and Maclean Storer for their constructive hole-poking in a couple of early drafts. Holly Ueda and Simon Varnam provided their proofreading skills, and performed acts of heroic criticism, over and above the call of duty, to help make this a better book. Even if I didn't accept all their suggestions, they forced me to look at what I'd written with new eyes.

Oh, and I, like Kenneth Sharpe, am British. This book is largely written in British English (some Americanisms may have slipped in, though—living in a polyglot community tends to do that to your writing style).

Hugh Ashton
Kamakura, June 2010

Preface to the 2013 edition

SINCE THE FIRST DRAFT of this story was written in 2007, many things happened. Wall Street collapsed, and the earthquake that I described in the original draft did not occur. It therefore seemed sensible to me in early 2010 as I prepared to publish the first edition of the book that the original fictional earthquake should be replaced by the real Wall Street debacle. This actually involved quite a lot of work, since I had originally set the story in the winter, and the Lehman collapse occurred in the autumn. Much of the action therefore took place in late summer.

This meant that I had to turn off heaters and turn on air-conditioners, take off coats and roll up sleeves. At one point, Sharpe and Mieko are eating fruit. This fruit was originally *mikan* (mandarin oranges) which are a winter thing in Japan, and come from various specialist areas which I named. For summer, I had to change the mandarins to peaches, and the place of origin to Yamanashi. Such are the penalties of accuracy.

In any event, the change was made. And then less than a year later, we actually did experience a massive earthquake in Japan. Much more devastating than the one I described, in so many ways. Tens of thousands died in the resulting tsunami, and three nuclear reactors melted down. I foretold a mere few hundred deaths and a potential nuclear disaster which was averted by the quick reactions of the plant workers.

But when I think about it, how much difference is there between Tokyo Electric Power Company and Lehman Brothers? Both were known to be engaged in risky activities, skirting, if not actually breaking, the law, and the regulators winked at their transgressions. Both considered themselves (wrongly in Lehman's case) "too big to fail".

In the end, both of these corrupt systems: America's financial world, and Japan's energy industry, caused disasters—and not just to my fictional hero and his friends.

To me, the real tragedy here is the fact that virtually nothing seems to have been done to prevent these things happening in the future. Yes, Japan has shut down its nuclear reactors (though at the time of writing, the present government seems determined to re-open them). There is some more interest in renewable energy. But the root of the problem—the blind chase for profit at the expense of safety, or even common-sense, remains, as it does in the financial services sector.

Don't get me wrong—I'm not blindly anti-nuclear or anti-banker. I just think if you're going to play with fire, it's a good idea to have a bucket of water handy, and if you burn yourself, you learn from the pain and stop it happening again.

Sermon over. Enjoy the adventures of Kenneth and his friends.

Thanks to Jo at Inknbeans Press for letting me share my thoughts with youin a previous edition of this book. She is sadly missed, almost a year to the day after she left us.

MY SINCERE THANKS GO to Robert Whiting for his wonderful introduction to the history preceding the events described in this novel.

He has also been kind enough to correct me in one or two places where my knowledge has been somewhat at fault. For example, he points out that Koreans in Japan can acquire Japanese citizenship if they wish, but for a variety of reasons, many choose not to do so.

He also makes the point that Hello Kitty has been with us here in Japan since 1974—nearly 40 years, rather than 20. That's a long time for a mouthless cat.

And also he (and I) would like to emphasise that the obnoxious inhabitants of the various Embassies described here are fictitious, and have no existence in reality. They are pure (or rather, impure) figments of my imagination.

Hugh Ashton
Kamakura, April, 2013

At the Sharpe End

Hugh Ashton

j-views Publishing, Lichfield, UK

Chapter 1: Tokyo

It had been an aggravating day for Kenneth Sharpe as he trudged his way round central Tokyo. A stranger, an Australian backpacker from the look and sound of him, had dug his hooks into Sharpe on the morning train, and bent his ear with some crazy story about giant insects and a theme park. Sharpe didn't really remember or care about the details – he'd turned off after a couple of minutes, writing off the guy as a first-order loony. Next, when he turned up to his client's office for a meeting that had been arranged two weeks previously, he found that his contact had been transferred to Singapore the day after the meeting had been arranged, but had neglected to tell him. Now, nursing a consolatory cup of coffee while killing time before his next meeting, he was being accosted by yet another stranger, this time a Japanese businessman.

"Sorry?" aggrieved, but still polite.

"Excuse me, but I want to tell you something," Sharpe's interlocutor replied in almost fluent English with an accent that hovered between American and British, with almost no touch of Japanese in it, and with a curious slightly husky tinge to the voice.

Sharpe used a paper napkin to wipe his face, looked

down at his flies, checked to see his briefcase was still beside the chair. No problems in those departments. He sighed. "Go ahead."

"I am in trouble. I work for a small electronics company. You probably haven't heard of Katsuyama Electronic Devices," (Sharpe shook his head in agreement), "but we will soon be very important players when it comes to putting AI image-recognition algorithms onto silicon."

"Meaning?" Actually, Sharpe had a fair idea of what was meant here, but wanted to be sure. As it happened, one of his clients who made digital cameras was looking for something that sounded like this kind of technology as a gimmick to build into their next generation of products.

"Meaning that within a year, we can build face recognition into a chip-set costing less than ten dollars in mass production."

"With what kind of figures for false acceptance rate and false rejection rate?" Sharpe asked, more to show off his knowledge of the jargon than because he was seriously interested in the answer. "Wait a moment." Sharpe stopped to think for a second. "How did you know that I would be interested in what you're talking about?" Sharpe started to come awake as he realised that this wasn't the sort of information that would be passed on to random strangers.

CONFIDENCES PASSED TO HIM BY STRANGERS seemed to be part of his life now. People he'd never met before kept coming up to him and telling him the most amazing stories of their lives, or those of other people. It didn't seem to matter whether these people were Japanese or not. And it didn't even seem to matter about the language. Once a little old Japanese man came up to Sharpe and started talking earnestly to him in what seemed to be some Eastern European language he couldn't recognise. This went on for a full ten minutes, broken only by Sharpe's "Da"s of incomprehension (it was the only vaguely relevant Slavic word he could remember at the time). And another time, an elderly Japanese lady sitting next to him on the Tokyo underground train had spontaneously launched into a long story in Japanese of how her son had been eaten by an exceptionally large octopus, the recounting of which had lasted from Naka-Meguro to Akihabara (Sharpe was pretty sure it had been that way round – the octopus doing the eating, that is – but then again, Japanese is a notoriously vague language, and Japanese cuisine features quite a lot of octopus, so it might have been that the son had died while or after eating an octopus. Sharpe didn't really care either way).

An ex-girlfriend had disabused him of the notion that he had a kind sympathetic face, when he'd mentioned this phenomenon. "Sometimes when you're not concentrating, you look kind of stupid, and people think you might give them money," she had explained.

Well, thanks, he had thought to himself. Always nice to be appreciated. But the thing was, he reflected later, none of these people had ever asked him for money, and it was difficult to see how most of these long involved stories, half of which he didn't really understand anyway, could ever end up being a pitch for a confidence trick. This one seemed to be a bit different.

"**Less than 0.2 per cent FAR and 0.15 for FRR.** Impressive, no? And I'm pretty sure you're interested. Believe me."

Sharpe and the Japanese businessman regarded each other over their empty coffee cups. The Japanese saw a rapidly balding, paunchy, middle-aged Englishman, wearing a light grey summer suit that looked as though it could have been replaced to advantage at any time in the past couple of years. Sharpe saw an eminently forgettable Japanese face below a full head of neatly styled longish hair, above an equally forgettable dark blue suit. But the eyes stood out from the rest of the face as a memorable feature. They reminded Sharpe of the eyes of someone he'd once known – a kindly and sympathetic martial arts teacher who had later been accused and convicted of sexual offences with young girls.

In the meantime, his new-found companion looked as though he was about to burst with the information he wanted to pass on. Too many espressos in the past hour, thought Sharpe.

"Better than 99 per cent, on both counts, eh?" Sharpe asked. A silent nod in response. "How about some fresh air?" The same nod. Sharpe's new friend reached into his pocket and put on a surgical mask – a Japanese trait that always annoyed Sharpe – some days the train looked like a surgeons' convention. Sharpe packed his computer away into his briefcase and the two went outside where the humid Tokyo atmosphere struck Sharpe with an almost physical shock after the air-conditioned coffee shop.

Without saying a word, Sharpe's new friend led the way down a side-street towards the river, and a few minutes later the two men were standing side by side, looking straight ahead at the brown water of the Sumida River swirling towards Tokyo Bay. A farting barge passed, carrying a load of something heavy and messy-looking. The Japanese man's nervousness seemed to have disappeared.

"So what's the trouble?" Sharpe asked, picking up the conversation from where it had left off in the coffee shop. "What's so strange about all this business? Do you want me to sell it for you?"

"I know too much about this technology. I'm being approached by the American security services to give them the details."

Sharpe stole a sideways look. He seemed serious. And to Sharpe's eyes he didn't seem that paranoid. But Sharpe didn't view himself as an expert in these matters.

"CIA or FBI, then? Not the KGB or MI5?"

"I'm serious. These agents have threatened to harm my family if I don't co-operate."

Humouring him. "What does the president of your company want to do with the technology? Isn't it up to him?"

"I *am* the president!" he exploded. "It's my company."

"But?" At this moment, Sharpe actually thought longingly of the Isle of Mantids, as had been related to him by the Australian. Meter-long killer insects seemed relatively safe and sane compared to this.

"But it's not my money backing the company. My wife's parents helped me to go to Stanford University to do research, and lent me the money to expand my company. Excuse me—" and he dived into an inner pocket, apparently for a business card. Sharpe told himself that if you were to try to save someone from a burning building in Japan, they wouldn't agree to be rescued until they'd swapped cards with you. Sharpe mirrored the move, diving into his own pocket, and the two men emerged with their respective 91 x 55 millimetre pasteboard rectangles, exchanged with due ceremony.

Sure enough, the card presented to Sharpe was from Katsuyama Electronic Devices, with a fancy-looking modernistic logo, and Sharpe's new friend, Masashi Katsuyama, with "President" as his job title. The card given in exchange, which gave the company as Sharpe Practice, also listed a "President", Kenneth Sharpe, and had an equally flashy logo, but Sharpe was willing to bet that Katsuyama Electronic

Devices consisted of something more than one person, a telephone, a Web site and an e-mail account, which was the basis of his own business, a freelance technology consultancy in Tokyo – Sharpe's way of describing his bumming his way through life, getting paid for playing with new technology toys by companies, mainly banks, with no time or inclination to do it for themselves. He found this way of making a living much more congenial than teaching English – the standard "foreigner" job in Japan for those not employed by companies, and he had never bothered to learn to read Japanese well enough to work as a translator.

More than once it had occurred to Sharpe that running his own show and living on his wits was hardly a way of guaranteeing a secure retirement. Some of his friends were ensconced in Japanese companies, but from his days when he had worked as a language teacher seconded to some of these companies, he doubted if he could survive the high volume of bullshit that seemed to be shovelled over the workers there on a daily basis. He had a feeling that Katsuyama's company might be a little different, but he wasn't going to rush into asking for a job from someone who claimed that the secret services of the USA were after him.

"Thank you," Katsuyama said, tucking the card carefully into a small alligator-skin case. "Let me explain a bit more to you. My wife's parents helped me build up the business when I took it over from my father. They hold a controlling interest. And they don't want to sell to the Americans. You see," and his voice dropped to a lower tone, "they're Korean."

Sharpe considered some of the implications of this. It was more than a matter of simply "so what?" As it happens, Sharpe reminded himself, "Korean" as used in Japan doesn't necessarily mean simply "born and bred in Korea". Japan actually used to regard Korea as part of Japan before World War Two, and many Koreans came over to Japan, some of them against their will, to work for Japanese companies. Come the end of the war, many of those from the North couldn't go back to Korea, for a variety of reasons, mainly on account of Japan's not recognising the North Korean state. Nor could they acquire Japanese citizenship, so a compromise was reached whereby they were granted permanent right of residence in Japan, but remained as Korean citizens, as did their children and grandchildren. To this day, these "Koreans", some of whom may have Korean towns given as their official place of birth, although they have never been to Korea, make up the largest percentage of "foreigners" living in Japan.

Many of these "Koreans" have close ties with the Stalinist North Korean regime, and some, discriminated against by Japanese, find it easier to get jobs on the legal fringes of society than to work at "respectable" jobs. The situation's complex, and the details of the explanation depend on who you talk to and when you talk to them, but the basic facts are roughly what are outlined here.

These things went through Sharpe's mind as Katsuyama went on, "My wife's parents are basically kind people – actually, I suppose they've been really good to me – but I have to admit that my father-in-law has connections I'm not happy about."

"Oh?" Sharpe raised his eyebrows.

In response, Katsuyama held up his left hand with the little finger tucked into the palm – a sign representing underworld yakuza connections. "And they're very sympathetic to the North. That's where their family comes from. Half of them are still living over there," he added.

Sharpe grunted in sympathy.

"I started publishing the results of my work at Stanford. I came up with the idea that you could break down a face into a series of discrete components. Standard things like eye spacing and nose width – that sort of thing. Then I realised you could use some funky little DSP convolutions – you know, in-chip digital signal processing – to match these up almost in real time against a compressed database consisting of modelled combinations of these primary components. And then I started getting messages from some very strange places around Washington. This kind of technology's very exciting for them – they see it as a way of picking faces out of crowds. Security screening. Finding suspected terrorists. The Americans have been trying to make this kind of thing work, but they've not got as far as they hoped. They want to use my technology as a shortcut."

Sharpe grunted again. The current American obsession with security against the hordes of terrorists infesting politicians' brains, and the handful of actual terrorists, irked him every time he had to fly to Seattle or San Jose. Last time, one of the young gum-chewing security workers had plunged his hand down the front of Sharpe's trousers without warning. He'd imagined there were constitutional amendments against that sort of thing, but apparently not. "Speaking for myself, I wouldn't want to give them more ways of playing Big Brother," he said.

"Me, too. And you can imagine what my wife's family would have to say about it. I and my invention would probably be disappeared to North Korea or something. So I came back to Japan as soon as I had my doctorate."

"It's all very interesting, but why are you talking to me?"

"I saw a paper you'd written on image-processing algorithms a year ago."

It was true – such a thing actually did exist. One of Sharpe's clients had requested an "independent research paper" which promoted their advances in the field and which they gleefully reprinted and distributed as promotional literature. As a result, he knew more than the average technical journalist about this kind of thing.

"But there are other experts in the field. Not that I'd call myself an expert," Sharpe hastily added. "I'm really only a journalist."

"The others in this field I know are all American. Or Japanese. You're the only one from a neutral country who seems to know enough about the subject to get things published."

Sharpe had his doubts about the "neutral", given Britain's recent role in the Iraq invasion and occupation, but he held his tongue.

He realised that he must have been drinking too much coffee earlier that day, or too little, or something, because the full meaning of the conversation only now hit him.

"But what you're telling me means that you knew who I was before you started talking to me?" Katsuyama nodded. Sharpe thought back. "You weren't in that coffee shop when I came in?" Another nod. "So you've been following me around all day?"

"All week," Katsuyama corrected.

Sharpe turned his back on the Sumida River, propped himself against the concrete wall dividing the footpath from the river bank and looked up. A little girl was riding a tricycle round and round the balcony of a third-floor flat. She stopped her endless circuits and looked down at the strange foreigner looking up at her. Sharpe waved. She considered gravely, waved, and continued on her course. Still watching her and avoiding Katsuyama's eyes, Sharpe exploded in a sudden burst of temper. "Jesus Christ! That's pretty damned presumptuous. Why the hell couldn't you just phone me? Or was that too simple for you bloody rocket scientists? Why do you have to play these stupid games?"

"Phones can be tapped," Katsuyama pointed out. "Even

cellular ones. And in any case, I've stopped carrying a mobile phone round with me. They can trace your movements through your phone, you know." Sharpe nodded. He did know.

"Go on," Sharpe said. He was breathing more calmly, but was still more than a little peeved. He felt in his pockets for a cigarette before remembering that he'd given up smoking several years previously. All he could feel there was what felt like a toffee-like object that had escaped from its wrapper and had spent the last few years collecting pocket fluff. Maybe it was time to start smoking again.

"What I need is someone to describe the algorithms I used to break down the faces. They're actually trivially obvious." Sharpe stared at Katsuyama, hoping his expression appeared sarcastic. "If you're into that kind of thing, I mean," added the other, interpreting the stare the way Sharpe had hoped he would. "But it's not easy to string them together in the right combinations and the right order. That's where my value-added bit came in, and that's the part that's not public."

"So what happens if I describe the exact process? Don't I get the boys from Langley after me, then?"

"Not Langley. Fort Meade. These guys are from the NSA, not the CIA. No, you won't. If everyone knows about this thing, it's useless as a secret. We would draw its fangs. Think about it – there's no point in them chasing me any further if the whole world has it." To Sharpe, it sounded as though Katsuyama was trying to convince himself more than he was trying to convince Sharpe. "I really want you to have a very good look at this thing and find out what it can do and tell everyone about it."

"So why don't you publicise it yourself, then?" It was Katsuyama's turn to look at Sharpe. "OK, I get it. You publish your findings, and they know that you've stiffed them. And they take it out on you."

"Right. They've already threatened my family," Katsuyama reminded him. "So you do it. As far as the world is concerned, we've never met. You worked it all out from first principles, and based it all on my published work. I can lie low for a month or two until it all becomes public through you."

"And you stay safe?"

"That's the theory." He smiled. "Of course, I'm an engineer, so I know how theory has a habit of running contrary to practice." He paused and thought. "I think I mean it that way round."

"All right, so I've never met you. Now what? How did I come to find out and understand what you were up to?" Sharpe asked.

My published work's all on the Web in English – no sense in my giving you copies – you can just look it up. Work it all out from there. The one thing I do want to do now, though, is give you this to look after." He reached into his shoulder bag and brought out a flat cardboard box about the size of a magazine, decorated with the ubiquitous Hello Kitty character, a mouthless overly cute cartoon cat originally marketed to five-year-olds about twenty years previously, which still manages to grace the bags, pencil cases, lunch boxes and other accessories of half the female population of Japan under fifty. Sharpe remembered one girl who'd attracted him on account of her common-sense and maturity – until he'd discovered all her underwear was decorated with Kitty-chan. That had been a big turn-off.

"Thanks," he said, looking at Kitty. "Always been a big fan."

"Don't be stupid. This is a prototype of the entire system. In fact, it's the only working example of my theories. And it's much safer if I don't know where it is. So just take it and put it somewhere safe, and then I can swear with a clear conscience that I have no idea of its whereabouts."

"You're still assuming I'm going to do this, aren't you?" Sharpe hoped he still sounded peeved.

"Of course I am. For three reasons." He lifted his hand and started counting on his fingers, Japanese-style, where you fold the fingers down one by one as you make the points. "First, you will get a lot of favourable publicity out of this. I reckon any consulting job in the field is yours from now on. Second, you like me, and you're doing it for a friend." Katsuyama paused and grinned. "Aren't you? And lastly," the third finger went down, "you're going to become quite rich doing this. I know that, because I'll be paying you the equivalent of several million dollars. Tax-free, offshore. We'll make the final arrangements together later. OK?"

"Well, since you put it that way ..."

"I thought you'd come round to my point of view in the end. So you take this, and like I said, you put it somewhere that I can't guess."

Sharpe took the box, gingerly. "Can I look inside?"

"Sure you can, but I don't know how much it's going to mean to you. The real secrets are all in here right now until you dig them out from my work." Katsuyama tapped his head. "We'll meet again in a week or so. Probably less. Don't worry about when and where, I'll find you. I've done it before, remember."

"That's it for today?" asked Sharpe. "That's all?"

"That's it. You have my card, but don't bother calling the number on it. I won't be there. And my secretary answers my e-mail at that address, so don't try that, either. You can look up the company, if you like. We're real, you know. Quite profitable, too, in our little way. That's where your money's coming from." He gave a half-wave and vanished down a

At the Sharpe End

small side alley, leaving Sharpe standing by the bank of the river, holding a cardboard box decorated with a mouthless cartoon cat.

The tricyclist on the balcony had stopped her obsessive pedalling and was looking down at Sharpe. Or more accurately, she was looking at the box.

"That's Kitty-chan, isn't it?" she called down in Japanese.

"Yes, it is. Clever of you to notice it."

"I want it!" Sharpe shook his head. "I want Kitty-chan!" she screamed. Time to take off, Sharpe decided, ducking down the same side alley that Katsuyama had taken, pursued by the little girl's frustrated wails. Japanese children can be such brats, he thought.

He didn't see Katsuyama on the way to the station, but then he hadn't expected to.

Even though Sharpe continued doing consultancy work for the client whom he met later that day, he found it impossible to concentrate on the meeting and he subsequently had absolutely no memory of it at all.

What on earth was in the box that he had accepted so casually and was now resting beside his case under the table while he talked to clients about a report he was due to deliver? Anthrax bacteria? Sarin nerve gas? A small radioactive dirty bomb? And he'd taken it from a stranger he'd only met for the first time a few minutes earlier. He must be suffering from premature senile decay, he told himself.

Sure Katsuyama talked up a blue streak, Sharpe reasoned to himself, but so could Sharpe himself with the wind behind him. Katsuyama's business card seemed legitimate enough, but then so did Sharpe's own. None of the previous Tellers of Tall Tales (as he tended to think of them) had ever thought to leave this kind of evidence of their lunacy with him. He thought about leaving the box in the train, or simply throwing it in the trash, but things in Japan have a habit of miraculously returning to their owner, so that probably wasn't going to do much good. And if he did that, there was the question of what to say to Katsuyama next time they met. There was no doubt in Sharpe's mind that there was going to be a next meeting.

As for going to the police – that was out of the question. Sharpe had little confidence in the ability or utility of the average Japanese policeman – remembering that this was a country that saw its top policeman shot in public in broad daylight by the lunatic Aum Shinrikyo cult, and more than twelve years later, was still seeking the evidence to convict the self-confessed assailants. In any case, Sharpe had quite liked the little he'd seen of Katsuyama, despite his sneaky habit of following people around for days without their knowledge. Maybe this was one of Sharpe's flaws. He tried to analyse himself in the style of his school essays on Shakespeare: Q. Describe the fatal character flaw in Kenneth Sharpe's character that leads to his final undoing. A. Despite some flare-ups of temper, a naïve tendency to display an unwarranted trust in the good intentions of complete strangers.

But could Katsuyama really be trusted? That was the 64 million yen question that Sharpe kept asking himself that evening on his train ride back to the eastern Tokyo suburbs (actually it was Chiba if he was honest with himself, but "Tokyo suburbs" sounded a little more impressive). He'd moved there several years previously, finding that it was possible to rent a relatively spacious and more modern flat for considerably less money than he would have had to pay for the dubious privilege of living close to the centre of Tokyo. The 40-minute train ride to the commercial district was a small price to pay, considering that he did a lot of his work from home in any case.

He walked up the stairs to the second-floor flat, let himself in, kicked off his shoes, and walked into the kitchen, Hello Kitty still tucked firmly under his arm. He hadn't even broken the tape to look inside the box. As he walked through the kitchen door, Mieko, his live-in girlfriend of just over two years, saw the box.

"Present for Kumi-chan?" she asked. Kumi-chan was her sister's three-year-old daughter Kumiko who came to visit sometimes. Mieko and Kumi-chan formed a mutual adoration society, and Sharpe himself, in sentimental moments, admitted he was not immune to Kumi-chan's charms.

"No, it's something else inside a Kitty-chan box. Something from a client." And wasn't that the truth, when you thought about it? he reasoned.

In the small spare bedroom he used as a home office, Sharpe logged onto his main computer while unpacking the day's work from his briefcase. After dealing with the evening crop of e-mail, he browsed the Katsuyama Electronic Devices Web site.

Sure enough, the picture of Sharpe's new friend smiled out from the list of corporate officers. No-one who looked like a North Korean gangster (whatever one of those people looks like) had their photo up there, though.

The company itself, if the accounts sheets were to be believed, was a profitable little business, as Katsuyama had said. Somewhat lower-tech than Sharpe's usual line of client, dealing in commodity semiconductor components, rather than in leading-edge technology, but obviously with an edge that enabled them to continue high-profit sales to larger corporations. Sales and profitability had increased dramatically since Masashi had taken over from a Hiroshi Katsuyama (his father, obviously) a few years previously.

And all this was without the wonder technology, the sole example of which was apparently reposing in a Hello Kitty box close to Sharpe's feet.

A quick Google search for Katsuyama's name revealed reprints of several technical papers, some of which listed him as a co-author, and one or two where he was apparently the sole author. Most seemed to list Stanford University as the place of origin, and listed Katsuyama as an Associate Professor there. The papers weren't exactly light reading, and there was no way Sharpe was going to pretend that he understood them after a quick skim through, but sure enough, they seemed to deal with image processing and pattern recognition software algorithms, and the journals where they had appeared were eminently respectable, with peer review and a high standard of contributor, if the academic honours and titles were anything to go by. He decided not to waste paper by printing them out just yet, but bookmarked the sites so he could find the papers easily in the future.

It was Mieko's turn to cook that night. She called to Sharpe that dinner was ready, and they ate grilled fish and rice while she told of her day's adventures with the local neighbourhood women's association, who had somewhat grudgingly, on account of her overseas education (she'd been to school in Britain where her father had been working for a Japanese car manufacturer), divorced status, and her unmarried cohabitation with a foreigner, admitted her to their ranks, and taken a trip to a new shopping centre in Yokohama. The idea of forty middle-aged Japanese ladies invading a single store en masse would strike fear to the core of most Western shopkeepers' beings, but the Japanese shopping malls encourage this kind of visit – shopping is often listed as a favourite hobby by Japanese women.

As Sharpe was drying the last of the dishes, the doorbell

rang. Draping the cloth nonchalantly over one arm, he flung open the door. A very young and nervous-looking uniformed policeman was standing outside. His uniform seemed several sizes too big for him, and Sharpe had the absurd feeling that maybe he'd grow into it, as Sharpe had been assured he would when he was a child and his mother had bought jackets whose sleeves had reached his fingertips.

"Er ... You're a foreigner?" the young policeman stammered in Japanese.

Yep, I am, kid. Stick with those powers of observation and you'll make detective in no time, Sharpe thought, but kept this to himself, mentally adding this incident to his list of the strange things that happen sometimes when Japanese come into contact with foreigners. Instead, his reflexes sent him to grab his "gaijin card", or more officially, the Certificate of Alien Registration from the Ministry of Justice, issued by the local city hall, that is meant to be carried at all times and produced on demand to the police. The policeman waved it away.

"Please ... we need ..." he started in terrible painful English. Sharpe had the feeling that it must have cost him a week's brainpower to get those few words out.

"Don't worry about speaking English," Sharpe said to him, in Japanese. "Maybe you'd like to come in and have some tea?"

Relief spread over the policeman's face. "Yes, please. Excuse me. Thank you very much," and he continued to make the appropriate Japanese polite noises of gratitude as he unstrapped the strange ankle boots that Japanese policemen wear, and arranged them neatly by the tumble of Sharpe's oversized shoes in the hallway (Mieko's, of course, were neatly stashed away in the cupboard provided for shoes).

"*Oi, o-cha!*" Sharpe shouted to Mieko in the kitchen,

using an old-fashioned disrespectful way of talking to one's female partner and asking for tea. The policeman caught Sharpe's eye and allowed himself to exchange a faint grin. All boys together.

The two men went into the living room, and Sharpe turned off the TV, which was showing yet another of the inexhaustible store of food programs. As they sat down, the policeman removing his belt, with all the police paraphernalia attached, Mieko started to come in. "Do you want to share a peach with me?" she asked. "I found some really nice ones from Okayama today—" and then stopped as she saw the policeman. "Sorry," she said, running back into the kitchen, only to return what seemed like only a few seconds later, fully composed, with a clean apron, and a tray with three cups of tea, and three plates with segments of peeled peach. "Sorry there's no cake," she said to the policeman. Sharpe envied her and all Japanese women of his acquaintance the mysterious gift of moving from a state of complete panic to total unflappable calm in five seconds flat. Of course, the reverse was also true. Mieko could reach a state of advanced hysteria in seconds over what Sharpe perceived as being trivia.

"Please don't worry," the policeman replied. "Did you say these were from Okayama? How wonderful. My parents grew up near there and we always used to get a box of peaches from my aunt every year when I was a boy." Japanese people can go on for hours about food, and the places it comes from and how to serve it, Sharpe thought to himself. He was often reminded of the French obsession with food, but multiplied by a factor of about five.

Everyone made the usual polite remarks and started to eat and drink. When the policeman had finished his fruit, he turned to Sharpe.

"Thank you for the tea. I am sorry that I have to ask you a few questions." He pulled out a notebook and pencil.

"Please go ahead."

The policeman asked various questions that seemed to have come out of a manual, though Sharpe couldn't see for the life of him what relevance his date of birth had to anything. He was almost surprised that he wasn't being asked for his blood type (a favourite way of determining someone's character, according to many Japanese). At the end of the routine questions, Sharpe felt that things seemed to be pretty matey by now, so he wasn't expecting the next words.

"When did you last see Dr Masashi Katsuyama?"

Better to tell the truth, if there was going to be any trouble, Sharpe thought to himself. "About 3:15."

"Where did you last see him?"

"By the Sumida river embankment. Near Asakusa-bashi station. Can I ask why?" The policeman made a note in his notebook, slurped some tea and looked up.

"He fell off the platform at Shinjuku station earlier this evening in front of a train. He died, and your business card was found in his pocket."

Sharpe sat a little straighter. A faint noise something like "Oh my God," in English emerged. Tea went down his chin. "Shut your mouth, you look stupid," Mieko mouthed to him silently. He hadn't realised that his mouth was open.

"What time did you come home tonight?"

"I arrived here about 5:45, if I remember right."

"Did anyone see you, apart from your wife, of course?" Sharpe didn't correct the mistake.

Sharpe reflected. "Yes, I said hello to old Mrs Watanabe who lives on the fifth floor of the block. She was just coming back from the supermarket, and we came up in the lift together. I asked her how the neighbourhood trip to Yokohama had gone."

"Thank you. Dr Katsuyama's accident was at 6:07, but I had to be sure that you weren't involved. There was only your card in his pocket, you see. No other cards or identification, so you were the first person we wanted to talk to ."

"You're sure it was an accident?" Sharpe asked, biting off the words as the implications struck him.

"What else would it be?" The policeman seemed to turn suspicious. "I think it would be a good idea in any case for you to come and talk to my chief tomorrow morning. Please don't go to work tomorrow morning. We'll phone you, and let you know when you should come round to the police station." He stood up and was once again the charming young man with an aunt who sent him peaches. "Thank you very much for the tea and fruit," he said, bowing to Mieko. "And thank you for answering my questions," bowing to Sharpe. "Sorry to have troubled you," bowing to both.

Sharpe escorted him down the hallway, where he put on his boots. "Thank you once again," he said, bowing. Sharpe returned to the living room, picked something up and raced back to the front door. "Mr Policeman!" he yelled (it's not nearly as rude in Japanese as it sounds in English). "Your belt and pistol! You left them under the table!"

He turned round, a look of horror on his face as he patted the place where his pistol should be. "Thank you, thank you, thank you," he babbled. Sharpe handed the heavy belt to him as he kept muttering things to himself which sounded like the outpourings of pure relief. Pity the poor soul, Sharpe thought to himself, if he turned up at the police station and had to explain that he'd left his pistol somewhere in a foreigner's flat while he was drinking tea.

"Thank you very much." This was accompanied by a deep bow and seemed to be the most sincere thing he'd said in a long while. "Good night. Good luck tomorrow," somewhat mystifyingly.

"And what was all that about?" asked Mieko as Sharpe returned to the living room again.

Sharpe grinned. "Didn't you see? He'd left his belt and pistol behind."

"That's really odd," Mieko frowned. "You'd think a policeman would have a little more sense than that, wouldn't you?"

Sharpe agreed. "And he seemed surprised that I wasn't Japanese when I opened the door. Very strange."

"Anyway, that's not what I meant. What were you and this dead man talking about? Who is he?"

He shrugged in reply. "Someone I met today. I really don't know who he was. We were talking business. I'm sure I'll find out more about everything tomorrow." He didn't feel nearly as confident as his words, though. Why did he have to go to the police station? Why couldn't they send someone more senior to question him?

And with that, they opened two cans of beer, and started their nightly game of cribbage before turning in for the night. Mieko won, as usual, even though she'd only learned the game a few months before.

Chapter 2: Tokyo

THE NEXT DAY ARRIVED with the sound of the alarm clock. Sharpe woke, wondering why he had a sinking feeling in the pit of his stomach which reminded him of similar feelings on exam mornings at school years ago, but he couldn't place the reason until he remembered the appointment at the police station later that morning. He showered, going through the day's tasks in his mind, and made a mental note to make a couple of calls to clients and invent an emergency dentist's appointment. In Japan, it's almost automatically assumed that if the police want to talk to you about anything you must be guilty of something – and it's not a good idea for a consultant to advertise the fact that he's been called by the police to assist them with their enquiries.

He decided to improve the shining hour by putting a final polish on a couple of reports, and using the Web to do research for another report. The call came a little before 10 o'clock.

"Mr Sharpe? Please come to the main city police station at 11 o'clock precisely," the voice at the other end said in efficient Japanese. "Do you know where that is?" with a slight inflection of doubt, as if a foreigner couldn't be expected to know these things.

"Yes, I do, and I'll be there at 11. Excuse me, but who am I talking to?"

"Ask for Inspector Sugita."

"Thank you," bowing as he replaced the receiver before he could catch himself – an irrational habit he'd noticed a lot of non-Japanese acquire very soon after starting to do business in Japan.

Since he hadn't shaved or dressed up in a suit when he got up, he padded off to the bathroom to shave and ask himself if Hello Kitty should go to the police station with him.

He made the decision, while rinsing the last flecks of foam from behind his ears, that she should stay at home. When he'd dried his face, he moved the box into the cupboard among the toys that Kumi-chan played with when she came to visit. It looked quite at home there.

If you're going to be talking to the police, it's important to look your best, he told himself, picking out his best light-weight suit and a white shirt. Maybe he couldn't give the impression that he outranked them, but he could at least prevent them from seeing him as an uncouth barbarian.

As he knotted his tie, Mieko came into the bedroom. "Are you sure you don't want me to come with you?" she asked, continuing a discussion that had started last night in bed. Notwithstanding the horror stories of foreigners who'd reportedly been beaten by the Japanese police into sign-ing confessions written in Japanese that they couldn't even read, Sharpe decided he was reasonably safe.

"No, but it's not a bad idea if you call me on my mobile a little before 12 if I'm not back or I haven't called you by then, and ask about lunch. At least the police will know that someone knows where I am. If it looks like I'm in trouble that I can't handle, I'll tell you I don't want fish for lunch. If

I say that, or if I'm not answering my phone at all, get hold of the Consulate at the British Embassy and tell them I'm in the police station, and something odd is going on. The embassy number's in the Rolodex on my desk. It's an Inspector Sugita that I'm meant to be seeing, by the way. But if I say I want fish, everything's fine and you don't need to worry." Ridiculous, he thought. Stupid little code words.

"No fish means trouble?" she confirmed, and smiled. "Take care. I've polished your best black shoes and put them out for you."

"Love you, darling," Sharpe replied. And he really meant it.

"Love you, too," she said and kissed him goodbye as he opened the front door and slipped on his gleaming shoes.

IT WAS ANOTHER UNPLEASANTLY HUMID WARM MORNING, but getting to the police station was an easy walk down a shallow slope, so he set off a little early and arrived about five minutes ahead of time without being his usual sweat-covered self. The receptionist at the front desk asked him to take a seat, and Sharpe parked himself on a slippery plastic-covered bench. Since he'd brought nothing to read, he was forced to pick up a copy of the *Asahi Shimbun* which was lying around and read that as well as he could.

He'd just finished deciphering something about the latest cabinet reshuffle, and was feeling quite pleased that his Japanese reading ability seemed to be improving (and so it should after all this time, he told himself), when his light was blocked by the policeman who'd drunk tea at the flat the previous night. He stood up and bowed.

"Please come with me. Inspector Sugita is ready for you." He smiled at Sharpe as they walked down the corridor together, and patted his pistol significantly. Sharpe had the feeling that he'd made a friend.

"In here," opening a grey steel door. It took a few seconds for Sharpe's eyes to adjust. The first thing he saw was a metal table. A powerful desk lamp standing on the table shone into his eyes, making it difficult to see who or what was on the other side. The small room had no windows, and as far as Sharpe could make out, the concrete block walls were rough and unplastered. The only furniture visible apart from the table was a metal armless chair with its back to the door. There was an unpleasant chemical smell which Sharpe couldn't quite place and which was almost overpowered by the smell of rough tobacco smoke filling the unconditioned air. Sharpe coughed, but he couldn't work out whether it was because of the atmosphere or because of nervousness.

"Please sit down," came a soft voice in Japanese from the darkness.

"And can we do something about the goddamned lighting?" added a plaintive-sounding American-accented voice in English.

The desk lamp promptly went out, and there was darkness for a fraction of a second before a ceiling fluorescent light flickered into life. Sharpe sat in the chair and looked across the table at the two men facing him.

The first was presumably the one in a police uniform that seemed a little too tight for him. The face matched the voice, being one of those childish faces that sometimes stay with Japanese men until late middle age.

The second speaker looked like a caricature of himself. Lean Western face scarred by pockmarks, with crew-cut grizzled hair, a dark grey suit and white shirt with a plain dark narrow tie. Oversized gold ring with some kind of emblem, worn on the right hand. Had to be one of the American spook agencies. Sharpe sneaked a glance at his feet. Right. Black wingtips to match the cliché. He was the one smoking a small stinking cigar of some kind. Sharpe noticed his hand shaking as he stubbed out the end of one cigar and immediately lit another. "That's better," he remarked, looking up at the light. "Not a hell of a lot better, but better." He looked at Sharpe, and then at the other man, who was presumably Inspector Sugita. "Why are we in here anyway, Inspector?" he asked the policeman in Japanese which sounded much better than Sharpe's, although with a strong American accent. "Can't we be somewhere with a window or something?" He started whistling "A Room With a View" to himself, but it seemed to go over Sugita's head.

"You told me you wanted an interrogation," replied Sugita. "So I booked this room."

"Well, maybe I used the wrong Japanese word. Sorry." He didn't sound it. "All I meant was that I wanted to talk to Mr Sharpe on a semiformal basis."

He turned to Sharpe. "Sorry about this," in Mid-Western English. It didn't sound much more sincere than his Japanese apology. "Next time we'll get the Imperial Suite reserved for you."

Sharpe gave up on the attempt to think of something witty to say in reply, and ended up saying nothing.

"What did Katsuyama want to talk about?" asked Sugita abruptly, in Japanese.

Sharpe replied in the same language. "He wanted me to write a research paper for him. I sometimes write market research papers for my clients which advertise and publicise the advances they have made in their fields."

"What was the subject of this one to be?" asked the American in English. He stretched out his arms, yawned and added, "Pardon me. Late night last night. Call me Ben if it helps you to have a name to give me. You do a lot of this? Is this your main line of work?" he threw out.

"No, not a lot. And it's not my main line of work."

"And your main line of work is ...?" Sugita, in Japanese.

"Consultancy."

"Covers a multitude of sins," said Ben. "I guess you must be one of these techno-geeks." It wasn't a question. In fact, the way it was spoken, it sounded like an insult. Sharpe decided that even if it was meant that way, he wasn't going to rise to the bait.

"Can we speak one language only, please?" Sharpe asked in Japanese. "I'd prefer English, if possible, but maybe Inspector Sugita would prefer Japanese."

"One language sounds much more sensible," said Sugita. Much to Sharpe's surprise he started to speak very reasonable British English. "Thank you for your concern, Mr Sharpe, but I am happy with English as the language for this meeting. And even if I am not very happy, Ben here will be happy, and our translators will write down the recording we are making."

"So what was the subject of your conversation with Katsuyama?" asked Ben again.

"Image processing. Computer recognition of faces so that you can spot a known face from a crowd photo." Silence. Sharpe went on blindly. "Something to do with algorithms and deconstruction of facial features. And a way of doing all this in hardware using digital signal processors – a kind of special chip." There was no way for Sharpe to see if any of this was making any sense to the others. They just sat there. He started floundering. "If you do this sort of thing in software, you need large and expensive computers to do this. If you can put it onto a chip, it makes life easier. Cheaper. You know."

He couldn't tell if they knew or not. Ben sat waiting in the hideous fluorescent light, his scalp gleaming pinkly through his crew-cut, thin at the top. He seemed to be expecting more, so Sharpe obliged, turning to Katsuyama as a subject.

"He told me he'd done research at Stanford and published a few things already. He claimed they were on the Web, and I found a few papers with his name as author."

"And?" Ben probed.

"And what?" Sharpe was starting to sound annoyed, and not all of it was an act. "What has this got to do with his death?"

It was Sugita who answered. "The problem is, Mr Sharpe, that Dr Katsuyama was in possession of intellectual property which was not, strictly speaking, his."

"In other words," Ben interrupted before Sugita had quite finished speaking, "he stole his concepts from the research labs at Stanford where he was working, which were being funded by outside sources. Concepts, furthermore, that are crucial to the security of the United States."

"Oh, bollocks," Sharpe said before he could stop himself. There was a puzzled look on Ben's face. "Oh, never mind," he added. "It's a British slang expression, not worth translating."

"In any case," continued Sugita (Sharpe could have sworn he saw a faint smile cross his lips for half a second in response to Sharpe's explanation), "as Ben has explained, there are important matters involved. We would like to avoid an international scandal regarding the theft of intellectual property, if possible."

"Another scandal, you mean?" Sharpe asked, referring to a recent case in which Japanese researchers had walked out of American labs with biotech material to give Japan's ailing pharmaceutical industry a shot in the arm.

Sugita nodded sadly in reluctant agreement. "It's possible, you see, that Dr Katsuyama did not die by accident," he went on. "The police are attempting to investigate this possibility right now." This seemed to be a rather strange and roundabout way for Sugita to express himself, seeing that he was wearing a police uniform himself, but Sharpe let it pass.

"More specifically," said Ben, who seemed to be chain-smoking his way through a whole tin of his vile little cigars, "we're interested in recovering a prototype device that we believe he may have brought with him from Stanford. He never showed you such a thing?"

"No." Sharpe shook his head. That much was strictly true, he rationalised to himself. Katsuyama had only given him a box and had never showed him what was inside. "What are we talking about, anyway? A box the size of a refrigerator? A small truck? A cigarette lighter?"

"A circuit card to go into a personal computer." About this big." Ben sketched a shape and size in the air with his hands. "Sorry," he added sarcastically, "you're a technical consultant, aren't you? You know all this already."

"Why do you think he would have shown it to me, anyway?" dodging the sarcasm. "Wouldn't you expect it to be at his company? Or at his home?"

"Believe me, we know it's not at his home," said Ben, and then bit his tongue, aware that he'd said too much. "Forget I said that," he added, drawing further attention to his slip.

"He didn't give you the key to a coin locker or anything like that?" asked Sugita but, it seemed to Sharpe, without much hope that he would get an acceptable answer.

Sharpe shook his head again.

"Speak up for the record," snapped Ben. "We can't read that from the tape."

"No, he did not give me the key to a coin locker or anything like that," Sharpe answered dutifully, taking the internal line that a Hello Kitty box containing goodness knows what counted as "anything like" the key to a coin locker.

"Thank you." He exchanged shrugs with Sugita. They sighed in near-perfect unison. Maybe they practised these things, thought Sharpe.

Sugita leaned forward. "Did Dr Katsuyama mention any connections with North Korea?" Both men waited for the answer.

"Yes." It seemed safe to talk about this, at any rate. "He said that his wife's family – her parents, I think, were sympathetic to the current regime."

"Did he also say that he was in deep debt to these relations?"

"No, he said that they'd helped him through Stanford and re-financed his company through a loan. He didn't mention that it was a major outstanding debt."

"Thank you, Mr Sharpe. Since, according to the reports," he shuffled through some papers, "you seem to have been nowhere near Dr Katsuyama when he died, I have no further questions. Ben?"

"Just one. Mr Sharpe, what sort of fee was Dr Katsuyama offering you for writing his report?"

Sharpe thought back and once more decided to oblige with a half-truth. "The exact amount wasn't discussed. He gave me to believe it would be very generous."

Ben gave a hollow laugh. "I wonder what he'd have used for money?"

Which gave Sharpe pause for thought, given what had been said earlier about debt. He also wondered about the accuracy of the annual accounts on the company Web site, given the usual lax standards of corporate accounting and auditing in Japan.

"That's it, then. For now, anyway." Ben turned to Inspector Sugita.

Sugita in turn swivelled to face Sharpe. "Are you intending to leave Japan soon, Mr Sharpe?"

"No, not unless a client asks me to do some research overseas, and then I might have to go away for a week or two. But there's nothing definite in that line in the immediate future."

"If you are going to leave Japan, Mr Sharpe, please make sure you let me know in advance." He pushed a card across the table with simply the two characters for "Sugita", and a mobile telephone number printed on it. Sharpe wondered for a moment if Ben was going to give him a card, but only for a moment. He scooped up Sugita's card and tucked it carefully into his wallet.

"Thank you for visiting us today," said Sugita.

"Yeah, thanks for nothing," added Ben, lighting yet another cigar.

Sharpe stood up and turned to leave.

"Oh, one more thing," called Ben to his back. "What was Katsuyama wearing when you met him? Was he carrying anything?"

Sharpe turned round, half-closing his eyes in a conscious attempt to appear as a co-operative witness. "Dark blue suit. Pale blue shirt. Dark red tie with patterns on it. Yellow patterns. And he was carrying a black attaché case and had a shoulder bag over one shoulder. Dark grey. The bag, not the shoulder." The others ignored this last.

"OK, you actually did see him," replied Ben. "I was beginning to wonder."

Sharpe ignored this, and left, closing the door behind him. He walked along the corridor to the entrance lobby, enjoying the sunlight as he opened the door. His mobile phone started to ring as he started down the steps. The display told him it was Mieko.

"Hello, dear," he said.

"Are you coming home for lunch?" she asked.

"Yes, and I think fish would be a good idea for today's lunch."

"You can eat fish?" she confirmed.

"Yes. Maybe only small fish, though. But I can certainly eat fish."

"Good," she said, and rung off.

AS HE STARTED TO WALK HOME, Sharpe had time to think. Who was "Ben", for example? NSA? Katsuyama had claimed they were the ones chasing him? FBI? CIA? Or any one of a number of shadowy three-letter agencies infesting the area around Washington who seemed to treat Tokyo as a second home, if Roppongi barroom gossip was to be believed? And who was Sugita? Not a policeman, despite the uniform, Sharpe was willing to bet money on that.

Had he lied to them? Sharpe replayed the conversation, if that's what you wanted to call it, in his head, and considered. He certainly had told them the truth and nothing but the truth. But it wasn't the whole truth, so help him God. But then they hadn't asked, and he certainly hadn't been on oath.

And how much of the truth had Katsuyama told Sharpe? There was probably more than a grain of truth in his story. What if Ben's crowd had got their story wrong? Sharpe reflected. It wouldn't be the first time that the Americans had made mistakes of this kind. Suppose Katsuyama had actually done this research, but it really was his own technology that he'd developed by himself, not stolen from Stanford, as Ben was claiming?

And more importantly, what was in that Hello Kitty box sitting in Kumi-chan's toy cupboard? This was something he was going to have to find out soon, if only because the curiosity was burning a hole in his mind. The more he thought about it, the more surprised he was with himself for not having opened it earlier. Another thing struck him as he turned into the bush-flanked entrance of the "mansion" (Japanese English for "block of flats") where he lived; what was the legal status of whatever was inside it? Did it belong to Katsuyama's estate or his company? To Sharpe? To Stanford University? To the company that had funded the research?

Sharpe had hardly ever seen Mieko so pleased to see him. "I was really frightened I was going to have to get you out of there. I've never heard of anything quite like this happening to anyone."

"I'm glad you didn't have to," returning her embrace. "But really, you don't have to worry."

"What was Inspector Sugita like? Scary?"

"No, actually. I quite liked him, in fact," Sharpe said, a little to his own surprise. But when he thought about it, it was true. Sugita had behaved politely and reasonably. But he thought it better not to mention the American at this stage. It would only complicate things.

They ate lunch, deliberately steering round the topic of the morning's events. Sharpe had assigned the afternoon as a "work at home" time, so he shut himself in his home office after finishing the meal, willed himself not to open the Hello Kitty box, and worked solidly until about five o'clock. A little after five, Mieko popped her head around the door. "I'm going to aerobics tonight, remember? I changed from Tuesday this week."

"Oh, that's right. What and when do you want to eat, then?" It was Sharpe's evening to cook the evening meal.

"Shrimp curry? We've got some shrimp in the freezer, and I'll put them out to defrost," Sharpe nodded. "About 6:30?"

"OK, just give me a few minutes to finish these paragraphs and I'll make a start."

SHARPE HAD ALWAYS FOUND he could do a lot of constructive thinking while cooking – mixing things, chopping vegetables and so on. He enjoyed the creative process and the feel of doing something physical after working with words all day. The only real problem was that he liked to do things in the kitchen in his own way, which wasn't always the approved way or even the most efficient way. It meant no-one else could help, or even be in the kitchen while Sharpe was cooking. It was bad for the nerves of all parties. Mieko had discovered this early on in their relationship, and she now kept out of Sharpe's way while he prepared any meal. If he wanted to see things in a philosophical light, Sharpe considered that his kitchen technique could be taken as a metaphor for his whole life – a basic incompatibility between his way of doing things and that of the world at large.

Sharpe was heating the garlic and spices in oil when the great thought struck him – so hard that the mixture turned a very deep shade of brown before he noticed and snatched it off the stove.

Vishal! Of course. Vishal (his family name was something multi-syllabic and unpronounceable for Westerners) was an Indian friend from Bangalore who lived nearby and worked at the Tokyo branch of one of the international investment banks. Maybe it was the smell of the curry that had reminded him. Sharpe always felt that one of the joys of the international life in Tokyo was the chance to make friends with people from different countries whom you'd have little or no opportunity of meeting in "normal" life.

His friends ranged from Czechs, Hungarians, Latvians and Russians, through New Zealanders and Australians, and Chinese from Hong Kong, Singapore and Canada, through to a large number of Indians, imported by the large international finance houses to manage their computer systems (for a variety of reasons, it usually proved impossible to hire Japanese of a sufficiently high level of competence for these positions).

Vishal, one of these Indians who had been living in Japan for nearly four years now, had an almost intuitive gift for understanding computers and things related, and as a result his job title at the bank seemed to become more impressive every time Sharpe saw him. They'd first met while Sharpe had been called in on a project at the bank where Vishal worked, and something had clicked on a personal level, especially when they discovered they lived close to each other in the wilds of Chiba (as the Tokyo-dwellers regarded it). He was the perfect person, Sharpe reasoned, to say what the Hello Kitty box contents (if they were anything like what had been promised) actually were.

He finished preparing the curry base of onions, coconut milk and a little lemongrass, and left it simmering while he went back for the box. Cutting the tape neatly, he looked inside for the first time since he had been given it over 24 hours earlier (had it really been that long? he asked himself).

Inside was a long circuit card, obviously meant to be fitted into a PC, wrapped in a transparent protective anti-static plastic bag. Looking through the plastic, a mass of extremely large chips, presumably digital signal processors, were visible, arranged in an array on the card. He slid the card out of the bag, holding it carefully by the edges, and looked more closely. It was obviously a multi-layer board, not just a prototyping board, and it was extremely complex in terms of the number of connections between the chips.

There were a few "kludges" on the back side – small strands of thin wire making additional connections – added after the card had been assembled.

Also in the box, under the card, was a CD in a case. It was a recordable CD-R, with about half the space used (Sharpe used the trick of holding the disc at an angle to the light to tell how much had been written) and the words "Rev 0.94/71c" and a date about a month ago hand-written in black felt marker.

He put everything back in the box and closed the lid. Vishal was going to have fun tonight, he thought, heading back to the kitchen. Between stirs of the saucepan, Sharpe called Vishal on his mobile number and confirmed that he was ready to receive visitors that evening.

The curry was nearly ready. Sharpe tossed in the shelled shrimps and some quartered hard-boiled eggs and waited a few minutes for them to heat through. Mieko came in from the living-room and the curry was speedily demolished, together with rice and home-made green tomato chutney (a speciality of Sharpe's).

"What are you going to do tonight? Rent a video?" asked Mieko as she was going out of the door.

"No, I thought I'd pop round and see Vishal. Haven't seen him for a long time."

"Say hello to him and Meema for me, then? Do you want to take some sweets? You know how Meema loves those *daifuku* you can get from the store on the corner? They're open till eight or so, so you should be able to get a few if you start off fairly soon."

"Good idea. Have fun at the aerobics." She set off, and after washing the dishes, Sharpe picked up the Hello Kitty box, and set off, locking the door behind him.

SHARPE ARRIVED AT **V**ISHAL'S about twenty minutes later, having stopped, as suggested, to buy the Japanese goodies along the way. He'd never seen the point of owning a car in Tokyo, even though some of his foreign friends felt it necessary to proclaim their status by owning costly lumps of metal, which sat unused in their expensive parking slots except for a week or so each year when the owners went on holiday, often stuck in traffic jams for up to six hours at a stretch. And then they had the nerve to charge you for the use of these so-called "expressways". Sharpe told himself that the benefits of walking everywhere the trains wouldn't take him offset most of the damage to his health caused by his largely sedentary life-style.

Vishal's absurdly beautiful wife Meema answered the door. Sharpe, although he remembered and usually obeyed the commandment about not coveting your neighbour's wife, found it difficult to obey all the rules in Meema's case. Happily for all concerned, the level of covetousness stayed at a very minor flirtation level, at its maximum, which didn't happen very frequently anyway, due to some self-restraint on Sharpe's part and (he assumed) a complete lack of interest on Meema's. It stayed at that level, but certain irrelevant thoughts sometimes intruded while Sharpe was showering. He was pretty sure that Meema didn't suffer from similar problems.

Sharpe passed her the *daifuku* he'd picked up on the way, and she greeted them with the expected rapture before showing him into Vishal's home office, which looked more like an elephants' graveyard for elderly computing equipment every time Sharpe visited. Vishal met him excitedly halfway across the room, almost leaping from his chair to perform the greeting.

Much as Sharpe liked Vishal and respected him as a person, his accent was always an inexhaustible source of amusement. He always sounded to Sharpe like a British co-median's imitation of an Indian who has only just started to learn English, and Sharpe had found that if he didn't con-sciously stop himself, he found himself imitating Vishal's verbal mannerisms after only a few minutes' conversation. Highly embarrassing, even if Vishal never seemed to notice, or was too much of a gentleman to comment if he did. His Japanese had the same accent, and Mieko also found herself speaking Japanese with an Indian accent after an evening with him and Meema (Meema's English and Japanese were both almost fluent and accent-less, by the way).

"Well, Kenneth-san, and what can I be doing for you this evening?"

Unfortunately, all too many of Sharpe's visits to Vishal in the past had been based around requests for technical assis-tance of one sort or another, ranging from CD-ROMs stuck in drives (Sharpe had inadvertently inserted two at once) to dealing with a particularly evil virus infestation (save the data, reformat the hard disk and re-install everything). This evening, Sharpe explained a little about how a client had presented him with some hardware and a CD-ROM, and no adequate way of explaining them. Not too far off the truth, when you thought about it, really.

"Well, have you not brought them round? What can you expect me to do for you if you are not going to co-operate fully?"

Shades of Inspector Sugita, Sharpe thought to himself, handing over the Hello Kitty box.

"Oho, yes. Most interesting. Most interesting indeed. Well then, we are going to have to find out about you, aren't we?" he said, looking at the box. "I think we'll start with you," picking up the CD-ROM and putting it into the drive on his computer. Listening to Vishal's infuriating habit of talking to inanimate things as he worked, Sharpe always thought it would drive him mad if he ever had to share an office with him. Since he didn't, he always said nothing.

Vishal picked up another disc and put it into another CD drive attached to the same computer. "First, we'll make a copy of you, won't we? Just in case you get scratched or something." Sharpe said nothing, but drew up a chair and peered over Vishal's shoulder. Watching Vishal at work, he got a feeling like the one when a good doctor starts probing the sore spot that's been bothering you, and you know you're in good hands now.

When the copy was done, Vishal ejected the original, put it back in its case and wordlessly handed it back to Sharpe. Then he turned his attention back to the computer screen. "Aha! So you are being Linux?" he asked the disc. "Very good, but we can still play!"

He restarted the computer, which had been running Microsoft Windows, and pressed a few keys to start up a different operating system – in this case, the free Linux system, which is used more and more in banks and scientific laboratories. It didn't surprise Sharpe that Katsuyama had used Linux for his work. In fact, he'd recently written a paper on the prevalence of Linux as the system of choice in Japanese research institutions, and he used it more and more in his own work following the virus outbreaks of the mid-2000s.

At this moment, Meema came in with a tray loaded with a plate of food and some cans of beer. "Samosas for you boys?" she asked. Knowing what the reply would be from both, she put her burden down on the table beside Vishal.

"Thank you," said Sharpe. Vishal said nothing, so Meema gently cuffed the side of his head. "Thank you," he grunted.

"That's better," she said. "One of you has some manners, anyway," looking at Sharpe. "Hmm. Interesting," bending down over the open Hello Kitty box. "That's a DSP array?"

Sharpe always considered it an unfair distribution of gifts on the part of Providence that a PhD in applied electronics working on trading strategies at a major brokerage should also be a beautiful woman and a superb cook, but Meema was all of those things. "Getting into image processing?" she asked Sharpe.

"I think so," Sharpe replied.

"Well, why were you not telling me that, then, instead of wasting your time talking to her?" Vishal asked Sharpe.

"Because your samosas stink and hers don't," Sharpe replied, biting into one of Meema's marvellous offerings. Everyone laughed. Vishal's cooking skills could burn a boiled egg. "How did you know?" to Meema.

"Because those are 64-bit processors. Too much for audio work. You might be going in for some other kind of signal processing, but video has the most applications these days. Very trendy. Do you really need all that floating-point capability, though?"

"Why am I wasting my time talking to Vishal?" Sharpe asked rhetorically.

"Because I get my hands dirty. She's just into theory. And she knows nothing about software," replied Vishal. In this case, reflected Sharpe, "nothing" was a highly relative term. Meema only knew as much about software as the average computer science PhD who happened to design trading systems for exotic financial products at the bank where she worked with Vishal.

"Well, I'm in the kitchen getting my hands dirty if you want any more help," said Meema, leaving the room with an air of offended dignity and her pretty chin in the air. Sharpe knew her well enough to know that she wasn't really that offended. Sparring like this seemed to be a continuous game between her and Vishal.

A few more minutes typing and clicking with the mouse

and, "Oho! So now we see who's right!" Vishal dramatically pressed the Enter key and a message appeared.

"Connect camera to computer," it said, in English.

"See, Meema was right. It is about video," Sharpe couldn't resist saying.

"Yes, but could she have decrypted the source code and built the program as I've just done?" Vishal asked in return. "I have to say that there's a lot of code there, and I don't really have much understanding of what the half of it's about."

Sharpe didn't even bother trying to answer that question, but thought to himself that if Vishal really could immediately understand the work of a top Stanford researcher, either Katsuyama had been lying about his work, or Vishal was even brighter than Sharpe thought he was.

"But what sort of camera are we talking about?" Vishal asked the computer, which of course didn't reply. Receiving no response from the machine, Vishal tried second best. "Any input ports on the back of that card you brought along?" he asked, turning to Sharpe.

Sharpe looked. "No. All looks self-contained to me."

"Well, let's be trying this," continued Vishal, reaching for a digital camcorder and connecting it to the computer through a FireWire port. The message didn't go away.

"Maybe if you tried quitting the program and restarting with the camera connected?" suggested Sharpe.

"I was just going to try that," replied Vishal a little testily.

This time, there was no message of complaint from the computer.

"Don't you say 'told you so,'" warned Vishal. "But now what are we to be doing?" The computer screen showed one blank window with some menu titles over the top.

He selected the 'Faces' menu, and picked the 'Match' option. Immediately the message came back, "No Katsuyama card fitted".

"I am supposing that is a Katsuyama card that you have brought with you?" asked Vishal.

"I suppose so," Sharpe answered. It doesn't have any markings on it, but I have good reason to believe that it is a genuine Katsuyama card."

"I am not going to ask you how you know these things, but I will make the assumption you are correct here," replied Vishal, shutting down the computer.

They fitted the card into the computer. For all Vishal's genius on the keyboard, Sharpe knew from past experience he was surprisingly clumsy with a screwdriver, so Sharpe did the work while Vishal sat back and munched on a couple of samosas. When the case was finally screwed back together again, Vishal was more than halfway through his can of beer.

"Thank you very much. Just don't let Meema know you did that, or she'll have you putting up shelves in the bathroom in no time at all," warned Vishal. "She's been after me for months to do it."

This time there was no answering message of complaint from the computer, but on the other hand, nothing seemed to be happening.

"Kenneth, do you have any ideas of what this is for?" asked Vishal.

"I have a few, but I am not going to tell you just now," Sharpe replied guardedly.

"I have no idea why you are saying that. So if it is games that you want to be playing, please face the camera and say 'cheese'". Sharpe complied, and Vishal fooled around with the mouse and keyboard.

"Now look here," he requested. Sharpe's face was on the screen. "I'm going to add this to the database, I think." Click, click. "Good. Now, let's compare. Smile for the camera again." Sharpe did so. Click, click. "Oh, look."

"It says 'Not enough records in target database for match'," read out Sharpe.

"So what it is saying is that we must have some more faces."

"Vishal," Sharpe said slowly. "How do you know that this program is for face recognition? You've only been using this a few minutes and I didn't tell you anything about it, did I?"

"It's because I'm a bloody genius, that's why, man," he answered, finishing the last of his can of beer.

Sharpe shook his head. "And I had a little help," confessed Vishal, opening a window that announced "Welcome to the Katsuyama Face Recognition Program. Version 0.94 Build 0.71c".

Sharpe laughed. "You're still a bloody genius." Vishal popped the tops on a second can of beer for each of them and they clinked cans together. "So, bloody genius, what do you think this does?"

"I'll need a little more time to work this out absolutely. Can you leave this with me?"

"Sure, why not? You have a copy of the disc, and the card's not going out of your PC, is it?" I'll leave it all with you. How long do you want with this?"

"I will be needing about a week, I am thinking. Come back this time next week, and there will be some answers ready for you. It would be quicker, but you understand that we are having an audit at work and this is taking much time. Damn nuisance, but that's life. Let's go and talk to Meema."

The next half-hour passed quickly enough in conversation, mainly about Vishal's cousin, who wanted to come to Japan, but was having problems with his visa application.

"Thanks, you two. I really must be going. I'll be round next week to see what you've discovered, Vishal, and then the two of you must come over soon for a meal."

"Looking forward to it," replied Meema.

Sharpe trotted off happily into the night, bearing a bag containing some samosas to take back for Mieko that Meema had thoughtfully hidden where they wouldn't get eaten.

WHEN HE ARRIVED BACK AT THE FLAT, Mieko was in hysterical tears, standing in the hallway. Sharpe dropped the bag of samosas and rushed to embrace her.

"What's the matter, darling?" She said nothing, but led him by the hand into the living room. Sharpe had heard the expression "it looks as though a bomb's hit it", but never experienced it in its full glory before. The furniture was upside down, every book was out of the bookcase, the cupboards were open and their contents littered the floor.

"… And … it all happened while we were both out," she sobbed, taking his hand and leading him to the bedroom. The story was the same.

"What about your jewellery?" he asked. He knew Mieko loved jewellery. Not expensive things, but all good taste, and she collected it quite seriously. All with some kind of sentimental value, marking birthdays, friends' weddings, trips abroad, and the like. None of it was really valuable, but was all good quality, no trash, and it was loved, as much as anyone can love inanimate things, and was a real part of her life.

Mieko's face crumpled. She dropped to her hands and knees and started sifting through the wreckage of cosmetics and lingerie by her dressing-table. There was no way Sharpe could see that he was going to be of any use, so he stood and watched, feeling slightly sick at the invasion of their privacy. After a few minutes she looked up, smiling through her tears. "I think it's all here. One thing missing. That sapphire brooch that we bought together in Thailand in April, remember ... Oh, here it is!" She held it up triumphantly. "That's everything!"

"I am glad," Sharpe said, and really meant it, hugging her. He realised that her jewellery did mean a lot to her, silly as it might sound. Maybe it was to do with her terrible first marriage where her husband walked out, taking her two children, whom she'd never seen again (losing one's children completely in this way is not that uncommon in Japan, though it is usually the mother who gets custody). Then the Big One hit Sharpe. What about his office? He rushed into the next room to view chaos once again. He'd taken the laptop to Vishal and Meema's, so that was OK. But the main desktop computer was trashed. When he looked at it, he could see the cover had been removed, and the hard disk had been taken out. Ouch, he thought. Better not look at the desk. He did. Ouch again.

Mieko was behind him. "Who was it?" she asked.

"How the hell would I know?" he snapped, instantly aware that he wasn't being fair. "Sorry," calming down immediately. "Look, get ready to go out again. I'm going to call Meema and ask if you can spend the night there. I'm going to be talking to the police, and maybe they'll want to talk to you. When you get to Meema's, start writing down everything you can remember about how you came in, what you saw, what lights were on, and everything like that. It'll help the police, I hope." He pulled out his mobile.

"Meema? It's Kenneth. Can Mieko spend the night with you?" He quickly explained the situation. "You'll send Vishal round in the car to collect her? Bless you, Meema."

He explained to Mieko that Vishal would be round in a few moments. "I'll just get a toothbrush and things," she said.

Sharpe reached in his pocket, opened his wallet, and looked at the card Inspector Sugita had given him earlier the previous day. He dialled the number on the card. There were a few clicks and beeps, and a phone started ringing.

"Yes?" came the answer in Japanese.

"Inspector Sugita? My name is Kenneth Sharpe. We met this morning."

"Of course." The voice sounded affable.

"My house has just been burgled."

"What?" He sounded shocked. "Of course, I am sure you will realise that this is not my usual work as a policeman—"

"Yes, I'm sorry about that, Inspector Sugita, but I felt that you would be interested."

"No, no, Mr Sharpe, you misunderstand me. What I was going to say was that although it is not my usual line of work, I will make sure that the patrol cars come round immediately. Please allow me to help. I also will be coming to see you personally as soon as possible." He didn't leave any room for argument. The line clicked dead.

The doorbell rang. Sharpe opened it and let in Vishal.

"Oh my God!" he exclaimed as he saw the chaos. "Who in the world would be doing such a terrible thing?" He seemed as upset as Sharpe and Mieko. "Oh, Mieko, I am so sorry to be seeing all this terrible terrible thing," he said, as she emerged from the bathroom.

"Now, you take care of yourself and have a good night's sleep if you can," Sharpe said, hugging Mieko goodnight.

It's good to have friends you can trust like this, thought Sharpe, as Vishal gallantly escorted Mieko to the car. Of course he had made many other friends in his time in Japan, but Vishal and Meema really turned up trumps when you needed them. He hoped they felt the same about him.

"Vishal!" Sharpe called out to him. "I won't be coming round to visit you tonight, but I may call you."

"Any time. I really mean that. Any bloody time you like." They drove off, and as Sharpe finished waving, he thought he saw some movement behind the camellia bushes at the side of the parking area. He certainly wasn't going to go out there and investigate, though, and he went back to the flat to wait for the police.

He didn't have long to wait. The doorbell rang, and he answered it. His uniformed friend from the previous night was there, grinning nervously from behind two colleagues in plain clothes.

"Mr Sharpe," the taller and older of the two plainclothesmen asked. "I am Detective-Sergeant Kurokawa, and this is my colleague, Detective-Sergeant Yatabe." He spoke excellent American English, with hardly a trace of a Japanese accent. Sharpe's pistol-forgetting friend, who continued grinning in the background, was not introduced.

"Come in, please." They removed their shoes and stepped into the hallway.

"This is bad," said Kurokawa, peering into the wrecked living room. "Very bad. This is not just an ordinary burglary." He translated this into Japanese for the benefit of his colleagues. "Would you mind if we spoke Japanese, Mr Sharpe? My English is not so good." Which hardly seemed to be true, of course, but it saved the face of the other two.

"That's fine, but there may be some words where I will need your help," Sharpe answered in Japanese. Smiles all round.

The police went into their routine and took Sharpe methodically through checklists of what he had seen, what he had touched, what was missing, and so on. They walked through the flat together, looking at the damage and taking notes. Sharpe started to feel sick as the full scale of the vandalism and invasion of privacy started to sink in. They asked about Mieko, and when he explained that she had gone to a friend's house, they took the details as he gave them.

"Will she be asleep, do you think?" asked Yatabe. He was

slightly shorter than Kurokawa, with a friendly round face and a bushy moustache.

"Probably not."

"Then I will make a phone call. What number?" he asked. He dialled on his mobile and got through to Mieko quickly.

"You're writing it down?" he asked the phone. "Excellent idea. Thank you. It was his idea?" he looked over at Sharpe and gave a thumbs-up sign and a grin. "You're nearly done? Can I come over and collect it in about fifteen minutes? Maybe ask a few more questions? Just me and the policeman who visited you last evening. Thank you." He hung up.

"One thing," Sharpe added. He described the shape he had half-seen in the shadows of the parking area. "But then, I might have been imagining things," he finished.

"Or you might not," said Yatabe. "Let's find out, shall we? Which side of the parking area? The left? If we go out of these windows and take the fire escape, can we get round there without passing in front of the lighted building entrance? Good, then that's what we'll do. Come on," he said to Sharpe's uniformed friend.

They went to the hallway and collected their shoes before sliding aside the broken French window which had obviously been the point of entry and exit for the burglars, and moving almost soundlessly towards the fire escape along the balcony.

"Kenji-san enjoys that sort of thing," commented Kurokawa in English, chuckling. "Me, I feel too old."

"Your English is really very good," Sharpe replied.

"Police academy in Sacramento. Part of the foreigner liaison course. So we'd know how to deal with ignorant barbarian foreigners who don't know how to behave in civilised Japan." His smile was clearly genuine, and there seemed to be no insult intended.

Sharpe felt the least he could do was to smile back. "Glad to see you, anyway."

"Well, I can get the fingerprint boys round, but it would be a waste of time, I'm sure. This isn't a burglary, really, is it? No jewellery taken and no cash missing."

The doorbell rang.

"Excuse me," Sharpe said, and opened it to let in Inspector Sugita, who was in plain clothes.

"Sorry to meet you like this," he said. His reaction on seeing the wrecked room was the same as everyone else's. "Oh dear, dear, dear," he exclaimed in Japanese.

"Please relax, Sergeant," he said to Kurokawa, who'd leaped to attention when Sugita walked in. "You're working, this isn't a—" The last word defeated Sharpe's Japanese skills, and he sent a non-verbal signal for assistance.

"Parade-ground," Kurokawa translated for Sharpe.

"Excellent, Sergeant. It was a good move to send you to Washington, wasn't it?"

"I was in Sacramento, sir." Kurokawa coughed, and Sharpe thought he saw the suspicion of a wink pass between the two men.

"Of course, Sergeant. Sacramento, wasn't it?"

"So what's missing?" Sugita asked Sharpe in Japanese.

"As far as I can tell so far, only the hard disk out of my desktop computer."

"What does that contain?"

"Client data, research materials, database software, reports. My whole business."

"You don't seem very upset about it."

"I'm not very upset, as a matter of fact," said Sharpe. "I make backups every night to another disk which I disconnect and keep in the back of the drawer where I keep my printer paper. I've checked and it's still there. No-one seems to have noticed it. I've lost maybe half a day's work, I

At the Sharpe End

suppose. Whoever's got the disk knows a little of what I do, but most of it is— 'Encrypted'?" Sharpe asked Kurokawa the last word in English.

"*Angouka sareta*," Kurokawa explained to Sugita, who nodded.

"What on earth is this?" Sugita was now looking at the remains of the contents of Kumi-chan's toy cupboard. "Are your children all right?" He sounded genuinely concerned.

Sharpe explained about Kumi-chan and how he and Mieko kept her toys here for when she came to visit.

"Someone hates Kitty-chan," Sugita remarked, poking through the remains of a child's painting set, decorated with pictures of the popular mascot, and a boxed jigsaw puzzle of the mouthless feline, both of which seemed to have been singled out for particular violence. A chill went down Sharpe's spine. Why had Kitty-chan been specially trashed in this way?

The doorbell rang again. It was Sharpe's uniformed friend, with a leather-clad Japanese youth in tow. Sharpe noticed the prisoner holding his hands oddly, and then realised he was handcuffed. "Thank you, Mr Sharpe," said the policeman. "We found this one just where you said he would be. Permission to call the station to send someone for him now, sir?" he asked Sugita, saluting.

"Of course. Well done, Mori. Where's Yatabe?"

"He's gone round to the friend's house, to talk to Mrs Sharpe, sir."

"Get the station to send someone to be with him, will you? No, on second thoughts, you go over there, Kurokawa, when the others arrive. Mori, call in to the station to get this garbage picked up and let's get a full incident team over here."

Mori made the call. No-one said anything for a few minutes.

Sharpe examined the youth, slouching beside Mori. An ordinary sort of face. Pinched-looking. About 20 years old, permed hair dyed brown, black leather jacket and jeans. Expensive-looking cowboy-style boots which the police hadn't made him take off before bringing him into the flat. Odd, he thought. Or maybe it was just impossible to take them off while he was wearing handcuffs. He wondered why they'd brought him into the flat in the first place.

"Nice boots," Sharpe said in English, on impulse.

The youth looked up and smiled. "Thanks, mate. Cost me two hundred dollars. Real crocodile," he replied in an Australian accent.

Sugita, Kurokawa and Sharpe exchanged glances. "Oh, shit," said the youth in English. He laughed, showing a terrible set of teeth. "Now you know I speak English."

"If it's not too much trouble for you," said Sugita to Sharpe, "I think it would be a good idea if you came down to the station tomorrow. I'll call you when we want you to come round. We'll put you on the other side of the table this time." He smiled. Sharpe didn't think the joke was funny, and didn't bother smiling back.

And then the house was full of policemen. Mori and his prisoner went off with a couple of the new arrivals, Kurokawa set off for Vishal's, and the rest stayed, dusting, counting, asking questions, taking photos, making endless notes on clipboards. Sugita kept his distance from the mass, occasionally being consulted by the others.

After about thirty minutes, Sharpe felt like the proverbial pork chop at the bar mitzvah – useless. Sugita came over and put his hand on his shoulder.

"You look tired," he said in English. "Don't worry, they'll be gone in a little while. Where are you going to sleep?"

"Thanks, I'll be all right. I can drag out a futon and sleep somewhere on the floor."

And that's what he did when the last of the boots departed some forty minutes later. Contrary to his expectations, he didn't dream at all, not even of poor mutilated Kitty-chan.

Chapter 2: Tokyo

Chapter 3: Tokyo

SHARPE WOKE UP TO A NIGHTMARE VISION of overturned furniture and general chaos. He went into the kitchen to see if it might be possible to make a cup of coffee, and retired hastily. Someone was going to have to clean up the kitchen some time, but it wasn't going to be him just then, he reckoned.

He remembered that somewhere in the place was the stash of samosas Meema had given him for Mieko the previous night, and was just starting to hunt for them when his mobile went off. It was Vishal. "Listen, man, I've got to be getting to work now, but I'll give you a hand this evening getting the heavy stuff sorted out, right? Get over to our place now. Meema's expecting you for breakfast."

"Bless the pair of you. I really appreciate it." He put the phone back in his pocket and the doorbell rang.

It was Mrs Miyata from the neighbourhood association.

"Last night … I heard … Is there anything …" Sharpe knew what she wanted, and decided to let her off easily. He had always found her to be charming, a bit butterfly-minded, and always dressed a little too young for her age, but a good soul, and the leader of the association, so he calculated that this was the best thing to do. At least the truth would circulate around the neighbourhood, and any lurid rumours would be stopped in their tracks.

"Please come in, Mrs Miyata. Mieko's not here. No, we didn't have a fight. Yes, they were policemen last night. Come this way, and you'll see—"

She turned white at the sight of the living room, and Sharpe almost expected her to faint. She collapsed against the back of an overturned chair and gasped for breath. To a typically obsessively clean and tidy housewife like her, this must have seemed like blasphemy or sacrilege.

She asked the first question that everyone always asks.

"No, they don't know who did it. They arrested one person last night, and I may have to go to the police station today to talk about it more."

She asked the next question that everyone always asks.

"Nothing much. No money or valuables, anyway."

"Oh you poor things. Where is Mieko now?"

Sharpe explained that she'd gone to Vishal and Meema's. "It was too late to bother you," he lied. "You and your husband would have been asleep and we couldn't have woken you." That, and the fact that Mrs Miyata would have gone off like a siren if all this had been explained to her at the time.

She nodded. "Thank you. Meema's a nice person. So is Vishal, of course, but I can't always understand him," she added. Mrs Miyata had met them socially several times now, and the common Japanese prejudice against non-white foreigners seemed to have disappeared in Mrs Miyata's case. Sharpe was pleased to see that the tolerance had spread to the whole of the neighbourhood association. Vishal and Meema were always welcome now at community New Year parties and the like. In fact, the plates containing Meema's home-made Indian snacks were always the first ones to empty at the traditional Japanese festivals.

"Anyway, Mrs Miyata, that's what happened. I'm just going to Vishal and Meema's now to collect Mieko."

"Well, if we can help ..."

"Thank you. I'll tell Mieko." Sharpe wasn't sure if Mieko would welcome a gang of helpers who might be more interested in examining the inner secrets of a foreigner's household than doing any actual work. It would just be curiosity and there would be no malice intended, but it would be more than a bit nerve-racking for Mieko.

Sharpe escorted Mrs Miyata to the door. "Please tell everyone what's happened, Mrs Miyata." Sharpe guessed she would do so anyway, but this gave her formal permission to gossip. "And please don't worry. We'll be fine."

HE PICKED UP HIS BRIEFCASE, and locked the door (more out of habit than anything else) and then set off for Vishal's house. It was a typical Tokyo summer day, warm and sticky, although the sky was relatively clear. The cicadas were shrilling from the trees as he walked past—a sound of summer that always reminded Sharpe that he wasn't living in England any more.

It had taken Sharpe some time to appreciate the sprawling Tokyo metropolis. Sharpe had discovered he'd somehow fallen in love with the city without ever having intended to do so. The random piles of concrete didn't look any more beautiful to him now than when he'd first arrived—in fact, he hadn't even reached the stage where he could ignore its ugliness. But the imperfections had acquired their own peculiar charm. Somewhat like a plain girl, he thought, who makes no effort to be anything other than what she is, Tokyo had actually become attractive as a result of its honesty, and the imperfections had started to become points of attraction.

He reached Vishal's house, and Meema opened the door. "She's still sleeping," she said. "Those policemen last night were very nice, but they did stay for quite a long time. And I think the emotional shock must have been terrible. Come in and have some coffee while I wake her up."

Sharpe gratefully sipped coffee and listened to the feminine noises coming from the bedroom. Eventually Mieko appeared, without her makeup, and with her long hair unbrushed, looking slightly the worse for wear.

"All right, darling?" he asked.

"Fine," she replied, yawning. "Still tired, though. I didn't get off to sleep until about 3 o'clock."

"Breakfast, you two," called Meema. More coffee and toast seemed like a really good idea to Sharpe.

"Mrs Miyata called round just before I set off," he said to Mieko. "I had to explain to her that we hadn't had the mother of all battles last night. She wanted to know what was going on, so I told her."

"I bet she said she'd be round to help," said Mieko. "With an army."

"She offered," Sharpe replied guardedly.

"Well, I'm not going to have them all round. Mrs Watanabe's one of the worst. She'd be making rude comments on the state of your underwear as soon as she stepped into the bedroom."

"Vishal will be round in the evening," Meema reminded Sharpe. "He said the place really looked terrible and you'd be needing some help." She looked closely at him. "Any idea why this has happened to you? Is it anything to do with the stuff you and Vishal were working on last night?"

"What makes you say that?"

"Oh my God, it is. Are we next?" Meema's perceptions were disturbingly acute, even at this time of the morning.

From Sharpe's left, Mieko joined in. It was like being at Wimbledon – as the ball.

"Kenneth, what is all this? Is this something to do with that box you brought back the other day and the man who died?"

"What man is this?" shrieked Meema. Sharpe had forgotten how shrill her voice could be when she was excited. "And he died? What are you mixed up in, Kenneth? It sounds to me as though Mieko shouldn't be going home. You, you can please yourself where you go. And you keep Vishal out of this, you hear?"

"Wait a moment, Meema," he tried to explain. "I met a man the other day who gave me the box you saw last night. I didn't know what was in it until just before I came round to you, and I had no idea how or what it really was until Vishal explained it. And you, of course," Sharpe added quickly.

"And now this man's dead?"

"He fell under a train at Shinjuku station. I talked to the police about our conversation and I told them what I knew."

"Who else did you tell? The people who wrecked our home?" asked Mieko.

Sharpe was grateful that she referred to it as "our" home – usually she referred to it as "your", implying she was going to flit out of his life as casually as she had flitted in, but that was beside the point here. He thought back to Ben's casual mention of how they'd searched Katsuyama's home. "Maybe I did," he admitted grudgingly, thinking of Ben in the police station. Both women sighed together.

"What have you matched yourself to?" Meema asked Mieko. "A man who opens his house to bad men, to goondas and badmaashes."

"Look, I didn't mean to do it," Sharpe said helplessly.

"But you did," said Mieko. He was outnumbered and outgunned. And they didn't fight fair, recruiting feminine illogic to their cause. Sharpe was saved from outright abject defeat by his mobile phone.

"Yes?"

"Inspector Sugita here. Please come round to the police station as soon as possible."

"I can be there in about fifteen minutes?"

"Excellent. I'll be waiting for you."

Sharpe turned the phone off and started to speak before the double barrage started up again. "That was Inspector Sugita. He wants me to go round to the police station to talk to the man they arrested last night. Did they tell you?"

Both of them nodded.

"All right, I'll call you when I get out," he said to Mieko. "Thanks for the breakfast, Meema." She simply shrugged.

THE CICADAS' NOISE NOW SEEMED MORE LIKE AN IRRITATION than a sign of summer as Sharpe made his way to the police station. He wasn't in the best of moods when he walked up the steps and presented himself at the reception desk.

"He's with me." Inspector Sugita's voice came from behind Sharpe, addressed to the receptionist. "No need to sign him in."

They walked along the same corridor that Sharpe had previously used. Sugita seemed anxious to put him at his ease, asking about Mieko and about insurance cover.

Sharpe tried to turn the subject to the arrested man. "What charge?" he asked.

"Oh, we're just holding him right now," explained Sugita. Japanese police have the right to hold arrested suspects without benefit of a lawyer for over twenty days. And then they can bring another charge which allows another twenty days of unsupervised questioning. Japanese jurisprudence has very little in common with Western legal procedure, despite similar terminology in many cases.

They reached the interrogation room. "This side, today," explained Sugita, waving Sharpe to the chair that Ben had used. The room still smelled of his cigars. Sugita fiddled with the desk light, aiming it so that it would be shining in the eyes of whoever sat in the chair opposite.

The door opened, and the youth of last night came in, followed by Kurokawa.

"Sit," ordered Sugita, pointing to the chair.

With an effort, the youth sat. Sharpe noticed he kept his hands behind his back, and guessed he was handcuffed. Without any warning, Kurokawa unleashed a backhand swing at his face, which knocked him sprawling on the floor.

"I told you to sit down," snarled Sugita.

The youth struggled from the floor and sat on the chair once again. Blood trickled out of the corner of his mouth. Kurokawa hit him again in the face. Again, he went sprawling. This time, Sugita said nothing, but waited as he struggled to his feet and sat again.

Sugita held up his hand to Kurokawa. "Enough," he said. To the youth, "We expect you to answer our questions willingly and honestly and openly. If you don't …" He left the sentence dangling. "We know your name already, Osaki, and your address. Thank you for helping us with that last night, but we could have got that from the driving licence in your pocket. What your driving licence doesn't tell us, and you didn't tell us last night, is what the hell you were doing."

The mouth moved, but only blood came out.

"Take the cuffs off," ordered Sugita. "And bring a towel." Kurokawa fished in his pocket for a key and fiddled around behind Osaki's back. Osaki winced, and brought his hands in front of him, massaging his wrists. "Thank you," he said.

Sugita nodded. "Get that towel," he said to Kurokawa. "And some water."

They waited in silence for Kurokawa's return. Osaki kept massaging his wrists. Sharpe sat, embarrassed to be in the same room as the others. More than anything, he was embarrassed at his own almost sexual secret enjoyment of the scene – not something he wanted to admit to himself, or anyone else. And it was anyone's guess what Sugita was thinking, just sitting there like a Buddha.

Kurokawa returned and tossed a white towel into Osaki's lap. Picking it up, Osaki dabbed his face and spat discreetly. Sharpe thought he heard part of a tooth hit the floor. The towel turned red as he mopped his mouth.

"Water," Sugita ordered Kurokawa. A paper cup found its way into Osaki's hands.

"Thank you," he said again. He drank, rinsed, and spat into the towel.

"Now I've done something for you, you do something for me," said Sugita.

"Of course, Inspector," said Osaki. His voice was quiet as he sat very straight in his chair.

"Tell me and this gentleman here what were you doing outside his apartment building last night."

"Waiting to see who was coming in and out of his apartment. My job was to let the people inside know when someone was coming and call them by phone."

"Who hired you?" asked Sugita.

"I don't know his name," replied Osaki. "He was a foreigner."

"Korean or Chinese, maybe?" asked Sugita, somewhat hopefully, it seemed to Sharpe.

Osaki shook his head violently. "No, not at all. He was an American, or maybe a Canadian, but I would guess that he was American."

"Where did you meet him?"

Osaki shuffled his feet and looked a little embarrassed. Kurokawa tensed beside him, but relaxed in response to Sugita's raised finger.

"Well?" asked Sugita. "Where and when did you meet him?" he repeated.

"Special bar in Roppongi the night before last," replied Osaki. He squirmed a little in his seat as Sugita continued to stare at him, and Kurokawa moved a little closer. "Gay bar, if you really want to know."

"If you answer the rest of my questions the way I like, I won't bother asking you too many questions about what you were doing there. We might manage to forget about it, even. Name of the bar?"

"Mama Turkey's. It's just round the back of the Roppongi Hills building. In the alley just to the left of the Chinese restaurant at the bottom of the street. Pink sign outside the door."

"Thanks for the directions, but I don't think I'm going to want to go there very soon," replied Sugita dryly. "How did you meet him? Did he approach you or the other way round?"

"He approached me."

"And he said?"

"'Can you do something for me?' He was speaking English – he must have heard me showing off my English to my friends. Of course, I just thought he meant the usual. But then he made it clear that this was going to be something different when he explained."

"How much was he paying you?"

"Fifty thousand. Half in advance. Half after the job. Of course, I haven't got the second half yet."

Sugita laughed without any humour. "I don't think you're

going to get it any time soon, anyway. So, did this mysterious American have a name?"

"He said his name was Eric, but I'm pretty sure it wasn't his real name."

"What did he look like?"

"Tall, thin. Very short grey hair. Wore a suit and tie – not sharp – a bit old-fashioned. Really lame shoes. Marks on his face – scars, sort of. Kept smoking these stinking little cigars. Smelled a bit like this room."

Sharpe said nothing. Sugita said nothing. They carefully didn't look at each other.

"Was it him who went into the apartment?"

"Yes, it was. He had a couple of friends with him. They went round the back to go through the window there. You saw that. He came out of there just as your wife," nodding to Sharpe, "was going up the stairs to the apartment. I saw her coming in and I phoned him."

"How did you know it was his wife?" Sugita asked. Sharpe decided not to correct the repeated mistake, though he was sure that someone would have remarked the lack of a wedding ring, and the fact would be on file.

"He'd shown me pictures. And I'd seen her going out earlier."

Sharpe asked himself where the pictures of Mieko had come from. This was starting to get very scary.

"And you had photographs of Mr Sharpe here?" asked Sugita.

Osaki nodded. "One photo of him, one of her, one of both of them together, and a picture of where the flat was in the building." The shivers were really starting to chase each other up and down Sharpe's spine by now. Someone had cased the joint with a vengeance.

"Where are the photos now?"

"I don't have them. He never gave them to me. Just

showed them to me and made sure I could remember the faces."

Sugita changed tack. "What do you know about Hello Kitty?" he asked. "In connection with this incident? And don't get cute with me."

"Nothing, I swear," replied Osaki. He seemed puzzled.

What would Hello Kitty have to do with any of this? Sharpe wondered himself why Sugita had fastened onto that one point. As far as Sharpe knew, all Sugita knew of Hello Kitty was that he'd seen some badly vandalised toy the previous night.

"Maybe nothing," repeated Sugita. "And then you got collared while you were smoking a cigarette?" He seemed to be slightly amused by this.

"That's right. I was keeping a watch for Eric to come out again – if I saw anything, I was to call his phone, and so when I saw Mr Sharpe's wife go in, I called him, like I said."

"So why were you still there?"

"I was waiting for my money," replied Osaki. "Eric had told me that I would get the rest of the money if I waited there for him after the job had finished. Well, I saw the police car come up, and I thought to myself that Eric wouldn't be coming back while the police were around, so it would be a good time for me to have a cigarette. But it's an odd thing, I could have sworn there was someone else nearby watching."

"Did you see this other person?" asked Sugita.

"No, like I said, it was more of a feeling than anything else."

"Well, that's all very interesting. We'll be asking you to sign a statement about all this soon. Understood?"

Osaki nodded. "May I speak to Mr Sharpe, please?" he asked Sugita. Sugita signalled his assent.

Osaki lifted his head and looked into Sharpe's eyes. "I'd

like to apologise for my part in this," he said in his Australian English. "When I came into your flat last night, I really had no idea what a mess it was going to be. I didn't know that it was going to be this kind of thing. Of course I knew that it was going to be a robbery, but not that kind. I mean, if I had known what kind of job it was going to be, I wouldn't have … I mean, I'm bloody sorry about it all." He voice tailed off as he knelt on the floor and bowed.

"Get up and shut up," said Sugita, but his voice was not unkind.

Sharpe added, "Thank you for the apology." A slight bow in return.

"OK, take him away for now," Sugita said to Kurokawa, who'd watched this little comedy in silence. "And no need for the cuffs," he added, as Kurokawa reached for them.

"Well?" he asked Sharpe in English as the door closed. "Do you want us to keep him in jail? Charge him with being an accessory? We can keep him for a long time, you know, before we charge him with anything."

Sharpe had never been put in a position like this before. "I really have no idea."

"OK, then. What do you think of his story? Do you believe him?"

"Do you?" Sharpe countered.

"I'm sorry to say that I do," replied Sugita, shaking his head. "Usually I would never have believed Ben would do such a thing. But I do know that his agency is very concerned about the Katsuyama case."

Sharpe thought the matter over for a while, "Can we reach a compromise?" he asked. "I'm not going to excuse that kid everything, of course. But at the same time, he's not really guilty of anything serious, is he?" Sugita shook his head in agreement. "So how about keeping him in the cells for tonight, and then letting him out tomorrow morning?

Tell him I don't want to press charges or anything?" Sharpe reckoned this might save Sugita the embarrassment of his complicity with Ben and his agency. Much as he liked the idea of Ben getting his comeuppance in public, he saw no point in unnecessarily provoking Sugita and his group of whatever they were. He was sure by now that they weren't the regular police.

Sugita nodded. "I like that idea. It would be a waste of time and trouble for us to take him to court. That's what we'll do, then."

Sharpe was on his way home from the police station, and was just pulling out his mobile phone to call Mieko and let her know where he was, when he heard a voice behind him.

"Here, mate!" Sharpe turned. To his dismay, he saw the Australian who'd been telling him on the train about the Isle of Mantids the other day. One of the last people he wanted to see. "Here," his unwelcome companion panted as he caught up with Sharpe. "Let me buy you a coffee or something. Put you straight for me bending your ear with that load of bollocks the other day." He grasped Sharpe's elbow and firmly steered him to a nearby branch of a national chain of cheap restaurants. There was no wriggling out of it without making more fuss than the occasion seemed to warrant, so Sharpe submitted with a bad grace.

When they were seated at an isolated table, the Australian ordered coffee for two from the waitress, a plump moon-faced girl who looked as though she'd be happier doing anything other than her current job. Maybe it was the unflattering absurdly short skirt that formed part of her uniform that was depressing her. While they were waiting for the order to arrive, Sharpe sat with his arms folded, feeling sulky. He hoped it showed. His companion kept him company in his silence. Maybe he'd got the message, Sharpe thought.

The coffee came, borne by the miserably mini-skirted waitress, and the Australian pulled the sugar bowl towards him.

"Sorry about this," he remarked, spooning sugar into his coffee. His Australian accent and attitude was gone, replaced by a British upper-middle-class accent. It didn't go particularly well with the shabby black T-shirt with a fluorescent koala design. "Can't be too careful where Sugita's concerned."

Sharpe tried to keep a straight face, but failed. "How the hell do you know about Sugita?"

"My job, old boy." He reached in an inside pocket and scaled a laminated plastic card across the table. His photograph was printed on it, with a name, Jonathan Campbell, and impressive-looking lettering identifying the bearer as an employee of Her Britannic Majesty's Government.

"MI5? Or 6?" asked Sharpe. "I can never remember which is which."

"Don't be silly. Nothing as grand as that. British Department of Trade and Industry – we don't like to advertise our presence too widely sometimes. I'm not James Bond, I don't have any kind of license to kill, and I don't have a cigarette lighter hidden in my micro-camera. Or even the other way round. Cheers." He lifted his cup, swigged the coffee, and made a face. "That stuff is bloody awful. Wonder what they put in it."

Sharpe looked suspiciously at the contents of his cup, and sipped gingerly. It tasted much the same as always to him. "Seems OK to me."

"You've been here too long, that's your trouble. What's it now, fifteen years ago that you came here?"

"About that," Sharpe agreed.

"Now me, I've only been here a few months, and I can still remember the taste of Seattle coffee. That's where I was before. There and Silicon Valley."

"Chasing Bill Gates and Steve Jobs?"

"Something like that," the other admitted. "Why did you come to this benighted part of the world in the first place, anyway?"

"Came here as an English teacher after I lost my job in the UK. I was also running away from a rather painful divorce. The pay was reasonable, and it sounded exotic in England at the time, but the reality is actually incredibly boring and frustrating. So I got out of that as soon as I found a company that could use my UK experience in the technical field, and then I started working for myself about seven years back."

"Why did you start working for yourself? Why not for a company? I'd have thought it was incredibly risky, setting yourself up as any kind of consultant in a country as weird as this."

"I'm not a joiner," Sharpe confessed. "I don't want to get too deeply involved." It was true, he told himself. He tended not to become a full member of anything he was associated with, preferring to stay on the outside and observe with what he hoped would be taken for cynical detachment. A fear of getting too deeply involved and then getting hurt, if he rationalized it to himself. Maybe that's why he had stayed in Japan—he could be a perpetual outsider, with no chance of getting sucked into the mainstream of society. His English divorce had hurt him more than he wanted to admit to himself.

"In any case," he responded, "what and who the hell are you? Technology police or something?"

"That's a lot closer to the truth than you might imagine, you know." He took another sip of his coffee and called the waitress over. "Put simply, we keep an eye on technology developments which could be of interest to HMG."

"Officially sanctioned industrial espionage, then?"

"That's about the size of it. We don't actually steal trade secrets or anything, but we do give discreet little nudges behind the scenes to make sure that deals go the way we want." He studied the large glossy menu, and eventually pointed out a picture of a plate of miniature doughnuts to the depressed waitress, who seemed to have just discovered yet another reason why life was not worth living.

"To British companies?" asked Sharpe, watching the rotund backside and chubby thighs move slowly towards the kitchen.

"Where possible. But often it's just a case of making sure the deal doesn't go the wrong way, rather than making sure it goes the right way."

"Atomic secrets to North Korea?"

"That's an extreme example, but yes, that's the sort of thing. Remember that deal where the maglev technology was going to go to the Frogs and then didn't?" Sharpe nodded, remembering how the French had been interested in purchasing superconductor magnetic levitation from Sumitomo to make their next-generation high-speed train, the UGV. The deal had fallen flat, and the license had gone instead to a Singaporean company developing a rapid transit system in Brunei.

"Well," continued the other, accepting the doughnuts from the waitress, "that was me making sure that the deal didn't go through. Or rather, not me, but my boss here."

"I thought we were friends with the French?"

"Friends, sure." He laughed mirthlessly. "Come off it. Anyway, us poor bloody infantry in the trenches just do the pushing. The owls in Whitehall give me the direction to push in." He bit into a doughnut. "Jesus Christ! What's in this thing?" holding it out towards Sharpe.

Sharpe inspected it. "*Anko*. Bean jam."

"If it's been jam, what is it now?" Sharpe sat silently. "Don't bother laughing. It's not that funny in any case. Want one?" gesturing to the plate. Sharpe shook his head. "Don't blame you. How do you stand this bloody country, anyway?" Sharpe continued to sit in silence. "Don't bother answering that one, either."

Sharpe stirred in his seat. "Actually, I do have a question or two for you to answer. Why the hell were you following me around the other day, and what was that load of crap about the island with those insects?"

The other took another bite of the doughnut, winced, and put the uneaten half on the plate. "I wasn't really following you, if you want to know. I was following Katsuyama, who, as I am sure you have found out, is no longer around to be followed, and I needed to talk to someone in the train that he was in. You didn't notice him there? I don't think you were meant to. You were the only other Westerner in that carriage that day. You turned up in almost every public place that he visited since we started trailing him, so it was pretty obvious who he wanted to talk to. He was just waiting for the moment. Like it or not, your name and face are quite well-known round this town, and it's fairly easy to get hold of basic information such as where you live and so on. And as for the Isle of the Mantids that I was talking about, it's basically bullshit. Sort of entertaining, but still bullshit."

"Well, thank you for the explanation or confession or whatever you want to call it. Now I feel much better, and I'm sure you feel better as well for having got all that off your chest. Now go in peace and sin no more. Go on. Piss off."

"What's eating you, then?"

"Can't you bloody guess? First thing is I find I'm being tailed by a mad scientist with North Korean connections, who falls under a train the same evening I meet him. Then I get grilled under the bright lights by the Japanese police and the CIA playing tag-team. Then my place gets worked over and trashed and my stuff is stolen. Then I have to sit and watch the Japanese police beat up some poor sod who's only involved by accident. And then James Bond comes crashing into my life telling me that he's been following me around as well, and now he wants me to play on his team. All right," as the other held up a warning hand, "you're not James Bond. You can be Austin Powers if you prefer," referring to the James Bond parodies. "But if it was you, wouldn't you feel a little pissed off at this stage of the game?"

"OK, OK, you have a point. Several points, I suppose. Let me explain a few things to you. Want to stay here, or walk outside?"

"Walk and talk? We can't be bugged outside, right?"

"Oh, don't be so bloody stupid. No-one's bugging us." Sharpe let the other collect the bill and pay for it. After all, he'd ordered the uneaten doughnuts.

As they were leaving the restaurant, Sharpe asked, "What's your name? What do I call you?"

"Which?"

"I assume there's a difference between your name, and what I call you, then? Like Ben?"

"We'll come to Ben in a moment, if we're talking about the same person, which I am pretty sure we are. Call me Jon. Without the 'H'. It's the name on my card, if you didn't notice, and actually happens to be my real name, if it makes you feel any better."

They walked side by side, with Sharpe taking the lead in determining the direction. After five minutes of silence they arrived at a line of trees flanking a small stream, deep-set in its concreted banks. "Great in April when all these cherries are out in flower," remarked Sharpe. "Not so wonderful right now, but let's walk along the bank anyway. We come to a station in about a kilometre, and you can take the train back to the embassy from there – I take it that's where you'll be writing up your report?" Jon said nothing. "Oh, please yourself. Now tell me whatever it is that you think I'm entitled to know. Need-to-know – isn't that how you people work? Well, I need to know quite a lot."

"OK, what do you know about Sugita for starters?"

"Inspector in the police who's a nice guy, or likes to be seen as one, anyway," leaving it vague as to whether it was as a police inspector or a nice guy that Sugita liked to be seen. "Plays good cop in the good cop, bad cop game."

"Let's start with him. First, his name's not really Sugita, as you might guess. It's Ishihara – and yes, there is a very vague family connection to the Governor of Tokyo, but it's not a strong one. I think we can ignore it in this case. He certainly doesn't share his relative's xenophobia. Next, he's not really a police inspector any more. You'd probably worked that out. You don't think that the police would let an inspector appear in a uniform fitting that badly, do you? I've seen him in it a couple of times, and nearly wet myself laughing whenever he bends over, waiting for his trousers to split."

"Go on." Sharpe wasn't sure if was better to be questioned by a fake policeman or a real one.

"He's actually sort of my opposite number, I suppose. Employed by the Ministry of Justice – in one of their special departments which actually aren't their departments. It's complicated. There are quite a few of them, and I don't know all the ins and outs of how they're organized. Some seem to be focussed on anti-gang activities, some on military intelligence, some on economic intelligence, and so on.

Most of these funny little groups seem to be based out of the police headquarters in Kasumigaseki, and they're almost always headed by ex-police. Ishihara actually was a pretty good criminal investigator, specialising in things like intellectual property theft and related white-collar crime, and his sidekick Kurokawa is an impressive performer, too. Went to Quantico as joint liaison with the FBI at one time."

Sharpe remembered the way Kurokawa had backhanded the lookout man, and thought "impressive" might be the wrong adjective to describe him.

Jon went on. "You know that Japan has no intelligence service worthy of the name?" Sharpe shook his head. "What they have instead is a collection of pretty amateur agents in every ministry and department, as well as the military intelligence arms. And of course, a lot of the work is effectively outsourced to the large conglomerates, who pass on to the government some of their industrial and other interesting material that they pick up, as a patriotic duty. But there's no central co-ordination – silly buggers. Anyway, your Inspector Sugita is pretty much the number one man in his field, which is the sort of thing you're involved with. Technology and that sort of thing."

"What about the police working with him? I mean the ones who came round last night."

"Well, the one who came by to ask you about Katsuyama's death – don't worry, I know most of the facts, and I'll explain how in a while – is also one of Ishihara's men, but he's one who's never been in the police. Do you think a real trained police officer would leave his gun behind like that? Come to that, do you think it was a real gun?"

Sharpe thought about it, more than a little surprised and shocked by the knowledge that Jon seemed to have of his actions and meetings over the past few days, but it all seemed to make a sort of sense. "Go on," he repeated.

"As I said, Kurokawa is Ishihara's man, of course, and so is Yatabe. In fact, the four we're talking about make up the mainstay of the team. The other police who came round to your place last night are active-duty bona fide 24-carat police. But they have standing orders to subordinate their activities to Ishihara when he demands it. They hate doing it, of course, but they do it."

"And Ben?"

"Oh, 'Ben'? The thing you know as Ben is a real piece of work. Real name is Al S. Kowalski, believe it or not. Ex-spook. Very much ex. He was sent over here about fifteen years ago, and was one of the principal parties in a very nasty scandal involving a teenage male prostitute found naked and bleeding to death in a Roppongi back street one morning. Very nasty place to be bleeding from, as well. Seems like Al likes a bit of rough in his sex life. Japanese police couldn't touch him – diplomatic immunity and all the rest of the crap, but they were mightily pissed off, I heard. Added to which, Big Al hits the bottle and goes on uncontrollable benders for a couple of weeks at a time. So the Agency kicked him out, and there's a warrant waiting for him if he ever shows his face in the good old US of A again. Which of course, he never will."

"And so he's doing Ishihara's dirty work in exchange for immunity from extradition and prosecution by the Japanese authorities?"

Jon looked at him. "Very good, Kenneth," he said softly. "Go to the top of the class."

Sharpe walked on in silence a little further, Jon slightly behind him. "All right then, Kurokawa's your man inside who's giving you all of this? You're not plucking this out of thin air, are you?"

Jon gave Sharpe another look. "Ooh, you *are* good," he

said, affecting a camp voice. "Not quite right, though," he added. "Nine out of ten."

"Well, I don't think it's Yatabe. Ishihara himself?"

"I never said a word," confirmed Jon. "Want to join our lot? Mostly indoor work, no heavy lifting, guaranteed pension. You really could become quite good at this game, you know."

"What have you got on Ishihara, then?"

"Would I tell you? And with you not even signing the Official Secrets Act?" asked Jon rhetorically. "As it happens, nothing. He came to us of his own free will many moons ago. Fed up with what he saw as the graft and corruption in the Liberal Democratic Party. Plus he'd had a couple of years at Cambridge as an exchange student, and really admired what he'd seen of England." He paused and regarded the river for a while. "Should have brought those bloody doughnuts for those ducks. Silly bugger," he added inconsequentially. It wasn't entirely clear whether the "silly bugger" referred to Ishihara's admiration of the British, or his own forgetting to bring suitable nourishment for the ducks.

"Do the rest of his team know?"

"Hell, no, but we do cooperate with them from time to time. Ishihara sent Kurokawa over to the States to learn a few things from the FBI. Since then, we've learned quite a lot about the way the Yanks' counter-intelligence operations work overseas. Damn, now you really are going to have to sign the bloody thing."

"It's all right," countered Sharpe stiffly. "I know how to keep my mouth shut." They walked on in silence.

Sharpe stopped short. "Bloody hell! You bastards!" Once again, he realised that someone had been taking an interest in him without his having been aware of it. His own ignorance angered him as much as the sudden realisation of the fact.

"Keep your voice down. What is it now?" in the voice of someone humouring a fractious child.

"My flat. Who the hell burgled it?"

"Al S. Kowalski. And a hired hand. Don't know who that was. Plus the kid you met this morning as a lookout."

"With your blessing? Or Ishihara's?"

"With Ishihara's reluctant blessing. Cover, you see. If Ishihara left the British alone while turning over the houses of all the Japanese involved in this thing, it would look a bit fishy, wouldn't it?"

"So what's "this thing", anyway, when it's at home? All this crazy shit is about what Katsuyama has developed?"

"Yes, it is. How much do you know about it?"

"What Katsuyama told me about it. That it's a cheap way of identifying faces in silicon."

"Have you any idea what that's worth?"

"Not a hell of a lot, surely? I mean maybe to a digital camera maker who wants to be able to automatically tag the kids' photos as you take them, it's a useful gimmick, but not much more than that."

"No more than that? Think bigger than your poxy little digital camera makers." Jon seemed to be considering inner options. "What arrangements have you got for this afternoon? I want you to cancel the lot of them. Now. Use your mobile. We're off to the embassy after lunch, and then I want you to meet a friend of mine. Go on, I'm going to stand over you while you cancel those arrangements. Tell them you have a fatal case of diarrhoea or something. Tell your woman you're busy, as well."

Sharpe felt he was in no position to argue. He made the calls, leaving a message for Mieko, who appeared to be out of the house, and wasn't answering her mobile. Jon made one short call on his own phone, but he turned away from

Sharpe while he was making it, so it was impossible to hear or guess what he was saying.

After lunch in a hideously pretentious Italian restaurant in Azabu, for which Jon (or rather, the British taxpayer, Sharpe thought cynically) paid, they set off for Hanzomon, where the Tokyo British Embassy is located in a spacious garden compound facing the Imperial Palace. Sharpe knew the embassy only from passport renewals, international economic or technical forums to which he got occasional invitations, and following Princess Diana's death, when he had joined the long line of emotional Tokyo-ites to sign the book of condolence (kept in the Ambassador's residence, not the embassy itself, given Diana's ambiguous status at the time). Usually the hired Japanese security guards at the entrance searched bags, and demanded ID, but Jon's magic plastic card let them straight through the gate. Sharpe fought the urge to salute the civilian rent-a-cop back.

"This way," said Jon, leading Sharpe past the Consular section, where he usually renewed his passport, round to the back of the compound. A brass plate on the door said "Jonathan Campbell, Special Liaison". Special Liaison to what? Sharpe wondered to himself.

Jon unlocked the door and they entered a small room, furnished sparsely with standard office furniture. The room had absolutely no trace of personality, other than a smart pinstripe suit and shirt and tie, on a hanger on a peg behind the door. The desk was bare, except for two telephones. Jon picked up the red one.

"Internal line," he said, covering the mouthpiece with his hand. To the telephone, "Major Barclay's annexe if you would please, Jill." He covered the mouthpiece again. "He works outside the embassy walls for some reason I've never been told, and visits are by appointment only. Like royalty." He spoke into the phone again. "Tim? Jon here. There's someone you ought to be speaking to. Yes, the man himself. No, we've eaten, but thanks for the offer. Yes, within fifteen minutes." He put the phone down.

"We're off to see the wizard," he announced. "One stop down the line to Kudanshita, or do you feel like walking? We can do it in fifteen minutes if you'd prefer."

"Walking's fine."

"Let's go." Jon locked the door carefully behind him and they set off.

As they walked out of the embassy compound, Sharpe gave in to temptation, and returned the quasi-military salute thrown at him by the uniformed private security guard at the gate, which caused momentary confusion in the guard box, and a smirk to appear on Jon's face. They made their way through small side-streets to a building which appeared to be an empty shop with shuttered windows. Jon pulled the key to the locked front door from his pocket, and led the way through the room, filled with empty showcases, to the back of the building, where a solid-looking door barred their way. It looked much newer than the rest of the building, with heavy-duty hinges and a fearsomely complex-looking lock and some electronic gadgetry that looked like a fingerprint reader.

Jon pressed the buzzer beside the door and identified himself over the intercom. The lock clicked, presumably having been opened by a remote control. "This is as far as I go," explained Jon. "I could tell you it was lines of demarcation and bailiwicks and all that but actually, I can't stand being in the same room as the bastard for more than two minutes at a time. I'll be seeing you in the near future, I'm sure. Good luck." Sharpe wasn't convinced that was what he wanted, but it didn't seem to be his choice to make.

THE FIRST THING HE NOTICED ABOUT THE ROOM when he entered was the acoustics. All the sound seemed to be soaked up by the walls and floor, and replaced by a soft hissing sound. In contrast to the technical soundscape, the windowless room was comfortably, if somewhat garishly, furnished, with a loud floral wallpaper and a brightly-coloured Turkish carpet, in an attempt to turn the space into a study in a private house. A private house owned by someone with questionable aesthetic sensibilities, thought Sharpe, but still an improvement on standard government issue.

The next thing that he noticed was the heat. It was uncomfortably warm in the room, to the point of stuffiness, even compared to the humid weather outside. The air-conditioning was obviously not turned on.

The diminutive Major Barclay made up for his lack of height with an overly fussy manner which seemed intended to put visitors at ease, but didn't succeed in its task. Sharpe had the absurd impression that he moved on wheels as he came from behind the desk and motioned to a pair of matched armchairs.

Sharpe sat down, but the other hovered. "Coffee, tea, or something a touch stronger? The coffee's *fabulous*, though I say it myself. Comes straight from Indonesia. Special beans reserved for the Indonesian President and the Cabinet. Suharto *adored* it – drank gallons of the stuff. *Do* say yes." Sharpe obliged, recognising the source of Jon's earlier imitation.

The Major ("*Do* call me Tim, or if you like, you can think of me as Major Tim, a bit like the song, not that I really take *any* notice at *all* of ground control") fussed with coffee beans and a shiny glass and metal contraption in an alcove in one corner of the office, throwing out small talk about the weather ("I *adore* the cold dry mornings in Tokyo winters – so *bracing*, don't you find?"), the England cricket team's chances in the New Zealand Test match (Sharpe, who had hated cricket since he broke his finger catching a ball at the age of seven, switched off at this point), and the recent Japanese cabinet reshuffle ("such *bullies*"). Eventually the coffee got made, and after more fuss with the milk and sugar ("I *detest* that Japanese white paint-type muck they give you, don't you?"), Tiny Tim, as Sharpe now mentally referred to him, settled himself in the armchair and inhaled the steam of his coffee.

"Fabulous," he breathed. Sharpe politely sipped his coffee, and agreed. It was good, he had to admit.

"So Jon picked you up," Barclay remarked, reaching behind him to pick up a beige folder lying on his desk.

"If you like to put it that way," responded Sharpe.

"No, no, the question is how *you* like to put it." Sharpe looked at him over the top of his coffee cup, but there appeared to be no deliberate double entendre involved.

"Excuse me," he said, after a pause. "But just who the hell are you?"

"It says on the door. Or it would do if I'd ever bothered to put up a nameplate. Barclay. Timothy Augustus Neville. Major. Late of Her Majesty's 33rd Corps of Mounted Sanitary Engineers."

"And now?"

"Oh, you *are* nosy, aren't you? I suppose we'd better get this thing out of the way, then, hadn't we?" He removed a set of folded printed sheets out of the folder. Sharpe noticed the words "Official Secrets Act" in large type underneath the Royal coat of arms. "Here, here and here," he said, turning to the last page, and proffering a silver fountain pen to Sharpe.

"And if I don't?"

"Well, much as I'm enjoying our little tête-à-tête, I suppose we'd have to say that rain stopped play, wouldn't we?"

"And if I signed it, and then went back on what I'd signed?"

"Ooh, you just *want* to be awkward, don't you?" Tiny Tim patted his immaculately coiffed silver hair as if making sure it was still there. Sharpe had a feeling that if he pulled hard enough, it might come away in his hand, and expose some bald spots. But then again, hair transplants were big in Japan. "Well, we can't extradite you for that, of course. But there might be some *very* butch heavies from the Special Branch waiting for you if you *ever* decided to go back to dear old Blighty. Much better to sign, really, and do it as though you meant it. Just close your eyes and think of England," moving the pen towards Sharpe again.

Sharpe skimmed through the paragraphs of legalese. "Oh, for God's sake, man," cried Barclay. "No-one actually *reads* the bloody thing." Sharpe ignored him, and ploughed through the jungle of "hereinafters" and "notwithstandings". Years of reading confidentiality agreements had taught him to skim legal documents fairly fast and reliably. He rapidly came to the conclusion that he'd met commercial non-disclosure agreements which were better worded and armed with more teeth than this. He signed.

"Oh, well *done*," exclaimed Barclay, as if applauding an infant who'd just been coaxed into swallowing an unwanted spoonful of food, and retrieving the papers from Sharpe. "Now we can chat properly," tucking the signed document into the buff folder. "More coffee, by the way? I will," moving towards the coffee machine. Sharpe declined. "So where shall we start? How much did Jon tell you?"

Sharpe repeated the gist of what he had been told earlier that day.

"Silly boy sometimes, our Jon," commented Barclay. "Says just a *little* too much for his own good sometimes. You really didn't need to know *all* of that. Words will be had, I can assure you." He made a motion as if smacking a child's wrist.

"Who the hell are you to decide what I do and don't need to know?" snapped back Sharpe. "It seems you and your crew have had a pretty good go at taking over my life for the past few days. Isn't it only fair that I'm allowed to know what's going on around me?"

Barclay was instantly conciliatory. "Dear me, there's no need to take it all so *personally*," he purred. "I'm not sure you realise *exactly* what kind of high stakes are on the table right now. Any other pearls of wisdom I can throw in your general direction? Not that I would regard it as casting pearls before swine in *your* case," he giggled.

"Why is Katsuyama's gizmo so important?" asked Sharpe.

"Oh, *right* in the bull's eye or his arsehole or something," exclaimed Barclay. "I must say, that is a *remarkably* good one to start with. Why is this little box of tricks so important, he asks?" He sat back in his chair. Sharpe noticed his legs didn't reach the floor, but stuck out slightly in front of him. "Well, where Katsuyama was such a clever boy was that he found a way of doing things cheap and fast. And small. Just think, you could put the thing on one of those absolutely *super* spy satellites that no-one is meant to have, get it to count the spots on a gnat's dick, and get it to send back the information to us. 'Spotted dick gnat located at x degrees, y minutes and z seconds north, and a-b-c west, proceeding in a southerly direction along the M1 up to London.'"

"Yes?" Sharpe didn't see where this was leading.

"As opposed to sending *thousands* of photos of gnats with no spots on their dicks to the boys in the back room, who'd then have to spend their days counting spots on gnats' dicks until they find the picture of the one they want. By which time, the bloody thing has flown up the M1, bitten the Prime Minister on the bum, and returned home to Mummy and is safely tucked up in bed with a hot water bottle. Now replace a gnat with spots on his dick on the M1 with a suspected terrorist in Afghanistan. See the use now?"

Sharpe saw. "OK, if the thing's that smart, what do the Japanese want with it? They don't have satellites that good, do they?" Tiny Tim just smiled faintly. "Well, they don't have the bloody launchers. That H2A booster is flakier than ..."

"A Kellogg's factory?" Barclay suggested helpfully. "Yes, Kenny– I may call you Kenny?"

"I prefer Kenneth, or Ken, if you really must abbreviate it."

"Ken, then. New planet swims into his," he mused to himself. "Yes, you're right, Ken. The Japanese space capability is sadly limited by their inability to actually *do* anything. Shame, really. They have such bloody *wonderful* ideas. Robots running around on Mars building cities, and all that crap."

"But Katsuyama's idea is a useful bargaining chip when it comes to defence negotiations with the US?" Sharpe suggested. "No pun intended."

"Very, very good, Ken," applauded Barclay, patting his tiny hands together. "Of course, the Yanks claim it's really theirs, having been made in Stanford, but between you and me, I think our late lamented friend Katsuyama deserves *some* credit here, don't you? And in this case, finders are keepers, don't you think?" Without waiting for an answer, he continued. "Of course, that always presupposes that we know just *who* the finder is. If it happened to be one of Her Majesty's subjects, that would be a fine thing for the UK, don't you think? Hurrah for bloody old England and all that?"

"Indeed it would," said Sharpe, as offhandedly as he could manage.

"So where the bloody hell is it?" Barclay asked, more sharply. "Katsuyama gave it to you, and it wasn't in your flat, was it?"

"It wasn't found in my flat." Let the petty-minded bastard chew on that, he thought to himself.

"All right, we'll let you keep your little secrets for now," somewhat testily. "We'll find out sooner or later."

"Is this thing really so important if you already know everything that Katsuyama was up to?"

"Strange as it may seem to you, yes. From what we know, Katsuyama is – or rather was," he corrected himself, "one of those mad geniuses who come along once in a blue moon, and no-one can follow their reasoning. Let me make a wild guess. When you met Katsuyama, was he asking you to write up his work based on what he'd published at Stanford, in order to put the Americans off the scent? Something like that?"

Sharpe sulkily admitted that this was indeed the case, but something told him that this wasn't exactly a wild guess on Barclay's part.

"Let me tell you, Ken, that you wouldn't have stood a virgin snowball's chance in hell of managing it. No offence to your education and intelligence, which I'm sure are vastly superior to those of the average member of God's creation. It's just that Katsuyama was progressing by leaps and bounds. And when you leap and bound, you leave precious few footprints behind you for anyone to follow. See where I'm driving?"

"How do you know so much about him?"

"My dear Ken, please give us *some* credit for recognising genius, even in little out-of-the-way backwaters of academia like Stanford University. Anyway, the upshot is that without the combination of the hardware and the software he wrote to make it sit up and beg, we're stuffed, to coin a phrase."

"All right, I think I get what you're driving at. Where does the North Korean connection fit into all of this?"

"Ah," lacing his fingertips together. Some of the former playfulness crept back into his voice. "That *naughty* Kim Jong-il. The Dear Leader and his henchmen. Oh dear, *what* a mess."

"Yes?"

"Well, let's try and imagine North Korea. Not the poor buggers starving to death – unfortunate as they may be, they play *no* part in our discussions. What we're seeing right now – those of us with the eyes to see, that is – is a struggle between the Party and the Army as the old order changeth. And they're *not* the same at all, no indeed they're not," he insisted, wagging a warning finger, although Sharpe had shown no sign of promoting any view to the contrary. "The Party would like to see their country as a proud independent state true to the spirit of Iosif Vissarionovich, God damn his soul to hell, free of all contaminating influences – that old *juche* self-reliance thing of Daddy Kim's. The Army generals, bless them, being hairy-chested men of action, take a somewhat more practical view, and feel that their country needs the helping hand of another."

"Like China?" asked Sharpe.

"*Just* like China. Absolutely. And with China trying to win gold medals in the space race, you can see that Katsuyama's doodad would actually be quite a feather in their cap. So put two and two together?" he invited.

"Katsuyama's in-laws are on the military side of the argument. They want the imaging technology to give to China. China backs the military against the Party. Military wins. Katsuyama wants to keep it out of their hands, for obvious reasons."

"Very good indeed," Barclay applauded again, moving his hands together soundlessly. "Of course, I forget that you do this kind of thing for a living, in a slightly different field, of course. Fancy joining our little mob?"

"Thank you, but no. Jon's already asked."

"Has he now? That was a very naughty thing for our Jonnie-boy to do. He has absolutely *no* authority to go round saying that sort of thing. We shall *definitely* have to have words, I can see that."

Sharpe found it hard to summon up much sympathy for Jon's fate. He decided it was time to change to a more urgent topic of conversation. "So what happens to me now? Am I going to be pursued and harassed by renegade CIA agents and North Korean spies all the time? "

"No, don't be so silly. We'd be keeping an eye out for you."

"Just like you kept an eye out for Katsuyama?"

"Touché there, Ken," acknowledged Barclay, shaking his head, though whether in sorrow at Katsuyama's death or not, it was impossible to tell.

"Who killed the poor sod, anyway? Do you know, and would you tell me if you did?"

"No and no," replied Barclay calmly.

"And just like you kept an eye on my flat while Ben or Al or whatever he calls himself this week turned the bloody place upside-down?" Sharpe was aware that he was starting to shout, but he didn't care. It felt good.

"Temper, temper," Barclay admonished him. "You may consider Al as an elemental force of nature. Like the wind, he bloweth where he listeth. The only thing that can faintly be described as a control over Al is the thought of a future in a small secure room in the USA shared twenty-four hours a day with three other men, who might not always respect the fact that Al likes to be the one on top in his little games. And believe me, Ishihara reminds him of this possible change to his lifestyle at reasonably frequent intervals." He patted his hair once again. "Not that it always seems to do a lot of good," he added.

"What about the kid that they pulled in who was watching my flat? Where does he come into all of this?"

"He sounds like Al's bit of rough for the night who got called on to do a bit of extra. From what I hear, he's the original tart with a heart. Might even like to meet him myself when all this is over."

"I think that was my point – when is all this over?"

"I'd have thought that was *rather* obvious, Ken," replied Barclay, smiling like a panther. "The answer is in your hands, isn't it? Or if not actually in your hands, it could be within a few minutes, I am sure." He got up out of the chair and moved to the door. "Well, it's been *fabulous* meeting you today, Ken," reaching for the handle. "You know my name, and you know where to find my little nest. I'm sure we'll be seeing each other *very* soon." He pulled the door open. "*So* nice to have met you. Good-bye, or should I say au revoir?"

Sharpe didn't bother to say anything in reply, but picked up his things and walked out.

As he made his way towards the station, Jon came running up to meet him. He had changed from the Australian hitchhiker look to a business suit. The tattoos seemed to have vanished as well. He could have been taken for any of the yuppie bond traders Sharpe spent much of his spare time avoiding in Roppongi bars.

"How did you get on with our very own poison dwarf?" he asked. "*Fabulous* coffee," he breathed.

"Piss off," growled Sharpe.

"Don't blame you there. I had to take you to meet him, though."

"You, lad, told me a damn sight more than you should

have done, and you are now in deep shit with Major Tim Bloody Barclay," answered Sharpe with some satisfaction.

"So what's new?" responded the other. "Can I buy you a drink later this evening? Meet you at the Press Club in Yurakucho? Meet a somewhat more attractive companion or companions than the one you've just been talking to?"

"You're not referring to yourself there, I take it? Wouldn't be hard to find something more attractive, I agree. OK, as long as you're buying. I'm not a member. What time?"

"Quarter past seven. See you in the bar. Here's my mobile number," handing over a piece of paper. "Just in case you get held up."

"Or you do."

"I never get held up – always on time – that's one of my virtues, as I am sure the poison dwarf informed you? No? He should have done. Well, I'm back to the embassy now. See you later." He set off down the street as Sharpe descended the steps to the Metro station.

Now Sharpe thought about it a bit more, he was beginning to get an understanding of the value of the thing. Did that mean Vishal and Meema were in danger? If so, he'd have to do something about it. Such as moving the contents of Hello Kitty to a bank deposit box? But that was an obvious thing to do, and he had no doubt that Ishihara/Sugita and his organisation would have little difficulty in obtaining permission to open such a box, or opening it anyway, even if permission were not forthcoming.

Like most people, Sharpe found it difficult to maintain a concentrated train of logical thought. Thoughts of Meema led to other things, and before he realised what he was doing, he found himself in a semi-erotic daydream. That in turn led to slightly guilty thoughts of Mieko. He decided to call her, realising that he hadn't actually spoken to her since he'd left her and Meema shouting at him that morning as he set off for the police station.

There was no answer at the flat. He left a message on the answering machine and checked his watch. Probably out shopping. He called her mobile number. No answer, not even the recorded message telling him her phone was off-line and asking him to leave a message.

Sighing, he wrestled with his mobile phone's interface and sent a short text message to her mobile telling her that he'd be out that evening, and she wasn't to wait for him or cook for him. He hoped to God she wasn't out shopping now – she became righteously angry when she bought and cooked food that he was unable to eat as the result of a late-running meeting or last-minute work coming his way.

He decided to call Meema's to see if Mieko was still there. There was still a stiffness in Meema's voice.

"No, she left me about an hour after you went. No, she didn't say where she was going. She told me she was going to cook something for you and Vishal when he comes round tonight. I think she's forgiven you. I must say, I wouldn't." There was an distinctly audible sniff of contempt at the other end of the line.

Hell and damnation! He'd arranged for Vishal to help out with getting things straight, and now he had to put him off, and appease Mieko. Or put off the meeting with Jon. Two against one. Jon lost.

The phone was answered after five rings. "Jon, it's Kenneth Sharpe. Look, I can't make tonight – forgot I had something else on this evening. Can we make it some other time?"

"Sorry to hear that. Same place, same time tomorrow OK by you?"

"Can't promise anything right now. Let me call you to-morrow and I'll let you know."

"Fine. You take care of yourself, right?" and the phone clicked off. Sharpe was left wondering exactly what he meant by that last phrase.

Time enough to make his way back home and try to make his peace with Mieko. On the way from the station to his flat he stopped and bought a small bouquet of flowers. Not large enough to look like an obvious bribe, but large enough for a serious peace offering, he thought.

THE FRONT DOOR OF THE FLAT WAS UNLOCKED. Not like Mieko, he thought. She was usually obsessive about locking the door whether she was in or out of the flat. Like many Japanese recently, she was worried by the media reports of a "crime wave" in Japan, as the result of the wicked foreigners (mainly Chinese) coming in and taking over. The fact that the Japanese organised crime families had effectively been running the country through their Liberal Democratic Party stooges since the end of the war never bothered the media, but half-a-dozen burglaries a month in a city of twelve million were blown up into a civilisation-threatening crime wave. Silly to think about all that, though, when the place had just been thoroughly worked over.

"Hello, I'm home," he called. No answer. He walked into the living-room. It looked just the same as he had left it that morning – overturned furniture and mess everywhere. The wind was blowing in through the smashed window. Have to do something about that. Not urgent, though – it wasn't exactly cold.

No-one in the kitchen, which looked almost normal. Someone had been tidying up. No-one in the bedroom, or his office, which both looked exactly as he had left them that morning. Feeling a bit of a fool, he even knocked on the toilet door, but there was no answer.

Chapter 3: Tokyo

Weird, he thought, opening the fridge for a glass of milk. He saw a pack of crab claws – one of his favourite foods, which Mieko also loved – which he didn't remember having seen the night before. Must be her shopping for this evening. Mieko's attempt at a peace offering, he told himself.

But where was she? He called Meema again.

"Kenneth here, Meema. Mieko hasn't called you recently, has she?"

"No, isn't she at home?" A little of the chill had gone out of Meema's voice.

"No, no sign of her, but she's done some shopping."

"Perhaps she's with the neighbours?" suggested Meema.

"I'm sure you're right," agreed Sharpe. "Thanks."

He wasn't sure of his last words, though. As the unmarried once-divorced partner of a foreigner, Mieko was tolerated, but not openly welcomed, as a part of the neighbourhood association. She wasn't that close to any of the neighbours, and he didn't think she'd be sitting there gossiping while the flat was in such a mess.

Maybe her parents' house? He took a deep breath and dialled, hoping it was her father who picked up the phone. It wasn't. Damn. "Mrs Nishimura? Has Mieko been round to see you today? No, we haven't had an argument, but we had a bit of an accident in the flat last night, and I thought she might have wanted to tell you about it. All right. Thank you. And best regards to your husband." He put the phone down and sighed. Mrs Nishimura seemed to want to blame him for everything that had gone wrong with her beloved daughter's life, even though he'd met Mieko more than a year after the failure of her marriage.

Happily, her father was a much more practically minded man who welcomed the idea of an exotic connection to the family, and happily exhibited Sharpe to his friends at the local pub as a sign of his international broadmindedness.

Sharpe usually woke up the next morning with a deepened appreciation of Japanese generosity, and an aching head.

Well, wherever Mieko actually was, someone had to get the evening meal ready. Sharpe dumped his briefcase in the study, put the flowers into water, and rolled up his sleeves. As he put the carrots into the sink for washing, he noticed a slip of paper beside the sink – a till receipt from the local supermarket listing some vegetables and a pack of crab claws. Looking at it more closely, he noticed the time and date – about four hours ago. Mieko's apron was draped over the back of a chair. So where was she?

His mobile phone rang, and he snatched at it with dripping hands, but it wasn't Mieko.

"Hello, Vishal."

"Look man, I am very very sorry. Bloody boss needs me to explain the new procedures to the New York office on a conference call, and that means that I am not going to be able to be helping you tonight. He is fixing this bloody thing for half past nine o'clock this evening and I am having a meeting with him before that."

"I understand, Vishal." Actually, Sharpe was a little relieved. If Mieko wasn't back, it might be embarrassing to try to explain her absence.

"No, man, I really am sorry. Let me come round to you tomorrow evening, I swear, yes?"

"No problem. Just let me know a few minutes before you come round, right?"

"Sure. Very very sorry."

"Vishal. Just shut up. You can buy me a beer some time if you really feel that bad about things, but it's not your fault. Don't worry about it, OK?"

Sharpe continued washing and peeling the carrots. He'd just sliced them and had put them into a saucepan when the doorbell rang. Probably Mieko, forgotten her key, he hoped to himself, opening the front door.

He was wrong. Standing on the doorstep was a slightly built woman in a dark raincoat with a headscarf concealing her hair and most of her face, which was turned away from him. He couldn't for the life of him work out who it was.

"Yes?" he asked in Japanese.

Without revealing her face, she spoke to him in Japanese with a noticeable accent that he had difficulty placing. "Sorry to bother you. My name is Tomiko Katsuyama. I believe you knew my husband. May I come in?"

She slipped through the door quickly, glancing behind her.

"Is someone following you?" asked Sharpe, closing the front door.

"I hope not," she replied.

Sharpe led the way into the living room, momentarily forgetting the state of the room. As she entered the doorway, Mrs Katsuyama froze. "Oh goodness," she said, her hand fluttering to her mouth. "I never thought it would look like that."

And what the hell was that meant to mean? thought Sharpe, tidying a chair for her to sit on. He decided to let it sort itself out in the course of conversation. "Excuse me a minute," he said. "I was just about to fix that," pointing to the broken window, though which the wind was continuing to blow.

He went to his study and came back with a roll of duct tape and a cardboard box. She watched in silence as he taped cardboard over the broken window panes before drawing the curtains. Only then did she seem to relax.

"Please, I know it's not that great here at the moment, but please try to make yourself as comfortable as you can," said Sharpe. "Tea or something?"

"If it's not too much trouble, I'd like a little whisky." Sharpe noticed her hands were shaking. "Just a little. Straight, please."

Whisky was one of the few alcoholic drinks that Sharpe didn't really like. However, grateful clients kept showering him with expensive Scottish malts and bourbons, so he was well-stocked.

"Wait a moment," going into the kitchen. When he returned with a small glass of whisky for her, and a vodka and orange juice for himself, he nearly dropped the drinks. She had removed her headscarf and coat, and even in a black "formal" funeral dress, she was one of the most attractive women he had ever seen off a cinema screen, and the tightly fitting black dress appeared to be cut considerably lower in the front and have a much shorter skirt than seemed appropriate for mourning. However, Sharpe had never considered himself an expert on women's fashion. Perhaps this is what the well-dressed widow wore these days. He remembered Mieko's more "comfortably rounded" figure and tried unsuccessfully not to think disloyal thoughts. Although he was convinced his eyes were popping out of his head like chapel hat pegs, as his Derbyshire grandmother used to put it, somehow he managed to cross the two miles of floor to her chair without collapsing, spilling the drinks, or otherwise making an obvious fool of himself. Beautiful women always had an unfortunate effect on him, it seemed, making his feet twice their usual size and making them trip over anything in their path that was higher than a matchstick, and increasing his natural clumsiness factor by several hundred percent.

"Is this all right?" he croaked like a raven, handing her the glass. At least, he assumed it came out as a croak. His throat was so dry and constricted he was surprised he could make any intelligible sound at all.

"Thank you," she said. He put down his glass, heaved the sofa into some kind of normality, and collapsed into it.

He was about to make some cheerful and flippant toast, when he remembered that he was in the presence of a recently bereaved widow. "To the memory of your husband," he said, lifting his glass solemnly.

She said nothing, but raised her glass in reply. The finger of whisky he had poured for her went down with no apparent pause, and no apparent effect. Sharpe sipped his drink, trying desperately not to stare too hard at her profile. There was a silence that lasted for a minute or so, during which Sharpe managed to gulp most of his drink. The sound of his drinking sounded in his head like feeding time at the zoo, and the ice swirling in his glass crashed in his ears like the iceberg that hit the *Titanic*, but she didn't seem to notice anything out of the ordinary.

"Another?" he asked.

"Yes, please." There was almost no expression in the small quiet voice. He went into the kitchen to pour the drinks, and picked up a bag of rice crackers which he shook into a bowl. She accepted the glass with a word of thanks, and started sipping, and then coughing.

"Are you all right?" asked Sharpe. More coughing. As gently as he could, he moved beside her and started to pat her on the back, uncomfortably aware of the feel of her body through the thin black dress, which seemed to be all she was wearing in that area.

She stopped coughing and turned to him, her lovely face distorted in an ugly mask. "Please..." she gasped, and fell sobbing into his arms, gripping his clothes with both hands as though he was a life-belt. Feeling like a fool, he held her, stroking her hair and feeling her body shake as she wept. His feelings were definitely and inappropriately erotic. Eventually she stopped and loosened her grip on his shirt, and in response he unwound his arms from around her shoulders and moved a little way away from her.

"I'm sorry," she said. "So sorry. I never realised that it would come to this."

"Come to what?" Sharpe asked her.

"My father and his brothers. They're terrible men. That's why I ran away from them and married Masashi, so that I wouldn't have to live with that kind of thing any more." She started sobbing again, but less violently than before. Even though he wanted to, Sharpe didn't put his arms around her this time.

"What have they done?" he asked, when the sobs had died down a little. He remembered what Katsuyama had hinted about his in-laws' gangster connections.

"It's your wife," she said, quietly. Turning to look him in the eyes. "They were here an hour ago and took her."

Sharpe was on his feet instantly. "Where?" All his worst fears leapt to the surface.

"They mentioned the river," she answered. She had completely stopped crying and seemed to be in control of herself. "They were talking about a construction lot near the station where there's a new block of flats being built."

"What were they going to do?"

"They didn't say. Maybe hold her for ransom, maybe … I don't know. I must go now before they notice I've gone."

"Where have you come from?" asked Sharpe, already on his feet. He had no firm ideas in his mind, but part of him had already cast himself as a white knight riding to Mieko's rescue.

"Staying with relatives. Now I must go." As he was helping her on with her coat, the sleeve of her dress rode up, exposing livid bruises on her arm.

"What's that?" asked Sharpe. "Who did that?" The

bruises were about the size and shape that a man's hand would make if he gripped a beautiful woman's arm tightly.

"Nothing. No-one," she answered too quickly. And then the coat was on, and she was off before Sharpe could stop her.

There was no doubt in his mind that he would go after Mieko. None at all. He thought for a moment about taking a weapon, and dismissed the idea. The odds were that he would be outnumbered by people whose way of life included violence as part of their daily routine, and the closest thing to a real weapon that he could find was likely to be a kitchen knife anyway.

Walking fast through the barely-lit streets (after a couple of decades of desk-based life, he was in no condition for extended bursts of running), he began to be afraid. It was years since he'd been personally involved in any kind of violent action. He'd studied a little kendo in the past, but fencing with bamboo swords hardly qualified as a practical method of self-defence in the 21st century. Usually he relied on his wits and his skill with words to talk his way out of difficult situations, but he had his doubts as to how effective this would be in this case.

Searching his pockets, he remembered his key-ring had a small light attached. Although it was meant to help find a keyhole in the dark, it was brighter than it needed to be, and might prove useful. And that, apart from the keys themselves, comprised the contents of his arsenal against ... what?

He tried hard not to remember what he'd read in the past about some of the more gruesome habits of gangsters in Japan, and then asked himself why on earth he was being so possessive about Katsuyama's gizmo. Let them have it, he told himself. It's not yours. Hell, they probably have a legal right to it, if they're his relatives. Perfectly reasonable.

Except that Katsuyama had given it to him, and he'd liked Katsuyama. Not that that made any difference. He was getting illogical. Time to slow down and think it through.

All right, he finally decided to himself. If they want the bloody thing so much, then let them have it. He'd have to go to Vishal's place and pick it up. But then he'd have to involve Vishal and Meema, and there was no way he was going to get them involved if he could help it. He'd have to talk.

Sharpe felt his heart was pounding fast and hard as he walked fast. He was rehearsing what to say in his best Japanese when he felt a heavy hand on his shoulder.

"SHARPE DESU KA?" ASKED A ROUGH VOICE as another hand grabbed the other shoulder – hard. He tried not to wince as the fingers bit into muscles that he'd forgotten existed.

"Hai," he replied. There seemed to be little point in denying his identity and he wasn't going to start complaining about the missing honorific.

He was dragged towards a large black car of the type that Sharpe automatically associated with gangsters. It seemed to be one of those things which were far too big for Japanese roads, and had incongruous dainty lace curtains behind the tinted windows.

"In," said one of the men behind him, opening the door and shoving him inside. The central locking mechanism clicked, locking all the doors together. Sharpe found himself sitting next to a large older man, with tightly permed hair, wearing a dark shirt and light-coloured tie. Why on earth did gangsters in Japan always have to live up to their stereotyped image? Sharpe thought, but then reminded himself that all Japanese seem to find the image more appealing than the reality of actually being something.

"Where is my daughter's husband?" asked his companion in almost completely fluent unaccented American English.

Sharpe choked back a number of possible answers and simply replied, "I'm sorry. I don't know your daughter and I don't know her husband." The pain exploded in his head without warning. As he shrank back against the back seat of the car, giving an involuntary cry, he heard an answering cry from the front of the car. Screwing up his eyes against the pain, he looked, to see Mieko sitting in the car's front seat, her arm gripped by the driver.

The man in the back seat beside him was reflectively fingering the gun with which he'd just pistol-whipped Sharpe. Sharpe didn't know if it was a real gun or not – Japanese firearms regulations are incredibly strict, but there had been reports of Russian pistols finding their way into the hands of local gangs. He decided not to try and find out. "My daughter's husband's name is Katsuyama. Maybe that refreshes your memory," said his captor.

Despite the pain and the oncoming dizziness, Sharpe noticed the use of the present tense. He decided to ignore it for the moment. "He's dead. Fell off a platform at Shinjuku and was killed by a train. Didn't the police tell you?"

The pain of the blow was worse this time, because he was half-expecting it. He could feel something warm and wet trickling down his cheek, but decided not to wipe it off. "Yes, the police did tell us, but they lied to us. The body my daughter and I identified as Masashi's was that of a stranger."

Sharpe looked at him, his mouth slowly opening. "But the police came to me that evening because they found my business card in his pocket," he objected. "And later, I described his clothes to the police and they agreed that's what he was wearing when I met him."

"You didn't see the body yourself, then?" Katsuyama's father-in-law was shaking his head.

"No, of course not. Why did you think I had?"

"Never mind why. Yes, your card was found in the pocket of the dead man. And the pocket belonged to a jacket that belonged to my son-in-law. But the body inside those clothes was not that of my son-in-law."

Sharpe could think of nothing useful to say, and so kept his mouth shut. "But you did meet my son-in-law?" was the next question.

"Yes, I did. The afternoon the day he d— I mean, the day that Mr X fell off the platform at Shinjuku."

"Mr Ecks?" There was a frown on the face. "Who is this Mr Ecks? The man who died? You know him, then?"

"I mean X like X, Y, Z," explained Sharpe. "We don't know his name, so we call him X."

Relief. "Oh, I see."

"May I ask a question?" asked Sharpe, half-tensing against a further blow. The other nodded. "Why did you say to the police that the mystery man – Mr X – was your daughter's husband when he wasn't?"

"It seemed like a good idea for everyone to believe he was dead, especially if the police had kidnapped him and decided he was better off officially dead." This made no sense to Sharpe. If the official bodies, whoever they might be, had indeed kidnapped Katsuyama, why on earth would they call in someone to identify a strange body in this way? And why would his nearest and dearest aid and abet such a conspiracy? Something seemed to be very wrong with all this, but he decided to hold his tongue. Maybe all would be revealed in time. The gangster continued. "Now a question for you. What did you and Masashi talk about?"

It seemed like a good idea to keep telling the truth. After all, it wasn't just him who was going to suffer if he got caught out in a lie. "His work. He claimed that the Americans were chasing him."

"Did he say anything about me?"

Honesty is the best policy, Sharpe told himself once again, but a little unconvincingly, and took a deep breath. "Yes, he did. He said that you were very well-connected in certain special circles." He tensed himself, waiting for the gun in his face again, but it didn't arrive. "He also said that you came from Korea. The North," he added.

To his relief, his questioner was smiling. "Well, that sounds fair enough. Did he give you anything?"

Damn, thought Sharpe. The big one. Even though he'd made up his mind in advance to return Katsuyama's gadget, he wished he didn't have to answer questions about it. Being hit in the face tends to prejudice your opinion of a man. He answered anyway. "Yes, he did."

"I won't insult your intelligence by asking you what it was. Is it safe?"

Sharpe nodded, dumbly.

"Will the Japanese police find it?"

"Probably not," replied Sharpe, wondering why he hadn't been asked where it was.

As if reading his mind, the other said, "I'm not going to ask you where it is. Frankly, I'm not sure I want to know right now, as long as you have no intention of going to the police with it."

"I'm certainly not going to do that," replied Sharpe, truthfully. He'd had enough of Sugita, or whatever his real name was, and he wasn't going to help him, let alone that bastard Ben or Al or whatever he wanted to call himself, who went round wrecking other people's houses. As for the British Embassy and the gang of nut-jobs there, he couldn't care less. He stated, with a little more conviction, "There's no way I'm going to talk to the police about this."

"That's fine. Keep it that way."

By now, Sharpe was thoroughly confused. "Excuse me, but your son-in-law told me that you wanted to pass his invention to North Korea."

The other laughed. It seemed like genuine laughter, but Sharpe couldn't be entirely sure without a clear look at the man's face. "No, that's not what I want. The Dear Leader could never pay me enough for it. I want this for my own use and I may well explain that to you some time in the future. But more than anything else right now, I want my son-in-law found. Will you help me find him, Mr Sharpe?"

"I'm not a detective," answered Sharpe.

"But I believe you have friends in interesting places. And you must be good at finding things out, otherwise Masashi would never have trusted you. Will you help?" The voice was insistent, and Sharpe could feel the man's hot breath on his face as he leaned close, gripping Sharpe's jacket sleeve in a vice-like grip.

"I can try." Damn it, it was as much as he could promise.

"Find him, and I'll make you rich, Mr Sharpe. Fail to find him, and I'll ..." The voice tailed off.

"You'll kill me?"

Again the laughter. "No, Mr Sharpe. I'm not the monster you think I am. I was going to say that I'll pay you for trying, but not as much as if you find him."

"Oh."

"And I apologise for all the rough stuff just now. You see, I thought you'd been working together with the police to cover up Masashi's kidnapping by them. Now I'm sure we're friends. Shake?" The grip on Sharpe's sleeve relaxed, to change to an outstretched hand. By now thoroughly confused, Sharpe shook it, and felt something small and hard pressed into his palm. As he withdrew it, he opened his hand to look at the metal key with a number stamped on the tag attached to it.

"A man of your talents, Mr Sharpe, who passes through Tokyo station almost every day, should have no problem knowing what to do with this."

"What about—?" Sharpe jerked his head towards the front seat, where Mieko was still sitting in shocked silence.

"Of course she goes when you go, in a minute. We had to get your attention somehow. Again, my apologies."

"So you sent your daughter to see me and tell me where you were?"

"Of course."

Sharpe considered asking about the bruises on her arm, but decided against chancing his luck. Enough questions for one night. But there was one other practical matter. The small part of Sharpe that took care of business showed itself.

"Look, I'm going to be looking for your son-in-law. I'm happy to do it. I liked him when I met him, and I'm glad it wasn't him who went under the train at Shinjuku. But how do I get in contact with you to let you know how I'm doing?"

"You don't. I contact you. It's much safer that way. Now both of you, get out and go home." The driver pushed the button to unlock the doors. Sharpe opened his door, and Mieko opened hers. Sharpe got out, and faced the two gorillas who'd dragged him to the car.

"Leave them alone. They're going home in peace. Make sure they get back safely," came the voice from the car, speaking Japanese.

Sharpe went round to the other side of the car and took Mieko's arm, steadying her. She seemed to be in reasonable shape – better than Sharpe, anyway. He had the feeling she was steadying him. Galileo or Copernicus or whoever it was had been right, he realised. The world was definitely spinning round.

"Are you all right?" he asked her.

"OK," she said.

"Let's go," he told her, and they started off back home, hand in hand, followed at a discreet distance by the two thugs.

THEY RETURNED TO THE RELATIVE SAFETY of the wrecked flat, and Mieko shrieked at the sight of his cut face, now she could see it clearly in the light. Sharpe went into the bathroom and looked in the mirror, exploring the lumps on his cheek with his fingers. Nothing seemed to be broken, but one side of his face was covered in blood. He was glad that they hadn't met Mrs Watanabe or any of the neighbours on their way back. When he dabbed the blood off gently, and had splashed some antiseptic over the cuts, it stung, and he walked back into the living-room, wincing.

Mieko had found the whisky bottle, and the glasses that he had used earlier that evening and was examining them curiously.

"There's lipstick on one of these," she accused.

"You heard what he said," replied Sharpe. "He sent his daughter round to let me know where you were. She said she needed a drink, so I gave her some whisky."

"Oh." She didn't seem totally convinced. "Did you think she was pretty?"

"Yes," Sharpe answered. Honesty seemed to be the order of the day. It seemed to work. Mieko seemed to become a little calmer, and she started stroking his face.

"*Itai!* That hurts!" complained Sharpe. She stopped touching his face. "Why, did you meet her?" Mieko nodded. "Anyway, you haven't told me yet what happened to you."

She shrugged. "Nothing much. I was just putting away the shopping when the doorbell rang, and I went to answer it. The two men who brought you to the car were standing there, and they forced me to go along with them. I really couldn't struggle out of their hands, and one of them showed me a knife. I was too frightened to scream or anything. They took me to the car and then we went to this building somewhere near Shinagawa. I'm not sure exactly where. They talked to me for a couple of hours, and then we got back in the car and went to where you found me."

"Did they hurt you?" asked Sharpe. He was aware that it was a bit late to be asking this question, but Mieko hadn't seemed hurt, or even unduly upset by her capture. In fact, she seemed to be much more upset by his state. He noted, though, that she had said she'd been snatched as she came back from the supermarket, four hours before Sharpe's return, according to the till receipt, while Katsuyama's wife had said the kidnapping had taken place only an hour before. He decided not to press the point.

"No, not at all," replied Mieko. "The older man who was talking to you was very kind and polite. He even gave me tea and cookies and he and his daughter talked to me. I agree with you, she is good-looking – to some men, I suppose." Sharpe smiled inwardly at the qualification.

"What did he say to you?"

"Not a lot that seemed important. He asked a few questions, though, all about you. Where you work, who you work for, when you come back home. That sort of thing?"

"Anything else?"

"He asked about that Kitty-chan box that you brought back the other day. How on earth he knew we had it, I don't know. I told him that I hadn't seen it since you brought it back. Why is it important, anyway?"

"Don't worry about it. It really isn't that important." Was

it really not important? He wasn't sure. Anyway, it was better not to mix Mieko up in this too deeply.

"I'm hungry," Mieko said. She really had an amazing ability to hop from subject to subject like a mountain goat, thought Sharpe. And not just from subject to subject, but from level to level.

"Sorry," he said. "I suppose I am, too. I saw that you'd bought some crab claws, but I don't feel like cooking right now, and I'm sure you don't want to, either. Shall we order a pizza or something? Ordered pizza wasn't something that they went in for very much – after all these years, Sharpe was still unsure of the merits of Japanese pizza, which could include ingredients such as potato, sweet corn and squid all covered in mayonnaise, and all in the same overpriced pizza – but it was an occasional last resort.

She nodded.

"Tell them to hurry," added Sharpe. "You choose what you want to eat. I don't really care."

She phoned the pizza company and while she was doing that, and they were waiting for the pizza to be delivered, Sharpe picked up one or two items from the floor and started to make the place look a little more habitable.

When the pizza arrived, Sharpe went into the kitchen and fetched plates and a couple of cans of beer. "I think we need one of these each," he said to Mieko. "And you need these," he added, handing her the vase of flowers that he'd bought earlier. Was it only that evening? It seemed like weeks ago.

"Oh, thank you," she said, leaning over to kiss him. He twisted his face to avoid the kiss landing on his sensitive cheek. "What's going on?" she asked, reaching for a slice of pizza. He was relieved to see that she'd ordered something relatively straightforward, rather than go for the Japanese "put everything on it and call it a luxury pizza" approach.

"I wish I knew. Something really odd."

"And what did he give you in the car?"

Sharpe fished in his pocket and produced the key that he had been given.

"Looks like the key to a coin locker," said Mieko. "It's got a number on it".

"Well, he did mention Tokyo station," said Sharpe. "I think I should probably try and find out what's in locker number," he squinted down at the key, "7415."

"You need new glasses."

"I know. I'm getting older, and I feel it every day," he replied, leaning over for another slice of pizza. "Ouch! I really am getting older," as a sharp pain shot through his back.

For no good reason, Sharpe was now beginning to believe that things would sort themselves out fairly quickly. Maybe it was the effect of the pizza and half a can of beer. He reckoned that if he spent half of next day cleaning up, this room would be nearly back to normal. Perhaps even less time than that.

Then there was his office. He hadn't lost much data when the hard disk had vanished, but he'd have to buy a new hard disk for backup. Well, that was easy enough to manage. He doubted if anything else was missing. One problem was that he usually worked in a state of barely-controlled chaos, so it might be a long time before he realised that something was missing out of there.

Was it really only last night that the flat had been broken into? He wiped his fingers on one of the paper napkins provided with the pizza, and finished the last of his can of beer.

"How's the bedroom?" asked Mieko.

"Still messy," replied Sharpe. "Sit down for a few minutes and I'll clean up what I can. I'll leave you to tidy up your own stuff. I don't know where it all goes." Don't even know what half of it is, he said to himself. Time he got to understand a bit more about women at his age.

As he was sorting through the mess of clothes thrown randomly around the room, he discovered an empty cigar tin, which had once contained cheap small Dutch cigars, and which had somehow been overlooked by the police. No prizes for guessing where that came from, Sherlock, he thought to himself. What an arrogant fool to make it so obvious, was his next thought.

As he had promised Mieko, he didn't try to tidy up her clothes, but when he went back into the living-room he found her fast asleep stretched out on the sofa, her half-empty beer glass on the table in front of her. Oh well. He went back into the bedroom, and used a bulldozer technique to clear enough space for the futon, which he then spread on the floor before spreading the bedclothes on it. Then he went back into the living-room and carried Mieko onto the futon, where he gently undressed what he could without waking her up. As he slipped off her blouse, she half woke up and put her arms around his neck.

"Ken-chan," she murmured, and kissed him. He kissed her in return, and she responded, waking up. He bent down to kiss her again, tracing a path from her lips down her neck to her chest and breasts, which he freed from her bra, and turned the light out, moving over her. It was some time before he and Mieko finally went to sleep.

Chapter 4: Tokyo

THE NEXT MORNING SAW SHARPE UP BRIGHT AND EARLY, repairing the damage to his computer and to his office. Mieko was still sleeping, snoring slightly, as he made his way to the shower to wake himself up for the day ahead. His face still felt sore, and he decided not to shave that day. As he'd said to Sugita/Ishihara, there was little work that had been lost, but there was still a mass of papers and general level of messiness in the room that exceeded even the usual standards for the place. Looking through his appointments, he realised that there was nothing that couldn't be put off for a day or so. He sent off a couple of e-mail messages to take care of a progress meeting demanding a report (yesterday's neglected task), and attendance at a lecture given by a technical society that Sharpe only attended when he was on the prowl for new clients.

As he strolled into the kitchen to make the coffee for breakfast, he heard waking-up noises from Mieko. He could almost hear her smile as she walked into the kitchen behind Sharpe and flung her arms around him, pressing her breasts against his back. She was stark naked.

"Get dressed, you lewd and lascivious wench," he said,

turning in her embrace, returning her kiss and playfully slapping her backside. She put on a pout of mock annoyance, and sashayed out of the room.

By the time she returned, dressed and made up for the day, the coffee was ready, and they sat down to discuss the day ahead, as they usually did. Sharpe told her that he wasn't going to go to the customer today, and was going to get on with the work he should have done earlier, and Mieko informed him in return that she was going to go round to Meema's to pick up a few things she'd left there. Sharpe wasn't aware that she'd taken enough with her for one night to be able to forget anything, but he knew from experience that Mieko was capable of leaving a trail of belongings behind her wherever she went – one reason why she put up with his own messiness, he supposed.

"Aren't you going to Tokyo station?" asked Mieko.

"What for?" he replied, and then remembered the key he'd been given the previous night. "Oh, yes. I suppose I'd better find out what it's all about. I'll do it when I find a place to stop in the report I'm meant to be writing. It shouldn't take me more than an hour to go there and back. And I can buy a spare hard disk while I'm there."

He carried his third cup of coffee of the morning to his office, and started on his report for a major investment bank (not the one where Vishal worked), who had the idea that they might save some money by outsourcing some of their information technology to India, so that all their Tokyo databases would be managed from Bangalore. Sharpe's job was to analyse the possible risks and downsides of this approach, as seen from the Tokyo end.

As it happened, Sharpe thought this proposal was one of the silliest ideas he'd heard in a long time, but he was finding it difficult to put his thoughts into diplomatic language, so after an hour or so, he put on his jacket and walked to the station to catch the train for Tokyo. On the way there he passed a small builder's yard, and made a mental note to call in there on the way back to get the broken window fixed.

THE JOURNEY TO TOKYO STATION WAS QUITE LONG, and involved two changes of train. He spent the time on the train idly reliving last night's adventures, from the time he'd rushed out of the house to rescue Mieko, to the time when they'd fallen asleep contentedly in each other's arms. On balance he decided that he rather liked Katsuyama's father-in-law. At least he seemed to say what he meant, unlike Major Barclay, for one.

On arrival at the vast sprawling complex of Tokyo station, which was home to any number of Japan Railways lines and a number of subway lines, he wondered where to try first. The Yaesu side of the station was the busiest side of the station, so he decided to try his luck there. Pushing his way through the crowds of middle-aged ladies, all of whom seemed to be determined to block his way by moving in front of him before stopping dead in their tracks and standing rooted to the spot, Sharpe entered the underground area near the Gin-no-Suzu meeting place, where many of the coin lockers were to be found. A look at one bank of coin lockers there showed that they were of a new electronic keyless type where his key would obviously be useless. The next bank had numbers which were completely wrong, and the key tags were the wrong colour. By the time he'd checked the tenth bank of coin lockers around the meeting area, he was beginning to get more than a little discouraged. He guessed that the lockers at platform level would be of the same type, but felt he had to check them, all the same. A trudge up the stairs confirmed this.

His next stop was the other side of the station — the

Marunouchi side. Remembering a factoid he had heard once, that more people use Tokyo station every day than live in New Zealand, he fought his way to the other side against the flow of human traffic with some difficulty, passing a couple of other banks of lockers in the underground passage, neither of which seemed to offer anything useful. Nothing there which looked promising. The coin lockers had keys, but one bank had a completely different set of numbers, and the other banks seemed to use a different shape and size of key to the one in his pocket.

Time for the subway lines. He couldn't find the coin lockers at the Marunouchi line for some time, as the area was under construction, but emerging from that area, he spotted a small isolated group of lockers opposite, in an area with relatively little traffic, and somewhat off the beaten track. He saw that the top row contained locker 7415, there was no key in it, and his key fitted. He swung open the door to disclose a large bag with the name of an electronics retail chain on it, drew out the bag and peeked inside. His first thought was that Al Kowalski wasn't going to be burgling any houses in the near future. His next was that he had to find a place to be sick very soon, preferably out of the way, where he would not draw any attention to himself and the locker with the bag and its ghastly contents.

He stuffed the bag back where it had come from and re-locked the locker quickly, pushing in three 100-yen coins to do so, trusting that no-one had seen him. He walked fast, almost running, following the signs for the toilets and dashed inside.

He thanked God that at least one cubicle was empty, his stomach heaved, and what seemed like the whole of last week's meals erupted to fill the porcelain. Flushing the mess away, he wiped his chin with toilet paper, and staggered out to the basins where he splashed cold water over his face.

He drew a few curious looks, but not that many – Japanese seem less shy about exhibiting the contents of their stomachs before the world than do the British, but this usually happens usually late at night. Mid-morning was a slightly unusual time for public vomiting.

Time for a drink, he thought, looking around for a drinking fountain.

As he bent over the water spout in the corner of the room, he felt a hand on his shoulder, and heard a vaguely familiar Australian voice. "You all right, mate? Strewth, you look like death warmed over."

Sharpe looked up. "What the bloody hell are you doing following me about?" he asked Jon, who had reverted to his Australian backpacker look.

"Shut up, and let me get you a coffee. You look as though you could use one," replied the other. "And what the bloody hell happened to your face?" looking at the scabs on his cheek.

"You're the one who should be shutting up," replied Sharpe. It wasn't the most witty bit of repartee going, but he didn't care. "Now get out of my fucking way and stay out of my life. OK?" He prodded Jon firmly in the chest with a pointing forefinger.

"No way," said Jon, pointing a finger back. "There's no way I'm going to let you walk away from this without finding what's going on. Tim Barclay's going to have my balls for breakfast if I come back with no answers."

"Then I wish him *bon appétit*," replied Sharpe. "Now, if you'll excuse me—" His stomach gave a sudden unexpected lurch to port, and he dashed for the cubicle again. When he came out again, Jon was still standing there waiting.

"Oh, for God's sake, buy me a coffee or something," snapped Sharpe. "I suppose you're going to find out all about this sooner or later, so I might as well get a cup of coffee out of it."

"Good man," said Jon. He made as if to take Sharpe's elbow, but Sharpe shrugged him off.

They found a Starbuck's in the underground mall adjoining the station, under one of the new office blocks that were going up on the Marunouchi side. "We'll sit near the door," said Sharpe. "I need the air, even if it is underground. And mine's a double espresso – no sugar. I'll get the table, you get the coffee. Don't worry, I'm not going to run away. I couldn't if I wanted to."

He was telling the truth – he didn't feel like running anywhere. Sitting down at the table, the memory of the bag in the locker came back to him, and he retched again, but there was nothing in his stomach to back it up.

Jon arrived with the coffees.

"Thanks," said Sharpe, and winced as he took his first sip. Jon just sat, waiting.

"Well, aren't you going to ask me any questions?" asked Sharpe.

"No, since you probably aren't going to answer them. I'll wait until you talk." Jon sipped his iced latte in silence, and folded his arms behind his head. Neither man spoke for a few minutes.

"Did you see Katsuyama's body?" asked Sharpe, breaking the silence.

"No, why the hell would I have done?" replied Jon. "All we knew was what we were told by Ishihara."

"Did he see the body?" asked Sharpe.

"I suppose so. Why? What's strange about it?"

"I heard a rumour that it wasn't Katsuyama's body and that Katsuyama himself is still alive."

Jon put down his cup and stared at Sharpe. "I think you're serious."

At the Sharpe End

"Well, the person who told me this was certainly serious about it. His view was that Katsuyama had been kidnapped by the Japanese authorities, which I personally think is a complete load of bullcrap."

"Is that the same person who did that?" pointing to Sharpe's face.

"Could be, could be," replied Sharpe.

"Well, I suppose we can always get an exhumation order to find out whether this is a load of bovine excrement or not?" suggested Jon. Sharpe began to laugh. "What's so bloody funny?"

"You haven't been here that long, have you?"

"You know I haven't. Why?"

"First off, no-one's buried here in Japan. It's all cremation by law – you're not allowed to bury the dear departed. Next, they don't hang about here when it comes to disposing of each other. Usually there's a sort of wake affair the day after they pop their clogs, and the funeral's the day after that. You have to wait 24 hours, but most people go ahead with things very fast indeed. The contents of the coffin with Katsuyama's name on it are probably a little pile of grey ash and bone in a white urn by now."

"They do things that fast even when there's suspicion of foul play?" asked Jon.

"Seems like it."

"Jeezus. No wonder there are so many unsolved crimes in this country." He took a pull at his coffee. "So if he's not dead, where is he?"

"I don't know. And if I did, why would I want to tell you?"

"Oh, good God, you really are touchy today, aren't you?" retorted Jon.

"And just how would you feel if you'd just come across a severed head in a station coin locker?" replied Sharpe. The words were out of his mouth before he could bite them off.

Jon dropped his paper coffee cup, which fell into his lap. The last drops spilled over his trousers, but he didn't seem to notice. "A what?" he croaked. "You're joking, right?"

"I never joke about that kind of thing. Why the bloody hell do you think I was puking my guts up? For the fun of it?"

"OK." Jon's mood was one of humouring a lunatic. "A head, you say? Just sitting there in the locker?"

"No, the thing was in a damn' Yodobashi Camera bag."

"Severed?" repeated Jon, stupidly.

"Of course the bloody thing was severed," replied Sharpe. "You couldn't stuff a whole body into one of those lockers, could you?"

"Jesus Christ. Weird things do seem to be happening to you, don't they? Do you know where the head came from?"

"Yes. From the body of Al Kowalski."

Jon's eyes bulged. "Who would have done that? And why?"

"I think it was meant as a present for me. A sort of peace offering from someone who wants me to see them as a friend."

"You have some fucking weird friends, I'll tell you that much for free." He started mopping his trousers with a paper napkin. "Who's the mystery friend, then?"

Sharpe ignored the question. "So what are you going to do about it?"

"'What am I going to do about it?' he asks. Why the hell should I have anything to do with it?"

"Well, I'm certainly not going to get involved with this. You've probably got diplomatic immunity or something, haven't you?"

"I do have a kind of diplomatic standing," Jon admitted. "In any case, I suppose that I stand higher in the eyes of the Japanese authorities than you do. Did you touch anything?"

"Well, I had to, to lift up the bag and look inside, didn't I?"

"So your bloody fingerprints are all over everything? Oh, bloody wonderful. I'm going to have to tell Ishihara about this, you realise? I suppose the bag can be sanitised somehow before we tell him."

"Can you keep me out of it, then? I really don't need any more hassle about this."

"God knows how, but we can try."

"We?"

"Well, I'm going to have to tell the poison dwarf about this as well, you know. Major Tim bloody Barclay's going to love the melodrama. He'll probably wet himself with excitement. Oh, how absolutely *thrilling*," he mimicked.

"Again, keep me out of it with him. I don't want to have any more to do with him if it can be helped," said Sharpe.

"I don't really see how I can manage it." Jon was thinking aloud. "I mean, how do I go about stumbling over severed heads in station lockers unless someone guides me there?"

"A tall dark stranger presses the key into your hand as you get off the train at Tokyo station?" suggested Sharpe.

"Come off it."

"All right, it arrives in your mailbox with a little note saying 'Tokyo station'?"

"Better, I suppose. Why the hell should I shield you, anyway? You're hardly being co-operative with us."

"For very good reasons," Sharpe pointed out. "My place gets turned over by a friend of yours, my girlfriend gets abducted," Jon showed great surprise at this, "and I get beaten up last night. Where the bloody hell are you while all this is happening? And then, when I really need you lot like I need a hole in the head, you turn up."

"All right. There's not that many of us, you know. We

can't provide twenty-four hour coverage for you. And what's this about your girlfriend being abducted?"

"Believe me, I really don't want to tell you anything about this. How many of you is 'not many', then?"

"Two or three," Jon confessed, shamefacedly.

"And that's you and Tiny Tim and someone else when he's not got anything better to do?" asked Sharpe. Jon nodded.

"Why the hell don't you two work with the real professionals in this game, if things get this rough? All right, so I'm sure there's some stupid Whitehall reasons about turf and bailiwicks and whatnot. But wouldn't it be simpler if you just got out of this and left me to it or handed it over to people who are more used to the idea of severed heads in coin lockers? I don't see that you're doing a lot of good, frankly."

"We need to stop the North Korean military getting hold of it, and we're the best people to do that."

Sharpe sighed. "I'm not sure I believe that load of cobblers any more."

"Please yourself. I don't have that luxury. Someone's got to tell our lords and masters in London that Al Kowalski is no longer around to work his magic touch on the youth of Tokyo, and that the late lamented Katsuyama may well not be so late."

"Like I say, leave me out of it."

"If I can, I will. Now, I suppose I'm going to have to check out this story about Katsuyama still being alive."

"You're not going to tell Ishihara about that, are you?"

"Not if I can help it."

They left the table and dutifully dumped their rubbish in the cans provided, sorting out the paper and plastic as requested by the signs. Jon turned to look at Sharpe.

"You look a bit better than you did," he remarked. "Not that that's saying that much, really."

A thought struck Sharpe. "Look," he said. "You're

short-handed, you say. I need some extra work. Why don't you take me on as a temporary or something?"

"You'd have to sign the Official Secrets Act," pointed out Jon.

"Signed the bloody thing yesterday," objected Sharpe.

"And you'd have to come clean," Jon added. "Tell us everything you know and hand over everything you have."

"Forget it," Sharpe replied. "I'd probably be too expensive for you cheapskates anyway."

"You do believe in playing hard to get, don't you?" Jon said. "But you might be right about the money, anyway. I won't tell you about the pittance I get paid for leading my life of international glamour and mystery. It might embarrass us both. Look, I'm not going to be able to stay with you and make sure nothing else happens to you. But I will try to make sure that someone from the embassy keeps a quiet eye on your place, especially at night."

"Thanks. I'd appreciate that."

"In the little matter of gratitude, actions speak louder than words, remember," Jon called out as they went their separate ways.

WHEN HE ARRIVED HOME, Sharpe had no wish to continue with his everyday work. He had no doubt that he was now mixed up in some very dirty business indeed. It really would be a lot simpler to hand over Katsuyama's gadget and software to Tiny Tim and Jon. Earn the grateful thanks of Her Majesty's Government and all the rest of the package, which probably included a pair of concrete overshoes from North Korea. No thanks. After the previous night, Sharpe had no faith at all in the British government's ability to protect him against any assault by Katsuyama's family and friends. Or his enemies, come to that.

In any case, he'd decided by now that he really did have a certain kind of liking for Katsuyama's father-in-law, if he ignored the fact that he'd been hurt pretty badly by the man for almost no reason. There had been something about the man's manner that seemed refreshingly honest. He wasn't pleading any phoney-sounding cause of "national security" or patriotism. And he'd seemed decent enough once he'd realised that Sharpe wasn't playing on the Japanese or the American side, and he hadn't hurt Mieko, by the sound of it. Sharpe decided that he'd sooner throw in his lot with the mystery gangster than any of the other players in the game. He realised he didn't even know his name, but he had no doubt that should he ever need to contact the man, it would be easy enough. Maybe Mieko would remember a little more about the building or something, which would make it easier to trace him.

But to get on the good side of the man and his people, he'd have to find Katsuyama, and that was a real needle in a haystack sort of job.

The phone rang, jarring him out of his thoughts. It was Vishal.

"Listen, man. What was it that you were giving me the other night?"

"I thought you'd worked it out. It recognises faces."

"Yes it does do that, as we saw, but there's something there that you are not telling me. There is something very strange here. Meema is saying to me that a man has died because of this. I do not think I am wanting this thing in my house any more, you understand, Kenneth, my friend?"

"I understand," replied Sharpe. Damn, now he would have to find somewhere else to keep the board and software safely. And he'd probably lost Vishal's and Meema's friendship. He was wrong about that, though, as Vishal's next words proved.

"I am coming round to your house to help you with the furniture and all your things that were disturbed, don't forget that. And then we can go back to my house where I can be showing to you the strange thing that I have discovered. And then you can be taking the damn' thing out of my life and Meema's life pretty bloody quick."

"Sure, Vishal. What time can we expect you this evening?"

"Some time after seven o'clock. I will be calling you when I am leaving the office."

"Great. Look forward to seeing you."

Mieko came into the room. "Who was calling?" she asked.

"That was Vishal. He's coming to help pick up the furniture and get everything back in place."

"Oh good. Is Meema coming too?"

"I don't think so. He's coming straight from work, a little after seven."

"Oh, I'd better make sure he has something to eat and drink when he arrives." She scuttled off to perform mysterious tasks in the kitchen and then popped her head round the door again.

"What was in the locker at Tokyo? Did you find the right one?"

"I did, but I'm not sure what last night's friend was doing. It was only a bag full of rubbish."

"Strange, *neh*?" She disappeared back to the kitchen.

Sharpe swore to himself as he realised that he still hadn't bought a replacement hard disk for his computer. Finding Al Kowalski's head in a locker had driven all other thoughts out of his own. He suspected there was a sick joke there if he wanted to make one, but he couldn't be bothered. Looking at his watch, he reckoned he just had time to get to Akihabara, the electronics district, buy the disk and make it back before Vishal arrived. He grabbed his coat and a credit card and shouted to Mieko where he was going.

"All right, make sure you're back in time for Vishal," she reminded him.

Sharpe walked fast to the station. He was vaguely aware of someone who might or might not have been Jon following him at a distance. Quite frankly, he didn't care too much. What did bother him a little more was that not one, but two, shadows seemed to have attached themselves to him by the time he reached the station to catch the train to central Tokyo. One of them seemed to be, from the little he could make out at a distance, one of the goons who'd escorted him to and from the car the previous evening.

By the time he'd got on the train, and watched his two shadows get on the next carriage, he was sure of this. He still wasn't sure of the other watcher's identity, except that it wasn't Jon. He wondered how long it would take before the two became aware of each other.

As he arrived at Akihabara station, he decided to keep life simple, and not to play silly games with his trackers. He found the hard disk he wanted at the computer store, paid for it and went straight back to the station, rather than window-shopping through the store, which was his usual practice on such occasions.

He was amused to see his shadows also apparently examining computer peripherals for the exact length of time that it took him to buy his hard disk, and decide that there was nothing that they wanted to buy at the exact moment he made his purchase and started to walk away from the register. By now, he told himself, they must have recognised each other. Maybe they would start co-operating with each other, taking shifts to relieve each other at times.

Fat chance. As he travelled home, he noticed both of them in the next carriage, sitting opposite each other, studiously avoiding looking at each other and him, and they followed him back to his apartment, walking on opposite sides of the road, each about 20 meters behind him.

Arriving home, he was pleased to see them stop outside the gates of the apartment building. He could always sue them for trespass if they entered private property. Probably get a judgement against them in ten years' time or so, given the glacial pace of the Japanese legal system.

Once he was back, he started to replace the hard disk and make a backup. He had watched the progress meter creep about halfway across the screen as he copied the data from the old disk to the new, when the doorbell rang.

HE OPENED THE DOOR TO VISHAL, who was carrying his backpack.

"Hi, there. Come in," he said.

Vishal kicked off his shoes and made his way to Sharpe's office. "Have the bloody thing back, man," he said, holding out a plastic carrier bag to Sharpe. "I thought that maybe I should bring it straight to you. Meema's not being very happy with you right now, if you understand what I am saying."

Sharpe mumbled some sort of apology and opened the bag. Inside was the Hello Kitty box, and inside that were the Katsuyama card and the CD. "Thanks," he said. "I'm really grateful to you for helping me out on all of this. Fancy a beer?" Vishal nodded, and Sharpe reached into the refrigerator beside his desk (tax-deductible as an office expense, it held beer, as well as the soft drinks and ice-cream vitally necessary for Sharpe to carry on his business in summer). "Here you go."

Vishal opened the ring-pull, chugged away at the can and belched. "That's better. Thanks," he sighed. "Kenneth, my friend, what are you not telling me? About all this, I mean?"

"I don't know how much I can tell you, but I was given this lot," he gestured at the plastic bag, now lying on the desk, "by someone who wanted me to represent him. Later that day he was found dead at Shinjuku station. It seems he fell off the platform in front of a train."

"So what about your flat getting burgled? That is part of it, I am thinking?"

"Right you are. It is. Someone else wanted this. But they're now dead, as well."

Vishal shrugged. "I'm not really that surprised, I suppose. I found out something most interesting about all this, though."

"OK, what is it?" Sharpe popped the top of his own can, and leaned back in his chair.

"Well, I found I was becoming more and more interested in how this worked, so I started to examine the source code very closely."

Sharpe nodded. Computers don't speak human language, they talk to themselves in complicated sets of instructions, moving electrons around in chips. To talk to the machines, programmers use programming languages that are easier for human beings to understand. This is the "source code" that Vishal was referring to.

"Well, it didn't seem to me at the beginning as though there was anything very interesting there. All the really clever stuff was in pre-compiled modules which were on the disc."

Before a computer can run a program, the source code needs to be changed, or compiled, into instructions that computers can understand. Programmers often write and compile building blocks, or modules, of large programs, and then link the modules together. This saves the trouble of compiling the whole lot every time.

Vishal went on, "So I started to have a look at the inside of some of those modules."

For a human being to read a compiled program is difficult, if not impossible, and needs a special kind of brain. Apparently Vishal was one of those people with such a brain.

"Of course, there wasn't very much I was finding in there that was obvious. But I found some ASCII strings in there which didn't seem to be fitting what the program was all about."

ASCII (Sharpe couldn't be bothered to think of the meaning behind the acronym right now) is a code used to translate letters of the alphabet to computer values. When Vishal said that he had found "ASCII strings", he meant that he had found ordinary English text inside the code which even someone like Sharpe could read and understand, if he knew how and where to look. "Like what?" he asked Vishal.

"Well one of them was 'Bloomberg feed not connected', and another was 'FIX prices not available'. Do you understand what I am talking about?"

"Of course," Sharpe replied. "They're market data feeds, the kind of information that traders have coming into their workstations round the clock. They cost a fortune for the brokers to install and maintain. Why on earth would they be part of a face-recognition program?"

"That's what I was asking myself, my friend," replied Vishal. "So I am doing a little more thinking and a little more digging."

"And?"

"And I discovered a long list of currencies. The standard three-letter abbreviations like EUR, USD, JPY, that sort of thing, all in ASCII again."

Sharpe thought for a few moments. "So it's a currency-trading program pretending to be a face-recognition program or something along those lines?"

"That's what it looks like to me, man. What the hell have you been playing with? Who are your friends?"

Sharpe ignored this. "So how do we fire it up?"

"Well, to run the program, the card's got to be installed in the PC. We found that out the other day, didn't we?"

"All right. Wait until I've finished backing up my data and then we can slip the card into this computer."

"But, Kenneth, remember that this is being a Linux disc and you will be needing a Linux system to run this program. If I am remembering rightly, this is a Windows system alone?"

"Oh, shit." Actually, the disk that had been stolen was capable of being started in Linux or Windows, but he hadn't bothered to copy the Linux side to the backup disk he was using now, since he mainly used it for experiments.

"And I am guessing that you don't have a Bloomberg feed here. Am I being correct in this?"

"Damn' right you're being correct." The market data feeds supplied to commercial houses cost several thousands of dollars per month for each trader using the service. Even if Sharpe played the markets, which he didn't, there was no way that he could ever justify the cost of a commercial market data feed to his house.

"Well, there's only one answer to this problem, isn't there?" Vishal grinned. "I take it into work and install it on one of our development machines."

Sharpe thought about it. It made a sort of sense. There was no way that anyone with the same sort of ideas as Al Kowalski regarding the ownership of Katsuyama's hardware and program would be able to get through the high security surrounding the IT workers and equipment at Vishal's bank. Only one problem.

"Vishal, if you don't mind, I'd like to be able to play with this system as well."

"No problem, man. I can arrange for you to come in as a consultant. We are needing someone to look at our compliance rules, so it's real work for you at your usual rates. But it will mean that you have to spend some time in our development section. And if you happen to work late, well, that's what you consultant wallahs are always doing, isn't it?"

"You're a real friend, Vishal."

At that point, Mieko poked her head around the corner with a plate of rice crackers and tiny grilled fish wrapped in *shiso* leaves spread with *umeboshi* – pickled plum – paste. "Not as good as Meema's samosas," she apologised as she left the plate beside Vishal. "Sorry." She turned to Sharpe. "Any beer left in the fridge?" she asked him. He opened the fridge door and wordlessly handed her a can.

"Thanks," and left.

"Can you get me that consulting gig, then?" Sharpe asked Vishal.

"No problem, man. I'm up to my balls in alligators right now, and I really honestly need some help with the bits that aren't much fun."

"Usual rates? Pass us one of those fish, would you?"

"Sure, would I let you down on this? I'll give you a call in the next couple of days to let you know when you can come in and sign the contract and the rest of the shit."

"Great. Take all the Katsuyama stuff with you then, so it can go into work with you tomorrow. I'd feel a lot happier with it all behind your security system than out in the open."

"OK." Vishal started to pack the card and CD back into the plastic bag and then into his backpack.

"And before we drink all the beer, would you mind giving

me a hand with some of the heavier bits of furniture? Let's get the place a little tidier while we're both a bit sober, right?"

"Fine," replied Vishal good-naturedly, and they went into the other room to put things straight. With the two of them working together, and Mieko standing around offering advice and encouragement (as well as a steadying pair of hands sometimes), the job didn't take nearly as long as Sharpe had feared it would, and it didn't seem long before Vishal and Sharpe found themselves sitting down drinking beer again, and feasting on a selection of small Japanese snacks prepared by Mieko.

"Thanks, Vishal. It would have been so much more difficult on my own. I really appreciate it."

"No problem." He looked at his watch. "I have to be getting back now. No offence, Kenneth-san, but it's a long day tomorrow."

"I understand. Thanks for everything."

Sharpe let Vishal out of the door and went back to the office. The computer had finished the backup process by now, and he had just started to clean up some of the papers that seemed to breed like rabbits whenever his back was turned, when the doorbell rang. He looked around for something that Vishal had left behind, but couldn't see anything.

OPENING THE FRONT DOOR in answer to the repeated ring, he was surprised to see Jon standing there in his "young executive" outfit.

"All right, come in. And take your bloody shoes off," he snapped, as Jon started to step into the hallway.

"Gone native, have we?" smirked Jon. "All right, keep your hair on," as he slipped out of the black oxfords.

"You'd better come in here," said Sharpe, gesturing to the office and the chair that Vishal had just vacated.

At the Sharpe End

"Thanks," said Jon, accepting the fresh can of beer that Sharpe had extracted from the fridge. He took a swig. "Who was that who left just now?"

"Vishal. He's a friend of mine – don't ask me to give you his last name right now – it's long and Southern Indian – works with one of the banks in Tokyo. He came round to help me move some of the furniture back after Al Kowalski's Martha Stewart efforts at home makeover, and he talked about a consulting job at his bank."

"Which bank?" asked Jon. Sharpe told him. "What department?"

"It doesn't matter which bank, and he's in Fixed Income Commodities and Currencies." That was true. For some reason, unique in Sharpe's experience, the bank where Vishal worked put its developers into the divisions for which they developed programs, rather than into a centralised IT department.

"OK. Any news of Katsuyama?" He accepted one of the small dried fish that Sharpe held out to him.

"You're meant to eat the head, you know," pointed out Sharpe as Jon started to lay the remains on his plate.

"You're joking?"

For answer, Sharpe ate two fish, heads and all, in quick succession.

"All right," said Jon, who'd watched the performance somewhat dubiously. "Here's looking at you, kid," he addressed the fish head he was holding, and crunched his way through it. "Not too bad," he conceded. "A bit like fish-flavoured pork scratchings."

"And talking of heads …?" Sharpe asked. "What about friend Al over at Tokyo station?"

"Bloody thing's still in the locker. It would make life a bloody sight simpler if you gave us the key, you know."

"All you had to do was ask," grumbled Sharpe, as he fished in his pocket for the key, and passed it to Jon.

"Why didn't you give it to me this morning?"

"Why didn't you ask?"

They glared at each other over the beers and were still trying to stare each other down when Mieko walked in.

"Has Vishal gone yet? Oh?" as she caught sight of Jon.

"Jon, Mieko. Mieko, Jon," introduced Sharpe. "Jon works at the British Embassy. He's taken over from James Bond." Like many Japanese, Mieko was a fan of James Bond, especially the earlier Sean Connery films.

"Autographs later," smiled Jon. Sharpe reached into the fridge, and without being asked, passed her another beer.

"Thanks," said Mieko. "I really wanted to know if you would be ready for dinner in about ten minutes. I can make it serve three, if Mr Bond is staying. It's sukiyaki."

"That sounds delicious," replied Jon, before Sharpe had a chance to answer. Mieko smiled and left the room.

"Sorry to intrude like this," said Jon before Sharpe could say anything. "But you have no idea what it's like not to eat home cooking and to have to rely on the embassy canteen and eat out at restaurants where you don't even understand the menu all the time. My many finely-honed skills don't extend to the kitchen."

"All right, but for God's sake don't say anything about the whole Katsuyama thing to Mieko. She's upset enough as it is. Were you following me today on the way to the electronics store?"

"Not personally I wasn't, but we had people on you all day, and there's one outside right now. And we're not the only ones following you around."

"I'd noticed that."

"Aren't you going to tell me who they are?"

"I don't know. I like to think they're on the side of the

angels, and it makes me feel nice and safe with two lots looking after me. Just co-operate with whoever it is, that's all I ask. And again, don't say anything about all this to Mieko."

"Do you think I'm stupid?" asked Jon. "Oh, don't answer that," he said as Sharpe opened his mouth to reply. "Of course I'm not going to say anything."

"What will you do about the package in the locker?"

"Me, personally? As little as possible. We have people to deal with that kind of thing. Miles and miles away from the likes of me, let alone Major Tim Barclay. As soon as I get the key to them, they'll make their way to Tokyo station in the wee small hours of the morning, and probably leave Al's head in a suburban park somewhere before sending an anonymous fax to Ishihara."

"They can trace faxes, can't they?"

"Of course they can, but the fax will be sent from some large multinational corporation somewhere. All enquiries end at the automated switchboard and Ishihara's not going to make a fuss with Mitsui or Toshiba or Fujitsu about it, you can be sure. And you can be sure that will be the last that you, or anyone else will ever hear about the late Al S. Kowalski. May God have mercy on his immortal soul."

"Sounds like there's a bigger secret embassy presence than I ever imagined, doing things I've never heard about."

"Quite probably. Unlike our American cousins, our boys don't take up valuable drinking space in Roppongi pubs, telling the world what they're up to."

Mieko called them from the other room, telling them that the food was ready. "If you want to wash your hands?" offered Sharpe, indicating the small room on the left of the passageway.

"Thanks," replied Jon and ducked inside. When he came out, Sharpe guided him to the main room, and they sat down to the table.

The conversation throughout the meal was lively. Jon quickly explained to Mieko that he was not actually James Bond (she protested flirtingly that she didn't believe it for a moment), but kept her entertained with comic stories of diplomatic bedlam in Paris, Bangkok and Seattle.

"How did you come to know Kenneth-san?" she asked Jon.

"Oh, we bumped into each other at a coffee shop a few days ago," replied Sharpe quickly, "and we started talking. We found we had some friends in common."

"Kenneth's been really helpful to the embassy, and we hope he's going to continue to be useful to us in the future."

Sharpe stifled the urge to kick Jon hard under the table.

"Well, that would be nice, working for the embassy, wouldn't it?" asked Mieko.

"Yes, it would, as long as I was working with Jon, I'm sure. The problem is that sometimes you don't know who you're working for, when you work for the government."

"That reminds me," interrupted Jon, "of a driver we had in Bangkok. Charming old gentleman, but he often got somewhat confused as to the rank of his passengers ..." He skilfully spun out the story so that it ended at the same time as the meal, and then helped to clear away the dishes at the end.

"We might even invite you round again," said Sharpe as he and Jon sat together in the office demolishing some fruit.

"Thanks," Jon replied with a disarming simplicity. "I enjoyed myself being in someone's home and eating real food for a change. I'm not really a tough guy or a spy, you know, and even we civil servants get a touch homesick now and again. If you could try to see me as an ally, it would be helpful for both of us, I think. I'm sure there's a use for you with our people, and we'd probably be able to scrape up some money from somewhere to pay you well, even by your demanding standards, for your help."

"As long as I don't have to be friends with your poison dwarf boss," Sharpe remarked.

"Confidentially, I think he's on his way out, or at least on his way back home," replied Jon. "There are stories that he's feathered his own nest a little too well on the proceeds of insider trading. And even though he has full diplomatic immunity, any scandal about a diplomat making an illegal killing on the Tokyo Stock Exchange would be enough to finish his career. Not to mention that the whole thing would probably blow Ishihara sky-high."

Sharpe thought back to the definitely non-governmental appearance and furnishings of Major Barclay's lair, and nodded. "I can see where that would make things complicated. If Tiny Tim goes back in disgrace, would you take over from him?"

Jon shook his head in an ambiguous gesture. "If there was any justice in the world, I would do. I have the experience in the field and the track record. But I don't have the Japan experience that someone like you does. I'd need someone like you to work with me. It could be a nice little career for you."

"And what would you want in exchange for this fine favour you're offering me?"

Jon sighed. "I can't put anything over on you, can I? Fuck you. Of course I want that Katsuyama shit from you. If I had that to pass on to Whitehall, I'd have the pick of whatever job I wanted in Japan, and the right to pick my own assistants."

Sharpe remained silent.

"Well, I can't force you to hand something over," continued Jon.

"Especially if I don't have it," retorted Sharpe.

"Oh for Christ's sake, don't play silly buggers. All right, let's get theoretical. If by some strange chance you happened to have Katsuyama's gizmo, and if you were to pass it on to HMG through me, I can tell you there would be a lot in it for you."

"I'm sorry, Jon, but you don't know the half of it. And neither do I," he added quickly, as Jon opened his mouth to protest. "Just drop it for now, can you? Maybe in a few weeks' time I'll be able to tell you some things you want to hear. But not right now. OK?"

Jon closed his mouth and nodded. "OK. I hear you."

"OK, take that bloody locker key, and get out and do what you have to do, or get other people to do your dirty work for you. And who knows, behave yourself, and you might find yourself invited round some time soon."

"Thanks. I appreciate it."

Jon struggled into his shoes, and Sharpe, sighing heavily, closed the door on him.

"Thank you, Mieko," he said, going into the kitchen. "You did a good thing there."

"He was fun," she replied. "Can we invite him round for a proper dinner some time?"

"Probably," Sharpe replied abstractedly. He seized a cloth and started to dry the dishes. "Want to play cribbage tonight?" Mieko won again.

Chapter 5: Tokyo

THE WEEKEND PASSED PEACEFULLY ENOUGH. No police suggesting that he drop round to watch suspects get beaten up. No unexpected body parts turning up in public places. No strangers abducting those near and dear to him, and beating him about the head with a pistol. A pretty boring couple of days, all told. He used them to catch up on his e-mail and do Web research for a magazine article he'd promised to write.

On Monday morning, Vishal rang from his workplace.

"Kenneth-san, can you come in this afternoon at three to talk to our team leader about the project we talked about the other day?"

"No problem."

After lunch, Sharpe put on his best suit, armed himself with a stack of business cards, and set forth on the train to the centre of Tokyo. Once again he noticed two minders behind him, but he didn't recognise either of them this time.

He left them at the doorway to the building housing the bank's offices, which it shared with a number of other companies. As he rode the lift up to the twentieth floor, he was annoyed, as always, by the obsessive need of Japanese to push the "close door" button in the lift the instant they stepped inside. The practice seemed to be restricted to the Japanese workers in the building – the others seemed content to leave the lift to do its own thing, which it did in a matter of seconds, but the Japanese workers had actually worn the markings off the button. Come to that, Sharpe thought, the button probably wasn't connected to anything anyway. He'd noticed the same tendency with Mieko, who never seemed to trust the automatic programs on washing machines or microwaves and so on, and insisted on making manual settings instead, often with disastrous results (Sharpe still had a once-white shirt that was now a streaky pink). The lift announced its arrival at the twentieth floor in Japanese and English and Sharpe stepped out, noticing wryly that someone was pushing the "close door" button even as he was stepping out of the lift. The door still took another three seconds to close.

He'd been to Vishal's bank often enough to be recognised by the receptionist, and he accepted his visitor's badge along with a smile. After he'd waited for about five minutes in the reception area, Vishal came to meet him.

"Thanks for coming along, Kenneth-san. Come this way." He led the way to a meeting room on the floor above the reception area and closed the door.

"Now, about the compliance contract?" he asked Sharpe.

"Shouldn't we wait for the project leader?"

"I am the bloody project leader on this one, Kenneth-san!" Vishal laughed. "So I got the approval this morning to hire you for a month or so. Usual rates."

"Great. Thanks a lot."

"Sure. No problem. It's not being a special urgent thing anyway, but we must be making sure the Bloomberg feed to the traders' desks after the back end has processed it is presenting the same basic information as we receive. The SOX and J-SOX requirements are starting to hit us," referring to the US legislation and its Japanese equivalent, supposedly designed to promote transparency in financial affairs.

"Sounds quite a job."

"Not as bad as it is sounding and we don't have the FSA on our back, so you are not having to do it yesterday. Anyway, I've set up a workstation for you with a Bloomberg and a FIX feed, and a special hardware attachment." He winked. "And I'll be spending quite a lot of time helping you get everything set up and working."

"Oh, I see," said Sharpe as the meaning sank in. "Thank you very much."

Vishal dropped his voice. "The work should actually take about two weeks, even at your slow speed, so you can spend a fair bit of time on the other stuff." He grinned.

"I think you're starting to enjoy this," said Sharpe.

"I am indeed," replied Vishal. "I wish I had the opportunity to do this kind of thing myself all the time. But it's almost as good if you are being here to do it. Can you start next Monday?"

"No problem. There is one small thing, though? Can we make the first two weeks four days a week rather than five so that I can tidy up a few things?"

"Fine, if that's what you want to be doing."

Sharpe was whistling to himself as he made his way back home and stopped off at the local supermarket to buy a bottle of slightly better wine than usual. Quite apart from trying to solve the problems of the mysterious Katsuyama package, the money that he would earn over the next four weeks was going to be a useful boost to his bank balance. Worth a modest celebration, he told himself.

As he came out of the supermarket, he looked for the two men tailing him. One seemed to have stopped following him, or maybe he'd become a little better at his job and had learned to keep himself hidden. The other was obviously from Katsuyama's father-in-law. Sharpe made a sudden decision and started to walk back the way he'd come from, directly towards his shadow.

The gangster appeared to panic, and stopped short, turning towards and away from Sharpe alternately, seemingly unable to make up his mind. A few more quick strides, and Sharpe was within speaking range.

"*Matte* – wait," he called in a low voice. "Listen," he went on in Japanese, "I am going to be working at that bank for one month. I have not forgotten about Mr Katsuyama, and I will do my best to find him when I am not working. Please tell your boss that."

The other coughed, seemingly embarrassed at the impropriety of his quarry turning and talking directly to him. "Thank you," he replied in gruff Japanese. "I will tell Mr Kim."

So Katsuyama's father-in-law was called Kim? Well, not exactly a useful fact to know. Over 20% of Korean people shared that name, Sharpe had read somewhere.

Sharpe turned round and resumed walking in his original direction. He caught sight of the street behind him reflected in a car window at one point, and noticed his shadow – still only one, it appeared – continuing to trail him at a respectful distance.

Mind you, he mused as he walked, it was one thing to say that he was going to find Katsuyama, and quite another to actually do it. In reality, he had absolutely no idea where to start looking.

ENTERING THE BLOCK OF FLATS, he picked up the mail from his box at the bottom of the staircase, and sorted through it as he walked up to his flat. Circulars, credit card bill, and a postcard from ... where? Hanoi? He turned it over curiously, since he had no idea who might have been writing from Hanoi – none of his friends had mentioned a pending holiday there, and as far as he knew, none of his clients had an interest there.

The card was written in ball-point pen, in English, and simply said, "Keep looking. K."

K? Kim? Katsuyama? Kitty? The K on its own was a bit Kafka-esque, Sharpe, who had never actually read any Kafka, but kept meaning to, thought to himself.

And keep looking for what? Very strange. For Katsuyama or what?

As Sharpe had said to Vishal, he had some work to do before he started at the bank, and he got as much as he could safely out of the way before he started the month's contract. When he wasn't clearing the decks, he continued to think about Katsuyama, and how, if possible, to find him. He went back to the Katsuyama Electronic Devices Web site, and looked at all he could see about Katsuyama. Aha! There was a link to Vietnam – there was a factory there making components for the Japanese parent. He looked up Thang Long Industrial Park and learned that it had been founded by a Japanese corporation, and was located just outside Hanoi. The plot thickens, he told himself.

So just how likely would it be that Katsuyama would take himself off there? Possible, he supposed. He wasn't sure of the relationship between Vietnam and North Korea, apart from the fact that both were single-party states, nominally Communist (whatever that meant these days). But even supposing that Katsuyama had taken himself off to Vietnam, for whatever reason, how did that help Sharpe? Hanoi is a big place with a population of (he looked it up) over four million people, and even assuming that Katsuyama was there, there was no way to know exactly how to find him.

Was there anything else in the postcard that could help?

The picture showed a view of the Ho Chi Minh mausoleum, which didn't seem too much of a clue. Sighing, he put the card on one side and returned to a report on object-oriented database design, which had fallen out of fashion in the West, but was being touted as a breakthrough technology for hand-held devices by a Japanese software house. The report was due for delivery in a few days, and Sharpe wanted to present it in person – a tactful reminder of his physical presence to those responsible for paying him, and a subtle (he hoped) hint that more work from the same quarter would be welcome in the future.

IT WAS ALWAYS SHARPE'S HABIT, after completing the first draft of any extended piece of writing, to print it out and go outside the house with a couple of red and blue pencils to correct it. In fine weather, such as that of the day after he had been to Vishal's bank, he would visit the local park next to the apartment building where he lived. Goodness knows what the young mothers indulgently watching their offspring cavort on the playground equipment made of the foreigner scribbling incomprehensible marks on a piece of paper, but Sharpe didn't care. The advantage of this method of working was that it insulated him from unwanted interruptions (he didn't take his mobile phone with him) and stopped him wasting time on diversions, such as computer games, surfing to irrelevant Web sites or using the time as an excuse to clean up his desk. It also gave him the chance to sit in the relatively fresh air and see something other than a computer screen.

He printed out the draft of the report and set out with a clipboard holding the printout, shouting to Mieko that he expected to be back in about an hour, if anyone were to call. Finding an unoccupied park bench out of the breeze, he sat down and started to correct the mistakes and stupidities with which his report, which had seemed almost perfect only twenty minutes earlier when he had looked at it on the screen, now seemed to be riddled.

As he reached the bottom of the second page, he became aware of someone sitting down beside him. A quick sideways glance revealed a youngish, prematurely balding and somewhat overweight man, American by the look of him, dressed in a rather loudly striped business suit and white shirt. Al S. Kowalski's younger and dumber cousin, thought Sharpe to himself. But with a little more class. His new neighbour was breathing hard and was rather red in the face. High blood pressure or something, Sharpe thought to himself. Looked as though he was about to blow at the seams.

The other caught Sharpe's glance and spoke, confirming all suspicions about his nationality.

"Say, you're Kenneth Sharpe, aren't you?" he asked in what sounded to Sharpe's ear like a Southern accent. "I've seen your photo in *Japan Business Monthly*". The magazine referred to occasionally took articles from Sharpe on technical subjects, and had started printing a somewhat less than flattering photo of him at the top of each article.

Sharpe nodded silently, unwilling to be drawn into conversation, and turned ostentatiously back to his work.

"Hi, I'm Kermit Winslow and I'm with the embassy here." He handed over his card, which Sharpe accepted without offering his own in return. Would any post-Muppets parents really name their child Kermit? Sharpe asked himself. Was this guy for real? He noticed that the business card further identified Kermit Winslow as the third of his ilk, so the poor sod probably actually was called Kermit. His position in the embassy was listed as Second Secretary in the

Commercial Service. Sharpe fought the impulse to do Miss Piggy impressions.

"All my cards are at home. Thank you for your card, but I really do have to finish this report," turning slightly away from the American.

"No, listen. We need your help."

Oh crap, Sharpe thought. As if it wasn't bad enough to have Jon hanging round my neck, I've now got his American counterpart doing the same thing.

"Go on," Sharpe said wearily.

"We have reason to believe that you are in possession of technology that's vital to the security of the free world." Sharpe listened in silence. Let the pompous little shit carry on. "The war on terror needs the Katsuyama technology to which you have access."

Sharpe still said nothing, and the other, mistaking his silence for approval, continued in his overblown manner. "As a representative of the United States of America, I demand that you make this available to the US Federal government so this technology can be utilised to spread freedom and democracy round the globe. You'd be providing vital assistance to the policeman of the free world," he added, noting Sharpe's hesitation.

Sharpe laughed. It was not a happy laugh, and it caught Winslow by surprise. "What was the phrase you used, sonny-boy? 'Policeman of the free world'? Dirty Harry, or KGB thug of the world, more like. When you people recognise international law and international courts, it may be time for you to start asking for your badge back. As far as I'm concerned, you people, and your psychopathic moron of a president, have forfeited any claim to any moral superiority. And your so-called 'war on terror' is the knee-jerk reaction of a bunch of gutless cowards who can't stand the sight of their own blood but don't mind how much they spill of other people's."

"You're against freedom and democracy? You support the terrorists, then?"

"I'm all for freedom and democracy. That's why I'm against the current regime of the USA that's illegally invading other countries, destroying its own freedoms, and pissing off people around the world big-time through an insane combination of arrogance and moral hypocrisy. Listen, if I could find toilet paper with the Stars and Stripes on it, I'd use it every day with the greatest satisfaction."

Winslow's face had been growing more and more angry as Sharpe carried on with his rant. "You called my President a psychopathic moron."

"Too right, sport. Want to hear what I call your crazy bloodthirsty crook of a Vice-President and lunatic ex-Secretary of Defence?" All of Sharpe's built-up resentment of what he saw as American hypocrisy and bullying was coming to the fore.

"And you said you'd desecrate my country's flag!"

"Big fucking deal. It's a piece of cloth, not a bloody holy relic."

By now, Sharpe was wondering if he'd gone too far. Winslow was almost literally going black in the face with rage at this latest insult to his sacred cows.

"You— you— un-American traitorous son of a—!" he illogically half-screamed, launching himself at Sharpe. Sharpe dropped his clipboard, and put up an arm to ward off the expected attack, which never came. From behind Winslow, Kim's man, whom Sharpe had noticed following him to the park earlier, swiftly appeared from among the trees. He stepped behind Winslow and threw a muscular arm around Winslow's neck while using the other arm to grab one of Winslow's hands, twisting it back. Winslow seemed to be screaming something, but the pressure on his throat was too great for any sound larger than a small squeak to come out.

Sharpe's unexpected protector looked directly at Sharpe and made a "go away" gesture with his head. Sharpe quickly picked up his clipboard and moved away. As he looked back, he could see the hapless American being dragged behind the bushes by the gangster. Sharpe felt little pity. Major-league numbskull, he said to himself.

Amazingly, the whole thing seemed to have taken place so quickly and quietly that no-one had noticed. The mothers on the other side of the park were engrossed in their children playing, and the children themselves were engrossed in whatever engrosses children. Only one toddler stood solemnly staring wide-eyed at the bushes behind which Winslow had disappeared.

SHARPE WONDERED WHAT HIS NEXT STEP SHOULD BE, as he let himself into his flat. He now had (he ticked them off on his fingers) a Japanese agency, a British agency, and an American agency, not to mention a North Korean gangster outfit, all much too interested in him for his own good.

Hanoi was beginning to seem like a good place to be for a couple of days. He picked up his Internet telephone and dialled the Katsuyama factory in Vietnam listed on the Web site.

"Do you speak English?"

"Yes, a little." Thank God for that. Sharpe's Vietnamese was completely nonexistent.

"May I speak to Dr Masashi Katsuyama?"

"I'm sorry, he's not at here now. Maybe you try his hotel?"

"Sorry, what's the number of his hotel? He gave it to me,

but I lost it, so I thought I'd try you." She slowly and carefully read out a telephone number.

"Thank you very much."

"You're welcome, sir."

Sharpe dialled the number he'd just been given.

"Sofitel Metropole Hanoi," came the voice at the other end.

"Do you speak English? *Parlez-vous anglais*?" asked Sharpe, with an inspired memory of Vietnam's colonial past.

"Of course, sir. How may I help you?" replied a suave American-tinged voice.

"I'd like to speak to one of your guests, please. Dr Masashi Katsuyama."

"Thank you, sir. That's room 378. Ringing for you now, sir."

Sharpe broke the connection, writing down '378' on a piece of paper.

A few more clicks on the Web site of a travel company and a few more on a Hanoi hotel Web site. He hit "Print" a few times.

He shouted to the kitchen, "Mieko, how do you fancy going to Vietnam tomorrow for a few days?"

"Tomorrow? I have my yoga class then." Mieko displayed her amazing talent for reducing the cosmic to the trivial yet again. If you told her the world was about to end in half an hour's time, she'd calculate that it just gave her time to bring in the laundry before the fire and brimstone came raining down.

"I'm serious. What are you doing now? Stop doing it, whatever it is, and come to the Vietnamese Embassy to get our visas."

"Don't we need air tickets and hotel reservations and things?"

"Probably, but I've got them already. Just booked them on the Internet."

"Won't it take a long time to get the visas?"

"I don't think so. Remember Roger and Mariko who went to Vietnam last year? They said they got their visas done on the same day while they waited."

"You're mad," coming in to stare at him in disbelief.

"No, I'm not. Please, Mieko. I'm serious about this."

"All right. In twenty minutes. Is this all to do with that stupid thing?"

Sharpe nodded.

"I thought it was. I'll be with you soon."

"Fine." That suited Sharpe. "I'll be out of the house for a few minutes and then I'll come back and we'll be off."

He owed Kim a favour, he supposed. Several favours, maybe. Time to start working off the debt. Again, there was only one obvious minder around, a different one from the one who had saved him from the deranged American. The British team seemed to have called off their watch. Sharpe made straight for his shadow.

"Masashi Katsuyama. In Hanoi. Sofitel Metropole hotel. Room 378," he said in Japanese, pressing a piece of paper into the other's hand. "And thank your friend for his help today."

The man grunted. It might have been thanks, it might have been surprise. He bowed. "Thank you very much indeed," he growled. "I will make sure the boss gets this information."

Sharpe bowed back, and walked back to the flat.

"Your mobile was ringing," called Mieko from the bathroom, where she was doing nameless things to her face, preparatory to going out. "It stopped just as I got to it."

The mobile was on his desk, and Sharpe pressed the buttons to call back the number that had called him.

"What the fuck's going on?" were Jon's first words.

"What do you mean?"

"Who the hell is beating up US diplomats? Is this yet another of your hidden talents?"

"I don't know anything about it."

"Oh, come off it. Kermit Winslow III of the American Diplomatic Corps has just staggered into the British Embassy minus about half his teeth and with a crushed larynx and a dislocated shoulder and the first person he wants to speak to is Tim Barclay, complaining that the British are attacking him. Tim Barclay being safely tucked away inside his little cave, I get the job of soothing some very ruffled feathers, don't I?"

"He's got it wrong. He was talking to me. He was going to attack me because of something I said to him. Someone else restrained him, fairly heavily, I admit. And why the hell would he go to Barclay, anyway?"

"Because, you stupid sod, he and Barclay, and I, come to that, are all doing the same thing, and we're all of us on the same side," explained Jon. "Theoretically, at least," he added after a pause. "Kermit the Frog-Faced Wonder is convinced that you are now working alongside the British Government to assist us with the destruction of democracy and freedom and the rest of the bullshit. It took all of my powers of persuasion to stop him going to our Ambassador and having your balls cut off and stuck on spikes above the US Embassy gate as a warning to anyone who dares to assault an American."

"I didn't assault him. I never laid a finger on him," protested Sharpe.

"All right, who was it then?"

"Probably the same one who did for Al Kowalski. And by the way, where are your bloody people when I need them?"

"Nights only from now on. Sorry. I did what I could.

So it's the North Korean mob acting as your protectors?" Sharpe said nothing. "I said to you once that you have some pretty fucking weird friends. I see no reason to change my opinion about that."

"Suit yourself," replied Sharpe. He considered letting Jon know that there was no need for a watcher for the next few nights, but decided against it. It might be a good idea if someone kept an eye on the flat while he and Mieko were away.

"You're not going to give the thing to the North Koreans, are you?" asked Jon incredulously. "I mean, you don't believe in the Dear Leader and all that bullshit, do you?"

"Credit me with a little common-sense," replied Sharpe.

"All right, I'll do you that favour. But I notice that's not a 'no'," replied Jon. "Anyway, well done."

"What do you mean?" Sharpe answered, a little thrown by the sudden change.

"Pissing off Winslow so much he took a swing at you. Pompous little prick's had that coming to him for months."

THE RECEIPTS FOR THE AIR TICKETS and hotel booking that Sharpe had printed were sufficient for the smiling Vietnamese at the embassy to provide him and Mieko with visas while they waited.

"Well, if that's Vietnamese bureaucracy, that's incredible," he remarked to Mieko as they walked down the hill from the embassy toward the station.

"Wonderful," she agreed. "Why are we going, anyway?"

"I think it's a good idea for us to be out of the country for a few days. Please, trust me on this."

"What's the weather going to be like in Hanoi?"

"According to the Internet, hot, and probably very humid. Even more unpleasant than here. Sorry."

"So why Hanoi?"

"I have a little bit of business to do there, and I wanted you to come along too. You can see the sights while I do my business. Ever heard of Halong Bay?"

"No."

"I'll show you pictures on the computer when we get back. It's a World Heritage site, and meant to be fabulously beautiful. Maybe I can come with you if I can get my business finished early. And there's lots of other things to do there. I hope my business won't take more than half a day or a day. And then we can come back on Sunday, and I start at Vishal's bank on Monday."

"Sounds fun." She snuggled against him on the train ride home, and sang softly to herself in the bedroom as she picked out clothes to pack.

Chapter 6: Hanoi

Hanoi airport turned out to be large, modern, and virtually empty. The road to Hanoi, along which they travelled in a Japanese-built taxi, was likewise nearly empty, and seemed to have been in a half-finished state for some time.

The hotel which Sharpe had booked was located near the old French quarter of Hanoi, and was housed in an early 20th-century colonial building. As soon as they had left their luggage in the room, Mieko excitedly dragged Sharpe out of the hotel, and they wandered through the narrow streets of the traditional Hanoi markets, dodging the motor-scooters and cycles threading their way through the warm rain and the noisy good-natured crowds.

A few shopkeepers, seeing Mieko and Sharpe together, addressed her in Vietnamese, but when she shook her head and replied in English, they switched effortlessly to English and apologised to her. Sharpe and Mieko bought cheap Vietnamese plastic rainwear, and although Mieko usually hated rainy weather, the novelty of the surroundings overcame her usual dislike of getting wet.

Mieko had a passion for shoes as well as for jewellery, and when they reached a street of shoe stalls, Sharpe prepared himself for a long wait while she tried on pair after pair of seemingly identical footwear, demanding his opinion at every stage.

"Why don't we go to the West Lake?" suggested Sharpe, in a desperate attempt to escape the inevitable. Much to his surprise, she agreed. It was an easy walk to the lake, with the central Post Office dominating one side, and groups of people sitting around chatting under the trees, even in the light rain.

"These people look as though they're happy with their lives," said Sharpe. He didn't know quite why he said it, but it seemed to be true. They were definitely not as well dressed as Japanese people, and they almost certainly didn't get as much to eat, but there was a certain contentment on their faces that was missing in the average Tokyo resident.

"Maybe," said Mieko, dubiously. Having grown up in post-war Japanese society where wealth and happiness were considered synonyms, she found it a little difficult to believe that poverty and happiness could coexist.

Sharpe's mobile phone rang. He had been pleasantly surprised when he had turned it on at the airport to find that he was able to use it in Vietnam, but the call was unexpected.

"Where the hell are you?" asked Jon.

"Not in Tokyo, and that's all I'm saying," replied Sharpe. "Maybe it will show up on your next phone bill."

"Look, we have a problem," said Jon.

"Who's 'we', Jon? You may have problems, I may have problems, but I can't think of any I want to share with you right now. I'm coming back on Sunday night. Talk to me then, but not before." He hung up and turned the phone off to prevent any further calls.

"Just business," he lied to Mieko. "Want to see the temple on the island?" They wandered through the temple, Mieko taking a photo of Sharpe by the guardian tiger carved on the gatepost, and later bought glasses of hot Vietnamese coffee, with condensed milk at the bottom.

When they got back to the hotel, Mieko yawned. "What shall we do for dinner tonight?" she asked. "Shall we just try the hotel restaurant? I don't want to go anywhere far." She yawned again.

"Fine by me," replied Sharpe. "Why don't you rest for an hour or so while I find out a few things? I'll take the room key with me so I don't have to wake you up when I come back."

He slipped downstairs, and asked the whereabouts of the Sofitel Metropole, discovering it was only a few hundred meters behind the Post Office on the lake that they had passed earlier that day. The friendly desk clerk passed him a map, with the route clearly marked, and Sharpe set off.

He enjoyed strange cities, especially the sights and smells and sounds of them. Maybe that's why, even though Japan and the Japanese way of doing things sometimes drove him to distraction, he continued to live and work in Tokyo. He took his time going to the Metropole, ducking into little stores selling landscape and abstract oil paintings, which he admired, but did not buy, a tiny supermarket, where he bought some cashew nuts, and a tourist souvenir store, where he bought a few postcards to send to family in England.

The Metropole itself was unmistakable – an elegant lump of colonial architecture taking up one side of a tree-lined avenue with a ministry building opposite, restored to its former glory, and entered through an imposing doorway. Inside the marble-floored entrance, a cheerful Vietnamese girl dressed in traditional *ao dai* sized him up, greeted him in English, and asked how she might be of service to him.

Sharpe asked for Katsuyama, and she conferred with the

reception desk staff before handing him a telephone which was ringing.

"*Moshi moshi*," came the voice at the other end after about five rings. "Hello."

"Dr Katsuyama," Sharpe said quickly in Japanese. "We met in a coffee shop and walked by the Sumida River the other day. Maybe we can meet again and you can explain some more to me?"

"Certainly," came the half-remembered voice with its husky overtones, still speaking Japanese. "Tomorrow at ten in the morning. At the place on the postcard." The line went dead.

And that was that. Sharpe didn't think there would be anything gained by hanging around the Metropole, so he made his way back to his own hotel, checking out the hotel restaurants as he went in, and woke up Mieko.

"Ready for dinner, dear?" he asked her. "We've got a choice of Vietnamese, French, or a bar with snacks."

"Vietnamese, of course." It was one of the things that Sharpe liked about Mieko – unlike many Japanese, she didn't regard foreign food with suspicion. In fact, every new item on the menu was a potential Everest waiting to be conquered.

Some spring rolls and chicken fried with vegetables later, washed down with 3-3-3 (pronounced "ba-ba-ba") beer, they were sated. "That was great," said Mieko.

"Agreed," said Sharpe. "There's no nightlife in this town, apparently. Let's go up to the room and make some of our own." Mieko giggled.

THE NEXT MORNING IT WAS RAINING AGAIN, but only drizzling. Sharpe's suggestion that they visit the Ho Chi Minh mausoleum was halfheartedly endorsed by Mieko.

Like many Japanese of her generation, she had a surprisingly vague idea of modern history, and seemed to be under the impression that Vietnam had threatened to invade the USA, and that Ho Chi Minh had been responsible for the bombing of Cambodia, hence the USA's intervention to contain the rapacious Vietnamese.

Sharpe attempted to set her straight on the facts as he saw them, and explained that Ho Chi Minh had actually been an enemy of the French and the Japanese colonial systems before becoming leader of a Communist state, but he wasn't sure how much had actually gone in. Part of it was the problems with the technical political vocabulary. Mieko's English in that area was stronger than Sharpe's Japanese, but not by much.

Although he had visited both Moscow and Beijing in the past, Sharpe had avoided visiting the mausoleums of the Communist demigods in either city, so he was unprepared for the formality and seriousness with which the usually smiling and easy-going Vietnamese treated the visit to Ho Chi Minh's tomb. Visitors were divided into Vietnamese and foreigners, and were required to line up silently in single file. Cameras were forbidden, and hands were to be respectfully at one's side or in front.

The whole process seemed designed to produce a serious and solemn atmosphere, as well as to magnify the importance of "Uncle Ho", and it seemed to work. Sharpe found himself seduced by the theatre of it all, and the dramatic lighting of the inner chamber in which the embalmed corpse lay only served to enhance the effect. In fact, Sharpe found himself so caught up in the whole business that he forgot that he had originally come out to meet Katsuyama.

As they filed out of the "silent zone" surrounding the mausoleum, Sharpe actually felt as though he'd had some kind of religious experience, and so did Mieko, if her face was anything to go by. Wonderful what you could do with the right lighting and psychological preparation, he thought, raising his camera to take a picture of Mieko standing in front of the square, Stalinist-style mausoleum. As he squinted through the viewfinder, a familiar husky voice asked in English if he wanted the speaker to take a photograph of him and Mieko standing together.

"Thank you, that would be very kind," Sharpe said, handing the camera to Katsuyama. "You just press this halfway down to focus the camera, and then all the way down to take the picture."

"I think I can manage to work that out," replied the other. "Have you managed to work out *my* little toy yet?"

"Well, it's a face-recognition program, as you said. I got it working, yes. And there's something to so with currency trading as well, but I've no idea how to make it all work."

"Well, you're about halfway there, I suppose. Just remember the big K and use it," said Katsuyama, enigmatically. "I really don't want to tell you any more than that."

"Is this some kind of intelligence test?"

"You might call it something like that. Now move over and join your lady so that I can take the picture."

Sharpe sheepishly went over to Mieko, and Katsuyama took two pictures of them together. Sharpe went over to collect the camera.

"I had to tell your father-in-law where you were. Of course he knew it wasn't you who died at Shinjuku that day when he saw the body at the police station," said Sharpe, hoping he might get some information about the whole affair. Katsuyama's face darkened, but he didn't seem about to provide any details of the incident.

"I would have preferred it if you hadn't done that. But no real harm done now that I'm dead, I suppose," he said without a trace of humour. "But get to the real purpose of that program, and you'll have a lot of fun and make a big difference to things, if you don't tell my father-in-law all about it."

Oh, not again, thought Sharpe. Why did everyone seem to think a simple program and hardware device was going to change the world? Were the contents of a Hello Kitty box really more important than the whole of what thousands of Microsoft engineers and billions of Bill Gates's dollars had achieved?

He left Katsuyama and rejoined Mieko. Once out of the solemn oppressive atmosphere of the mausoleum grounds, the Vietnamese seemed to revert to a state of easy-going normalcy, and Sharpe felt his spirits lifting, as they walked around the park surrounding the monument and saw the unusual One Pillar Pagoda with its foot in the lake, Uncle Ho's house, where he reportedly spent his last years pottering around in his garden, and the rest of the sights.

SHARPE WAS PRETTY SURE that there would be no more messages forthcoming from Katsuyama in the next few days, and decided he was free to enjoy his time in Vietnam. He and Mieko stayed in a modern hotel in Halong, with its thousands of green enchanted islands scattered throughout the bay, shopped in the old quarter of Hanoi (Mieko restricted herself to only two pairs of shoes) and discovered the joys of *pho*, the Vietnamese rice noodles that form a traditional Hanoi breakfast. As a memento of the trip, Sharpe bought Mieko a pair of ruby earrings she had admired in a small local jeweller's.

"That was a good break," said Sharpe to Mieko as they sat in the plane carrying them back to Japan.

"Yes," she agreed, still a little shaken from the taxi ride. The driver had tried to avoid paying the highway toll, and had taken them on a tour of what seemed like every water-buffalo track within a 20-kilometre radius of Hanoi. At one point, Sharpe had been almost convinced that they were about to be taken into the wilderness and robbed of all their possessions, but the smiling driver had pulled up to the airport terminal, seemingly unconcerned about the damage he had undoubtedly caused to his vehicle's suspension, and the worry he had caused his passengers, and in plenty of time for them to catch their plane.

"I never saw you do any business, though," Mieko pointed out to Sharpe.

"Oh, I got most of it done while you were asleep the first evening," replied Sharpe.

AT NARITA AIRPORT, WHEN SHARPE TURNED ON HIS MOBILE PHONE, it reported a flood of missed calls, all from Jon's mobile number.

"Excuse me," he said to Mieko and called back.

"Where the bloody hell have you been?" asked Jon.

"Hanoi."

Sharpe could hear the smack of Jon's palm against his forehead. "Hanoi. Of course. How fucking obvious. How could I possibly have missed that? I was thinking somewhere a bit closer to home, like Timbuktu, or the Lost City of the Incas. Where are you now?"

"Narita, waiting for our bags to come round on the carousel."

"Call me again as soon as you get home, then. And don't bugger off like that again without letting me know. Or without letting Ishihara know. He told us some time back that he'd told you not to leave the country without letting him know first. And he may not be real police, but he can probably make life pretty unpleasant for you, even without the assistance of Al Kowalski."

Oh shit. The scene with "Sugita" and "Ben" in the police interview room came back to Sharpe and he swore aloud. "You said something?" enquired Jon sarcastically. "You want me to smooth over your troubled waters one more time? You owe me one, pal. Actually, you owe both me and Ishihara more than one. Life would be a lot simpler for you if you let us know who your other friends are – you know, the friends who cut off other people's heads on your behalf. Assuming that's not something you do yourself in your spare time, that is."

Sharpe exploded. "No, it is not! What the hell are you accusing me of?"

"I know, I know. You're too busy trolling off to foreign climes without letting us know. Keep your hair on."

"Thank you for nothing. I'll call you when I get back home. A couple of hours, probably."

"Make sure you bloody well do."

Sharpe rang off, and in a temper pulled Mieko's bag from the carousel as it passed him. It was heavier than he had expected it to be, and he nearly felled an elderly Japanese gentleman as it came off the belt, striking the poor man hard across the back of the knees so that he staggered badly. Mieko offered copious apologies in ultra-polite Japanese, while Sharpe stood by, bowing feebly and feeling totally useless.

His own case went by and he made a desperate lunge for it, carefully lifting it clear of those around him. Mieko and he loaded up their baggage cart, and with a few last bows in the general direction of Sharpe's victim, who was still standing waiting for his baggage, left the baggage area and went through customs towards the escalator leading to the underground train stations.

An express train, from which they only had to make one change to arrive at their local station, was leaving in only ten minutes, so they bought reserved seats on it, and had a smooth and easy journey home. As soon as Sharpe had carried their cases into the bedroom, he apologised to Mieko. "Look, you know that I'd normally help you get the meal ready, but I promised to make this call." She sniffed. Sharpe wasn't sure of the deep significance of the sniff – Mieko's sniffs had various meanings and interpretations, but he knew that this one was not a good omen. He closed the office door and dialled Jon.

"Thanks for calling back. That was a quick journey from the airport."

"We were lucky with the trains. So what's up?"

"I assume you remember pissing off Kermit Winslow III? Well, it seems that he intended to return the favour. Our man watching your place at night recognised him going into your apartment building the other night, and followed him up the stairs. Do you know, the bugger had a can of lighter fluid and a lighter on him?"

"Hardly a crime."

"Might have been if our man hadn't stopped him. He was soaking rags in lighter fuel and dropping them through your front door's letterbox, and he was about to send a lit version of the same after them when our man stopped him."

"Thank you." Sharpe thought for a minute. "There were no rags on the floor when we just came back."

Jon coughed in a slightly embarrassed fashion. "Er, no. One of our people picked your lock and removed them for you."

"I suppose I should say thanks again, but it seems a bit more difficult to do this time round."

"We'll consider ourselves thanked, then," replied Jon.

"And what about our frog-named friend?"

"Well, he is a diplomat of a kind, so we can't officially do anything. But apart from being one of these ultra-nationalistic

Republicans, and a complete nutter to boot, he also has a penchant for dressing up in frilly maids' outfits." Sharpe laughed. "I can assure you that it's not a pretty sight," Jon went on. "I know. I've seen the photos. And so has he, with the understanding that if he tries anything else stupid, those photos go straight to the American Ambassador and to all the Japanese scandal weeklies."

"What does Major Tim Barclay have to say about it all?"

"Oh, he *loves* it. Especially those saucy frills around the knees. I really do think he's on the way out. Don't worry about him for now."

"Thanks."

"You owe us, Sharpe," Jon reminded him. The use of his surname underscored the stern tone. "We're going to have to collect soon. I want some names, remember."

"Understood," replied Sharpe, and rang off. He went to the kitchen and helped Mieko get the supper ready.

Chapter 7: Tokyo

THE NEXT DAY, SHARPE PUT ON HIS SECOND-BEST SUIT and took the early train to Vishal's bank. He already had an electronic access card, having worked there in the past, but it had expired, so he spent the first twenty minutes of the day being re-photographed and his details re-entered into the security database. It struck him at that point that Katsuyama's face-recognition database did indeed have many practical uses; but the currency-trading functionality that Vishal claimed to have discovered, how it was accessed, and what it did, remained an almost complete mystery.

Vishal led him to a small room with a desktop computer and a laptop and explained the details of Sharpe's assignment, which was a little more complex than he had originally explained (wasn't that always the way? Sharpe thought to himself). The regulatory authorities apparently wanted to make sure that all transactions made in a very specialised field of derivatives trading were being faithfully and accurately recorded in a secure database, as well as being accurately relayed in detail through to a central source linked to the bank's risk management team. Vishal explained that the software used for the trades had been written some years ago by a consultancy in New York, subsequently improved and adapted by another team of consultants in London, and finally localised for the Tokyo market by yet another consultancy in Hong Kong, who had made a poor job of it, chiefly because they'd failed to appreciate the problems involved in data processing in the Japanese language, and had subsequently gone out of business, leaving, as always in these cases, less than half of the software documented, with the rest being described in a weird Chinese version of English.

"I'm sorry, it's like pushing you into a pool full of sharks," said Vishal. "But none of us has the time to look at this, and we know you're good at these jobs. We have here a little of the source code which they were leaving with us, but not enough." He showed Sharpe where the relevant files were stored on the network. "And here," pointing to a shelf of loose-leaf files, "are the specifications and their notes. Some of them, anyway. The program's loaded onto this computer," pointing to the desktop machine, "and this is how you get it started," demonstrating. "And here's your user name and a temporary password. Change it as soon as you log onto the trading system. Test data is all in here," pointing to a printout of file names. "Use your login ID and password to access those directories. Now I must be going to another meeting, but I will be seeing you at lunchtime, all right?"

Sharpe sighed as Vishal left him with what appeared to be an insoluble technical problem. Mind you, he told himself, almost all problems started like this, and eventually resolved themselves into something a lot easier and simpler to understand. He ploughed through the introductory manuals, fetching himself several cups of coffee during the morning. Several people with whom he'd worked on previous contracts dropped by to greet him, and the morning passed quite quickly, and surprisingly productively.

Vishal came by at lunchtime, and Sharpe told him how

far he'd got on. "Better than I'd expected," said Vishal. "Don't finish too soon, though. Maybe you can spend the afternoon doing other things."

AFTER LUNCH, VISHAL EXPLAINED how the computer on Sharpe's desk had been supplied with the market data feeds that Vishal had identified as necessary for the operation of the currency trading program he believed to be lurking buried in the face recognition software, and the Katsuyama board had also been fitted.

"It said that you needed a video camera for the face recognition program, so I've left you with one just in case," said Vishal. "Now I must be leaving you for another stupid bloody meeting. Enjoy yourself, man."

Sharpe plugged in the video camera, and fired up the Katsuyama program. It looked just the same as before when he and Vishal had first run it and it invited him to register his face. What had Katsuyama said to him in Hanoi? 'Remember the big K and use it'? He pressed the K key, with and without the Shift key and the Control and Alt keys in different combinations. Nothing happened.

He quit the program and tried double-clicking its icon while holding down the K key and Shift key together.

"Holy shit!" The screen now showed something completely unexpected. He read "Katsuyama FX Predictor" together with a choice of exchanges to which he could supposedly connect. "Tokyo" was the nearest exchange, and he clicked that button.

He was asked for a name and password for trading on the exchange, which of course he didn't have, so he clicked "Cancel". To his surprise, the program didn't quit, but put up a message saying "Trading disabled. Use Preferences to set user name and password, and configure system." After clicking "OK", he discovered the Preferences panel (he'd used many commercial programs which were more difficult to use than this prototype) and entered a name and password with a few other details. "You are now authorised to view rates," the screen told him. "Press Continue". He did, and was presented with a list of currency pairs, and invited to pick up to three pairs. He picked the yen/US dollar pair and clicked "OK" again. After about 15 minutes fine-tuning the system (surprisingly easy) to use the Bloomberg and other data feeds connected to his computer, the message then told him, "Gathering data. Please wait."

He waited, and after about three minutes, the screen cleared and a line tracing a light blue graph started to make its way across the screen. A number, also in light blue, appeared at the bottom right of the screen and its value changed every five seconds or so, at irregular intervals as the line wriggled across the screen. The bottom axis of the graph went from 14:17 to 14:37, and the vertical Y axis started at 114 and went up to 117. Obviously the graph was tracing the up-to-date exchange rate as the data came into the system.

After about a minute, Sharpe noticed some odd things. The computer's system clock at the top of the screen was displaying the time as 14:15 – three minutes before the time marking the end of the light blue line making its way across the screen. He checked his digital watch, which was usually accurate to a minute or so. Yes, the graph appeared to be describing events three minutes into the future. And the part of the graph which had already been drawn wasn't staying still, either. As Sharpe watched, it twitched and wriggled slightly as the numerical values changed.

Sharpe was still staring at it and trying to work out exactly what was going on, when after three minutes a dark blue line started to appear from the left of the screen, almost perfectly overlaying the light blue line drawn previously. The time corresponding to the end of this new line now matched the time given on the system clock at the top of the screen. Another figure appeared at the bottom of the screen in dark blue, showing the current value of the dark blue line, and another changing figure, hovering around zero, which Sharpe came to realise was the difference between the values shown by the light and dark blue lines.

As Sharpe watched, the dark blue line grew in length, almost completely corresponding to the light blue line as it made its way across the screen. Only occasionally was a gap visible between them.

As the lines scrolled across the screen it hit him with full force what he was looking at. All of Katsuyama's techniques associated with pattern recognition, with the acceleration coming from the associated digital signal processing technology, were being used to interpret the current price data for a constantly changing exchange rate, extracted from the data feeds and treated as a pattern. The system was matching the pattern and extrapolating trends three minutes into the future. Any trader armed with this almost certain knowledge of the future could make a killing on the lightning-fast trades that made up the world of the currency markets using only simple trading strategies. If more sophisticated option trading was figured in, there was probably no limit to the money this program could make.

He found a program menu item allowing him to halt the march of the lines across the screen, and selected a trio of currency rates, involving the yen, dollar and euro.

Once again, the program predicted the three exchange rates three minutes in advance. The result seemed to be slightly less accurate than when it was predicting only a pair of currency rates, but it seemed almost completely accurate when it came to predicting whether the line would rise or fall and when the change in direction would occur – just the amount of change was slightly wrong.

How many people knew about this, other than Katsuyama and now him? Is this really what the Japanese, British and Americans, not to mention Korean gangsters, were all fighting over? Somehow, he doubted it. No-one had given him even the smallest clue or hint that this was what it was all about.

Using the laptop computer, he logged onto the Internet and did some more searches for Katsuyama's name and published work. There was nothing visible there that seemed remotely relevant to the trading program, except the papers on image processing that he had seen previously. Maybe, somewhere in the mathematics and equations of the papers, there was a clue as to the existence of this currency program, but it was a very good bet that no-one in the financial world had ever seen these papers, let alone understood their significance, and it was an even better bet that no mathematicians would ever have taken the trouble to apply these algorithms to foreign exchange trading.

After twenty minutes of fascinated watching, he stopped the program and let out a deep breath. He realised that he'd just witnessed the impossible – an accurate forecast of the future, and a technology that could quite probably turn its user into a multimillionaire in a very short space of time if deployed intelligently. How it all worked, he really had no idea. Nor was it his business to know. The immediate question was what he was to do with this knowledge. If he looked carefully at the contract that he'd signed with the bank, it probably said that anything he discovered during his time at the bank belonged to them. Stuff that. Much as he liked the people at the bank where he was now working, he felt that someone other than them deserved a break on this. What on earth would any government do with this, though? Could Jon and Major Barclay be trusted with this? Jon, possibly, but he didn't trust Tim Barclay an inch. He had very much the same feeling about Ishihara and his outfit. He made up his mind to keep the whole thing to himself for the moment.

Time to go back to the work he was being paid for, even if it was nearly impossible to keep his mind on the job. He ploughed through the almost incomprehensible mass of words that passed for documentation written by the defunct Hong Kong contractor, and attempted to make sense of the first stages of the process.

A few hours later, Vishal poked his head round the door. "Any luck with the other program?" he asked Sharpe, putting a significant emphasis on the word "other".

"Not a thing," Sharpe lied. He had no wish to deceive his friend Vishal, but he didn't want to put him in a position where he was deceiving his full-time employers. For Sharpe as a contractor, the situation was slightly easier in practical terms, even if he did break the contract. At least he couldn't be fired and lose his bonus and his pension benefits and all the other goodies that came with being a permanent employee. All they could do was cancel his contract and stop him ever working for them again. He doubted if they'd ever bring anything to a Japanese court, especially given the nature of his discovery.

"Too bad," replied Vishal. "Come on, let's go to the pub. One of our UNIX guys is leaving for New York, and we're all going for a drink."

"All right," said Sharpe, stretching. "Let me just clean up this lot first," gesturing to the papers and folders around the desk.

After a few minutes Vishal and Sharpe made their way to the faux-Irish bar which served as a watering-hole for many of Tokyo's foreign community working in the financial sector. Sharpe knew a lot of the faces at the bar, and even managed to remember some of the names to go with them, and he was soon involved in a heated discussion involving the relative merits of different database systems used by Vishal's bank.

A few drinks later he was on the train back home.

"Tadaima – I'M HOME," he called as he opened the door.

"*O-kaeri-nasai* – welcome back," answered Mieko's voice.

To Sharpe's surprise, Katsuyama's father-in-law, Kim, was sitting on the sofa in their living-room, drinking tea, and obviously very much at his ease. A single hulking body-guard perched uncomfortably on a chair behind him, look-ing completely out of place.

Kim half-rose, smiling, as Sharpe entered. "Mr Sharpe, you are a genius," he beamed, speaking his excellent English. "Thank you for finding my son-in-law."

"No problems?"

Kim appeared surprised by the question. "Of course not. Why should there be? As long as I know where he is, that's the main thing."

"So he's still in Hanoi?" Mieko looked at Sharpe curi-ously, but he didn't elaborate. Later, he mouthed silently to her.

"Yes, yes. Very safe and in Hanoi," a little testily. "I said I would compensate you if you succeeded in your search, and here you are." He said something in Korean to the body-guard, who handed a black attaché case to him. Kim stood up and used both hands to hand the case to Sharpe for-mally. Sharpe, equally formally, used both hands to receive it. "Open it," suggested Kim.

Sharpe snapped the catches and opened the lid. The case

contained five bricks of ten-thousand yen notes. Probably about ten million yen there, Sharpe thought to himself. He resisted the urge to pick up one of the bricks and count it.

"Is that enough, do you think?" asked Kim. "It's all the real thing, by the way," he smiled. "None of the fake rubbish that North Korea's been pushing over here." He was referring to the counterfeit foreign currency that North Korea had been producing in large quantities, to the embarrassment of the United States, Japan, and the other countries whose currency had been counterfeited.

"The thought had never crossed my mind," said Sharpe. The germ of an idea came to him. "Mr Kim, I'm not ungrateful. In fact, I'm more than grateful, and I thank you most sincerely for all this, but I'd sooner not accept the money at this time. I'd like you to keep it safe for me, but I may ask you for it in a little while." He closed the lid of the case and handed it back to Kim.

Kim raised his eyebrows. "You're turning this down?"

"No, not at all, but I'm asking you to look after it for me for a little while, if you don't mind."

"As long as you don't expect me to pay you interest." Kim laughed, and passed the case back to the bodyguard. "Can I ask why?"

"I don't feel this is a particularly safe place to have so much cash, and I'm not that happy about walking into a bank with all this money in cash." Sharpe gestured to the still unrepaired broken window, whose temporary cardboard was beginning to come adrift. "Thank you very much for all your help with the Americans, and so on, while we're talking about that sort of thing."

"I hope it didn't cause you too much trouble, especially the left baggage at the station," said Kim, blandly. Mieko looked curiously at Sharpe, then at Kim, and then at Sharpe again. She failed to gain anything from their innocent expressions.

"I think everything went as smoothly as could be expected, under the circumstances."

"Good, good," purred Kim.

Sharpe sat down in a chair facing Kim and accepted a cup of tea from Mieko. "I don't want to appear too nosy, but may I ask you a few questions?"

"You can ask them, but I don't promise you I'll answer them." Kim threw his arms behind his head and leaned back in Sharpe's sofa, making himself comfortable.

"Fair enough. First question. Your family is from North Korea, I understand?"

"Yes, indeed. I've been there several times in the recent past, but I've not actually lived there since I was a teenager. All my mother's family lives there and most of my father's family as well. The ones who are left, that is." He paused. "Many of my aunts and uncles have died in the prison camps."

"I suppose that answers the next question I was afraid to ask," said Sharpe.

"You were going to ask if I support the current government of North Korea, then? I fear that you might not have got a very flattering or accurate picture of me from my son-in-law, who believes I am a puppet or a stooge or some kind of agent for the North Korean government or *Chongryon* or something. He confuses my love of my country with a love of its government. I fled from those accursed devils of Kim Il-sung and his evil henchmen to the USA as soon as I was able to do so." Sharpe raised his eyebrows. "Forgive the melodramatic language, but I find it difficult to think of those people in any other terms. I did quite well in my line of work in America for a few years, but then moved my operations to Japan. The business opportunities were better, I found."

Sharpe decided not to enquire too deeply into the nature of Kim's business interests. "What about the military? Do you think they're a better future for the North Koreans, then, if they were to take over the country from the Party?"

Kim made a dismissive motion with his hand. "Who told you the Party and the soldiers were different from each other? They're just different sides of the same coin. You may think I'm totally mad, but I really believe that the only hope for the people of North Korea is for the people themselves to throw off the Party and ask to join the South."

So much for Major Barclay's theory about the military fighting the Party in North Korea, Sharpe thought to himself. "What about China taking over North Korea through a puppet party?" he asked. This had been a view put forward by a German journalist recently at a lecture that Sharpe had attended.

"China's just more of the same. Don't you think the people of North Korea have had enough of dictators pretending to be Communists? And there's no way that Koreans would put up with a foreign power ruling them yet again."

Sharpe had to agree that this sounded probable.

Kim continued, "I'm probably a little strange in my ideas. I do quite a lot of things that many governments don't like, but you know why I do these things, Mr Sharpe?" Sharpe obediently shook his head. "I do them to make money. But," and he held up a warning finger, "I don't make this money for myself. As I've just shown you," and he gestured towards the attaché case, "I'm perfectly happy to give large amounts of it away to people I like."

Sharpe nodded, and Kim continued. "You should see my house. Believe it or not, it's not that much bigger than this apartment, and it's not as well-furnished. I don't want to make money for myself, as I say. When my son-in-law needed money to help his business, I was there. When he needed money to go to Stanford to pursue his research, I was there. But mainly, Mr Sharpe," and here he leant forward, "I make money to help my people. If I can make enough money, maybe I can work for my people to gain their freedom."

He was sincere, Sharpe decided, but crazy. "Mr Kim, with the best will in the world, and even with lots of money, I don't really see how the people of North Korea can start to overthrow a government armed with tanks and missiles, even if they wanted to, which I believe is nearly an impossibility to start with."

Kim laughed. "You're thinking of pitched battles in the streets? No way. This would be pinpoint surgery to remove the disease from the country and inject some healthy elements. Some people might call it terrorism. I prefer to call it a fight for freedom."

Sharpe noticed that the teacups were empty, and poured more tea for his uninvited guests. Somehow, it seemed to be perfectly normal to be sitting around drinking tea with a gangster, calmly discussing ways to dispose of the present North Korean dictatorship through terrorist plots. It was still one of the more seriously weird situations in which he'd found himself since coming to Japan, though (and recently there seemed to have been many of them).

"Mr Kim, how much money do you think it would take to make your plans work?"

"In US dollars ..." Kim closed his eyes and appeared to be doing some rapid mental calculations. "I think about twenty-five million dollars in the right hands would be enough to get rid of the Party and to put a responsible person in a leading position to negotiate with the South. I've got a good way to go before I have enough money. That's why I am keen for my son-in-law to succeed with his ideas."

"Which ideas are those, Mr Kim?"

"Oh, his ideas and his research about reading faces on a computer. I'm sure that's worth a few million dollars to the right people."

Sharpe searched the man's face, as far as he was able, trying to determine whether he was hiding any knowledge of the currency trading program. It was impossible to tell for sure, but Sharpe didn't feel that it was the time to bring up the subject.

"Twenty-five million dollars doesn't seem like an awful lot of money, though, Mr Kim," he said. "I mean, it's more than I have available to me right now," he laughed, "but on a government's scale, it will hardly buy anything."

"Mr Sharpe, you come from a rich country, and you are living in a rich country," Kim said sharply. "I guess that the amount you charge your clients for one hour of your work would be enough to feed a North Korean worker's family for a month. In an economy like that, a little goes a very long way."

"I understand," said Sharpe, a little abashed.

"Forget the idea of the people taking to the streets," repeated Kim. "But a few key officials could suddenly find themselves removed very quickly and relatively cheaply. Trains could stop running, with lines being blocked. Electricity to key government and Party offices could be cut off. Police might fail to investigate various accidents. None of this takes an incredible amount of money. But it adds up when all's said and done."

"I think you have some very specific plans in your head, Mr Kim," Sharpe said, not without some admiration in his voice.

"Indeed I do. But I've done enough talking for today," said Kim. "I will leave you now, but one of my men will still be keeping an eye open for you. With your permission, that is?"

"Of course. Thank you," said Sharpe. "I do feel a bit safer with your people around."

"Good. And the money here," patting the case, "is yours whenever you want. Now, if you'll excuse me," and he went to the front door, preceded by his bodyguard, who carefully peered through the spy-hole in the door before cautiously opening it, revealing another bodyguard standing outside. Sharpe recognised him as the one who had rearranged Kermit Winslow's dental work.

And then, almost without Sharpe realising it, they were all gone, leaving Sharpe and Mieko somewhat confused and more than a little frightened.

"I THINK THERE'S A LOT YOU HAVEN'T TOLD ME," said Mieko.

"You're right, there is quite a lot. I didn't want to worry you."

"Who's in Hanoi? And why on earth did you turn down a whole case full of money?"

"The person in Hanoi is the man whom I met and who we were told had died at Shinjuku station by that policeman who came round and ate peaches that evening. We met him outside Ho Chi Minh's tomb. He was the one who took our picture there." Mieko's mouth opened wide.

"Why did they think he was dead, if he's not?"

"Because there was a body found at Shinjuku station wearing his clothes. It even had my card in the pocket, which was what brought that policeman round to us to start with, remember?"

"And it's all connected to our flat being burgled?"

"Yes, it is. But I do know that the person who did that won't be doing it again. Don't ask me how I know, but I do know."

At the Sharpe End

"And why did you turn down the money?"

"I haven't turned it down. I'm just asking him to look after it for a while for me. It's not a question of whether I want the money or not. It's a question of someone asking me where the money came from. And you know that money's not clean – look at what he does for a living."

"Don't you like him?"

"That's not very relevant, if the money's dirty, is it? Actually, I suppose I do quite like him, except that—" Sharpe stopped. He had just remembered Katsuyama's wife, and the bruises on her arm.

"What?" asked Mieko.

"Well, you remember the night he kidnapped you? And Katsuyama's wife came round to see me before I rushed off to see you?"

She nodded. "Yes, of course."

"Well, when she was here, I noticed that she had bruises on her arm."

"So did I."

Sharpe looked at Mieko curiously. "You weren't here when she was here," he pointed out.

"No, but I met her when I was with Mr Kim. And I noticed the bruises then. I told you about it, remember?"

"No." Sharpe racked his memory, but he had absolutely no memory of her mentioning this. Either he was losing his memory, or Mieko was. He suspected the latter, if truth be told. "So how did she behave around her father? Scared?"

"No, not at all. Are you really sure I didn't tell you all about this before?" Sharpe shook his head. "No, she seemed very friendly. Looking after him, and making sure he was warm and comfortable enough and that his teacup was filled and so on. Not at all scared."

"Did you hear what happened between them when she

came round here? Did you know she was coming round here?"

"Yes, he told her to come round here and to pretend he was a monster, to frighten you about me, and make you hurry up."

"And what did she say?"

"She laughed, and kissed his cheek."

Sharpe had to admit that this didn't seem like the actions of a woman who was frightened of her monster of a father. "What about the bruises?"

"Well, I don't think that he had anything to do with them. She wouldn't have been so friendly otherwise. And from what I saw of them, they weren't new. About two or three days old, I thought."

"How on earth would you know about a thing like that?" Mieko turned her head away. Sharpe could have bitten off his tongue, remembering her alcoholic ex-husband who had beaten her repeatedly, forcing her to flee the marriage. "Oh God, sorry I said that. Yes, I'm sure you know, and I'm sure you're right," putting his arms round her.

"My guess is that it was her husband who did that," added Mieko, sinking into his embrace, with her head nestling against his chest.

Sharpe wasn't so convinced by this idea, but he said nothing. The weird way that things were developing, Mieko might well be right about it.

"So you think Mr Kim's all right?" he asked Mieko.

"Well, don't you think so?"

"I'm sure he is. Look at the way that he's going to help those poor North Koreans."

Sharpe sighed inwardly to himself. The Japanese media had been demonising North Korea for some time now. A number of Japanese nationals had been kidnapped some twenty-five years earlier, for reasons best known to North

Korean spy-masters. A few had been returned, together with an American spouse (a deserter from the Vietnam war) and their children, but the parents of one so-called "abductee", whom they still believed to be alive in North Korea, were an almost nightly fixture on Japanese television speaking about the need to "resolve the issue" (whatever that was meant to mean), seemingly unable to come to terms with the fact that the bones of their beloved missing daughter were in all probability at the bottom of an undocumented mass grave outside a prison camp somewhere near Pyongyang.

"You think he's serious about it, then?"

"Oh yes. He had a lot of books about Korea in the place he took me, and a lot of maps. I think he's being truthful. Why?"

"Well, it's complicated."

"Our whole life has been getting complicated, ever since you came back with that Hello Kitty box. And where is that box now?" she asked, pushing herself away from Sharpe.

"In a very safe place where no-one can get at it, except the people who are meant to be able to," he explained. "You don't need to know where."

She relaxed a little. "Don't you want to explain a bit more?"

"No," replied Sharpe. She stiffened again. "It's not that I don't trust you, of course. But I think the fewer people who know what's going on, the better it is. I don't want to put you in a position where you might be forced to tell someone about something."

"You make it sound very scary."

"Aren't you scared? I am," Sharpe said. "There are a lot of really nasty things going on. And I really don't think it would be a good idea to have Kumi-chan round here for a little while. I'm not sure it's safe."

"I agree. We have to get that window fixed first." Sharpe

sighed to himself. That wasn't exactly what he'd meant, but it would do for now. "I'll see if they're open tomorrow morning when I'm on my way to the station."

"Oh yes, sorry. I'd forgotten that you were at the bank now. Shall I go instead of you, then?"

"If you like. Let's write it down so that we don't forget it."

"So I don't forget it," she corrected him.

Chapter 8: Tokyo

THE NEXT DAY AT THE BANK showed Sharpe that the previous day's currency predictions were no fluke. For over an hour, he watched fascinated as the line predicting the currency prices three minutes into the future was neatly overwritten by the line representing the actual currency rates. Though he had no specialised financial trading expertise or experience, Sharpe could see how even he could make money with this. In the right hands, it would be a deadly financial weapon, capable of controlling the markets and making millions. And, of course, millions of dollars was just what Kim was looking for. If Kim was serious, and honest about his wish to topple North Korea's Stalinist regime, then it seemed to Sharpe that putting the currency exchange program in Kim's hands would be a good idea.

He'd just decided that he'd have to take Vishal at least partly into his confidence, when Vishal himself walked in the door. Sharpe tried to shut down the program, but he was too slow.

"That isn't looking anything like pornography," said Vishal as he watched Sharpe's fruitless frantic attempts to clear the screen and return it to something more like a working environment. "Even if you were able to get to one of those sites through our firewall. But—" He stopped and looked at the screen. "That's not one of our programs, is it?"

Sharpe shook his head. "Close the door, and sit down, Vishal. This is really big." Mystified, Vishal did as Sharpe asked him. "Now, I really don't want you to tell anyone else about this. Can I have your word on this?" Even more mystified, Vishal nodded. "OK, now watch."

Sharpe explained the meanings of the two lines and how the currency price was being predicted accurately three minutes into the future.

Vishal refused to believe it at first, so Sharpe stopped the program and showed Vishal from the beginning what was happening.

"My God!" exclaimed Vishal, watching exchange rate fluctuations. "This is amazing, man! I don't bloody believe what's happening. Do you know what I'm working on right now?" Sharpe shook his head. "It's an ultra low-latency forex trading platform, designed to cut the time between the time that the price changes and the trades get placed. Now you're showing me something where you can place the trade before the price changes. The things you could do on options ... This could make someone very rich."

"Technically, it's your bank that gets very rich," Sharpe reminded him.

"Bugger that, man," snapped Vishal. "Shut that bloody thing down, and get the card the hell out of the computer. I am not wanting the bank to have anything at all to do with this. This is just you and me, man."

Sharpe looked at him. This was not the Vishal he knew, who usually acted as a good company employee, working all the hours he was asked to work without complaint or fuss and loyally defending the bank against any slurs or accusations. "All right," he agreed, shutting down the program and turning off the computer. "Got a screwdriver handy?" Silly question. Vishal was all thumbs, and was no more likely to have a screwdriver on him than a full-sized oxyacetylene welding kit. Sharpe rummaged in his case, and came up with his own portable toolkit. "Anti-static bag?" he asked Vishal, as he loosened the screw holding the card in place.

"I'll go and look for one," replied Vishal. Once he was out of the room, Sharpe asked himself about Vishal's strong and uncharacteristic reaction. What was it that had set him off like that?

Vishal appeared with a cardboard box with the name of a computer maker printed on it. Not, thank goodness, a Hello Kitty box, Sharpe thought.

"Here you go. They're putting new disk controllers in some of the servers, and these are now spare."

Sharpe swiftly removed the Katsuyama card, and placed it in the special bag, designed to protect the delicate components against stray static charges, and placed the bag in the box. He screwed the computer back together and looked at Vishal.

"Better get the software off here, as well?" he suggested. "Your job, I think."

Vishal slid into the seat that Sharpe vacated and used the keyboard and mouse. "That's it, I'm pretty sure. I've done a secure erase, so that no-one should be able to find out what was on the disk."

By now, Sharpe realised, he and Vishal had probably broken Japanese Financial Services Agency regulations several times over, not to mention internal bank rules, but it all seemed pretty minor compared to severed heads in station coin lockers. "Where's the original CD that I got from Katsuyama?" he asked.

"It is in the desk drawer here. I locked it," said Vishal.

He fished in his pocket, pulled out a bunch of keys and un-locked the drawer. "Here you go."

"Thanks," taking the disc and placing it in the box with the card. The box went into his bag. "Now, why are you so excited about all this?"

"Not here," said Vishal. "Come out to the coffee shop with me. That is much safer."

Sharpe picked up his bag, and followed Vishal out of the office building to the coffee shop next door. He looked at his watch. "I'm calling this my lunch-time," he said to Vishal. "Let's go to the Italian restaurant where they do the good espresso."

Somewhat to his surprise, Vishal demurred. "No, let's be somewhere where there'll be no-one else from the bank."

VISHAL LED THE WAY THROUGH THE TOKYO BACK STREETS to a small restaurant calling itself "Mumbai Cafe" with a garish red and yellow awning. Once inside, they found they were the only customers. "Deepak does most of his business in the evening," explained Vishal, gesturing at the grinning cook behind the counter. The menu was writ-ten on the wall, but in a script that Sharpe couldn't read, neither English nor Japanese. "Shall I place the order for us?" suggested Vishal, noticing Sharpe's bemusement. He spoke rapidly to the owner. Sharpe could make out a few words that he recognised from Indian restaurant menus, but wasn't sure whether he'd got them right.

"You'll like the food here. Not quite up to Meema's high standards, but I am thinking it is being a pretty good sec-ond-best," said Vishal confidently. "Now, there's a very good reason why I don't want the bank to get involved in this, you know."

"Go on," said Sharpe. A plate of spiced poppadums had

At the Sharpe End

just magically appeared in front of him, and he broke off a piece of poppadum and nibbled at it.

"My sister back in India is very sick indeed. She has a very rare disease of the kidneys and to enable her to live for another few years, she is needing treatment that can only be performed in the USA or Germany."

"Oh, that's terrible news, Vishal," said Sharpe. "When did you hear about this, and why didn't you tell me earlier?"

"We'd suspected for some time, but the last test results only came in a few days ago, and you seemed to be having your own set of problems. Of course, I am helping her by sending money to India, but my family still doesn't have enough money to be sending her to America or Europe for treatment. If we use this currency trading program ourselves, we could be making that money very easily."

"We could," admitted Sharpe cautiously.

"But are you knowing any foreign exchange brokers who could be trusted absolutely? After all, if we keep winning at this thing, aren't they going to become suspicious?"

"All right, so you are starting to come round to my own way of thinking," said Sharpe, "and that's a good point that you make there. So we set up our own brokerage with just three or four of us. You run the IT side of things, and Meema should be the trader. She knows a lot about foreign exchange strategies."

"You are absolutely correct there, Kenneth-san. Bang on. For the past six months she is doing nothing but that sort of very thing in the back office for the traders."

"Do you know how easy it is to set up a foreign exchange brokerage?" Sharpe asked Vishal. "I must admit that I've really only just thought of the idea."

"No bloody idea, man. That is your next job."

"Look, before we go too far on this, Vishal, I want to

know a few things. How much money does your sister need to go to America or Germany and have the operations?"

"The doctors are telling us that it will take at least one million dollars. Not as much as two million, but at least one million. If she has the operation, there is a very good chance indeed that she will live a normal life. About eighty or ninety per cent, I am being told. But without the operation," he paused, "it is about twenty per cent only that she will live more than five years." Steaming plates of curried vegetables, together with pickles, and a plate of chapattis, were placed in front of them, and Vishal seized one of the rounds of bread, tearing off a piece and dipping it into the aubergine curry. "I know it may seem to be a lot of money, but she is my eldest sister, and I am very fond of her indeed."

"I understand that, Vishal, and who's to say that you won't have the money and your sister will be cured? But quite honestly, let's think big. One or two million dollars is not a lot of money for this program to produce. I have a friend who needs twenty-five million dollars and I was thinking that we could use the program for that as well."

Vishal's hand stopped halfway to his mouth. A piece of vegetable slipped from the bread he was holding and dropped into his water glass. Vishal didn't seem to notice. "You are telling me twenty-five million dollars?" he asked, wide-eyed. "What sort of friends do you have? What will he do with all that money? Is he starting a competitor to Microsoft or something?"

"He's going to take over a country. Just a little one, though," explained Sharpe, taking his first mouthful of curry and watching Vishal's expression with amusement. "I think there's enough money in that program to send your sister to the USA, or anywhere else she needs to go, and to help my other friend, and to leave something for you and Meema, and me and Mieko. But you and Meema would almost certainly have to leave your jobs here, and work for the new brokerage. Conflicts of interest and so on."

"It's a terrible risk, Kenneth-san. I am thinking this may be being too much for me, after all."

"It's a risk worth taking, Vishal. You saw those lines on the screen. Anyone with a decent trading strategy could make a fortune. Remember the margins and the leverage in foreign exchange – you can trade with many times the amount of capital you actually put in. You can play with calls and options and all kinds of other fancy things. Meema understands them, even if you and I don't know it all. Even a small change in the rates could make us a lot of money."

"Yes, but I am thinking it will cost a great deal of money to get the Bloomberg lines and the data feeds and everything else."

"Vishal, you're just making problems for the sake of it. Those would be my problems to solve. I think I can get all this sorted out. You know I can. I've managed projects for you and the bank in the past." Sharpe didn't remind Vishal that he had had the full power of the bank behind him before, when he had needed to bully vendors into meeting delivery deadlines.

They bickered back and forth. Sharpe knew Vishal well enough to know that many of his objections were simply ways of ensuring that there would be no future problems, and that he was playing devil's advocate to make entirely sure of his ground.

"Who's the friend?" Vishal came back to the point. "And what are you talking about when you talk about taking over a whole country?"

Without going into too much detail, Sharpe explained about Kim, and his supposed desire for change in North Korea. Vishal was sceptical, but admitted that he knew very little about the country or its politics other than what he'd learned from the Japanese media.

"Now let me get on and enjoy this food for now," said Sharpe at length. "What's left of it. It's pretty good, by the way. I agree with you it's not as good as Meema's cooking, but it comes pretty damn' close."

"I'll be thinking about this all afternoon," said Vishal as they left the restaurant.

"Do that," said Sharpe. "I'd like you and Meema to come round to our place this evening, if you don't mind, and talk about it together with me and Mieko."

"I think we can manage that. About 7:30?"

THAT EVENING, SHARPE WAS PLEASANTLY SURPRISED to find both Mieko and Meema strongly in favour of the proposed currency exchange brokerage. He'd expected some opposition from Mieko against what seemed to him to be a rather risky proposition, but she had been reading a lot of prospectuses from banks extolling the virtues of foreign currency investment accounts based around exchange rates. This was a currently popular Japanese fad, since the exchange market was largely unregulated, and she was strongly in favour of the idea. Meema's reaction was, if anything, even more surprising, once she'd accepted the idea that a computer program and a collection of DSP chips could predict the future movements of the currency markets.

"I've spent the last few months working on trading strategies for a bunch of rich spoiled brats," she explained, referring to the traders. "You know I heard one on the phone to HR the other day. Guess what? He was threatening to go back to London the next day unless they changed the colour of the sheets in his company flat." Sharpe got the feeling that she would have spat in disgust if she had been sitting anywhere but in his living room. "It will be a pleasure to use these ideas for myself." She did raise one objection, though. "Who's this friend who wants to take over North Korea for himself?"

Uh-oh. This was going to take a bit of tact and finesse, Sharpe told himself. Last point first. "I don't think he wants to take over North Korea for himself. All he wants to do is to get rid of the lot who are in power right now and then get the South Koreans to take over."

"I'm sure it's going to be a lot more complicated than you make it sound," said Meema. "I don't have any experience at this sort of thing, but I can't believe it's going to be as simple as all that to merge the two countries. And who is he, anyway?"

"He's a gangster, I suppose," admitted Sharpe.

"He's very nice, though," Mieko added helpfully, to the horrified Meema, who sat there with her eyes and mouth opened wide.

"What do you mean, 'very nice'?" asked Meema.

"He kidnapped me once," said Mieko, as calmly as if she'd been describing an everyday conversation she'd had with someone.

"And you like him?" asked Meema incredulously. "I always thought you were a sensible woman, Mieko-san. You've been hanging around Kenneth too long. It's turned your brains, I swear."

"No, seriously," Mieko insisted. "I had no choice about going, but once I was there he treated me very well. Very kind and polite. And when he came round here, he couldn't have been nicer."

Meema was obviously far from being convinced by this. "What sort of gangster?" she asked. "Drugs, women, loan-sharking, gambling, pachinko?"

"I'm not sure," admitted Sharpe.

"Gambling, mainly, from what I heard," said Mieko. "At least that's what he and his people were talking about."

"Well, that's all right, I suppose," said Meema. "At least the victims choose to go their own way and it's their own fault if they suffer." Sharpe wasn't sure about the logic of this morality, but he was glad that she wasn't raising any stronger objections. As a postscript he added to himself the fact that the four of them were discussing a massive gambling operation, much bigger than the pachinko establishments or wherever Kim was probably making his money.

"What about the legal side of all this business?" asked Vishal.

"Well, it seems that we have to register with the Financial Services Agency and get a license. I'm pretty sure that's the case, even if we're not open to outside clients. It just looks like a formality, as long as we have the capital to back us up."

"That was going to be my next point," said Meema. "Quite honestly, Vishal and I can't afford to put a lot of money into this. I know we get paid well by the bank, but so much is going back to India, and our families are depending on it. And if we have no money coming in because we're not working at the bank ..." Her voice trailed off.

"I'm not asking you to put any money in there," said Sharpe. "I'm hoping that I can provide most of the starting money. And the rest – we need 120% capital compared to the at-risk assets, as far as I can tell – can be provided by our Korean friend."

"Is he serious about North Korea?" asked Meema, returning to an earlier point, as was her habit. "Like I said, I've never taken over a country's government, but it would seem to me that you would probably need a little more money than that to do it."

"That's exactly the point I made to him," replied Sharpe.

"His response was that we're thinking in terms of Japan or Europe. How far could you go in India with twenty-five million dollars?"

"A bloody long way," said Vishal, after a second's thought. "And India's being a damn' sight more advanced and expensive than North Korea, I am thinking. But it still does not seem to me as though it is being a really vast amount of money for the job that it has to do."

"I think we're talking about financing a surgical coup," replied Sharpe. "We're not talking about equipping a large revolutionary army or anything along those lines. More along the lines of assassinations and strategic stoppages of vital services."

"Isn't that called terrorism?" asked Meema, pointedly.

"Depends whose side you're looking at it from, I suppose. Technically, I suppose it is. But I don't think anyone in this room is too keen on what they've heard about the North Korean setup?" Everyone dutifully shook their heads. "So we're not financing terrorism, we're helping a liberation movement."

"You're beginning to sound like Ronald Reagan or one of those nutty Americans talking about the Contras or the mujihadeen or something," objected Vishal.

"I do," admitted Sharpe. "But I think I have a little more reason to sound self-righteous."

"Look, Vishal, we all agree that North Korea is bad and that almost any change is for the better," pointed out Meema.

"I think we all agree with that," chimed in Mieko. "And I want to add that I personally believe Mr Kim."

"One thing," added Sharpe. "I don't want my name anywhere on the company documents or anything. There are too many people who are interested in me."

"Oh?" Vishal asked.

Sharpe wished he hadn't brought up the subject, but he

ploughed on, giving a brief account of how Ishihara had interviewed him, and how Al Kowalski had been responsible for the burglary of the flat. Without going into too many details, he mentioned the British and American interest in the software, which they knew only as face-recognition technology, and talked a little about the times he had met Kim, as well as the trip to Hanoi.

"Kenneth," countered Meema. "All these spies and these funny people are interested in the face-recognition software, right?"

"No-one's said anything different," admitted Sharpe.

"So why would they be interested in a foreign exchange venture? I don't think you need to worry about this."

"I agree with you, Meema, in theory, at least. As far as I know, no-one knows about the currency trading side of things. But I really do want to keep somewhat out of sight on this. I don't want my head to appear above water for longer than is absolutely necessary."

"So whose company is it going to be?" asked Mieko.

"Yours, of course," Sharpe answered her. "It will be much easier if a Japanese person is named as the owner and president." Mieko looked a little dubious.

"I agree there," said Vishal. "Believe me, Mieko-san, it will make all our lives much easier."

"Haven't you ever wanted to be a company president?" Meema asked Mieko. "Now's your chance. But there's one more big thing. I want to meet your Mr Kim. You may be right about him. He may well be a wonderful person, but I have to meet him for myself."

"Good," said Sharpe. "To be honest with you, I haven't talked to him about it yet." Three mouths opened as their owners turned their heads to look at him. "Come on," he protested. "I wanted to know if you were interested before I started to talk to him. Vishal, if I'm late to work tomorrow, you know why." He didn't mention his secret fears to the others – that if he told Kim about the true purpose of Katsuyama's invention, Kim would simply seek to obtain it for himself, using whatever means were available to him.

When Vishal and Meema had left the flat, Sharpe told Mieko that he was going out for a moment. At the gates to the apartment building, he noticed Kim's henchman standing guard, but there was also another figure on the opposite side of the road who looked as though he was independently doing the same job. He went back to the building entrance and picked a leaflet advertising dry-cleaning services out of someone's mailbox, scribbled a note on the back of it, and set off through the gates again.

"Give this to your boss," he said as he passed close by Kim's man, passing the folded note to him, hopefully unobserved by the other shadow.

He went to the convenience store to buy two cans of beer, and came back, followed each way by both watchers. Ah well, he thought, letting himself back into the flat. Exercise for both of them.

As he was washing up the breakfast things the next morning, the doorbell rang.

"I'll get it," said Mieko. "It's probably the man to repair the window."

It wasn't. Kim stood in the doorway, his bodyguard behind him. "Is Mr Sharpe in?" he asked in Japanese. "I think he's expecting me."

"Kenneth-san!" called Mieko. "It's Mr Kim."

Sharpe emerged, drying his hands on a towel. "I was expecting you to telephone," he said to Kim.

"Telephones can be tapped," said Kim. "Even mobile phones. Get a coat and come with me."

Sharpe followed Kim to the large black car with the lace curtains, which was parked, Sharpe noticed, out of sight of the watchers at the gates. Kim chuckled as Sharpe showed his recognition of the car. "No need to worry about this thing. We're friends now, aren't we?"

"Of course," said Sharpe, getting into the back seat after Kim. The bodyguard shut the door after him, and climbed into the driver's seat.

"Forgive this melodrama," said Kim. "But you understand that meeting me may not be good for your health. So just keep your head down out of sight as we go out of the gates. I'll tell you when you can get up."

Feeling that this was being overly melodramatic, Sharpe did as he was asked. After a few minutes, Kim tapped him on the shoulder. "OK, get up now."

"Thanks. I feel really stupid."

"You shouldn't. There's a lot riding on this."

Sharpe took a deep breath. Now or never. "Do you know exactly how much is riding on it?"

"No, not exactly. I have a good idea how much the face-recognition technology would be worth to the right people, though."

"Think bigger. Much, much bigger," Sharpe told him.

Kim looked at him quizzically. "It's an interesting toy, but I really don't see it being very much more than that, even to the CIA."

"There are other patterns beside faces," Sharpe went on. "Patterns that people watch to make money." Kim continued to stare at him. "Like currency exchange rates," suggested Sharpe.

"I'm really not sure that I understand what you're trying to say," said Kim.

"All right. Very simply, the gizmo your son-in-law has invented and that everyone's looking for does a lot more than match faces in a database. You have a very clever son-in-law indeed, and he has developed a way of predicting currency exchange rate fluctuations extremely accurately, up to three minutes in advance."

"Is that important? Three minutes doesn't seem like a very long time." Kim seemed somewhat underwhelmed by the information.

Sharpe reminded himself that not everyone lived in the world of financial services. "Currency exchange rates, Mr Kim, change from second to second. Within fractions of a second. Maybe not by a lot, but they change. Many people in large banks all around the world watch these rates and try to bet on whether they'll go up or down. Buy low, sell high. Many times an hour in some cases. Three minutes is an eternity to these people. And there are all sorts of other games they play which I won't even bother to try and explain to you, even if I was sure I could. My point is that millions and millions of dollars change hands every day on the foreign exchange market. And so three minutes is a very long time to these people." He explained a little more about the Katsuyama hardware and software, and how it could be used in the currency markets.

"I see," said Kim, shaking his head slowly. "With my son-in-law's technology, we'd be betting on a horse race, but we'd know which horse was going to win before we made the bet?"

"That's exactly it," agreed Sharpe. "A really good way of looking at it."

"How on earth did you find this out?"

"Dr Katsuyama gave me a few hints, and so did a friend of mine."

"So," asked Kim. "Why are you telling me this?"

"Because we need your help," replied Sharpe, and explained the idea behind the proposed currency trading brokerage. "We think this could help you and your plans," he finished.

"You really think this idea could make the money I need?"

"I'm pretty certain it would only take a month or two to collect that sort of money."

"And they really allow you to gamble with money that you don't actually have?" asked Kim. "You're sure of that?"

"Yes, it's called leverage, or margins."

"These guys are crazy!" exclaimed Kim. "If I started to run my gambling businesses that way, I'd be bankrupt in no time at all. Why did no-one tell me about all this crazy shit before?"

"Well, they do have regulations, you know. It's not quite a casino." Sharpe wasn't quite sure of that last – actually, at times, the financial services industry seemed to him to be less like a set of bankers than a casino, merrily gambling with other people's money.

"Oh, regulations." Kim didn't seem too dismayed by this, though. "Anyway, tell me again what you'd like me to do, exactly."

"First, the money you offered me earlier for finding Dr Katsuyama?"

"Yes?"

"I'd like to use some of that to help set up the company. Rent office space, pay for the electronic data feeds, and so on."

"No problem. It's yours whenever you want it. I told you that the other day, and I meant it."

"Thanks. And there's a requirement that we have a capital adequacy to cover the amount that we're gambling. Will you help there?"

"As long as I'm allowed to put my money in there for you to gamble with at some stage in the proceedings."

"We were expecting you to do that," said Sharpe.

"How long is this going to take to set up?"

"I am pretty sure it's going to take at least a month and I don't want to start until I've finished my contract with the bank where I'm working at the moment, in any case. We need to get the license and so on, arrange for a building lease, and so on. And there's one more thing. I have friends who are going to be involved in this and they're going to have to give notice to the place where they're working now that they're going to leave. One of them wants to make a lot of money for his sister, who he says is ill and needs an operation. Anyway, they want to meet you to put their minds at rest."

"Sure thing. Where do you want to have the meeting? I don't think it's a good idea to have it at your place."

Sharpe was getting used to Kim's paranoia. Truth to tell, it was more than a little contagious. "All right, let's meet somewhere neutral."

"I own a very discreet club," said Kim. "It may not be entirely neutral, but I can promise you it's private."

"Sounds good." Kim passed a card over with the name and address of the club on it. The telephone number on the card was a mobile number.

"When do you want to meet? Tomorrow night at eight?" asked Kim.

"That sounds fine. I'll have to check with my friends, and if it's not all right, I'll let you know. Otherwise, expect us at eight. Four people."

"Fine. Now I suggest you go back. Wait a moment." He spoke to the driver and the car pulled over and stopped by the side of the road. The driver spoke into a mobile phone, and after a few minutes, another car drew up.

"Get in there, and keep your head down as they take you in," said Kim. That way it will be a different car coming back, and with luck, they'll never know you went out at all. Try and be careful when you come round tomorrow night. Try to make sure that no-one's following you, if you can manage it."

THE NEXT NIGHT SAW SHARPE AND MIEKO, together with Vishal and Meema, threading their way through the back streets of Shimbashi, south of Tokyo station.

"Are you sure you know where we're going?" asked Vishal.

"I know what the address is, anyway," replied Sharpe. Since Tokyo streets, for the most part, suffer from being un-named, the only sure way to find out the location of a place is by looking at a map, preferably on a computer, which can translate the apparently random district and building numbers into a meaningful location. Sharpe had typed the address into his computer and had printed out the Googled result.

"There you are," said Mieko, pointing to a tiny dimly lit white-on-purple sign advertising the existence of the club on the sixth floor. This was another thing about Tokyo – the place you wanted to get to hardly ever seemed to be on the ground floor once you'd found the building.

"I was expecting something discreet, but not quite this private," complained Sharpe as they staggered up the steep and badly lit stairs, the lift being marked as "out of order". "I doubt if they get any casual passing trade," he puffed. Damn, he was more out of shape than he thought.

At the door, identified only by a small sign, Sharpe spoke his name into an intercom system. Almost immediately they heard the sound of locks and bolts being undone, and the door was opened by a small middle-aged lady clad in ki-mono – the *mama-san* who managed the place. She seemed slightly taken aback by the sight of Meema – presumably non-Japanese females were infrequent customers, but she recovered her poise quickly and led them to a corner table, where Kim was sitting in solitary splendour.

"Glad you could all make it," he said, rising, and shaking hands all round as Sharpe introduced everyone. Unlike the *mama-san*, who now brought them hot towels to wipe their hands and faces, he didn't seem at all put out by Meema. "And what will you have to eat and drink?" he asked.

Mieko and Meema chose soft drinks, but Vishal and Sharpe, after only a little pressing, accepted small glasses of neat single malt Scotch whisky in Vishal's case, and a 20-year-old Havana rum in Sharpe's. Much to Sharpe's surprise, Kim himself seemed to be drinking orange juice. "Bad for my image as a big bold gangster, I know," he said, smiling. "But actually, I can't stand the taste of most alcohol, and in any case I have a very weak head for these things, so the few alcoholic drinks that I do like tend to knock me out very quickly."

The menu seemed to be mainly Korean food, so Sharpe suggested that Kim order on their behalf, trusting that there would be nothing too weird and wonderful making its way onto their plates.

While they were waiting, Sharpe once again summarised the position as he saw it, and waited for comments from the others.

"You're being serious about bringing down the North Korean government?" asked Vishal. "It really doesn't seem like a lot of money to be spending to make such a big change."

Kim smiled. "I explained to our friend here," gesturing towards Sharpe, "that you really shouldn't try to judge North Korea by Western, or even Indian, standards."

"So what is the money to be used for, then?" asked Vishal. "Are you going to be planting bombs?"

"We're thinking of bribes rather than bombs," replied Kim. "It's all a question of where to apply the lever. If you know the right places, you can do a lot of shifting with very little in the way of force and not much money. But there will be a few bombs, aimed against things, not against people. Mainly for effect and the bangs and flashes than to cause any actual damage."

"Don't you think it's going to be a bit more complicated than just causing some chaos and hoping the people will rise up?" asked Meema.

"No, I don't think it's going to be a bit more complicated than that," replied Kim. "I think it's going to be a *lot* more complicated. But there are enough good people in the South, and a lot of Korean people like myself living in Japan and America, who will help us once they see which way the wind is starting to blow, and that will make things easier."

"I have another question," said Meema. "How on earth is the South going to absorb the cost of absorbing the North? Germany had a bad enough time, and East Germany was a real land of luxury compared to the DPRK."

"That's a difficult one, I admit," said Kim. "But the plans I have don't include immediate reunification. Eventually, of course, I want it to come about, but it's not a top priority as far as I am concerned. Yes, a North without the Kim dynasty in charge would be a complete basket case, and the country would have to rely on international aid for some time, but it wouldn't be exclusively the South's responsibility."

"But you're not planning to put yourself into the Presidential Palace, or whatever it's called?" asked Vishal.

Kim chuckled. "Dear me, there's no way that I'd want to live there. I've been on what you might call the wrong side of the law for so long, I've almost forgotten how to do things on the right side."

"So are you being absolutely sure that you're the right

person to be doing this?" shot back Vishal. "Are the people of North Korea going to be grateful for their liberation at the hands of a common criminal?"

The atmosphere turned noticeably cooler. Kim put down his drink and glared at Vishal. From a corner of the room behind Vishal, a large figure appeared, and placed a heavy paw-like hand on Vishal's shoulder. Meema and Mieko froze, and Sharpe, worried for his friend, shifted forward in his seat to speak to Kim. Only Vishal seemed oblivious of the situation, taking a sip of his drink, and grinning, almost impudently, at Kim.

Much to Sharpe's surprise, Kim continued to glare at Vishal before changing his expression to a grin.

"You have balls, I tell you. Pak here," he jerked his head at the bouncer behind Vishal, who now relaxed his grip, "could break every bone in your body, and those of all your friends here before you had time to even think of calling for help. And no-one would find the pieces afterwards or even dream of asking any questions. It takes a very brave man to say something like you just did. Either very brave, or very stupid. And I don't believe you're stupid." He extended his hand towards Vishal. Vishal put down his glass and took the proffered hand. When his hand was finally released, Vishal massaged it ruefully with the other.

"Do I make my point?" asked Kim. Vishal nodded. "Good. Please remember that I am not a common criminal. I am a very uncommon criminal. I am first and foremost a patriot, and I want what's best for my country and its people. The fact that I work on the side of the law where most people fear to go is simply a way for me to make more money and to make it faster to achieve my goals. Understood?" Vishal nodded again. "Good. Now let us have no more foolishness about how I have made my money in the past, but let's concentrate on how you are going to help me make more money in the future to achieve my ends. Let me ask a few questions about you and what you do now and what you propose to do."

Sharpe let out his breath, with the realisation that he had been holding it for what seemed like hours. Meema and Mieko also relaxed visibly as Kim proceeded to ask Vishal and Meema courteously about the roles they would play in the new brokerage, displaying what seemed to be an almost complete lack of knowledge about the currency exchange business and the workings of the financial services industry, but a shrewd appreciation of the role of IT in business. Sharpe wondered idly what sort of computer systems Kim used to run his pachinko empire.

"So what exactly is your role going to be in all of this?" Vishal asked Kim.

"A customer," said Kim. "Very little more than that."

"But your money will be backing us, right?"

"Yes, if it's really necessary. I'm certainly prepared to provide some of the money for you to do the job properly, but it won't be my money by the time you declare it to the authorities," he pointed out. "I intend to keep a very low profile indeed on all of this."

"You're really going to trust us with all that money, and the money you're going to invest with us?" asked Meema.

"Indeed I am," replied Kim. "If your friend hasn't already told you," he nodded at Sharpe, "I have very extreme ways of showing my displeasure towards people who cross me. Mr Sharpe knows all about that."

Three pairs of eyes turned towards Sharpe, but he ducked his face into his glass, and refused to acknowledge the unspoken question.

"I would strongly advise you to keep tight hold of that money and not run away with it," added Kim. His tone was as casual as if he'd been discussing what they were going to order as snacks to go with their next drinks. "Of course, if my son-in-law's invention does not work as expected and you lose the money honestly, then there is no way that I can feel angry, is there?"

The questions back and forth continued, with increasing trust and goodwill on both sides, it seemed, and then drifted into small talk. It became obvious to Sharpe that his role in all of this was going to be bigger than he had originally expected – it wasn't just a question of renting some office space and sitting back watching the others do the work. It looked as though he was going to have to co-ordinate the whole setting up of the project and make sure that everything ran smoothly. Despite his hopes that it wasn't going to be too much work to get things rolling, it now appeared that it wasn't going to be all fun and games as far as he was concerned, at any rate.

He sipped his drink, and listened to Vishal, who now seemed to have accepted Kim at his word, explaining some of the intricacies of the Indian caste system.

Chapter 9: Tokyo

THE "M&M TRADING" CURRENCY BROKERAGE seemed destined to be a success. All four partners were actively involved in making the business work efficiently, and Kim had been as good as his word about sending on the money he'd promised to Sharpe for finding Katsuyama. This had arrived as bundles of cash, and now sat in a bank account. Sharpe had arranged to rent office space in a new building in a business park on the western outskirts of Tokyo. It was the other side of town, and a long way from their houses, but was on a reasonably direct train route, and came quite cheap, as the result of an initiative to move businesses into the suburbs. The main reason for choosing the office was that it came with a high-speed fibre-optic Internet link already in place, which made life a lot easier. Meema pointed out, however, that they were going to need a lot of voice lines and some sort of telephone exchange, or at any rate, some way of placing and receiving many calls at once.

"We'll do it as voice over IP," suggested Vishal, referring to the technology of using the Internet to make phone calls. "But we will be needing a few more traditional outside lines, too, as backup, I am thinking. Kenneth-san, it is your job to be asking the telephone company men to install at least four lines here as fast as they possibly can be doing it. It will be my job to be talking to my friends who are making these software telephone exchanges for the Internet phones and arranging for delivery and installation."

So Sharpe, aided by Mieko, cajoled and pleaded with NTT, the Japanese telephone company, to install six more lines into the building (he'd added two more to Vishal's original estimate for safety). After being told three times by different sales staff at NTT that the job could never be done in that particular building, he eventually managed to speak to a senior installation manager, who promised him that the work would be carried out within six weeks. He was about to explode over the phone and consign the whole of the Japanese telephone system to eternal damnation, but Mieko calmed him down, and he spent the rest of the afternoon fuming at the inefficiency of telephone companies in general and NTT in particular.

Much to his surprise, the NTT engineers arrived the next day and had completed the work within three hours. That's Japan all over, he told himself. First they tell you a thing is impossible, then tell you it's difficult, then they come along and do it perfectly in next to no time.

It had also been Sharpe's job to negotiate with the companies providing the market data feeds. He'd had enough experience in his consultancy with the Tokyo banks to be able to hold his own with the vendors, and to work his way through the long and complex contracts they provided, as well as fending off the constant offers of extra services for which he could see no possible need.

At the Sharpe End

THERE HAD BEEN A DISCUSSION about the name of the trading firm – Sharpe had rejected the use of his existing business, "Sharpe Practice", as the name, as he didn't want to draw undue attention to himself, and "M&M Trading", referring to Mieko and Meema, was the name that they'd all eventually agreed on, "even if it does make us sound a bit like a chocolate factory", as Vishal pointed out. Although Vishal's bank had been surprised to learn that he and Meema were to depart at the same time, they were used to a high rate of staff turnover, and Vishal seemed to have no doubt that, should he want to work there again, he could go back to his old position or, failing that, he could find a similar position at another financial institution. Of course, Sharpe thought to himself, if this venture succeeded as planned, there would be no need for Vishal to work for anyone other than himself ever again.

Vishal had worked hard to set up the complex network equipment necessary to use the data feeds efficiently and securely, in addition to sorting out the up-to-the-minute Internet phone system provided by one of his friends in Tokyo's rapidly growing Indian IT community. Sharpe was always impressed by the way that the Indians who'd come to work for the international banks in Tokyo had very soon established a reputation for being smart – they'd already set up an international school in the eastern suburbs of Tokyo where small children were taught in at least three languages – Hindi, English and Japanese – and recited their seventeen times table as happily as English or Japanese children recited their five times table.

Japanese TV programs featured these "wonder children" on a fairly regular basis, without ever questioning the reason for their being in Japan in the first place – the failure, for whatever reason, of the Japanese educational process to produce IT specialists of a truly international standard.

By the time Vishal had finished installing the phone system and had his friends making it work as he wanted, Sharpe was impressed. A small central computer was linked to the telephone lines entering the building and to the fibre Internet connection, and by using a control program on their computers, Meema and the rest of them could talk instantly to any one of a number of other brokers round the world whose numbers were stored in a central directory, connect many lines together in a conference call, re-route calls around the planet at almost no cost, or so it seemed, and perform many other tricks with the telephone system.

Sharpe was amazed by what could be done, and he was even more astounded when Vishal presented him with the bill for the telephone exchange computer and the programming done by his friends.

"This is about a fifth of the price that we'd have paid one of the big companies for a traditional exchange alone, you realise?" he said to Vishal, remembering some of the invoices he'd seen in the past for telephone systems in large companies. "And then they'd have charged us a fortune on top of that for setting the thing up and configuring it. Did you get a special price on this?"

"Of course I did," replied Vishal. "But twenty per cent discount is all the bastards were giving me."

"But even if you add twenty per cent to this, it's still cheap. Why aren't all the banks and businesses using this kind of thing instead of paying through the nose for the overpriced junk that's on everyone's desks and that no-one can use?"

"Ask me another," replied Vishal. "I was trying to get my bank to put in a system like this, at least for the fixed income traders, but they said it was untried technology, and preferred to spend a fortune updating the old system. And even then, it never worked properly."

"More fools them," responded Sharpe. "I think Meema's going to have fun with this toy."

MEEMA WAS DEFINITELY HAVING FUN, it seemed. Even before Vishal had connected the live data feeds, she had used a large part of the money Kim had given to Sharpe to purchase a database containing a minute-by-minute history of currency movements over the past six months, and was busy displaying the data in different formats, using a simulation program that Vishal had produced in one of the few moments when he wasn't busy with the networking and phone systems. She was using this data, which Vishal had persuaded the Katsuyama system to accept as a set of real-time market data, to develop the most advantageous strategies for buying and selling euros, dollars and yen, assuming that she had perfect knowledge of the prices three minutes into the future.

One day she looked up from her screens and called over to Sharpe, her face slightly flushed. "I did it!" she exclaimed.

"Did what?" asked Sharpe. He was on the other side of the room, deep in the throes of a complex official form concerning the number and quality of toilets provided for staff, which apparently had to be filled in and returned to the relevant authorities before trading was able to start.

"I made a million dollars profit in five minutes!" she cried. "That was my goal two days ago. And there was virtually no leverage! Most of it was real money!" Even though she had said "real money", Meema meant "play money" or "virtual money" that had no existence except in her simulation, as opposed to the "leverage" that allowed her to gamble with far more chips on the table than she could afford in reality. Even though the money she was talking about didn't actually exist, it was an impressive sum in a very short space of time.

"Bloody hell!" exclaimed Sharpe, taken aback. "If you carry on like that, Kim is going to be able to buy the whole of North Korea, lock, stock and barrel, not just fund a revolution."

"And Vishal and I will be able to buy the whole hospital, not just get an operation for his sister," laughed Meema. "You know," she added more seriously, "that's actually not a bad idea. We could use the money we make here to set up a hospital in India for this kind of thing and save people there a lot of trouble and expense if they have the sort of problems that Vishal's sister has."

The implications of what they were going to do hit Sharpe full force. "You know, until you start talking about things like that, I really had no idea how much power a lot of money could give you, especially when you don't really want it for yourself."

"Don't you?" asked Meema. "Want it for yourself, I mean."

"Well, I have to say, of course, that I like to be comfortable and it would be nice never have to worry about money for the rest of my life," replied Sharpe. "But beyond that, no, I don't really want a lot of money. I mean, you can only fly in one private jet at a time. What about you?"

"Oh, I wish I could say the same as you," replied Meema. "But I can't. I want money and all the things it can buy. It comes from having been quite poor when I was a child, I suppose. It doesn't mean that I don't want to use it to help other people. But I do want lots and lots of money for me and mine, and I really think we can make that happen."

"I've never thought of you as greedy for money," said Sharpe. Truth to tell, he was a little disappointed. He'd always thought of Meema as being somehow above that kind of thing, and it was a slight shock to discover these feet of clay.

"Not greedy, Kenneth-san. I just want the best for my child."

"But…" Sharpe had the feeling he'd missed something.

Meema patted her stomach. "Another seven months or so yet."

"Oh, congratulations! When did you find out? Have you told Mieko?"

"I found out last Friday, and I told her this morning."

"What did the proud father say when you told him, then?"

"Oh, he grinned. You know how he is when he gets really pleased? Well, multiply that by a factor of ten or so."

"Well, that's wonderful news, Meema." Sharpe felt a little less censorious about Meema's sudden lust for wealth now that he knew the circumstances. "You're feeling all right?" he added, a little worried.

"You mean morning sickness and that sort of thing? Only a little, and not enough to take my mind off the job, if you're worried about the job, rather than about me." She smiled, to show that she wasn't to be taken literally on the last comment.

"No, that's not what I meant at all," Sharpe lied.

"By the time things to get a little busy down here," Meema patted her stomach again, "I think we'll all be ready to pack up and go home. We'll have made all the money we want or need."

"One thing is worrying me, Meema, and it's nothing to do with you, or what you've just told me. If we're going to do so well at this, won't we actually have an effect on the prices? I mean, will the bets that we make on the future no longer be true, because our actions will be large enough to affect the movement of the market?"

Meema laughed. "Don't worry, Kenneth. First thing is, we're not going to be big enough to affect the market significantly. Do you know how much money gets moved around the money markets each day?"

"Billions of dollars?" Sharpe guessed.

"Trillions of dollars," Meema corrected him. "A billion here, a billion there. Pretty soon you're talking real money."

Sharpe laughed. "Is that Bill Gates talking?"

"No, it's me."

"Pretty good. Maybe we should adopt it as our company slogan. Hang it on the wall or something."

"And the other thing is that yes, these trades probably would have some effect on the market if they were big enough and sophisticated enough, but I can allow for that. One of the easiest ways would be to leave a three-minute gap between trades to allow the program to absorb the effect of my trades. But there are other strategies I can use. I can do some pretty smart things with short selling some options and exploiting the arbitrage gap between Hong Kong and Tokyo on the yen/euro ..."

Sharpe put his hands over his ears. "Spare me the details at this time in the morning," he groaned in mock dismay. "Some time, I'm probably going to have to ask you to write all this down, but not right now, please."

"But it's actually very simple," explained Meema. "Bring up this chair and have a look." She tapped a few keys on the keyboard, and brought up three different graphs in different windows on the huge expensive flat-panel screens that Sharpe and Vishal had connected to her computer a few days earlier. "Now. See how the dollar-euro spread is coming along?"

Sharpe leaned over to get a closer look. He couldn't help but notice that Meema's blouse was unbuttoned a little lower than usual, exposing more smooth brown skin than was normally visible, and also, as she leaned forward and more came into view, it was obvious that she wasn't wearing a bra. It was a highly distracting sight, with the reality somewhat better than his occasional fantasy, and he tried to avert his eyes before she noticed. Much to his embarrassment, he realised that she had been watching, and was obviously enjoying the effect the sight of her breasts was having on him. He switched his eyes to the screen, keeping them fixed there, and gabbled something inconsequential and meaningless about the figures.

She responded by pointing to another part of the second screen on the other side from where he was sitting. Again trying to avoid her eyes, he moved to have a better look. His hand accidentally brushed against Meema's blouse. She wasn't sitting there before, he told himself. She moved there so that I would have to touch her. Even so, he started to move his hand away quickly as if it had been burned, and began to apologise.

Much to his surprise, he found Meema's hand restraining his, and pressing the palm closer to her breast, so that he could feel her nipple through her blouse, rising and stiffening in his hand. It was obvious, even if he hadn't seen it with his own eyes a moment ago, that she wasn't wearing a bra. The reality of his past fantasies made him distinctly nervous and uncomfortable, and he tried to drag his hand away, but it was clamped in place by Meema's hand pressing it against her body.

Like many men who have had casual thoughts about adultery with their friends' wives, Sharpe found that imagination was much more to his taste than putting the idea into practice. It wasn't that he found Meema unattractive. Exactly the opposite, in fact, as he found his trousers becoming uncomfortably tight. But after all, Vishal, who was both his business partner and Meema's husband, not to mention the father of the unborn baby, was in the next room, and Mieko (another kind of partner) wasn't far away. This was far from being any kind of ideal scenario as far as seduction was concerned, quite apart from the whole business of her being pregnant, which to his mind somehow seemed to make it more wrong than it would otherwise be.

Meema moved her beautiful face closer to his and squeezed his hand tighter. "I think we should all be getting to know each other better if we're going to be working together on this," she whispered in his ear, and moved her other hand down to rest on his thigh. "Much better," she added.

"Listen, Meema," Sharpe said as he moved away, removing her hand from his leg with his free hand as gently as he could. "I know you're excited about all kinds of things. I know that you're doing great work for us all. Believe me, I'm as thrilled about it all as you are. But is this the right time for us to be doing this? One new thing at a time," quietly but firmly disengaging his hand from her breast. "Let's wait, shall we?" Her face started to become ugly with dismay. "Listen Meema, I like you a lot. An awful lot," he babbled. "I find you really attractive, honestly, but I don't want us to be rushing into anything just now, please." He kissed her lightly on the cheek, not wishing to engage in any more intimate contact. As his lips made contact, he realised that this was actually the first time that he had ever kissed her.

As quickly as the storm-clouds had gathered in Meema's face, they went away. As if a switch had been thrown, she returned to her businesslike and professional self again and resumed her lecture about the fluctuations in exchange rates as if nothing had happened.

Was it the pregnancy affecting Meema? Or was it the money? Sharpe remembered an old Hollywood film he'd once watched, starring Humphrey Bogart as a down-and-out who went gold prospecting in Mexico, and who lost his mind at the thought of so much wealth in his grasp. Was the same sort of thing happening here?

One thing seemed certain to him, he'd have keep his eyes wide open whenever he was alone with Meema until he was sure that whatever it was had worn off.

MIEKO SEEMED TO BE HAVING FUN, but in a rather different way. Before her marriage, she'd worked as a personal assistant to the ultra-wealthy president of a shipping company, arranging his business life for him as he travelled round the world, booking his hotels, reserving places at restaurants for his business meals and generally making sure his life ran smoothly. Thankfully, the tendency to arrange other people's time and activities didn't spill over too much into her personal life, Sharpe reflected, but she was having fun arranging the sort of things that Sharpe would never have considered, let alone actually put into practice. For example …

"Why are the gas people coming in tomorrow?" Sharpe had just received a telephone call from the town gas company arranging a visit by their installation engineers.

"To arrange the gas supply."

"Well, I'd guessed that, but don't we have gas laid on already for the water heater?"

"Yes, but this is for the trading room where Meema is sitting."

"Are we going to put a gas heater in there? I think the air-conditioner will take care of heating in the winter. Anyway, with all the computer gear in there, I think she'll be warm enough."

"No, we're putting in a gas cooker."

"In the trading room?"

"Yes, Meema says she thinks best when she's cooking, so we thought it would be a nice idea to give her a kitchen and make a partition for it in the corner of her office so that she can cook and trade in the same place. We're putting in a sink and so on as well. I told you about it, remember?" Sharpe had absolutely no memory of it. "Or maybe I forgot to mention it. And it'll be very convenient for us all if she's going to be cooking, so don't look so grouchy. It's going to be a bit expensive, but don't worry about it."

Sharpe groaned inwardly anyway. "You do realise that this will probably be the only foreign exchange brokerage where the head trader cooks kormas and biriyanis while she's calculating the point spread on the euro-yen rates? And it's a lot of work to get all this done."

"Yes, it is a lot of work, but other people are doing it all, and I've arranged for them all to come in before you and Vishal get the trading desk completely set up," said Mieko happily. "Fun, isn't it?"

" 'Mad' or 'loony' are more the words I'd use," said Sharpe, shaking his head.

Vishal agreed with Sharpe, but pointed out that once Meema had got an idea in her head, it was pretty useless to try and stand in her way. Sharpe, feeling the same was true of Mieko, agreed, and the two men worked on re-designing the layout of the computer room, including extractor fans to protect the computer equipment from the cooking fumes, something that both Mieko and Meema seemed to have forgotten in their enthusiasm for the idea.

"And get one of those plastic covers for the keyboard," said Sharpe to Mieko. "I don't want us missing a trade because a cardamom pod has fallen into the keyboard and is stopping the 'Buy' key from working."

But most of Mieko's time was spent on more mundane things, such as arranging for bank accounts to be opened, which required an officially registered seal with the name of the company on it, which meant first ordering the seal from a supplier, and then traipsing down to the local city hall to get the impression officially registered with the authorities, and then taking the certificate to the bank. It all took time and planning, but Mieko's unflappable nature helped things get done smoothly, and helped to prevent Sharpe from exploding at random intervals when he was presented with yet another piece of Japanese bureaucracy seemingly designed purely to obstruct honest citizens in the performance of their business.

SHARPE WAS IN THE CROWDED TRAIN on his way home from the new office when he was tapped on the shoulder from behind. Usually this signalled some kind soul picking up something he had dropped, and returning it to him, but not this time.

"Jon?" he exclaimed, none too pleased to see him again after a silence of a few weeks. "What's a boy like you doing in a nice train like this?" This time, Jon was in his "yuppie trader" outfit and looking very sleek and prosperous.

"Like the proverbial bad penny," agreed Jon grinning sheepishly. "Surprised?" Obviously some of Sharpe's displeasure had made itself apparent, even through his thick skin. "I've got news for you. And I'm sure you have some news for me. You've been keeping awfully quiet recently."

"I've been busy," replied Sharpe shortly.

"With what?" asked Jon. "No, don't tell me here. We'll chat over a friendly jar. Where are you off to now?" He dismissed all Sharpe's attempts to decline the invitation. "Just phone her up and tell her you'll be late." Gripping Sharpe's elbow firmly, he steered him off the train at the next station, watched over Sharpe while he made his call, and then guided them both into a branch of a chain that produced plastic imitations of English pubs. The place simultaneously managed to remind Sharpe of all the reasons why he no longer lived in England, and to make him feel homesick.

"Pint of Bass for me," said Jon. "They pull a good pint here. What's yours?"

"Mojito," said Sharpe, determined to choose a drink that fitted least with the ambience of the place. He had to explain the drink to the Japanese bartender, who regretted in atrocious English that there was no mint available. "All right then, a bloody gin and tonic, then," he snapped.

"A Bloody Mary with gin and no vodka?" suggested the bartender.

"No, a gin and tonic," said Sharpe in Japanese. "And make it a large one." He was slightly disturbed by the literal way in which this order was taken. What seemed like half a bottle of gin went into the ice-filled pint glass, topped off with a splash of tonic. Watching the performance, Sharpe had the feeling that he would regret this later.

"Cheers," said Jon, raising his glass, when they were settled at a corner table with their drinks.

Sharpe said nothing, but raised his glass in return. He took a sip. Jesus, it was almost neat gin. He would have to go back and get some more tonic water in there soon.

"Well, let me tell you the good news," said Jon. "Tim Barclay's on his merry way back to the UK, and guess who's taking his place?"

"Congratulations, I suppose you want me to say," said Sharpe. "Do you get the *fabulous* coffee maker?"

"To the victor belong the spoils, you mean? No, that's all his to take back. It's all very hush-hush, of course." He was obviously bursting to tell Sharpe all about this piece of gossip, but Sharpe was damned if he was going to feed Jon his lines. He got up and moved away from the table.

"Don't worry, I'm glued to your every word," he said ironically. "Just getting a little more tonic in here."

When he returned, Jon was still obviously determined to tell all. "It was Al Kowalski that did for Tim Barclay, you know."

"But Al Kowalski is dead, isn't he?"

"That's exactly where the problem lay. You see, Ishihara had been relying on Al for all kinds of special services. You know, those little things, like turning over your flat, that only Al could do, and he wasn't exactly too thrilled when Al's head turned up in the service lift of the headquarters of one of the larger Japanese electronics makers. Household name, too. And it was a company that had pissed me off big-time a year or so back over a trade deal back in the States, so I had great fun giving the orders to put the head there once they'd pulled it out of the station coin locker." He smiled unpleasantly.

"There was nothing on the news about it, was there?"

"Of course not, you great prannock. You don't think that a major brand with half a dozen appliances in your living room is going to broadcast the fact that its headquarters security is so leaky that any bugger can sneak in and leave miscellaneous body parts around the place, do you?"

"I see," replied Sharpe.

"And Ishihara put two and two together, knowing, because Barclay had told him, that you'd been round to see us, and he concluded that it was something to do with us not doing our job properly." He took a pull at his beer. "And he'd had his knife into Tim for years. I think they were both trying to play the insider trading game on the stock market, and it was a falling out between thieves. So it gave him great pleasure to drop a word in the ears of the Japanese Financial Services Agency, who talked to the Japanese Ministry of Foreign Affairs, who in turn held very delicate discussions with His Excellency the British Ambassador, with the happy result that Major Tim Barclay is now on his way home. Or rather, he will be in a few weeks. He's going to be out of that little hidey-hole of his soon, anyway, and he's just waiting out his time. 'Indefinite compassionate leave', they're calling it. And in the meantime, yours truly has effectively taken over the shop. Impressed?"

"Uh-huh," replied Sharpe in as neutral a tone as he could manage.

"So," Jon went on. "I offered you a job with us earlier without really being able to make good on the offer. Now it really is possible for me to offer you a job. No questions asked by anyone else. Coming on board?"

Sharpe shook his head. "No, thanks."

"Busy?" Jon asked. "Can I ask what's taking up your time these days?"

"Financial houses. The usual consultancy sort of thing."

"What about Katsuyama, then? Any idea where he might be? Or where the Katsuyama gadget's hiding itself these days? His wife's not talking to me as much as she used to."

"No and no, why should I?" Sharpe lied easily. Why on earth should Tomiko have anything to do with Jon, and where did she meet him in the first place? he asked himself.

"Keep thinking about it. If you find out, you've got my number, and my door's always open to you. Same goes if you change your mind about the job offer."

Something wasn't ringing quite right in Sharpe's ears. It wasn't just the gin, which remained at a near-toxic level in his drink, despite his having replaced three large blocks of ice with the equivalent volume of tonic water.

"You're sure about all this?"

Jon calmly took a drink of beer and stared at Sharpe impassively.

"Well, I can't say that you've exactly shaken my faith in

human nature as regards Major Tim Barclay. But it seems slightly strange to me. I really can't believe all that about Ishihara."

"It's a weird business that we're in."

"And I really don't like the idea of you shopping him to the authorities. Sounds like you're stirring up the shit just to get yourself promoted."

"We're all trying to get ahead, aren't we?" Sharpe heard the Estuary English sound of aggressive ambition, which worked on him like fingernails down a blackboard.

"Speak for yourself. I don't like what you're up to, though. Look, it's nothing personal," he lied, "but I have to be getting back. Your bill, I believe." He stalked out of the pub, ignoring Jon's protests.

Following a sudden impulse, Sharpe stopped at a mobile phone store on his way home and changed his phone for a new model, refusing the shop's offer to transfer the old number. It was going to be a nuisance for all his existing contacts to deal with the new number, but at least he could block any further attempts by Jon to reach him that way. Maybe Jon was on the side of the angels, and Tim Barclay was indeed a crooked little wheeler-dealer, but from where he was, they appeared to be different faces of the same coin. He would ask Mieko if they could change the apartment's phone number. Of course it wouldn't stop Jon from calling round at the flat in person, but somehow Sharpe thought that even Jon, whose attitude towards criticism seemed to resemble that of a duck's back to water, wouldn't want to do that.

THE NEXT DAY, KIM SHOWED UP at the M&M Trading office. "Nice," he commented, obviously impressed by Meema's trading station and its three enormous computer screens, and amused by the kitchen that by now had found its way into the same room.

"Do you have backups for the data feeds?" he asked.

Sharpe was slightly taken aback by this unexpected question. Kim had seemed ignorant of the details of financial technology when the whole business had been explained to him earlier.

"We do, but why do you ask?"

"I just wanted to make sure. Since you mentioned this plan, I thought I should find out a little more about what it was all about and how it worked, since I'm trusting you to make money for me with it. It seems that one of the main things you must make sure of in this business is that you are always on line and in touch with the world. Am I right?"

"Yes, you're right, of course." But Sharpe felt that it would be unusual for someone outside the business to seize on this as an important point.

"How are things going?"

Sharpe explained that they were still testing and verifying the system.

"So when are you going to stop spending my money and start making some real money for me?" Kim sounded stern.

"In a few days—" began Sharpe apologetically, but Kim slapped him on the back and chuckled.

"My little joke," he said. "I believe you're still using the money I gave you, and in any case, I can see you're working hard to get things finished. I'm sure you'll be ready soon."

"A question for you, Mr Kim?" Sharpe asked, when they were alone in the room. The other nodded. "Where is Dr Katsuyama right now?"

"Still in Hanoi. Why?"

"It's possible that we might need his expertise at some time in the future if his program goes wrong or doesn't work quite the way we think it should."

"Unlikely, I would guess. Your friend Vishal seems competent enough to fix any problems like that. In any case, I am glad that he's in Hanoi. I have the utmost respect for him and his work, but I don't want him anywhere near my daughter for a while."

Sharpe remembered the bruises on Tomiko Katsuyama's arm, and what Mieko had told him about her relationship with her father. Katsuyama's flight to Hanoi made some more sense now. "Vishal is highly competent," he agreed, "but he's not in the same league as your son-in-law."

"Well, if you ever find yourself really in need of him, let me know. Maybe I can do something about it." Kim took his leave of M&M Trading, making polite farewells to everyone, and inviting them all round to his club whenever they felt like visiting. "As my guests, of course," he added. "But don't expect the elevator to be fixed any time soon. We keep it that way to discourage anyone from just dropping in."

THIS WAS THE DAY that the market data feeds were to be turned on, and Vishal was on the telephone to three vendors at once as soon as Kim left. After about ten minutes of excited conversation, he turned to Sharpe.

"We are being almost ready to go." He launched a couple of programs on his own workstation, and watched excitedly as numbers flashed in front of his eyes. They meant little or nothing to Sharpe, except that something was happening, but Vishal seemed excited and satisfied.

"Time to fire up Katsuyama's gadget," he remarked to Sharpe, who went through the business of starting it, connected to the real-time data feeds for the first time.

"OK, Meema, select three currency pairs based on the New York prices," said Sharpe.

She selected the three pairs covering the euro, dollar

and yen, and the four partners of M&M Trading watched the lines of the prices predicted three minutes in the future creep across the screen, followed three minutes later by the actual prices, which tracked the predictions with almost perfect fidelity.

Meema burst into helpless giggles, and threw her arms around each of them in turn, kissing them, but without the passion that had marked her earlier move on Sharpe. It was still unlike Meema, Sharpe thought – usually she was physically undemonstrative, even towards Vishal, in public at least. "I can do it!" she exclaimed. "I know exactly how to do it! I want to start right now!"

"Not now, Meema," warned Sharpe. "Let's do a little more checking with the play money. Start on the real thing in a few days, or even the next week."

She pouted slightly, but Vishal backed Sharpe up on this. Somewhat sulkily, she agreed to do as they said, and continued to scan the screens. After ten minutes she reported, "It's working well, I'm making millions, this is magic – hey!"

"What is it, Meema?"

"Look at that! Something strange is going on, and it's not working our way." She checked the news ticker on another screen. "Oh, the spot price of Middle Eastern crude oil's just changed. That must be what's doing it."

And indeed, the Katsuyama prediction no longer seemed to correspond so closely to the trace of the real rate.

"If that had been real money, Meema," Sharpe asked her, "How much money would we have lost just then?"

"Not a lot," she admitted. "I was going to place a buy ten seconds before the news came through. If I'd done that, we'd have been in a bit of trouble."

"You are wanting me to applaud?" asked Vishal, a little sarcastically.

At the Sharpe End

"No," shot back Meema. "Just be thankful that I have some common sense when it comes to these things."

"Whatever," said Sharpe. "I think we have to look at this whole thing for another day or so, Meema, before we start putting real money into there."

Both Vishal and Meema nodded in agreement. "It's slightly different in real time," said Meema. "I can feel the pressure in a way that I couldn't when it was just a simulation. Look." She held out both hands in front of her. They were trembling slightly.

"But even now you are not playing with real money," Vishal pointed out. "If your nerves are shaking like this now, what are they going to be like when the real thing is arriving?"

Meema considered. "I'll manage," she said. "If things get too tough, I'll just log off the system and cook a korma or a dopiaza or something to calm myself down."

Privately, Sharpe was worried about his role in all of this. Although Meema had spent some time telling the rest of them about her tactics and strategies, she was so far in advance of them in the matter of trading that it was difficult to see how anyone could ever follow even the basics of what she had been doing. In the same way, Vishal was so far ahead of everyone else in the computer and IT aspects of the firm that he had made himself irreplaceable, and Mieko had such a firm grasp of the legal issues and the administrative work of the firm that it was difficult to see how the firm could survive without her. Truth to tell, Sharpe admitted to himself, he was the fifth wheel on the wagon (or to be more accurate, a fourth wheel on a tricycle). He said as much to Mieko one night as they were going home.

"That's not true," she corrected him. "You're the only

person who understands what everyone else is doing, even if you're not at the same level as the rest of us in our specialist areas. Vishal hasn't a clue what I'm up to, I don't know what he's doing at all with all his computers and cables, and Meema's lost the rest of us in her hedging and short-selling and options. You may not understand it all perfectly, but you know enough to be useful, at least."

It was faint praise, but it made him feel better.

"And there's another thing," she added. "Haven't you noticed that when there's a decision to be made, we're all waiting for you to say yes or no before we go ahead? You're the leader. So let's have no more of this 'I'm useless' rubbish. Time to come to bed." And that, thought Sharpe, was that.

Chapter 10: Tokyo

THE BIG DAY HAD ARRIVED. Sharpe and Mieko, Vishal and Meema had all contributed something to the initial holdings that were to be invested, and had agreed that the start of the week made a good time to start the trading process.

Meema had explained the concept of extended leverage to them, whereby they could trade many times the value of their actual assets, but Vishal had tried to veto the idea of this.

"We're going to be certain winners," he had pointed out. "Why be greedy and draw attention to ourselves by making stupidly large deals?" Sharpe had agreed in theory, but pointed out that the market typically expected leveraged trading. Meema had wanted to play with different trading strategies using leverage, and Mieko, who, in common with most Japanese, seemed to dislike the idea of debt on principle, agreed with Vishal's views. In the end, they all arrived at a compromise whereby they agreed to use only moderate amounts of leverage for the trading, and that if Meema felt the need to risk large amounts of borrowed money, she was to consult the others.

On the day, Meema claimed that she was nervous, and

didn't want anyone to be watching her when she made her first real trades on the system. All the same, Mieko, Sharpe and Vishal all found an excuse to wander separately into her trading room before she started, and make encouraging noises in her direction, accompanied by (at least in Mieko's case) a hug and a kiss.

The three non-traders then proceeded to invade Meema's trading room en masse, much to her visible annoyance. She shooed them all out, and after making fussy and unnecessary last-minute adjustments to Meema's computer, chair and desk, they tiptoed out of the room, and left her alone, closing the door softly behind them.

"I feel it's like looking after a racehorse before a race, or a ballerina or a concert pianist or something before a performance," said Sharpe.

"Or like a tightrope walker in a circus," said Mieko.

"Of course in the brokerages, it's usually only one or two traders who carry the whole floor. The rest of them just do as well as they would by sticking pins into a board blindfolded," remarked Sharpe.

"Or even a damn' sight worse," commented Vishal dryly. "Meema's got no-one else on the floor or at the next desk to cover for her if things go wrong. It's no wonder she's feeling the pressure."

"I'm making tea," said Mieko. "Will you two get away from that door? I'm sure Meema knows you're there and it's making her nervous." Obediently, the two men moved away from the door where they had been trying to listen surreptitiously to the goings-on within the room, and made their way sheepishly into the small kitchen area where Mieko was boiling water.

"Too bloody hot," complained Sharpe, taking a sip of his tea, and burning his tongue.

"Well, make your own bloody tea, then!" Mieko screamed

at him. "I'm going out," and flounced out of the room, shutting the door behind her with a bang.

Sharpe lifted his eyebrows. "What the hell did I say?" he asked Vishal, who only shrugged his shoulders in response. They drank their tea in near-silence, trying not to notice any noises coming from the other rooms, and studiously avoiding each other's eyes.

After half an hour of eternity, Meema opened the door, seemingly exhausted, but grinning widely.

"I've done it!" she exclaimed proudly. "I hardly needed to use any leverage on it at all. Almost all of it was done with our own money."

"How much?" asked Sharpe.

"Five hundred thousand US dollars. Plus change. Pure profit." She threw her arms around Vishal and kissed him with real passion, kissed Sharpe with somewhat less passion (he was relieved to notice), and looked around. "Where's Mieko?" she asked.

"Here," came Mieko's voice from behind her. "You're right," she said to Sharpe. "The tea was too hot." One of the reasons why Sharpe and she always seemed to get on so well was because even though both of them tended to flare up for no good reason, neither of them seemed able to bear a grudge for very long.

Meema threw her arms around Mieko and kissed her.

"Vishal, I think your sister's going to get better," said Sharpe to Vishal, shaking his hand.

"I hope so, man," replied Vishal. There were tears in his eyes. "Thank you, Meema." He put his arms round her.

"And thank you too, Kenneth," said Meema. "You didn't have to include us in this business, you know."

"That's true," said Vishal. "Thank you, Kenneth-san." Sharpe looked down at his shoes, unable to reply.

"How easy was it for you to do that?" Mieko asked,

obviously in awe of the unbelievable amount of money that had been made so fast.

"The actual trading was easy. Katsuyama's predictions were spot-on, every time. What's difficult is keeping cool. I wanted to take off my clothes and run around the room screaming every time I made a successful trade. I think I understand those lunatic traders a little better, now that I've done it myself."

"I see why you wanted us out of the room," commented Sharpe with a wry smile.

"Don't worry, I didn't do it," replied Meema. "Anyway, no more trading today. I'm exhausted and now I'm going to sit down for a few minutes and then I'm going to cook a vegetable biriyani for us all."

"I am thinking that half a million dollars plus change is quite enough for one day," agreed Vishal.

"I really can't believe it," said Mieko.

"Nor me," said Meema. She looked flushed, and was breathing heavily, as if she'd just run a long-distance race. "Now just let me sit down for a moment and do nothing and get my strength back."

After the next successful trading sessions a few days later (they had decided to leave the market alone for a short period in order not to draw undue attention to themselves) which netted at least another half million dollars each time, Sharpe talked a little more with Kim, and with several million dollars in profits, he decided it was time to start making money for Kim very soon.

Chapter 11: Tokyo

Sharpe was on the phone to Kim a few days later when the real problems started to take effect. Sharpe had just confirmed to Kim that the first transfer to M&M had arrived safely through a complex series of previously agreed financial cutouts, involving large amounts of cash being transported between different banks in different parts of Japan, when the conversation was interrupted by a piercing wordless scream from Meema's trading room.

"Excuse me," said Sharpe. "I've just heard a terrible noise, and I think I'm going to have to do something about it."

He put down the phone and rushed to Meema's room. Vishal was already there, with his arms around Meema, who was shaking and sobbing. Sharpe looked at Vishal.

"Not sure," he replied in answer to the unspoken question, "Something on the news feed. I haven't seen it yet. Something about Lehman Brothers, she said."

Sharpe moved over to one of the screens showing a news ticker. "Holy shit!"

"What?" asked Vishal, his head still buried in Meema's hair. "I still haven't looked."

"Lehman have gone bust. Official now. Chapter 11."

"Couldn't have happened to a nicer bunch of people," said Vishal sarcastically. The rivalry between Vishal's bank and Lehman Brothers was notorious. The implications hit him. "You what? You mean they're closing the Japan office?"

"No, the whole thing round the world is going into liquidation. Lehman Brothers is basically bankrupt. RIP. Rejected the Korean offer, and Barclays isn't going to buy them, it seems. Barclays don't want the bad debts, just the assets."

"What assets?" said Sharpe. "These people have been living on borrowed time, not to mention borrowed money, for ever and a day. Now their credit line has run out. Bet you no-one's interested in their repo business any more."

"Bloody hell!" said Vishal. He stared at the screen for a few minutes longer, apparently in shock. "What's the matter?" turning to the still weeping Meema. "You weren't that fond of them, were you?"

"It's … not … just … them," sniffled Meema. "Just take a look at the rest of the news."

Sharpe scrolled down the screen. "No!" he shouted. "This isn't happening!"

"Told you," said Meema, almost triumphantly.

"What's not happening?" asked Vishal, craning his neck. Sharpe's head was blocking his view of the screen.

"The whole financial world is just going crazy."

Meema answered. "All of this has sent the currency forecasts haywire. Just look at the screens there."

Obediently, they all looked at the Katsuyama program screen to see what was going on. As Meema had said, the line predicting the exchange fluctuations was only roughly following the actual exchange rate.

"I see," said Sharpe. "That seems to be real trouble." He continued reading down the screen. "What's this going to do to AIG? I mean, these guys are backing all the banks, and I bet that they can't cover all the losses."

"That means all the insurance for the banks has collapsed," said Vishal.

"Effectively, yes. Holy crap!" said Sharpe.

"But ..." wailed Meema. "I've lost all of Kim's money."

"What?" said Vishal. "But he sent us about two million dollars yesterday. We can't have lost it all just like that. Can we?" he added dubiously.

"We were doing so well with the other money that I made out of our trading that I decided I was going to start doing some real trading with real money."

"Two million dollars? All at once?"

Meema said nothing, but nodded dumbly.

"And that was Kim's money?" asked Sharpe.

"Yes, it was," replied Meema.

"Oh shit," said Vishal. "Ken, you're going to be the one who tells him."

"I was just thinking that myself," said Sharpe. "Are we really sure that we have to tell him?"

"Of course!" from a horrified Meema. "We can't just let two million dollars disappear like that without telling him, can we?"

"We don't have to tell him immediately, though," pointed out Vishal. "We could try to make it back."

"There's no way that we can make the money back right now," pointed out Meema. "Just look at the lines. They're even worse than they were a few minutes ago."

"It will settle down," said Sharpe, hoping he sounded a little more confident than he in fact felt. "Give it a few days and I think we're going to see something that's a little more reasonable and rational."

"So what are you going to tell Kim?"

"Nothing at all. We can use some of the money that we

made earlier. We made much more than enough to pay for your sister, Vishal. Once the markets have settled down a bit, we'll be clear, and we can make back the money many times over."

"It's worse than you think, Ken," said Meema. Her head was in her hands, and it was difficult to make out what she was saying. "It's not just Kim's money."

Vishal and Sharpe looked at each other. "Tell us. We're not going to bite your head off," said Sharpe.

"You will." She was sobbing again. Vishal put his arms around her again, and nodded significantly to Sharpe, who took the hint and went out of the room, closing the door behind him.

"What's happening?" Mieko asked him as he entered the room where she was sitting.

"The whole bloody financial world has collapsed. Lehman have finally gone under and they're taking the world with them. There's no way we can trade, no way we or anyone else knows what's going to happen next. It's that bad. It's worse than that bad. Meema's just lost all Kim's money." Sharpe felt as though he'd been kicked hard in the stomach. He felt sick and wanted to sit down. You don't lose two million dollars of a gangster's money and walk away in one piece, he told himself.

Vishal shouted for Sharpe and Mieko to join him and Meema. He looked shaken.

"We've lost everything," he said.

"Thank you for not saying it was me who lost it," said Meema. She had obviously been crying.

"It wasn't anything you did," said Vishal.

"You mean all our money as well?" asked Sharpe. "The money we made? What about Vishal's sister?"

"That's safe." She seemed a little calmer, but her eyes still looked red and puffy. "I put that into a sort of escrow and I promised myself that I wouldn't touch it. So I didn't. That's safe. But all the other money that we made has gone."

"So we're back where we started?" said Sharpe. Somehow the news didn't seem as shocking to him as it might. It's a lot worse to lose a gangster's money than your own, he thought to himself. The lead weight in his stomach refused to disappear.

"We're a lot better off," said Mieko. "We have the money for Vishal's sister."

"Of course."

"And we actually have some money of our own. I didn't lose it all. Not quite." Meema managed a weak smile. "And we don't owe anyone any money. We paid for all this," waving her hand around the office. "At least we're not going to have anyone chasing us."

"Except for Kim," Vishal pointed out.

"Maybe," Sharpe began, trying to convince himself as much as the others. "Maybe we can use whatever money we have to start again. Things are bound to settle down, and then everything will be back the way it was. And we'll all be millionaires again before we know what's happened.

"And if they don't settle down?" asked Meema. She started weeping again. "Come on, this is big news. Lehman are number three or four. They've just filed for bankruptcy and Merrill are shaky, and all the insurance in the world isn't going to cover the Lehman bad debts. They're not a brokerage any more, just in case you didn't know. They're a real estate investment trust selling fake bonds and equities on the side. This isn't just a dip in the market, Kenneth-san. This is bloody anarchy. All the trading strategies in the world aren't going to do us any good at all in this mess."

"Well, we still have enough to pay for Vishal's sister, and I think we may be able to pay back Kim soon. I'll just try to persuade him that he'll have to wait a little more time. I'm sure he can understand what's happening. He doesn't strike me as being exactly stupid."

"I don't know as much as you lot do about these things," said Mieko. "But if we're in trouble with all the special Katsuyama stuff that we have working for us, won't everyone else be in even more trouble? I mean, they won't have a clue what to do, will they? Surely we should be able to clean up as a result?"

"They won't know what they're doing, that's true, but I don't see how that's going to help us," said Sharpe. "I've never believed that having one eye in the country of the blind is that much of an advantage. Especially when someone turns the lights out on you."

"So we keep mum and sit it out?" said Meema.

"I've no better ideas for the moment." He shrugged. "Break time, children. All run outside and play till the bell rings."

Inside, he wasn't nearly as calm or cheerful as he sounded. If Meema really had figuratively put all of Kim's money on black, and the ball had turned up red, then they were definitely in serious trouble. As the others left the room, he brought up a spreadsheet on the computer and started to punch in a few numbers.

His earlier guess was almost right. If the money for Vishal's sister's operation was at the low end of the scale, there was a good chance that they wouldn't lose any more of their own money. Of course, the big unknown was the cost of the operation for Vishal's sister, which was still a large fuzzy number. Phone calls to American clinics and Internet research had proved fruitless when it came to tying down a definite number – something that Vishal in particular, as a computer engineer used to precise answers, found especially irritating.

One thing was certain. He wasn't going to tell Kim

everything that had happened. Memories of the bag in the Tokyo station locker were enough to disabuse him of that as an idea. However, he also had no intention of lying to Kim. That could also lead to a lot of trouble, he felt. He wasn't about to run away to Hanoi or anything, but he felt it would be best if he didn't answer the phone at home or work for a few days, and screened all calls on his mobile before answering it.

He saved the spreadsheet and joined the others in the next room, where they were watching one of the cable financial channels. It was like watching the planes crash into the World Trade Center on September 11, thought Sharpe. It almost seemed as if the whole of the Western financial system was dying before their very eyes and here they were, watching the hearse drive up to collect the body.

Every now and then, either Vishal or Sharpe would let out an expletive, and Meema would squeal. It was unbelievable that these major institutions, that had formed part of their lives for so long, seemed to be disappearing before their very eyes.

"We should have seen it coming when Bear Stearns went under," said Vishal. "The coming of the storm."

"Bullshit," replied Sharpe. "It's been coming for much longer than that, and Meema knows it better than anyone."

"Me?"

"Yes, you. You were the one making up those fancy trading strategies for the weird derivatives that were being sold. Putting together the packages of California no-doc mortgages and junk debt-funded LBOs."

"I was only—"

"—following orders. I know. No, it's not you who invented all these crazy credit default swaps and the rest of the shit, but tell me, did any of the managers off the trading desks really know what was going on? What was being sold?

How much risk was involved?" Meema shook her head. "There you are. You had a whole load of greedy bastards selling crap to other greedy bastards who happened to be more stupid than them, with no supervision."

"Oh, for God's sake shut up, Ken," said Mieko. "You've been saying this for the past year or so every time you come back home from a bank trading floor."

"Because it happens to be true," said Sharpe, a little stung. But he bit his tongue, all the same, as they continued to watch the reports on the Wall Street dance of death.

AFTER WHAT SEEMED LIKE HOURS of flipping channels, and watching the talking heads repeat the same phrases over and over again, Sharpe decided it was time to check the prediction lines on Meema's screens again. If anything, though, things seemed worse than before. An idea hit him, and he called into the next room.

"Meema. What would happen if you were to take currencies which weren't part of all this and use whatever we have left? Something like Thai baht or Malaysian dollars or something? God, even roubles. Don't you think that would be a bit more stable?"

"You're joking, Ken-chan," she replied. "It's all linked together. People are doing option calls on half the currencies that are being traded, and hedging the calls with the rest."

"Oh. Another good idea shattered," he muttered to himself.

"I honestly think you were right first time," said Meema. "Our best bet is simply to stay calm and wait till things get better."

"And to say nothing to Kim," added Vishal.

"Indeed, as far as possible."

"What happens if he calls and asks us what's happening?"

said Mieko. "He probably will. I'm sure he'll want to know what's going on here while the whole financial world is collapsing in ruins."

"Tell him some of the truth?" asked Sharpe. "That the markets are so chaotic that the Katsuyama gadget's useless at the moment. He should wait a bit, and it will all settle down? We don't have to mention to him that we've lost his money. Temporarily. We can tell him later if we want, when it's all safe again," he added, catching Meema's double-barrelled reproachful look.

"Sounds good enough to me," said Vishal.

"But how long is that going to keep him quiet, though?" asked Mieko.

"How the hell is anyone expected to answer that? Come on, we've been watching the greatest media minds on this subject, and they don't seem to have a frigging clue what's happening. How are we expected to know?"

IN THE NEXT FEW DAYS, a lot happened in the financial markets – various offers had been made and withdrawn for the stricken giant. In Japan, it seemed as though Nomura, the largest brokerage house in Japan, was about to take over large parts of Lehman's operations in Japan, but Sharpe had friends in the IT department there who had no interest in the buttoned-down culture of Nomura, and were proposing to sell themselves as a team to the highest bidder.

"Anyone we can find," Sharpe's informant had told him in an almost tearful (and Sharpe guessed at least partially drunken) late-night phone call. "Those bastards at Nomura just want to strip everything and they're not telling us a thing that's going on. All we've heard is that the trading desks are going to be paid enormous sums of money.

Guaranteed. Ha, ha. What about the poor bloody infantry? Fuck you, Nomura."

"That'll piss off the Nomura traders," agreed Sharpe. Foreign trading houses paid notoriously more than the Japanese equivalents, and the only thing that bound most traders to their employers was the size of their pay packets and bonuses.

"Yeah," giggled his friend (Sharpe was pretty sure by now he was drunk). "But where can they go? No-one's going to want a bunch of Nomura has-beens. Anyway, I don't think Nomura wanted the guys on our front desks anyway – just the technology that we'd been developing, and if I have my way, they're not going to get it. The whole of my team will come with me if I find the right place for us to work."

Later, Sharpe discovered that the whole of this specialist back-office team had gone to work for another more generous Japanese brokerage, leaving Nomura with a pile of technology that they could just about manage to use, but were incapable of enhancing, or even fixing if it went wrong. Just like M&M and the Katsuyama technology, really, if you thought about it.

"I wonder what has happened to our bank by now," said Vishal the next day, referring to the bank where he and Meema had worked before coming to work with Sharpe.

"You've still got friends there if you really want to find out," said Sharpe. "But my guess is that everyone's going to be in the same sort of mess." He typed a few addresses into the Web browser. "Well, like I said, everyone's in the same sort of shit. Your former playmates are as badly off as any of them. Well, not quite. You're better off than Merrill and a hell of a sight better off than Lehman. But in the hole by several billion dollars."

"Not surprised," said Meema. "Some of those derivatives deals I was helping with were pure smoke and mirrors, just like you said the other day, Ken. If the whole thing has collapsed, I'm not at all surprised. And I'm glad of it. I can't really say I'm proud of the work I did there, after it's all over." She sniffed.

"Well, what's happening in the trenches, do you think?" Sharpe asked. For answer, Vishal dashed off a few e-mail messages and sat back.

"Holy shit!" he said a few minutes later.

"Uh-huh?" replied Sharpe.

"I was just sending off messages to six people I used to work with. Four of them have gone to hell and bounced. 'No account exists at this address for—' blah blah."

"Did your friends jump or were they pushed?" Sharpe asked.

"Good question," replied Vishal. "I'll wait till I hear from the others that didn't bounce before I start asking questions like that. But it doesn't look like it is being a good time to be in the banking business."

"It's not a good time to be in the currency exchange business, either," Sharpe pointed out. "In fact, I would say it's a bloody awful time to be in any kind of business at all right now."

"Hang on," said Vishal. "I've just got a couple of replies back. No, things there are really grim right now. We were lucky to get out of there when we did." He scrolled down the messages. "Meema, you wouldn't be having a job there now if we'd stayed. Your department's been completely gutted. And I'm pretty sure I wouldn't be working there now, either."

When Kim called, there had been further developments, with the major American financial houses reverting to bank status, UK banks dropping like flies and being propped up by government loans, and even the American government adding its money to support the failed financial system.

"Well, I think you can guess," said Sharpe in answer to Kim's first question. "Since everything is in complete chaos, there's no way that your son-in-law's program can help us here. I'm afraid that you're going to have to wait until the markets calm down a bit before we can really talk about giving you the money you want."

"I thought that might be the case," replied Kim. "And I just want you to know that as long as my capital is safe, you can take your time over getting the profit to me." Sharpe heaved an internal sigh of relief. The next question down the line, which was one Sharpe had been expecting, was, "What do you think is going to happen next?" Sharpe got this question relatively often from people who knew he worked in banks, oblivious of the fact that he saw himself only as a glorified computer mechanic and really had very little knowledge of the financial businesses conducted by the banks. In Kim's case, maybe the question had a little more validity.

However, he gave the same answer that he always did when asked to perform as a prophet. "Well, we may see it get worse before we get better. Give it some time." As a piece of fortune-telling, Sharpe considered it to be on a par with "the sun will rise tomorrow morning", but as in this case, it usually calmed people down.

Kim rang off, and Sharpe felt that he'd just dodged a bullet the size of a cannonball. At least he wouldn't have to keep watching his back for some large knife-wielding Korean thug, he told himself.

Chapter 12: Tokyo

A week after Kim had called, Meema was sitting at the computer terminal, trying once more to create some order from the chaos of the markets.

"It's no good," she called to Sharpe in the next room. "I'm simulating all the trades, and it's all I can do to break even. If I let my concentration slip for a second – shit! Just lost a couple of hundred there."

By "a couple of hundred", Sharpe knew that she meant two hundred thousand yen of the simulated money. It wasn't a fortune, but for someone who had been winning consistently over the past few weeks, it was disconcerting to lose at all.

The phone rang, and he let Mieko pick it up.

"Yes? What?" he heard her say in Japanese. "Wait a moment, I'll get him for you."

"Who is it?" he asked, taking the phone from her.

"One of Kim's men," she replied. "Wants to speak to you, and you only." She sniffed. "Guess that sort of person doesn't think women are worth talking to."

"Hello?" Sharpe said into the phone in Japanese.

The person at the other end spoke very quickly and in an accent with which Sharpe was unfamiliar, so he asked him to speak more slowly. Even so, there were some words and phrases that he didn't understand at first, and he motioned to Mieko to pick up the extension.

"What's he saying?" he mouthed to her. "It sounds as though Kim's dead."

She looked shocked, but picked up the phone and listened for a minute as Sharpe continued the conversation. She nodded to him, and he lip-read, "Yes, he is."

When Sharpe eventually put the phone down, he asked Mieko, "Did I get that right? Kim is dead, and was found last night in his house with a knife stuck in him or something? And the wake's tomorrow night and the funeral the day after that and I'm expected to be there for at least one of them? They're going to fax the details of the place to me? Did I get that all right?"

"You did." Mieko put her phone down. Her hand was shaking. "Kenneth, are we safe?"

"I wish I knew, dear," was all that Sharpe could answer. "Maybe it's nothing to do with what we're doing at all. It may just be a gang war, and the people who killed him don't know anything at all about the North Korean business."

"I hope so." She shivered. "Ken-chan, I'm scared. I mean, Kim was a gangster, and he hurt you, but he seems to be – seemed to be, rather – as reasonable and decent as anyone like that could be. Maybe he was shielding us from all sorts of things he never told us about."

"Honestly, I think you're exaggerating. I mean, I know that it doesn't sound very much like accidental death, does it? But I really don't think that necessarily means we're in danger. We don't know half of what he was up to, or who his enemies in those fields were."

He heard the fax printing out a sheet of paper and went over to pick up the map that had just emerged. Meema and

Vishal were in the room, and he explained to them what he had just been told.

"Oh no," whispered Meema, who had listened in breathless silence to his story. "Are we safe here?"

"That's just what Mieko asked me. The answer is that I don't know, but I think we are." Why did everyone suddenly regard him as the fount of all wisdom? Sharpe asked himself as Vishal and Meema followed him into the room where Mieko was sitting.

"I'll go to the wake tomorrow evening. I've got a white shirt and a black tie somewhere, I'm sure. It all seems a bit quick. Do you think the police have been involved?"

"I wouldn't think they care one way or the other," replied Mieko.

"Do you want me to come with you?" Mieko asked.

"No, no need. I'll send your regards to Tomiko and put your name on the *kōden bukuro* if you want," referring to the envelope containing a substantial sum of money that is traditionally handed over by guests at Japanese funerals.

"No, I don't want that."

"And don't go putting my name or Meema's name on there, either. Or the company name. We have no idea who's going to be looking at the guest list," said Vishal.

Sharpe considered. It sounded a little paranoid, but he admitted it made sense, if there was any connection at all between the Katsuyama technology and Kim's murder. "So just my name, so I'm the one they come after?" he asked. He was only half joking. The others seemed to be quite serious in their worries, even if he could laugh them off.

THE NEXT EVENING SAW SHARPE DRESSED UP in a formal black suit, white shirt and black tie; the uniform for men attending funerals in Japan. Weddings are traditionally the same, except that the tie is white.

His pocket held the ceremonial envelope in which the money gift was to be presented at the wake. When he arrived at the point where his map software had located the address, in what Sharpe had always regarded as a somewhat seedy area of Tokyo, it seemed that the building had probably served as Kim's gang headquarters – at least, that's what Sharpe thought it looked like, from the little he knew of such places.

He was welcomed at the door by two of Kim's men whom he had previously met on other occasions. When he tried to present the envelope to them, it was politely but firmly replaced in his pocket. Unusually for a Japanese occasion, there was no book for the guests to write their names and addresses. Obviously funerals in this stratum of society were conducted slightly differently to those in other parts of Japan.

As he entered the room where the funeral was to be held, he noticed that it didn't seem to have many of the usual Buddhist trappings. He'd never been to a Shinto funeral, but what he knew of Shinto didn't seem anything like what he was seeing here. In fact, there really didn't seem to be any religious symbols at all that he could see.

He went up to the line in front of the open coffin, taking a white flower as he joined the line, and when his time came, laying it reverently on the lid. He looked at Kim, who seemed to be sleeping peacefully. If his violent death had been painful, it didn't show in his face.

He took a seat beside two large men who appeared, from the way they were being treated by Kim's men, as though they had come from another gang, and who viewed him curiously. He was, after all, the only Westerner in the place. As the room filled up, he noticed Tomiko enter, looking as stunning as he remembered, in formal mourning wear. Come to think of it, he'd only seen her in black. First for her husband, and now for her father. Hardly surprisingly, she didn't seem to notice him as she walked to the front, laid her flower by the coffin, and took her place in the front row.

The funeral service, if you could call it that, seemed to consist of a series of eulogies by assorted dignitaries from the underworld, if appearances were anything to go by. Some appeared surprised, and even embarrassed, if truth be told, when they were tapped on the shoulder and invited to speak. Sharpe was thankful that no-one asked him to say a few words.

After the last speaker, the congregation, if that's what it was, filed past the coffin to pay their final respects to the dead man and to his family. As Sharpe turned away from the coffin, his eyes met Tomiko's, who flashed a glance in his direction as she bowed deeply. It was something he didn't want to deal with, but he bowed in return.

Declining the beer and snacks that were offered to the mourners, he escaped to the outside world.

As he walked back towards the station, he became aware that he was being followed, and he stopped to adjust his shoes. His follower made no attempt to stop or to hide his presence, which was meant to be what happened in all the best detective stories, and instead he felt a hand grab his elbow in a painful grip.

"**WHERE THE BLOODY HELL** have you been all this time?" asked Jon. He stepped into the light, and Sharpe noticed that he was dressed in the same way as Sharpe himself – black suit and tie with a white shirt. Sharpe couldn't remember seeing him at the funeral, though.

"Trying to keep out of your way, and that of Major Tim Barclay, that's where," replied Sharpe. His arm was still being held in a painful grip that he didn't feel inclined to wriggle out of.

"Not very friendly," said Jon. He grinned. "I think it's time we had another of our little chats." He said this in a voice that didn't seem to leave any room for argument, and Sharpe felt he had no choice but to agree. "Let's walk, shall we? It's a beautiful night for a stroll."

Sharpe assumed he was speaking metaphorically. It seemed like an average Tokyo night to him.

"So, how's the Lehman collapse affecting you?" Jon asked. The question seemed casual, but Sharpe had the impression that there was more to the question than met the ear.

"Not too great."

"Meaning? You're not getting the contracts you used to from the banks?"

"Right."

"Bullshit!" Jon exploded. "I know what you and your slimy little Indian friends have been up to over the past few weeks."

"Can we have less of the personal insults, please?" Sharpe was angry, and it took all his self-control to stop himself taking a swing at the other.

"All right then, I know what you and your esteemed and worthy colleagues have been up to for the past month or so. Better?"

"Like what?"

"Like using the Katsuyama technology to make lots of money. Lots and lots." Jon licked his lips.

Sharpe was shaken. He had had no idea that anyone else was aware of the currency-trading aspect of Katsuyama's work.

"I told you that I was friendly with Tomiko," said Jon, seemingly enjoying Sharpe's confusion.

"I see." There really didn't seem to be much else to say.

"And what are you all doing now? Making lots of money for Tomiko?"

Sharpe wasn't in the least sure what he should be saying to Jon. How close was his relationship to the Kim clan right now?

"Shall we simply say that the market's in a difficult situation right now?"

"No, we won't simply say that," replied Jon. "I think you're going to have to be a little more explicit than that."

"OK, the market is in fucking chaos. We really don't have a clue what's going to happen next, and with the best will in the world, there's no way we can use the Katsuyama gadget to make money right now. Is that explicit enough for you?"

"Not the answer that I wanted to hear, and I'm bloody sure it's not the answer that Tomiko wants to hear either. On the other hand, it does sound reasonably honest, and the truth is always a joy to me in my old age."

"Glad to be of some use."

"You'd be a lot more use if you were to give her the money, I tell you that for free. She's going to need a fair amount of ready cash, and it seems that her old man sending his life savings to you left the piggy-bank pretty empty."

"Why does she need cash?"

"Taking over the family business. She's going to need money to pay her way. Grease palms, pay people off, buy loyalty, that sort of thing."

"Well, there's nothing we can do right now. I told you, the market's a right mess at the moment, and there's no way we can get the money to her."

"Is that including Kim's original investment?" Sharpe,

not trusting himself to speak, half-nodded. "She's not going to be happy about that."

"Tough. You're going to have to tell her?"

"I'm going to have to tell her something, I guess."

"Then I wish you joy." Despite Jon's protests, Sharpe disengaged himself and set off into the night, aiming for the station. As he turned the corner, he noticed Jon walking back the way he had come, presumably in his capacity as the bearer of bad news to Tomiko.

Chapter 13: Tokyo

THE NEXT AFTERNOON, SHARPE CALLED THE OTHER THREE TOGETHER at the office and told them of his conversation with Jon the previous night.

Meema was dismissive, pointing out that they could just about scrape together enough money to pay Kim's original stake back to Tomiko, even paying interest if she demanded. Although Sharpe pointed out that this could leave them with insufficient money to pay for Vishal's sister's operation, this didn't seem to make any impression on her. Sharpe wondered if her pregnancy was affecting her more than she wanted to admit.

Certainly she'd been acting strangely since the Lehman crash, and spent hours in front of the computer screen, watching the predicted lines from the Katsuyama program and the real lines from the data feeds. They were still far from matching up, and Meema seemed to be frustrated, using words that she didn't normally use (and totally incomprehensible to Sharpe in many cases – he had no idea what language she was swearing in). She was also constantly biting her nails down to the quick, a habit that Sharpe had never noticed before.

Despite the care that Vishal and Sharpe had taken to set up the kitchen in her trading office, she had hardly used it, except to make the endless pots of Japanese green tea that she had been drinking all the time she had been trading. Once, after a particularly short and successful trading session, Vishal had had the temerity to propose that she make a curry for them, and had nearly had his head bitten off for the suggestion.

Other than that incident, Vishal didn't seem to have noticed that there was any problem in the area of Meema's temperament, at least in public. He was busy trying to look inside the Katsuyama code, to improve it to take account of the new conditions, but although he was generally a kind and considerate husband, like so many geeks, once his mind was wrapped up in a computer problem, it seemed impossible for him to take any notice of anything else.

Sharpe felt that it wasn't his place to interfere between man and wife, especially when he regarded them equally as friends, but it was a source of worry to him whenever he noticed Meema's raw finger ends.

Although Sharpe was expecting it, the phone call from Tomiko Katsuyama was still a shock when it arrived at 2 o'clock the day after the funeral.

"So how much money have you made? Jon Campbell told me that you lost it all," in English. Sharpe was somewhat surprised, considering that she had spoken nothing but Japanese to him on his previous meeting, but given that she had lived in California while her husband was researching at Stanford, and possibly before that, when Kim lived in America, perhaps on balance it wasn't that surprising.

"We might be able to pay you back some of the money that your father gave us." Sharpe was as evasive as he could be.

"But I understand you haven't made the profits my father wanted and was expecting you to make?"

"No, of course not."

"What do you mean, 'of course'?" The tone seemed icy cold. It was hard for him to reconcile the voice, which seemed to come from the depths of an icy heart, with the gorgeous appearance of the speaker as he had seen her last.

"I take it you've been following the financial news?" Sharpe let any warmth drain from his voice. The temperature of the telephone lines carrying the conversation was now approximately zero.

"Well, I know something's happening."

"Let me explain it as simply as I can. All the markets are in chaos. There's no knowing from one minute to the next what's happening. No-one knows what on earth is going on, and there is no way we can make any money using your husband's ideas."

"Well, my father gave you that money for you to make money for him, to help him with his political aims. And that was several days ago. Now I want the money you've made from the money he gave you – loaned you." Her sentences were becoming shorter, and Sharpe could hear her breathing at the other end of the line. "I want it. Now."

"Are you all right?" Despite being annoyed by this conversation, Sharpe was concerned.

"I'm fine. Thanks for asking. Now where's the money?" Her voice sounded even more jerky and staccato.

"I've explained to you that we can't give you back the original money just now. Or rather it would be in no-one's interests right now." Sharpe tried to cover himself. "There's just no way we can give you back any more, because we really don't have it."

"We need it. All of the money you promised to my father. Now."

Sharpe sighed to himself, but noticed the "we" that Tomiko had just used. Something slightly odd seemed to be going on at the other end. He was certain that she hadn't sounded asthmatic or had any difficulty breathing when she had come round that evening.

"Look, I've explained to you that this is really impossible. The markets—"

She cut him off. "Do what my father wanted. Or else." The line went dead, and Sharpe was left stupidly holding his phone and swearing under his breath. He was just beginning to repeat himself when Mieko walked in.

"What's wrong?"

"That stupid Tomiko. She has absolutely no idea of how things work. She thinks her husband's invention is just going to make money for her magically. She doesn't understand what's what."

"Well, you can explain that."

Sharpe sighed. "I just did that, and I think that even Jon, God rot him, did the same. She wants all the money we promised Kim."

"Not just the money that he gave us? All the money that we were going to make for him?" Sharpe nodded. "Ouch. We don't have that money. We don't even have the money he gave us." Another nod and a groan from Sharpe. "And she's taken over as boss of a group of gangsters?" Sharpe nodded yet again.

"But," he pointed out, "although she is boss in name, she might need the money to keep the position and become a real boss with genuine power."

"All of the money?" asked Mieko. "I've never run a gang," (Sharpe couldn't help smiling at this – he found it hard to imagine anyone less likely than Mieko to be running a yakuza gang) "but I don't think you'd need all that money to do it."

"You're probably right. But whatever, I don't fancy the idea of a pissed-off gang boss who can't pay her gang members coming after me. Some of those guys are heavy." He closed his eyes and thought of Al Kowalski's head in the locker in Tokyo Station. He shuddered.

"What's the matter?" asked Mieko. "Ghost walked over your grave?"

"Don't say things like that," replied Sharpe, horrified, despite himself. Time to change the subject. "Any news from Vishal about getting the system working again?"

"No. Last time I saw him he wasn't talking to anyone. Just the computer, and it wasn't really a conversation. More like a stream of abuse."

Damn. Even if Tomiko held a knife to his throat (or worse), there was going to be no way he could meet her demands.

Sharpe walked out of the room, leaving Mieko doing something with cleaning rags and detergent that he didn't want to get involved with. He looked at his watch. Half-past five. Time to be setting off for home.

He called back to Mieko. "Do you really want to be starting that job now?"

"Yes, I do. If I don't do it now, there's no way to get the dirt off tomorrow."

What dirt? Sharpe thought to himself. He peeked in at Vishal, who appeared to be busy mumbling to his computer. "Vishal?"

"Piss off," without even bothering to look away from the screen.

Please yourself, thought Sharpe, a little offended. Aloud, "Well, don't work too hard."

A nod in reply.

He called back to Mieko. "All right, then. I'm going home. What do you want me to buy for supper?"

"It's all in the freezer. We can just pop it in the micro-wave when I get back. Won't take me more than a couple of hours to get this place clean."

Damn place looked fine, thought Sharpe to himself. No way was there a couple of hours' work there. He put on his coat, and was just opening the front door when he heard Meema behind him.

"Nothing for me to do, either," she said. "Come on, Ken-chan, let's go together. Wait while I get my coat on and fix my face."

SHARPE WAITED AS SHE SLIPPED INTO THE BATHROOM. After all, he told himself, he didn't have anything better to do with his time. Meema appeared. It did look as though she had done something to her face. She certainly looked a little different, anyway. Sharpe was still a bit vague about exactly how women titivated themselves for men, and how the whole thing managed to have an effect on the opposite sex, but in Meema's case, he decided it was something she'd done to her eyes. They looked bigger and darker than usual.

They walked down the street towards the station, and Meema looked at her watch. "There's time," she said.

"Time for what?" asked Sharpe. He didn't really want a detour. He felt drained by everything that had happened lately, and he wanted nothing so much as to get home, pour himself a very large gin and tonic, or something along those lines, and drink it.

"Time for a drink," said Meema, as if reading his mind. "We – Vishal and I – noticed this bar opposite the station the other day. Looked like a nice place from the outside." She led the way to an ornate door with brass fittings, set in a fake brick wall. The single window beside the door was lace-curtained, but it seemed that behind the lace curtains was a wall, stopping any view of what was inside. A small discreet sign just above the window said "Happy Times" in katakana. Sharpe couldn't see what had attracted her to the place.

Sharpe tried the door, but it was locked. "Not open yet," he said.

"No, you have to call," said Meema, fishing her phone from her bag and pressing the keypad. She turned away from Sharpe and started mumbling something in Japanese. As she put the phone back in her bag, the door opened.

"Welcome. Come in," said a female voice in Japanese from the dark interior.

Sharpe and Meema entered, and the door closed behind them. Sharpe heard the click of the lock after it had shut. The interior really was pretty dark, Sharpe thought to himself. Not just the contrast with the outside. At first, he could just make out the shape of a kimono-clad figure leading the way, but as his eyes adjusted, he could make out a little more detail. A woman in her early thirties, if the back view was anything to go by (mind you, it often wasn't). From the little that Sharpe could make out through the gloom, they appeared to be the only customers.

When they were seated in a corner booth, Meema echoed Sharpe's order for a gin and tonic, much to his surprise.

"Are you sure you should be drinking, in your condition?" he asked, a little worried. "And I've never seen you drinking G&T before."

"First time for everything," replied Meema. "In any case, I'm only going to try a bit. If I like it, that's the only one I'm going to drink all evening. Promise. And if I don't, I'll give it to you, so it won't be wasted." She leaned forward, and Sharpe noticed that the top of her dress seemed to have come unbuttoned a little. Almost automatically, he looked while trying not to appear that he was doing so, and realised he was once again staring at what appeared to be Meema's bra-less breasts. With a shock, he looked at Meema's face, and saw that she had noticed the direction of his look. He withdrew his gaze in panic.

The drinks arrived. Sharpe grabbed his and put it to his face to try to cover his confusion. A little less sweet than the usual Japanese apology for gin and tonic, and a good deal less toxic than the one he remembered drinking with Jon in the hideous parody of an English pub.

He put his glass down and watched as Meema sipped and winced slightly. "Not too bad," she proclaimed after swallowing the first sip. "I can see why you like it, I think."

"You're not drinking a lot, I hope?" asked Sharpe, a little worried. He had heard that pregnant women shouldn't drink alcohol, but he really didn't know much about these things. Babies had never been a part of his life.

"No, hardly anything," she replied. "Anyway, the baby seems to like it. Feel."

Without warning, she grabbed his hand and guided it through a gap in her dress, where it rested on her bare belly. He could feel her navel, which seemed to be protruding slightly, but couldn't make out any movement inside.

"Feel anything?"

"No, not really."

"Maybe a bit lower down?" She moved his hand to well below the equator of her bulge. He could feel coarse hair. "Or lower still?" moving his hand again. She didn't seem to be wearing any panties, and his fingers were now being pressed hard against her.

"Meema?" he asked, dry-throated. "Why on earth aren't you wearing anything down there?" It was the first thing that came to his mind. He wasn't sure what to say or to do in this situation, which seemed to be going further and faster than the previous occasion when she had made a move in his direction. He tried to move his hand away, but Meema had it grasped in a frighteningly tight grip, and he was worried that he would hurt her or the baby, or tear her clothes if he tried to break away, none of which was an alternative he wanted.

"Uh-huh," was all the answer he received. She was now pressing his hand hard against her crotch and moving her body against it with increasing speed and pressure. He could hear her rapid breathing, and feel her becoming wet, but in this semi-public place (he looked around anxiously, even though they had seemed to be alone in the place when they came in, and noticed with relief that even if there was someone else in the bar, he and Meema couldn't be seen by anyone else unless they actually came to that corner) he didn't find the situation at all erotic. "Kiss me, Ken-chan," she whispered hoarsely. Her body ground against his hand which she continued to press firmly against herself as her body moved rhythmically. He pecked her on the cheek. "No, properly. Come on," she replied, using her other hand to grab the back of his neck and press his face against hers.

He responded, but his heart wasn't in it at all. He felt as though he was taking part in a bad porn movie. "Ouch – shit!" he exclaimed as she bit his tongue hard and released his hand under her dress. "What the hell?" as he removed his hand hurriedly from inside her clothes.

She didn't answer, but sat there silently weeping. "Look in my bag," she sniffled at length. "There should be a pack of tissues there."

He opened her bag, and sure enough, there were the tissues, and beside them was a pair of panties which looked as though they'd been worn earlier that day. He handed her the tissues, and she blew her nose and wiped her eyes.

"So silly," she said. "Sorry. Did I hurt you? Sorry. I had to stop us both before I did something completely stupid. I was completely out of control, wasn't I?"

There seemed to be no answer to that, so he made none. They sat in silence for a while.

"What are you going to say?" she asked him.

This was one which seemed to demand an answer. "Who to?"

"Vishal? Mieko? Anyone?" She sniffed again.

"Why would I say anything to anyone? Unless you want me to?"

"I've behaved terribly." She turned her face away from him. "Why did I do this? What was I doing, anyway? Don't tell anyone."

Sharpe would have liked to know the answer to that question himself. "I'm not going to tell anyone," he replied. "But I think you should," he added.

She turned quickly to face him. "Why? What do you mean by that?"

Picking his words carefully. "Something's very strange about you right now, Meema. What happened just now isn't like the Meema I've come to know and respect. And this wasn't a sudden impulse, for sure."

"Why do you say that?" suspiciously. "But you're right. That wasn't the Meema you know. It's as if there are two people here – well, there are because I'm pregnant, but that's not what I mean – but a good angel and a bad angel fighting, if you want to put it in religious or mystical words. Except that the bad angel isn't really a part of me, but it's started taking over sometimes, like just now, and I have to stop things happening. Is this all rubbish that I'm talking?"

"No, not at all. It just means you're human. But I agree it's a bit worrying that you feel this way, and give in to these things."

"Why did you say that this wasn't a sudden impulse?" she asked again.

"Because I saw what was in your bag when I gave you the

tissues. I'm going to bet that you took those off just before you came out with me, when you were doing your face." She nodded. "I'm not going to ask you why. It's nothing to do with my overpowering and irresistible sexual allure, is it?"

Despite herself, Meema smiled. "No. Of course I like you, but there's never really been any thought about – I mean, any serious thoughts..." She trailed off, obviously embarrassed.

"Don't worry. I think everyone wonders from time to time what it would be like if they ... I mean, with their good friends, if ..." He, too, trailed off.

"Would you mind turning away?" asked Meema. "I want to put those panties back on again. I know it seems ridiculous to ask you not to look after what's just happened, but I'd feel happier."

"Tell me when it's safe to look," replied Sharpe, obediently turning his head away.

"All right," she said, after a short time. He turned back. "You know, that feels better. I've heard of women who never wear any underwear, and they think it's erotic. Me, I found it rather disgusting as soon as I walked outside, and I felt naked. I suppose Mieko always wears bra and panties?"

"I suppose so," he replied. "At least when she's dressed. And she always wears panties in bed. Most Japanese girls do, it seems. Except when ..." He reached for the drink, surprised that it was still there. He'd forgotten about it.

Meema reached for her drink, but put it down untasted. "What did you mean when you said I should talk to someone about it?"

"Exactly what I said. I don't mean a doctor or anyone like that, unless you want to. But couldn't you talk to Mieko about it?"

She shook her head. "I'm not going to do that. I'd have to explain what happened."

"Shall I explain what happened, and you can then explain why it happened? I'm lousy at keeping this sort of thing a secret, anyway. I have a guilty face or something, and it's bound to come out sooner or later, I'm afraid."

"But nothing really happened!" protested Meema.

"Exactly what I am going to say. If you want me to break the ice with Mieko, I will say exactly what's just happened, and say you want to talk to her about it, because you're worried about what's going on."

"I am worried, that's right. I mean, nothing like this has happened before."

"Except when you were showing me the new computer system before we started," Sharpe pointed out.

"Oh yes." Meema's face fell. "I'd completely pushed that to the back of my mind, what with all the other things that have been happening."

"Maybe you do have an overpowering crush on me, after all?" Sharpe laughed, hoping she would understand he wasn't serious.

"I don't think so. I really don't know what came over me then. Or just today. I suppose I was feeling sort of sorry for myself and ..." She trailed off again.

"I don't think I'm the right person to talk to about this, Meema. Talk to Mieko tomorrow."

"You're sweet, Ken-chan. Here I am, dragging you into this place—"

"What sort of place is this, anyway?"

"It's a place where people come to do the sort of thing I thought I wanted to do. Look, none of the booths can see into any of the other booths, and the staff never come to your table unless you ring the bell, so you're completely private."

"And you and Vishal came here?"

"No. I read about these places in a magazine and found

there was one close to here. This one. Anyway, as I said, you're sweet." She leaned over and kissed him on the cheek. It was far from the ravenous assault she had made earlier, and Sharpe returned the favour. There was hardly anything erotic in the gesture.

"You know, that felt almost … sisterly is the word I think I'm looking for," he said.

"Good, because that's how I think I feel towards you now. Now, when you've finished your drink, perhaps you wouldn't mind walking back home with me?"

"I'm not going to finish it," Sharpe decided.

"Fine." They got up, and Sharpe helped Meema on with her coat, careful to avoid touching her as he did so. "I'm paying. I chose this place, and I don't want you to feel responsible," she told him. The side of Meema that Vishal had once described as "steel wrapped in velvet" made an appearance. Sharpe wasn't going to argue.

The train journey and walk back together to Meema's flat took place almost completely wordlessly in a companionable silence.

As he left her at the door, and walked back home from her flat, Sharpe's thoughts kept turning to what would have happened if he hadn't resisted, and he had gone along with Meema's desires of the moment. One thing was certain – it would have made the conversation he was about to have with Mieko much more difficult.

Chapter 14: Tokyo

THE NEXT MORNING, AS THEY WERE EATING BREAKFAST TOGETHER, Sharpe and Mieko discussed the morning's campaign.

The previous night, Sharpe had explained the evening's happenings to Mieko, who had sat there incredulous as he unfolded his account of the incidents in the bar. Although he had tried to avoid giving the lurid details, she had forced him to spill every last one of the beans. Both of them had felt uncomfortable going to bed that evening and had been scrupulously careful to avoid touching each other unnecessarily. Any kind of sex had been completely out of the question, by unspoken mutual agreement.

"I think you should avoid going into the office this morning," suggested Mieko. "I think your presence there would only embarrass her. And if you can find a good reason to get Vishal out of the office, too, she and I can have a nice little all-girls-together chat, and I can find out what's eating her."

"Seems sensible. How on earth I get Vishal's nose out of that computer screen is beyond me, though."

"Call him and tell him you want advice on a new computer system or something."

"Not sure that would work. We're doing quite well with the one we have right now."

"Oh, come on. You can think of something. Just stay here so he's got to go out of the office and meet you."

She drank the last of her coffee and started to get ready to go out. "Wait about an hour before you call Vishal. And don't brood," she added.

Sharpe started. He wasn't aware that he had been brooding. "Was I?"

"Yes, you look incredibly worried and guilty. And there's no need to be. It sounded as though you behaved much better than anyone could have expected. You haven't hurt me, or Vishal or Meema."

"Only me who got hurt, right?"

"Stop it!" She kissed the top of his head as she passed him. "You have nothing to worry about or to blame yourself for."

He remembered what he had heard of Mieko's ex-husband, which made him feel somewhat virtuous by comparison, and kissed Mieko goodbye as she left. He settled down to doing some maintenance work on his computer, updating the operating system, putting in what seemed like endless patches to counteract hackers and viruses, until he felt it would be a good time to call Vishal.

"Hi there. Look, I'm stuck on one of these updates and I need your help. Can you come round and give me a hand?" Actually, this was basically true. He'd reached a point where he didn't feel safe going on with the update. There was an error message that he almost but didn't quite understand.

"Can you be giving me a bit more time, man? I think I've nearly got this working again." Vishal had "nearly got this working again" several times a day for a week since the Lehman's crash. Sharpe wasn't feeling bitchy enough to remind him of this.

"Oh, come on. You'll come to it with a fresh mind after doing something different. I really do need you here, and even when you do get it working, we're not going to start trading today."

At length, Vishal reluctantly agreed. "As long as you make sure I get lunch," he stipulated. "Meema didn't pack me up a tiffin this morning like she usually is doing. I am not being sure why that is."

Sharpe agreed to the bargain, and settled down to await Vishal, happy that he'd done his part to smooth over Meema's troubled waters. Unlike Vishal, however, he had a fairly good idea of why Meema hadn't made Vishal's lunch this morning.

When Vishal arrived, he immediately made a beeline for Sharpe's computer. "Oh, come on, Kenneth, this shouldn't be causing you any problems. This is pretty straightforward."

"Not to me, it's not. Maybe to a genius like you it's all plain and simple, but not to me."

Vishal sat down at the computer wordlessly. The mouse clicked, the keyboard clacked, the router lights flashed as the updates were downloaded from the Internet, and Vishal leaned back.

"A few minutes to load and then you're being done," he grinned. "How do you think Meema's looking these days? Pretty damn fine, eh?" still grinning.

Sharpe was taken aback, but tried not to show it. "I ... I hadn't really noticed," he said.

Vishal had his eyes closed, with a smile on his face. "I'm looking forward to being a father, I must say," he burbled to the ceiling.

WHILE HE WAS WONDERING WHAT ANSWER he was going to make to this, Sharpe was saved by his mobile phone going off.

"Yes?"

"Surprise, surprise. Jon here," came the unwelcome voice from the other end.

"I thought I'd changed my phone number," complained Sharpe.

"You did. And then you registered it with the embassy, you daft prat."

Damn! Yes, he had registered his details with the embassy in case of an earthquake or any other disaster.

"I thought those details were meant to be confidential?"

"Confidential, schmonfidential," scoffed Jon.

"So what do you want?"

"A few million dollars," came the answer.

Sharpe put the call on speakerphone and laid the phone down on the table, signalling to Vishal to keep quiet. "It's Jon from the British Embassy," he typed on the computer screen. Vishal's eyes went wide.

"And what makes you think I have that sort of money? A few million dollars?" he said to the phone.

"Come on, you had it. Have you lost it all?" came the reply. Vishal's bushy eyebrows went nearly to the back of his head, but Sharpe held up a finger, warning him to be quiet.

"And just how many million dollars are we talking about?"

"Whatever old man Kim was asking for. About fifty, sixty. Whatever it was." It sounded as though Jon was enjoying himself.

"Didn't I tell you we don't have that sort of money? Didn't Tomiko tell you that I told her? What's up with you people? Don't you understand what's going on?"

"She did. She also mentioned that you could make it in a day or so with the aid of her husband's magic box."

"Did she also mention that I told her that was a load of crap? The markets have turned to shit since Katsuyama had his flash of genius. Or hasn't that little thing sunk in yet?"

"I thought you had an Indian genius working with you who can fix anything." Vishal grinned, and then frowned.

"Well, he may be a genius, but since you know so much about these things, you probably know that your friend Tomiko's husband was a super-genius."

"Why are you using the past tense there?"

"Let me answer that question with a question about a question," retorted Sharpe. "Why do you feel that the past tense is not appropriate here?"

"Too deep for me to answer right now," said Jon. "So your answer to me, and to her, is that you don't have the money, right?"

"That's correct. We don't have that sort of money available to us. Nor will we have it available to us in the near future, it appears. Nor will we be in any position to change the situation. Clear enough for you?"

"I suggest you get your arse over to Vietnam pretty quickly," Jon answered. "I think you and your Indian friend are out of your depth here. And I don't just mean in technical matters. If you don't realise the full implications, you have a newly established, rather temperamental and somewhat edgy gang boss looking for money from you and your lot. And if she doesn't get it, I can imagine that she's going to be somewhat less than amused by the situation."

"I think you're putting it a bit strongly."

"I think I'm exercising a remarkable degree of understatement, quite frankly," replied Jon.

Sharpe thought for a bit. "Why should I go over to Vietnam?" he asked, hoping he sounded innocent.

Chapter 14: Tokyo

"For the same reason that you went before. Don't try and come all ignorant and baby-faced about this. I know a damn sight more about things than you realise. Probably more than you do, come to that. I have special, intimate knowledge." Sharpe could almost hear Jon leering as he emphasised the second adjective in the last sentence.

"There seem to be wheels within wheels," Sharpe agreed.

"You'll never know, boy," Jon told him.

"What's your share in all this?" asked Sharpe.

"I think that's my business, don't you?"

"And Tim Barclay? Is he in on this?"

There was a bitter laugh from the mobile phone's speaker. "Oh, he's history. There's no way he's going to be around here for much longer. Has he been bugging you, then?"

"Actually, I thought his future wasn't as black as you painted it. This might just be one of those rare occasions where my guess is a little more accurate than yours."

"Seems like we've both got ideas on this, doesn't it? We'll see who's right, won't we? I strongly advise you to get yourself to Hanoi as soon as possible, though. Having secrets isn't going to repair the Katsuyama gadget, is it? And time's a-wasting." The line abruptly went dead. Sharpe waited for Jon to call back, but the phone remained obstinately silent.

"I think you've got some things to explain," said Vishal. "Why the hell are you having to go to Hanoi?"

"That's where Katsuyama is hiding out."

"And what is this man from the embassy doing?"

Sharpe brought him up to speed on the relationships between Jon and Barclay, and Jon and the Kims, as he understood the situation.

"Kenneth, I have always been trusting you, even when you brought us in on the plot to take over North Korea. But this is being too much. I cannot be working with a hole-and-corner operation like the one you are running with us.

This is not being fair to me, and not being fair to Meema and not being fair to our baby." He stood up and it looked as though he was going to walk out, but Sharpe held up a hand.

"Vishal, please don't go until you've heard me out," he pleaded.

"Look, I am not wanting to work with all these secret spy chaps. Next you will be telling me that the CIA is involved in all this business."

"Closer than you think, Vishal." Sharpe told Vishal about Al Kowalski, and the raid that had been made on his flat.

"So that's what all that was about?" said Vishal. "So how are you knowing you are safe now? I feel that this is being a highly dangerous situation for us all, not just for you. And what about Mieko? Is she safe?"

Sharpe told him the story of his grisly find in the coin locker at Tokyo station. Vishal made a face. "If I didn't know you better, Kenneth, I would say you are an out-and-out lying bastard," he said. "Things like that just aren't happening in Tokyo. Maybe back home in India such terrible things might happen to the wrong sort of person, but to someone like you? You're not just making stories?" examining Sharpe's face. "No, I see you are not. And I know you too well to imagine that you might ever be that sort of person who makes stories like that."

"Want more?" asked Sharpe, and proceeded to recount his encounter with Kermit from the American Embassy.

"This is getting to be really serious," said Vishal. "I am not liking any of this at all. Why are you not telling this to Meema and me before? And have you been telling Mieko about all these things?"

"Because I felt all of this really was something you two and Mieko shouldn't be bothered with," replied Sharpe. It was at least half the truth. "Look, you're not happy about this at all, and I don't blame you at all for that. I really thought I could sort it out by myself without involving you."

"For now, I think you should be talking to Mieko, but I

don't want Meema to be knowing any of this, do you understand? She seems to have been acting a little strange recently, and I am not wanting her to be upset any more."

So you have noticed something? Sharpe thought to himself. I wonder just how much she's said to Vishal? He forced himself to try to look Vishal in the eye, but Vishal was looking the other way.

"All right," he said.

"Now I must be going back," said Vishal.

"I thought you were going to be staying for lunch?"

"I was, but I've just been thinking of something else that I could be trying to make the system work again." Sharpe wasn't going to call him on the lie.

"Sure?"

"I am being perfectly sure, thank you. No offence to your cooking, you understand? But I would really like to be fixing this problem before you have to go off to Hanoi and ask for help."

Sharpe let him go. Damn! He wasn't sure how closely Vishal would stick by him in the future if push came to shove. It was obvious that the revelations of severed heads and Korean gangsters beating up American embassy officials had shaken him badly.

A FEW MINUTES AFTER VISHAL HAD LEFT, Mieko called from her mobile phone.

"Well," she reported, letting out a long breath as she did so. "I think I did it. Is Vishal still with you?"

"No, he's gone."

"OK, come and meet me at the Italian place by the station."

Sharpe switched on the answering machine, got his coat,

At the Sharpe End

and made his way to the station. Mieko was waiting, a half-eaten plate of Caesar salad in front of her.

"Sorry to have started. All that talking has made me hungry."

Sharpe didn't really see how a few lettuce leaves and breadcrumbs could stave off the pangs of hunger, but he let it ride.

"So what have you discovered?"

"Meema's cracking up." Mieko put down her fork and looked at Sharpe, waiting for him to respond.

"I knew that, and so did you. Why?"

"Ah, that's the question." She picked up her fork and guided another mouthful of salad to her mouth. When this had been disposed of, she continued. "How long did you say the forex traders lasted at the banks?"

"A couple of years, I suppose. Then they burn out."

"And how old are they?"

"Early twenties, most of them. The pressure's too much for the older guys a lot of the time. Oh," as the thought hit him. "I see. She's a bit older than that, isn't she, and doing the same job?"

Mieko nodded. A waiter appeared, and Sharpe put in his order. The waiter took away the menu.

"It gets worse," she said. "What happens if a trader has a bad week? Makes a loss on the trading?"

"Well, the bank carries them, usually. It doesn't affect them too badly. They might not get so big a bonus at the end of the year, but that's about it."

"And what would happen if Meema didn't make money?"

"She did make money, though. She's surely not worried that this current chaos is making it impossible for her to trade?"

"It's a comedown after the success of the first few weeks."

Sharpe didn't see what she was driving at.

"Look, let me explain to you. We have a highly intelligent young lady, whose life has been spent making sure that half of the world – men, that is – know that she is at least as bright and capable as they are."

"And ...?"

"She did it. But it was a tremendous strain for her while she was doing it, and then she realises that she's pregnant and ... Oh, you're just a man. How can you be expected to understand?"

Sharpe looked sheepish.

"Oh, I didn't mean it. Well, perhaps I did. Basically, Meema is exhausted. Mentally, emotionally, physically. And now she feels completely useless. Except for being a baby machine."

"Look, you know me, Mieko. And you know Vishal. Neither of us would ever think of her that way."

"I know that, and so does Meema. But she's not rational right now."

"Tell me." The waiter brought Sharpe's pasta, and he took a fork and started eating without noticing what he was putting into his mouth. "Well, do you have some sort of solution?" He stopped suddenly. "What is this?" looking suspiciously at his plate. "Did I really order this?" pointing to the cold spaghetti garnished with dried seaweed and cod roe and drenched in vinaigrette dressing.

Mieko examined the bill on their table. "They think you did. Better eat it or let me have it." Sharpe pushed the plate over to her and repeated his first question while signalling to the waiter to bring the menu again. This time he got the waiter to repeat his order for carbonara back to him.

"So what is your solution?"

"Pack up and stop the operation. At least take Meema away from what she sees as the firing line."

"There are problems." Sharpe explained them, for the second time in a very short period.

Mieko started to bite her lower lip, always a sign that she was deep in thought. Sharpe started to speak, but she held up her hand. "Just let me think." He knew better than to interrupt. Typically Mieko just got on and did things, but sometimes she went into thought mode. The wait was usually worth it, even if it was irritating at times. He fiddled with a toothpick and drank half his water, crunching the ice cubes with his teeth.

"Don't do that," she said. "It irritates me."

In the middle of the enforced silence, his spaghetti arrived. He showered it with Parmesan cheese and started to eat.

"There isn't an easy answer, is there?" said Mieko, breaking the silence. "The first thing is that Meema and her baby must go away. Send them to India along with the money for Vishal's sister's operation and she can help arrange things at that end. That's the obvious easy part dealt with."

"Obvious? Easy?" Sharpe asked through a mouthful of pasta. He thought for a few seconds. "Yes, you're right. No argument from me, and I'm sure that Meema and Vishal will agree."

"The difficult part is how to avoid you being beaten up by Tomiko's gang."

"Or worse." Sharpe forked more pasta.

"Or worse," she agreed. "Then there's Vishal and me, of course. Maybe we'll get off a little easier."

"I don't like this at all," said Sharpe. "Don't you think we'd be better off somewhere else?"

"Like?"

Sharpe considered the problem. "All right, it's going to be nearly impossible for me to find the same sort of work anywhere else except possibly Hong Kong or Singapore."

"And Vishal's not going to be able to work in India in the same way as he works here."

"Oh, I'm not so sure about that. Maybe I could move to Mumbai or Bangalore or something?"

"Well that's not something I would enjoy," putting down her fork and crossing her arms. Sharpe knew her well enough that this signified a position from which she would only budge after a good deal of persuasion.

"It was only an idea. Not a good one, I admit."

"Something tells me you're going to have to go to Hanoi and talk to Katsuyama, don't you think?"

"Damn it, yes." He forked the rest of his spaghetti in silence, brooding. "All right, let's get back home. I'll get hold of Katsuyama and arrange to meet him."

SHARPE FIRST TRIED TO CONTACT KATSUYAMA through Skype, the Internet-based telephony system that had taken the place of conventional international telephones for him. However, there was no sign of anyone in the Skype directory called Masashi Katsuyama, either in roman letters, in either of the kana syllabic alphabets, or in kanji Chinese characters.

He guessed it was probably better to put things in writing, rather than try to explain things over the phone, so he started to write a cryptic e-mail message to the address on Katsuyama's business card before remembering that he had been told that Katsuyama's secretary filtered all e-mail.

It was doubtful whether he was still staying at the Sofitel in Hanoi – the place had certainly looked expensive when Sharpe had been there earlier, and didn't seem the sort of place where you'd dig in for the duration. Still, it was worth a try.

He connected his computer headset and "dialled".

Amazingly, it appeared that Katsuyama was still a customer there (Sharpe hated the term "guest" that hotels use to describe their customers – "guests" typically don't pay to stay with their hosts, he reasoned).

However, Katsuyama was apparently not actually in the hotel at that moment. Sharpe checked his watch. Well, early in the afternoon, he probably wouldn't be, would he? He left a message with the hotel asking Katsuyama to call him back on his new mobile number.

It was later that evening that the call came from Hanoi. Sharpe and Mieko had just finished their meal, and he was ready to start washing the dishes, when his mobile rang.

Sharpe explained the situation, asking for Katsuyama's help.

"There's no way I'm coming back to Japan. I'll meet you in Seoul," Sharpe heard, in the familiar husky voice.

"Where? It's a big city."

"Send me a message at this address when you know where you'll be staying and when you want to meet me. Stay in the hotel and wait for me." Sharpe took down a Google mail address.

"All right. I'll be there in a day or so to explain more. We can pay you well, you know." He heard laughter at the other end.

"I'm sure you can, if you worked out how to use my invention before all this crazy Wall Street shit started to hit the fan. Just make sure my wife doesn't get hold of it."

Sharpe was a little taken aback by this last. Why would Katsuyama want to keep the money from reaching his wife? Obviously their relationship wasn't that close, if they had been living in different countries for a few months, but this seemed to be taking things to some sort of extreme.

"Uh ... I hear you," replied Sharpe. "Maybe we can discuss this when we meet. You do know your father-in-law has died, don't you?" There was a long silence at the other end.

"No, I didn't know that," came the answer. "How? When?"

Sharpe filled in the details, wondering exactly what the relationship was between Katsuyama and his wife if she hadn't even bothered to inform him of the fact that his father-in-law, and principal business backer, had been killed.

"Have they caught the murderer yet?" was Katsuyama's next question, sounding somewhat irrelevant to Sharpe's ears. "Don't bother answering. Silly question. The Japanese police aren't going to waste time looking for the killer of a small-time gangster. See you in Seoul." And the line went dead.

"Mieko!" he shouted. "I need a ticket to Seoul tonight or tomorrow morning. Can you do it for me, please?"

"What? Why are you going there?"

"To see Katsuyama and try to get him to work for us to get the thing working again. Just the way we all decided it would be."

"But why Seoul, for God's sake? Why not Hanoi again?"

"Not my choice." Sharpe shrugged. "And I'm not the one calling the shots here."

"All right, if that's the way it's going to be." Soon, Sharpe could hear her on the phone, talking to a travel agent and making a reservation.

"I booked you business class on ANA," she said as she walked into the room a few minutes later. "It seems to me that you deserve to travel comfortably this time round, and we can afford it. Leaving at 9:20 tomorrow morning from Haneda. Arriving in Gimpo at 11:45."

Sharpe breathed a sigh of relief. Although he lived on the same side of Tokyo as the main international airport at Narita, the long train ride to Narita was never one he looked forward to. Haneda was opening up slowly as an alternative international hub, and was much easier for him to reach. "Thanks for that."

"Anyway, all the economy class seats, and all the flights from Narita were booked solid," she added, just as Sharpe was thinking how lucky he was to have Mieko to look after him.

"OK. I'll book myself in at a hotel then, now I know when I'll be arriving." He logged onto the Web site of the Grand Hyatt in Seoul where he had stayed in the past and made a reservation for two nights. He could always extend his stay if necessary, he reasoned. It wasn't that he had any particular liking for the hotel, but it was convenient for the centre of the city, and to his mind was less noisy and more civilised than some of the alternatives which he had used in the past. As soon as the booking was confirmed, he sent off a message to the e-mail address that Katsuyama had given him earlier. He wasn't really surprised when he received a reply within 10 minutes, confirming that Katsuyama would meet him in the hotel lobby the next day at 4PM, and adding the information that the Google e-mail address from which the reply had been sent would now be disabled.

"Looks as though I'll only be away for a night or so," he called to Mieko. I'll just take a couple of clean shirts and socks and things and not bother with any checked bags." He moved to the bedroom and started throwing things into an overnight bag. He'd almost finished when Mieko came in and, as always, removed his efforts at packing and put his things back in the bag for him neatly and tidily.

Chapter 15: Seoul

Sharpe arrived at the hotel and checked into his room, where he spent the time waiting for Katsuyama by lying on the large double bed, and making notes on his laptop for his forthcoming meeting about what needed to be done to the system and how much money could be offered.

The room TV was showing CNN in English, but after seeing the same headlines three times in an hour, and listening to the same vacuous comments, Sharpe turned off the set, and found some irrelevantly pleasant background music.

With Kim, Katsuyama's chief source of funding, now dead, Sharpe's main questions were whether Katsuyama would be prepared to return to Japan and help to get the brokerage back on track, and how much money would be required to persuade him.

There was also the problem, Sharpe mused as he swung his legs off the bed, splashed cold water over his face, and put on his jacket and tie before going downstairs to the hotel lobby to meet Katsuyama, of what someone who was reportedly dead was doing meeting him in Seoul.

He picked a place in the lobby that he hoped was

inconspicuous, but from where he could keep an eye on the main entrance doors and the reception desk so he could meet Katsuyama as soon as he arrived. Although he kept a careful eye on everyone entering and leaving the hotel, he could see no sign of Katsuyama.

He checked his watch. Katsuyama was almost fifteen minutes late – an unforgivable sin in most Japanese people's eyes.

Time to get up and check that Katsuyama wasn't hiding behind a pillar or something. As he reached the reception desk, a hand tapped him on the shoulder, and a familiar voice greeted him.

"Sorry if I made you jump," Katsuyama said to him as his heart-rate slowly returned to something closer to normal. "I prefer to come in through the side door."

Sharpe, who had no idea that there was such a thing as a side door to the hotel, let alone any knowledge of where it was, nodded.

"Do you think they're serving drinks?" Katsuyama asked. "I need one."

They made their way over to a quiet corner of the lounge bar area. Sharpe was quietly amused to notice that both Katsuyama and he automatically took places with their backs to the wall from where they could keep an eye on the comings and goings around them.

"Gin and tonic," Katsuyama ordered in English when the waiter arrived to take their orders. Sharpe followed his lead. When the waiter finally arrived with the drinks and had finished fussing with the coasters and a small bowl of cashews, and Sharpe had signed with his room number, Katsuyama took a pull at his gin and tonic, sighed, and leaned back in his chair.

"Tell me all about my father-in-law," he said.

Sharpe took a breath. "How much do you know already?"

"Nothing, apart from what you told me on the phone yesterday." Sharpe's surprise must have showed on his face, because Katsuyama explained, "I have as little to do with my bitch wife as possible. And the feeling's mutual. I'll tell you why in a bit."

"But even if you don't get on with her, surely someone must have told you something about what happened to him? After all, he was one of your principal backers, wasn't he?"

Katsuyama said nothing, but drained his glass, and set it significantly on the table in front of him. Sharpe signalled to a waiter for a refill. He had a feeling that Katsuyama was already several drinks ahead.

"All right," Sharpe said. "I can tell you what I know about him, which isn't much." He recounted a brief history of his dealings with Kim, and events up to the time of the funeral, and Tomiko's and Jon's demands for money. When he had finished, there was a long silence, broken only by the sound of the ice cubes rattling in Katsuyama's new glass, which was now empty.

"Who do you think killed him?" asked Katsuyama.

"I really have no idea. Members of a rival gang, maybe? The Americans? North Koreans? South Koreans? Martians? I really don't know enough to make any kind of guess worth more than a dart thrown at a dartboard. What's your guess?"

"Right. Too many possibilities," replied Katsuyama. "I wouldn't like to guess, either. I was just wondering if you knew more than I do about all this."

"I doubt it very much. Would the British have anything to do with it? Or the Americans?"

"Maybe the Americans. Why the British? What makes you mention them as possibilities."

"Oh, nothing." Sharpe didn't want to get too deep into this. "It's just that I know a couple of guys from the embassy who seem to monitor technical developments."

"One of them being this Jon Campbell you mentioned just now, and the other being his boss, who I have yet to have the pleasure of knowing the name?"

"Yes, that's right," said Sharpe, a little surprised. "Do you know Jon?"

"I know Jon Campbell only too well," said Katsuyama. "The bastard was in America not so long back, snooping round my lab, accidentally bumping into my graduate research assistants in bars and asking them questions about my work, that sort of thing."

"Yes, he told me he'd been in Silicon Valley. How well did you actually know him there?"

"Not nearly as well as my wife did, I can tell you that. She got to know him real close up and personal." Katsuyama grimaced. "You may have noticed that she's somewhat attractive? Have you fucked her yet?" Sharpe shook his head, appalled at the question. "Then you're probably one of the first men under 70 years old that she hasn't tried to get into bed with her." He looked at Sharpe critically. "Not that there's a lot of temptation for her to resist, I would guess." This time it was Katsuyama's turn to signal the waiter. Sharpe ordered a tonic water, without the gin. "Jon Campbell was always hanging round the Stanford campus, dropping heavy hints to anyone who would listen about how he wasn't James Bond or anything like that. So of course, all the women thought that he was, just because he said he wasn't. And my dear lovely bitch wife was one of them."

"So that's where he found out about the trading function of your technology?"

Katsuyama shrugged. "I would be somewhat surprised if he didn't get the idea from there. My graduate students only helped with some of the multicore and DSP scheduling algorithms. They thought that they were working on the image pattern recognition. Actually, that side of it works pretty well, but it was only intended as cover. Shame that it never hit the market. Of course, Jon being the kind of person he is, he might have got the skinny from anywhere."

They sat in silence for a while. "Why aren't you dead?" asked Sharpe. "No, you know what I mean. That's how I came into contact with your father-in-law, after all. He thought I was conspiring with the police to hide things. He thought that you'd been kidnapped by the authorities and that I was part of the cover-up. It seemed rather loony thinking to me, but that's what he told me."

"Ah yes, my father-in-law." Katsuyama sat staring in front of him. Sharpe had the feeling he had gone to sleep with his eyes open when he suddenly came out with, "What a fool. What a naïve and stupid fool to believe that he could buy his way into Pyongyang."

"Why couldn't he?" asked Sharpe, innocently. "From what I understood, he had quite a reasonable plan worked out."

Katsuyama laughed bitterly. "And I suppose he told you that he didn't want to be any part of a new government?" Sharpe nodded agreement. "I don't suppose he bothered mentioning to you that his family had played an important role in the original Kim Il-sung regime? And they got out while they could before being liquidated as enemies of the people?" This time Sharpe shook his head. "He never wanted justice or anything of the kind for the North Korean people. He wanted to get back into the country to recover the loot his family had stolen years before."

"What was going to be your share of all of this?" Sharpe couldn't help asking. This new twist on things was intriguing.

"I'd been promised enough money to keep the company

going and to expand it almost as much as I wanted. After all, that's a lot of money. And I could have done so much with it. Katsuyama Electronic Devices could have become a world leader in pattern recognition, and made the money back tens or hundreds of times over."

"What's your problem with that?"

"But that was almost certainly just a promise. I was pretty sure that I wouldn't live to see any of the money. I'd suffer an unfortunate accident just as Kim got the money he was after. I knew him and his daughter all too well. And so I decided it was time to get the hell out of Dodge. We had the factory in Hanoi, and it's easy enough to get yourself some decent protection there fairly cheaply. You probably didn't notice when you met me in Hanoi, but there were five armed guards surrounding us. The Vietnamese are good at that sort of thing." Sharpe looked around a little nervously. "Four today. One behind that pillar, and the other three at that table over there ..." Sharpe looked. He'd taken them for Korean businessmen.

"OK," Sharpe said. "I can see why you would want to skip town, given the circumstances. But why that way, and why the hell did you have to drag me into it?"

Katsuyama called for another drink – his fourth or fifth. Sharpe wasn't counting. His breathing seemed a little more forced, and his face was slightly flushed, but he didn't seem too drunk.

"I wanted them to believe I was dead. Didn't matter too much if it was suicide or what."

"But they were called in to identify your body. Kim and your wife, I mean. And not your body, of course."

"That wasn't meant to happen. The whole point of leaving your card in the jacket was that you'd be the one called to identify the body, and I did take the trouble to find someone who looked something like me. I didn't think that you'd remember me well enough to be able to say for sure it wasn't me. I really don't know how they bypassed you and went straight to Kim."

"Actually, they didn't bypass me completely. I was interviewed by some officials. Maybe there was something else in your pockets to identify you and that led them to your wife and her father?"

"I'm pretty sure there wasn't."

Sharpe thought for a moment. "Who are we talking about, anyway? The body wearing your clothes?"

"I don't know his name. He wore my clothes, I wore his."

"Why? What?" Sharpe shook his head in bewilderment.

"It's amazing what a hundred thousand yen will do. I told him I was being followed by my wife's private detective who suspected me of an affair." Mirthless laughter. "He thought it was funny. So do I, given my wife's habits. We changed in the toilets at the station."

"And where was all his ID? I assume you both hung onto your own wallets, and so on."

"I lifted it from his pocket along with the money I'd given him as we went down the escalator to the platform together. One of my minor talents."

Sharpe knew the answer already by now, but he had to ask the question.

"He never felt a thing," replied Katsuyama. "It was a crowded platform. It could easily have been an accident. It just so happened that it wasn't." He seemed totally unconcerned by the admission.

This wasn't a topic Sharpe wanted to pursue at any length. He felt more than slightly uneasy about talking to a self-confessed murderer. He changed the subject.

"When you met me the first time, you told me that you were being chased by the CIA and NSA. Was that a complete load of crap?"

Katsuyama smiled, but again without any warmth in it. "Not completely. They knew of the image-recognition work, and they were interested. Not as much as I led you to believe, perhaps, but they did make me several very serious offers. They didn't know anything at all about the financial side, of course. The main thing is that I wanted to get the thing off my hands to someone they would never dream of suspecting or following round."

"And then you went and planted my card in that poor bastard's pocket?" Sharpe asked. "That doesn't sound very smart. Leading the police straight to me."

"Best I could do at the time. Thought the police would have to keep an eye on you. That was other thing. Keep Kim and bitch away from you." The repeated gin and tonics were now starting to have a marked effect on him. His speech was slurring and his eyes were closed. His body was swaying from side to side, and each time he tipped to right or left, there seemed to be an even chance whether he would be able to right himself, but somehow he was still managing to keep his balance. There was no point, Sharpe reasoned, in trying to talk to him about putting the trading system to rights again. Even if he'd been capable of coherent speech, there was no way that Sharpe reckoned he could persuade Katsuyama into improving the system to meet current market conditions. In fact, given what he'd just been told about the ultimate destination of the money, Sharpe wasn't sure he wanted anything at all to do with Katsuyama or anyone connected with him ever again.

"Why did you want me to come to Seoul?"

Katsuyama didn't seem to notice the question, so Sharpe repeated it.

"Needed a change. Needed to buy some things," he mumbled with his eyes closed. He pitched forward, and Sharpe put his hand out to stop Katsuyama's head from crashing onto the table. As he slowly returned Katsuyama's body to an upright seated position, he was uncomfortably aware of the Vietnamese minders crowding round the back of his chair. While he was sure that they wouldn't try any violence in a public place like the hotel lobby, he felt the need to reassure them of his innocence.

"He'd had too much to drink. You were watching him and me. These were gin and tonics. I didn't make him drink them. They were his choice." The four men, compact and lithe in their dark suits, just stared at him. "Look, do you guys understand what I am saying? Do you speak English?" He tried repeating his words in Japanese. The same silence in reply. "Look, I don't speak Vietnamese at all."

"It's OK, man," said one of Katsuyama's guards in American English. "The boss gets this way quite often. Don't you worry yourself about him. We'll get him back where he needs to be."

Relief flooded over Sharpe as he realised he wasn't going to get the living daylights beaten out of him for something that wasn't his fault.

"You stay at this hotel for one more night," said the Vietnamese, holding up a single finger to show the number of nights Sharpe should stay. Or it might have been an insult. "Maybe boss will want to talk to you tomorrow. He'll surely telephone you before 2 tomorrow afternoon. So you stay here till then. If not, then go back to where you come from. Have a nice day." He bowed slightly. The bow was echoed by the other three, who picked up Katsuyama's slumped body, and guided him to the exit, watched by several concerned waiters and hotel staff.

A **WAITER CAME UP TO SHARPE.** "Is your friend all right?" he asked, with some concern. "Are those men his friends?"

"Definitely his friends," Sharpe answered. "And he's just had too much to drink, that's all."

The waiter shrugged, and handed Sharpe the bill to sign. Eight gin and tonics, he saw, six of which had been Katsuyama's. And doubles at least. No wonder he was out cold. He signed and handed the bill back to the waiter.

"Your billfold, sir," pointing to a brown leather wallet on one of the chairs.

"Not mine." It was Katsuyama's chair.

"Shall I give it back to him and his friends, sir?" asked the waiter.

"No, I'll do it. Maybe I can still catch them." He snatched up the wallet and rushed to the front door, but there was no sign of Katsuyama or his minders. He pushed open the revolving doors and tripped over a mat as he pushed his way through. He recovered his balance, but the wallet flew out of his hand and landed on the floor. As he picked it up, a few sheets of paper fell out. He stuffed them back in, hardly noticing that they were photographs. He scanned the area in front of the hotel for Katsuyama and his party, but they were nowhere in sight. As he returned to the reception desk, he took a closer look at the photos, which were still partly sticking out of the wallet, and received a severe shock. There was one picture of him and one of Mieko, and one of the two of them together, as well as one of the outside of his block of flats, with his flat circled in black felt-pen. They appeared to have come from a poor-quality digital camera, maybe a mobile phone camera, and had been enlarged and printed so that the individual pixels making up the picture were clearly visible.

He held them closer to examine them, and became aware of a faint, but distinctive odour that he vaguely recognized but couldn't place. He stuffed them back into the wallet, and went to the concierge's desk. As he reached the desk, the

Vietnamese bodyguard who'd spoken to him earlier came swiftly across the floor towards him.

"That belongs to the boss, I think," holding out his hand. Wordlessly, Sharpe gave him the wallet. "Thank you." He bowed and went towards the door.

One of Sharpe's peculiarities – at least, he'd never heard of anyone else who had the ability, or maybe they just didn't talk about it – was the ability to imagine smells and tastes in his mind. He tried to remember the smell of the photos and match it with his memories. A glaring fluorescent light and bare cement walls and Al Kowalski – "Ben" – and his cigars came back to mind.

What the hell were those photos doing there in Katsuyama's wallet? He remembered the kid they'd arrested – Osaki – talking at the police station about the photos he'd been shown by Al Kowalski. Were these the same ones? What sort of connection was there between Katsuyama and Kowalski?

TIME TO GET STRAIGHT BACK TO TOKYO, Sharpe reckoned. It really didn't seem like a good idea to be in close contact with, or even in the same city as Katsuyama, a man who seemed to be prepared to kill casually and without any sense of conscience.

Damn the man, he thought, as he stepped into the lift to return to his room. Maybe life wasn't wonderful before he stepped into my life, but at least it was nowhere near as complicated as it was now. He punched the button for his floor, and turned to the two other men who had followed him into the lift.

"Which floor?" No answer. Oh well, maybe they didn't speak English, but they made no move to push their floor button as the door closed.

As the lift started to ascend, one of them said, in a heavy accent, to Sharpe, "The same floor for you." He emphasised his words with a small pistol that he held pointed at Sharpe's navel.

"OK," Sharpe replied, holding his hands away from his body. "Whatever you say." He tried to behave as though having guns pulled on him in luxury hotels was an everyday occurrence. He failed and he was aware that his legs were shaking.

The lift stopped at Sharpe's floor, the doors opened, and Sharpe led the way to his room, highly conscious of the two men following him, and of at least one gun pointed at his back. As he reached for his card key to open the room door, he toyed with the idea of dashing through the doorway fast, slamming the door in their faces, and phoning the reception for help. The more he thought about it, the better an idea it seemed to be. Could he manage it? he asked himself, watching the red light in the electronic lock flash and turn green. He pulled the card key out of the lock and deliberately dropped it on the floor. "Damn!" as he bent to pick it up, the two goons offering no assistance, standing there passively. He watched the green lamp turn red and heard the door click locked again. Too long – at least three seconds while the lock stayed open. But there would be a chain on the other side. He could put the chain on and hold them off. Maybe.

He put the card in the lock again. This time his companions seemed a little more relaxed. And there was a laundry cart or room service being pushed along the corridor just round the corner. Better and better. As soon as the light turned green, he half-opened the door and slipped through the gap faster than he had ever done anything before in his life. He had time to slam the door shut and put the chain on before the two men outside appeared to react. He leaned his weight hard against the door, hoping to keep it shut until the autolock clicked. The door-handle rattled furiously as he tried to keep it from turning, but it held and suddenly he felt it stop twisting. Obviously the lock had clicked shut. There was a hammering on the door that stopped suddenly as he heard voices outside the door, and he seized the opportunity to grab the phone and dial the front desk. He had no time to try to make a simple English explanation, so he simply shouted the word "Police!" in English several times down the line, hoping that this and his tone of voice would be enough to do the trick. As he put the phone down, the shouting outside the door rose to a crescendo, and there was a loud bang, followed by the sound of breaking crockery. Sharpe thought he could hear footsteps running away from his room in the direction away from the lifts, but it was hard to say.

About a minute after he had heard the explosion, there was a loud knock on the door. He peered through the spyhole and saw several uniformed figures. Well, whoever they were, they weren't the people who'd been chasing him. He unchained the door and opened it.

Two hotel security men (or so he assumed – they certainly didn't seem to be official police) were standing there, with a young woman wearing a female version of the same uniform standing beside them. Behind her was a male figure in a white waiter's jacket and dark trousers, lying motionless on the floor. An overturned room service cart was behind him, with a red stain spreading across the white cloth that had been pulled off it, one corner still firmly in the waiter's grasp.

"I do not speak good English," said the older of the two men. "Miss Pak will speak for us." He turned to the young woman and said something in Korean to her.

"This is not your doing?" she said to Sharpe in almost impeccable English.

"Of course not. What happened, anyway? I was inside the room," said Sharpe.

"He has been shot," replied Miss Pak, without waiting for the security man's prompt. "He appears to be wounded, but not dead." She spoke in Korean, presumably translating this conversation. Another burst of Korean from the security guard.

"Who was it, then?"

"Two men." Sharpe described them and what had happened as best he could. "To be honest, they were behind me most of the time in the lift and while I was opening the door here. I didn't really get a good look at them." More translation. "One of them had a gun he was pointing at me. I suppose it must have been one of them who shot that poor man." At this point a team of medical orderlies carrying assorted medical equipment and a stretcher spilled out of the lift and clustered round the injured man. One clapped an oxygen mask to the victim's face, and the others gathered round, examining the damage and preparing the stretcher.

"Please wait here with us until the police arrive," the senior security guard said, speaking through Miss Pak.

"May I sit down on the bed?" asked Sharpe. "I feel completely exhausted." It was true. The adrenaline rush and the sheer terror of the past few minutes – he'd never had a gun pointed at him like that before – had exhausted him. Miss Pak passed on the request.

"Yes, you may," she replied. "And," in a quieter tone, "I would advise you to change your pants."

Automatically, Sharpe looked down, embarrassed to see that he had actually wet himself at some stage in the proceedings. "Thank you. I honestly hadn't realised that this had happened." Hardly surprising, he supposed. He really had had the piss scared out of him. He was only grateful it hadn't been worse.

"I guessed you didn't know. Don't worry, I won't look while you're changing." She gave a shy smile and deliberately turned away. Sharpe rummaged in his overnight bag for a pair of jeans – the only other trousers he had brought with him – and a clean pair of underpants.

"I'm going to have to go and wash myself," he called back over his shoulder.

An exchange in Korean, a little laughter from the men, and then "Go ahead" in Miss Pak's voice.

He went into the bathroom, cleaned himself up, and changed quickly, putting the wet clothes into a plastic laundry bag. He realised as he did so that the trousers belonged to one of his best suits, and would have to be cleaned in the very near future. When he emerged, there were two policemen standing talking to the security guides, as well as someone who looked as though he was from the hotel management. The medical team and the victim had disappeared.

One of the policeman came forward. "Mr Sharpe. Would you mind showing us your passport, please?" in English.

They seemed particularly interested in the fact that Sharpe was resident in Japan, and then, somewhat to his surprise, started to question him about Katsuyama, explaining that the hotel staff had noticed Katsuyama's performance earlier in the lobby. Well, they could hardly avoid noticing it, Sharpe told himself. Who was Katsuyama? they wanted to know, and where had he come from? Sharpe told them that Katsuyama was a business acquaintance whose technology his Japanese company had been using for some time and whom he was consulting to seek improvements. As far as he knew, Katsuyama was resident in Vietnam. No, he didn't know where Katsuyama was staying in Seoul, when he had come to Korea, or when he was returning to Vietnam.

"Please come to the police station with us." The words were polite enough, but the tone of voice hardly seemed friendly.

"May I make a phone call first?"

"Who will you call?"

"The British Embassy."

The policeman laughed. "We want to ask you some questions, but we are not arresting you. Do you really need your embassy to protect you?"

"No," Sharpe admitted. "But it would let my friends back in Japan know what was happening if they will pass on a message from me."

A nod. "Go ahead."

Sharpe looked through the hotel magazine, looking for the number, but the hotel manager coughed discreetly, and passed him a slip of paper.

"Oh, thank you very much."

He dialled, and when the phone was answered, asked to be put through to Consular. He explained that he was being taken by the police for questioning regarding a crime of which he was innocent, and asked that the Consulate do whatever they felt was necessary in such cases. He gave them Mieko's mobile number and asked them to contact her and let her know what was happening. And, as an afterthought, he asked the embassy to contact Tim Barclay at the Tokyo embassy and let him know what was going on. He wasn't quite sure why he did it, except that he knew that Barclay and Jon didn't seem to get on, and he wanted no friend of Jon's involved in this.

"All right," he said to the policeman as he put the phone down. "Let's go."

The hotel manager coughed. "Excuse me, sir. If you wouldn't mind settling the bill so far? Just in case ..."

Just in case what? Sharpe asked himself. In case he got hauled off by the Korean police, never to be seen again? It seemed like a strange sort of request, but the little party made its way to the hotel's checkout desk where Sharpe's credit card was processed. While he settled up, the police talked on their radios. "We'll keep the room open for you unless we hear otherwise," the manager promised. Again, that vague nebulous threat of something unknown.

Sharpe was hustled (there was no other way to describe it) into the back of a police car, where he sat between two officers, and they sped, siren screaming, through the streets of Seoul.

AT THE POLICE STATION, he was hurriedly whisked down a corridor to a bare-walled windowless room, similar to the one in Tokyo where he had first met Sugita/Ishihara and Ben/Al Kowalski. His uniformed escort saluted and left him alone in the room with an ascetically thin man wearing a light suit.

"Sit down." Sharpe sat on the hard chair facing the desk. It was just too close to the desk for comfort, but when he tried to move it back, he discovered it was fixed to the floor. Trying to settle himself into the chair, he also discovered that the front legs were somewhat shorter than the back legs, tending to pitch him forward, unless he braced himself, wedging his feet firmly against the floor. His thighs started to ache and his head was starting to hurt. The light was shining into his eyes. Just like all the bad films.

"Passport, please." Sharpe handed it over. It was examined briefly, some data entered on a laptop computer, and the passport then disappeared into a desk drawer.

"Hey! Can I have that back, please?" What right had they to confiscate his passport? He was innocent of anything – except maybe failing to report a murderer who had killed in another country.

The other held up a hand. "All in good time. Now, please describe to me what happened with the two men who held you up. I don't want to know about the other man for now."

Sharpe described the events in the hotel while the other tapped on the keyboard.

"You seem to have been lucky, Mr Sharpe."

"I agree. I was quite scared, to be frank with you."

"Perfectly natural reaction, I would say. Is there any chance you would recognize these men again?"

"I'm not sure."

"All we Orientals look the same?" A smile that appeared to have some warmth behind it.

"Of course not. I live in Japan, remember?"

"Sorry. Have a quick look at these." He turned the laptop so that Sharpe could see the screen, and started to display photos. Most of them seemed grainy and many of them were monochrome. Obviously not studio portraits, Sharpe thought to himself.

Suddenly, "Stop!"

Obediently, the other stopped the slide-show. Sharpe examined the face on the screen carefully.

"I'm not completely sure, but that certainly looks like one of them. The one who was holding the gun on me. I remember him better than the other."

"Not really surprising, is it? Thank you," making a note. "We'll come back to him."

This is where Katsuyama's face recognition gadget would be handy, Sharpe thought to himself. Ironic. The faces continued to flick past on the screen. On two of them, Sharpe indicated that there was a possibility they might match the other of his assailants, but he wasn't sure. At last the line of faces came to an end.

"Thank you, that has been most helpful. Let us continue." Sharpe's legs were aching from the uncomfortable position he had been forced to adopt to stay seated on the chair, but he nodded grimly. The first photo that he had identified re-appeared on screen, together with other, very similar faces. Despite the similarities, Sharpe stuck to his original choice.

"Now for the others." The process was repeated, but Sharpe couldn't single out the other face with any degree of certainty.

"Thank you, Mr Sharpe. That is most helpful."

"Am I free to go? Once you've returned my passport, that is."

The other spread his hands. "You are free to go at any time. Here's your passport. However, I'm going to tell you why you are here now."

"I'm helping you identify criminals?"

"Of course you are doing that. The main reason you are here, and not being interviewed at the hotel, which is where we would normally do these things, is for your safety?"

"Am I in danger now, then?"

"We believe so. The man you identified is known to us as a member of one of the DPRK intelligence agencies, specialising in assassination. Unfortunately, we have been unable to arrest and hold him, though we are aware of his activities."

"You're telling me that the North Korean spy service is trying to kill me?" Well, that completes the set, Sharpe thought to himself. Japanese, Americans, British, North Koreans. He wondered when the Russian KGB, or whatever had replaced them, was going to turn up and have a go at him.

The other nodded. "Quite frankly, with this man and his

accomplice at large, we feel you'd be safer here until you can be returned to Japan."

Returned to Japan, Sharpe noticed. Why the passive voice? Wasn't he considered capable of making the journey on his own?

The phone rang on the desk, and a brief conversation in Korean ensued before Sharpe's questioner switched to English.

"Yes? Major Barclay from Tokyo, is it? Yes, Senior Superintendent General Lee speaking. He's here now with me. At the National Police Agency. How long? When? About 10 this evening? We'll have a car to meet you at the airport and bring you here. Thank you." He put the phone down and addressed Sharpe. "As you may have gathered, your friend from the British Embassy in Japan seems to be looking out for your welfare. He will be flying here this evening and he will make sure you return to Japan safely to-morrow morning. According to my superiors, he has ways of ensuring your safety. Of course, we will provide complete protection to you and him on the way to the airport, and until you board the plane. After that, our jurisdiction ends."

"Someone's been bending some very important ears, it seems to me."

"I agree, it does sound like that to me. We would greatly prefer it if you would remain here until he arrives."

"Here?"

"Not in this room, for which I apologise, by the way. Quite honestly, until I'd had a chance to talk to you, your status was somewhat suspect. You might have been in league with these DPRK agents working against the man you spoke to earlier, Dr ..." he consulted his notes, "Katsuyama."

Totally cracked, Sharpe thought to himself, but he said nothing.

"Now that we've talked, I am satisfied that you are the

victim, not the perpetrator and we'll find you somewhere more comfortable to wait. I am sorry that we can't live up to the standards of the Grand Hyatt, but we can find you a nice quiet cell to yourself – the kind we use for our special guests. I assure you it won't be as bad as it sounds."

Aloud, "What about my bags and things from the hotel?"

"We'll have them fetched from there and brought to you. I believe you settled your bill already. I'm sorry about this, Mr Sharpe, but it does appear that you have become a target, and I would much prefer you out of the country for our own peace of mind, as well as for your own safety, of course."

"I hope you won't take it as a personal insult if I say that I will be glad to leave."

"Of course not. May I show you to your quarters?" rising. "Please follow me."

Sharpe rose to his feet, the muscles in his legs aching as he stretched. They walked down the corridor and into an elevator, which took them to the fifth floor.

"Not a basement dungeon?" smiled Sharpe.

"Far from it." The doors opened, and Sharpe was led to a comfortable room, which reminded him of the better class of business hotel in Tokyo. "Bathroom here," opening a door.

"This is a cell?" Sharpe asked incredulously.

"We have some very high-class criminals here sometimes. If they are found innocent or get pardoned in some political reshuffle, they tend to take it out on the police authorities later on. It's wisest to keep them as happy as possible while they're in detention."

"I see," said Sharpe. It seemed different from the British way of doing things. Well, maybe not that different, when he considered it a little more.

"We'll have something to eat sent to you, if you want."

"Yes, please," Sharpe replied. He'd skipped lunch, having been fed on the plane from Tokyo, and expecting to eat dinner with Katsuyama. Well, that hadn't turned out as planned, had it? He realised that he was actually ravenous. Maybe fear and adrenaline did that to you. He was left alone, but after about ten minutes, there was a knock on the door, and a uniformed policeman entered with a tray.

"Beer?" asked the policeman. Sharpe shook his head, both to decline the offer, and to indicate his complete bafflement at the increasingly surreal nature of the situation in which he found himself. He was left alone (he noticed the door was locked as it was closed) to eat a surprisingly reasonable meal of rice and grilled meat, with what seemed to be the traditional Korean soup of seaweed and sesame seeds.

After eating, he felt tired and lay on the bed and closed his eyes. It only seemed a few minutes later that he was awakened by the sound of the door opening, and a familiar voice calling to him.

Chapter 16: Seoul, Tokyo

"Wakey, wakey, Kenny-boy." Barclay was standing by the foot of the bed. Somehow Sharpe's baggage from the hotel was beside him. "Not quite the Hyatt, is it?"

"It's the best cell I've ever been in," Sharpe grinned.

Barclay looked around and sniffed. "I agree. Hell of a smell of garlic in here. Is that you who's taken up the habit?"

"Hardly a habit. I had some with my meal."

"And I've got to sit next to you on the plane back? Oh well, the things I do for Queen and country." He gave an operatic-scale sigh and sat on the edge of the bed. "*Do* tell," he invited. "I really want to know *everything* about what happened to you with Katsuyama and our friends from north of the border."

"Can it wait until we get back to Tokyo? Or at least we're on the plane?"

"If you must, I suppose. Maybe these walls have ears. I'd be disappointed in these people if they didn't, put it that way. I'll bid you a fond goodnight. I have the cell next to yours, it seems, and the management of this establishment have promised to give us a wake-up call at 6:30. See you in the morning." He left, and Sharpe prepared himself for bed.

Before he went to sleep, he tried calling Mieko using his mobile phone, but hardly to his surprise, there was no signal inside the room. He would have to call from the airport, he guessed.

TRUE TO THEIR WORD, the Korean police provided cars and an escort for Barclay and Sharpe the next morning. Motorcyclists with wailing sirens and flashing lights flanked their car as they sped down the highway to the airport.

"I feel somewhat important," Sharpe said to Barclay.

"Indeed. A bit like royalty. Always wanted to be a queen." Barclay smirked and started to move his arm in a parody of a royal wave.

"Oh, for God's sake, stop it. I nearly got killed by those two clowns yesterday and all you can do is make stupid jokes."

"All right, no need to get hoity-toity. Keep your legs crossed, Missy. But you're probably wrong about nearly being killed."

"You mean I *was* killed? News to me."

"Don't be so bloody stupid. I mean that my guess is that you would have been kidnapped."

"For what reason?"

"To get the Katsuyama gizmo."

"But I don't have it with me."

"So? They didn't know that, did they? And even if you didn't, I think you'd make a very powerful bargaining chip when it came to negotiations with your lady."

"And what if they did have it, what use would it be to them? Would they know how to set it up and use it?"

"Of course they wouldn't. But *you* know, don't you? And I'm sure that a few weeks in a North Korean prison, which, I am assured, is not nearly as nice as the pit whence I have just digged you, would make you more anxious to share that knowledge with your new friends. Not that I'm implying that you're weak-willed or anything like that. We all have our breaking points when we're stretched."

Sharpe considered this, as the landscape sped by the windows. "All right, I'll give you those points. How the hell did they come to learn of it anyway?"

"Oh, I don't think that there's a lot of point guessing that. Someone in Kim's little gang who was working both sides? Katsuyama himself, for reasons we can't even begin to guess at? Tomiko, likewise. I think we can rule you out of the picture," Barclay added, scrutinising Sharpe carefully. "Joke," he added, as Sharpe bristled. "Maybe Jonny-boy."

"Now that's another joke, isn't it?"

"Ha ha, only serious, sort of joke," replied Barclay. "Our Jonny's a prime little shit when he wants to be, and it might be him."

"Why not Ishihara, or any of his organisation?"

"Could be, could be. I'd put money on it being Jon rather than any of them, though, if you were to ask me for my expert opinion. The point is that North Korean intelligence seem to fancy you something rotten right now, as far as I can tell. Which means we're going to have to surround you with tender loving care, and get them out of your hair for good and all."

"And just how do you propose to do that?"

"Right now, my dear Ken, I don't have the faintest bloody idea. Just trust me, as the bishop said to the actress. Seriously," his voice dropped and his tone lost the bantering edge, "I have the glimmerings of an idea, but I need more time to work on it. Just be patient for now, and do what I tell you."

Sharpe considered carefully. He had no doubt that Barclay's primary interest was Major Tim Barclay. At the same time, he had certainly gone out of his way to keep Sharpe safe and sound in Seoul, and he had shown he had a pretty good handle on things. Maybe it was time to let him into the secret. "Listen, do you have the faintest bloody clue what all this is about?"

"I thought we'd been through this several times. Spy satellites and so on."

"Something quite a lot bigger than that. I'll tell you on the plane."

"You have me intrigued, I must say. But I'll bite my tongue for now."

The car sped on, and they arrived at the airport, where they were escorted through the check-in, security and immigration procedures with a speed Sharpe hardly believed was possible in the post-September 11 era.

When they were waiting for their plane, Sharpe suddenly looked up. "I came on ANA. This is a JAL flight. What gives?"

"Well, you're not on the flight you were meant to be coming back on, are you? We've got things arranged for you."

The boarding call came for first class passengers. Barclay stood up.

"That's for first class only. No rush," Sharpe reminded him.

"Look at your ticket, you silly sod."

Sharpe was amazed to see that he'd been upgraded to first class. There seemed to be no other passengers flying in first on this flight, as, other than the phalanx of uniformed police surrounding them, he and Barclay were the only ones walking towards the gate.

"That's right," replied Barclay when Sharpe mentioned it. "We bumped everyone else."

"We?"

"I'll explain things on the plane, dear boy," replied

Barclay, returning the farewell salutes given to them by the Korean police.

Sharpe had never flown first class before. He explored the glories of the large seat and its mass of audio-visual controls.

"Only a short flight though," Barclay reminded him. "But it's a lot simpler for security if we're the only passengers in this class. Our heavies are sitting in business, watching our backs for us. And if the flight crew turn out to be North Korean agents cunningly disguised as JAL pilots—" he shrugged. "We're stuffed. So sit back and enjoy it."

"Who are the 'we' who arranged all this? Surely the British Embassy doesn't have the power to rearrange JAL seating? Even you, with all your superpowers, can't arrange this, can you?"

"That's true," Barclay admitted. "Ishihara can, though."

Sharpe thought about this. "Oh God, that's all I need. The Japanese government, the British government, the Americans, the North Koreans. Probably the South Koreans. And the Vietnamese. Why the hell don't you bring the Libyans and the Israelis into it? Invite the whole damn' UN while you're about it?"

"Temper, temper, Ken. The Japanese were in this from the start, weren't they? You haven't told me what the gadget does, though."

"Nor have I."

"Now sit back and finish your champagne before we take off. Think about how you're going to tell me whatever it is you're going to tell me. When we're nice and safe 50,000 feet up in the air, I want you to tell me a bedtime story. All about poor little Ken, and how he met the bad wicked North Koreans who pointed a nasty-wasty little gun at him, and what led up to all that."

Chapter 16: Seoul, Tokyo

"All right. I can manage that. When we're up in the air. Now just shut up for a minute."

Mercifully, the flight attendant came round and fussed with seat belts and blankets before clearing away the empty glasses.

Once they were airborne, Sharpe kept to his word and started to talk to Barclay. However, there was something that Sharpe felt he had to know before he could trust the other very much further.

"Jon mentioned that he knew Katsuyama's wife some time ago, at the same time he tried to feed me a load of crap about how you were due to be sent home for insider trading. He said that you and Ishihara were in it together."

"Did he, now? How very interesting. I'm putting two and two together in my head right now, and it's all starting to add up to a damn' sight more than four."

"I take it you're not being sacked for insider trading, then?"

"Dear me, no. Not if I can help it, at any rate. I must confess that yes, there were some rather nosy little bastards from London poking their noses around my neck of the woods the other day, and it seemed to me that I smelled Jonny's dirty little fingers in there somewhere. I knew I should have shipped the little bastard off to Burkina Faso or somewhere some time ago. But I was able to convince the snoops of my innocence, for the simple reason that there is nothing to the story in the first place, and I have all the documentary evidence to prove it." He paused and sniffed. "So, Jonny knows Mrs K, does he? She's quite a looker, I believe, if your tastes run that way?" Sharpe confirmed this. "Well, well. There were always stories about Jonny and the ladies. You open my eyes, my dear Ken, you really do."

"Let me open them a little further. What if I told you that Katsuyama's gadget could predict the future?"

Barclay giggled. "I'd probably phone for the men in white coats to come and take you away."

"Well, it can. Or rather it could. In a very limited sphere, that is." Barclay looked incredulous as Sharpe explained what he had discovered.

The response was a stream of imaginative phrases, many of them new to Sharpe. "Well, bugger me sideways with a twelve-foot steam-powered barbed wire-wrapped dildo," Barclay finished. "You could make a fortune out of that."

"We did," said Sharpe, and explained how the M&M Trading organisation had indeed made money, and lost it, following the Lehman debacle. Barclay hung on his every word, every now and again taking a pull at the champagne, a full bottle of which had been supplied by the flight attendants. Sharpe went into detail about how Kim had abducted Mieko and subsequently invested his money, including the reasons he had been told why Kim had made the investment. It took some time to tell it all, with Barclay asking questions at appropriate moments, and they were asked to fasten their seat belts before he had finished.

"I'm impressed, dear boy, I really am," said Barclay, as the plane started its final descent. "Of course, a *wee* bit hurt that you didn't see fit to include me in your plans— All right, just my little joke," as Sharpe started to react. "It does seem as though you're somewhat in the shit, though. And I am sorry to say that one of my colleagues seems to be one of those who is squatting above you with his trousers down. Quickly, tell me about your dealings with Katsuyama and those North Koreans before we pull up at the terminal."

Sharpe gave Barclay a fully detailed account of his meeting with Katsuyama, and the North Korean agents who had attacked him. Barclay kept his mood surprisingly serious, compared to his earlier flippancy, and asked a number of incisive questions.

"Katsuyama lifted the guy's ID and so on before he pushed him under the train?" he asked.

"That's definitely what he said."

"Wouldn't have thought it was possible, even in a crowded place like Shinjuku. Seems a little odd to me. Remind me again, why did Kim and his daughter say they identified this mystery corpse as Katsuyama?"

"He simply said something like it was a good idea if everyone believed Katsuyama was dead."

"A good idea for whom, I wonder?" Barclay leaned back and popped a cashew nut into his mouth as the plane touched down and started to taxi towards the terminal. "This is the life, eh, Ken? And the nice thing for you is that Her Majesty is paying for this, and you're not even paying British taxes. Mind you, you're going to have to earn it by talking to Ishihara when we get to Tokyo."

"Why on earth?"

"Well, he *is* one of our best friends in Tokyo. We owe him several favours. Added to which, he can pull strings to protect you from the unwelcome attentions of our North Korean friends. *And* he is in a better position to get something done about a permanent solution to the problem."

"Permanent meaning what? A quiet mugging in a back alley or something and a splash into the Sumidagawa one dark night?"

Barclay tutted. "Oh dear me, no, Ken. Our Japanese friends are not into that kind of thing at all. Whatever Ishihara comes up with will be much more subtle than that. Which brings me back to those photos that you found in Katsuyama's pocket. Those are the same photos that you saw in the police station?"

"I never saw them. I just heard that lookout kid describe them."

"So you did. Just testing. But you did say that they smelled of Big Al's cigars?"

"I'm sure that was what they smelled like."

"*Filthy* things," remarked Barclay. "Always had to have the extractor fans on full blast for an hour after he came to see me. And *definitely* a distinctive smell. He must have had them specially imported from Inner Mongolia or somewhere where they added camel dung or a secret ingredient like that for that extra special something."

"Katsuyama told me that he skipped off to Vietnam immediately he did his stuff at Shinjuku." Sharpe shuddered. "It gives me the creeps."

"What does?"

"I was talking to him, thinking he was a normal person, and he turns out to be a bloody psycho. Someone who kills perfect strangers and doesn't seem to feel any regrets or any remorse."

"Then be thankful your dealings with Al Kowalski were limited. I never met Katsuyama, but it does sound as though he has some sort of charm to him. Charm was one feature that was conspicuously lacking from Al's makeup. But returning to your point about Vietnam. It takes time to get a visa and a ticket, even if it's only a day or so. That implies that the whole thing was premeditated. Including his first meeting with you."

"He told me he'd been following me for several days – in fact, I think he might have said a week. But it doesn't take as long as all that to get a visa and a ticket. I did it at a day's notice when I flew over there to see him in Hanoi. In any case, he probably wouldn't have needed a visa as a business owner."

"True." Barclay conceded the point. "But when would the photos have been given to Katsuyama if the lad he recruited for the burglary had them?"

"If I recall rightly, he'd been shown the photos, and never actually been given them. And who's to say that they were the same photos, anyway? You can make as many prints as you like. Shouldn't we be asking why rather than when?"

"That is going to lead us into some very murky waters indeed, don't you think? You're right, but I don't want to trouble my pretty little head about it right now. I think we're going to need a little more deep background before we start discussing much further."

Conveniently, the plane pulled up to the jetway as he spoke, and as first-class passengers, Sharpe and Barclay were the first to exit.

BARCLAY AND SHARPE WERE MET STRAIGHT OFF THE PLANE by one of Ishihara's assistants who had investigated the burglary.

"Kurokawa-san, isn't it?" asked Sharpe as they shook hands.

"That's right," smiled the other. "Come this way." He led them through a series of doors marked "No Entry – Official Business Only".

"How on earth did you manage that?" asked Sharpe, amazed. Kurokawa said nothing, but led them outside the terminal building to a waiting car. The driver was Mori, who had eaten peaches and drunk tea at Sharpe's flat before forgetting his pistol. He grinned at Sharpe as they got into the car.

The car pulled away, and fought its way through the airport maze before joining the expressway to Tokyo. Sharpe dug his phone out of his pocket and turned it on.

"Mind if I make a call to Mieko to tell her where I am?" he asked Kurokawa.

"No problem. Go ahead."

Sharpe turned on the phone and dialled. "Hello. Yes, it's me. I'm on my way back from Narita. What? Say that again? He's not hurt, is he? How's she? And how's the baby? Oh. When? Take care of yourselves. I've found out some things about him. No, I can't tell you over the phone. Not a good idea, there's too much to talk about." He hung up and turned to Barclay.

"Your bloody friend Jon. Why didn't you ship him off to Burkina Faso or somewhere when you had the chance to do it?"

"I had no evidence to justify that at all. Anyway, what are you talking about?"

"The guy's gone completely crackers, that's what. He came round to my friend Vishal and pulled a knife on him. Threatened to cut his throat or something unless Vishal told him the secret of how to use the Katsuyama gadget." Barclay held up a warning finger, indicating Kurokawa. "Anyway, Vishal's not hurt, but he's not happy about things. Apparently he's worried that Jon's going to go after his wife, who's pregnant, and he doesn't want that to happen."

"Can't blame him for that," said Barclay. "When did all this take place?"

"Last night, apparently. About eight o'clock."

"After you'd finished with Katsuyama and after the Koreans had threatened you. Coincidence, do you think? Kurokawa-san, what have you got to say about this? I thought your people were following him around the place to make sure that this sort of thing wasn't going to happen?" Sharpe must have shown his surprise, because Barclay turned to him. "Yes, I told you that I suspected something odd was going on there. I actually suspected something about his connections with Kim, or rather with Kim's daughter, but I really didn't know what or all the sordid little details. So I asked our friends here to help."

"There aren't that many of us, Major, you know that. We do our best—" Kurokawa sounded apologetic.

"Which doesn't seem to be good enough, does it? Let's find out a little more, shall we?" Barclay pulled out his own mobile phone.

"Who are you calling?" asked Sharpe.

"Embassy. See if Jon's there."

"Why not call him directly?"

"Softly, softly, dear boy." He spoke into the phone briefly. "Called in sick this morning," he reported as he put the phone back in his pocket. "Something tells me this is going to be a permanent sickness – I would be willing to bet that the embassy will never see Jon again."

"Why?"

Barclay looked at him. "You told me that he had openly thrown in his lot with Kim's daughter? And Katsuyama confirmed that? And now he goes around waving knives in people's faces. He's going to be in deep enough shit with the powers that be because of the accusations against me, which turned out to be a complete load of crap, and this latest trick isn't really going to earn him any brownie points, is it now? Unfortunately I don't have the power to actually fire the little sod, but if I did, he'd be gone in a flash, and I think my views are shared by enough people in Whitehall to justify him doing a runner."

"So I have the North Koreans after me, and Vishal's got a crazed British ex-civil servant after him?"

"Correction, Ken lad. Two corrections. One, you almost certainly have some gangsters after you as well as the aforementioned villains. Two, I think that not just you, but all your friends are in equal danger from all these sources. It may well be time for you and your friends to think about leaving Japan, at least on a semi-permanent basis. Kurokawa-san, I think it's time that you got the police involved at a more serious level. Can you arrange police protection for Ken here and his friends?"

"I think that can be arranged. Remind me of your address and your friends' home address, and give me your office address as well, please."

Sharpe did so, and Kurokawa-san in his turn got busy on the phone. "OK, we'll do that. Do you want your phones to be monitored as well? We can arrange that if you give us permission."

"I personally think that might be a good idea, but I think it's best if I talk to the others first about it. Would that be OK?"

"Sure," replied Kurokawa, and continued speaking into the phone. When he'd finished he addressed Sharpe. "You're getting a good team. They typically look after visiting dignitaries, but since no-one's visiting Tokyo right now, they're free to take care of you and your friends."

"Thanks, I appreciate it."

"You'd better call your good lady," said Barclay, "and ask her to be at the office with your Indian friends in about an hour's time. I think we should all talk together about this."

Sharpe sighed. "This is not going to be popular, I can tell you that right now."

"Cheer up. No-one likes being the bearer of bad tidings, but you're going to feel a lot better after all the cards have gone down on the table."

Sharpe called Mieko again, and she agreed to get Vishal and Meema to the office for the meeting.

THE CAR DROPPED SHARPE AND BARCLAY at the office.

"I hope you're coming in, too," Barclay said to Kurokawa.

"If we're going to go by protocol, it should really be Ishihara," replied Kurokawa.

"Stuff protocol. You're here, he isn't, so you're coming along." Kurokawa followed Sharpe and Barclay up the stairs to where Mieko was waiting.

"Hello, dear." Mieko offered a decorous cheek to Sharpe for kissing. She looked at Barclay and Kurokawa, trying to decide where she had seen them before.

Sharpe introduced them, and Mieko frowned. "I'm not happy, Ken-chan. This all seems dangerous and silly, being surrounded by policemen and spies. You're not some kind of super secret agent, you know."

"My dear girl," began Barclay, stopping and regrouping as he noticed Mieko bristling. He hurriedly repaired his tactical mistake. "Ms Nishimura, we are well aware that Ken is not James Bond, Superman, Batman or any other of the fictional characters who go around destroying villains. It is for that very reason that we have decided that it would be a good idea for all of you to be looked after and protected by the best professionals available. Kurokawa-san, maybe you can explain what is going to happen?"

Kurokawa started to explain. "In these cases—" he began, but Mieko stopped him.

"You say 'in these cases'. In which cases? Why are we one of these cases? You're frightening me."

"Good," replied Barclay. "I hope you are frightened, because you should be. Can we wait until your friends get here, and I'll explain why. Then maybe you'll be happier listening to Kurokawa-san's explanation."

"In the meantime," said Sharpe. "I'm going to put the kettle on. Coffee, anyone?"

Everyone wanted coffee, and Sharpe left the room. Better that Mieko discovered the joys of Barclay's company for herself, he reasoned, than him being the introducer.

When he returned with the coffee, Mieko and Barclay

seemed to be at least talking to each other. Kurokawa was standing up and examining the computer equipment.

"What sort of business is this?" he asked.

"Ah. Ken owes you all some explanations, as well as us having to fill you in on things. It's going to be an interesting time, I can tell."

At that moment, Meema came into the room, followed by Vishal. "I know you," she said, pointing to Kurokawa. "You came round to our place after the burglary at Mieko's and Kenneth's place, didn't you?" She looked down at Barclay. "But I don't know you, do I?"

"This is Major Tim Barclay from somewhere in Her Britannic Majesty's Government," said Sharpe. "He'll introduce himself properly later on. Vishal, I left some coffee on the hotplate in the kitchen. Grab a cup for yourself and one for Meema, come in, sit down and listen. This could literally be a matter of life and death." Vishal raised his eyebrows, but did as he was asked.

Sharpe started by asking Barclay to introduce and explain himself, which he did, with a broad touch of mystery regarding his actual department and responsibilities. "It may sound rather silly and melodramatic, all this hush-hush business, but I must ask you to bear with me. I have to ask you all, of course, to keep this quiet. Kenneth has already signed the British Official Secrets Act, and I will be asking you three to agree to the same terms in the very near future, even though you're not British citizens. Kurokawa-san and his team know most of what you're about to hear already, of course."

"If we don't agree?" asked Meema.

"Then I don't see how I can possibly extend any cooperation to any of you."

"What sort of cooperation?"

"We'll come to that in a little while. There's a lot of

ground to make up. Vishal? Can I ask you to explain to us all what happened to you last night?"

"It is all sounding rather silly, now that I am telling you in black and white. Like something out of a novel or a bad movie or something," said Vishal. "I had just gone out to fetch some beer from the convenience store when this man – not Japanese, European – came up to me and asked me if I was being a friend of yours, Kenneth. So I told him that of course that was true, and then he told me that he too was being a friend and that he did not want to see bad things happening to you. Of course, then I asked him what sort of bad things, and he told me that accidents happen sometimes. So I said to him that this is sounding like a threat and who did he think he was to be making such threats towards my friends. And then he pulled out a knife and held it to my face. Now I am not being frightened of such things as knives because I am quite skilled at fighting with kalari payat when I was younger and we learn about how we must deal with these things. I do not think I have lost all my skills in this area, so I was not being as frightened as some people might be. But he told me to tell you, Kenneth-san, that his name was Jon, and you should not be forgetting this, as he needed the money. So this, I am thinking, is the same stupid bastard who called your phone when I was with you the other day."

Sharpe nodded agreement.

"So I am thinking it is time to walk away from him, and I turn round and start going back to him. And then he threw the knife at me."

Mieko gasped. "You never told me that, Vishal."

He shrugged. "It really wasn't anything that you should be worrying yourself about. The knife hit me, but he has no idea of how to throw a knife properly, so it was only the hilt that was hitting my shoulder. Not even very hard."

"What did you do then?" asked Sharpe.

"I will tell you. I picked up the knife from the pavement and threw it back at a fence just beside him. And because I have been trained in throwing knives, it stuck in that fence pretty damn' hard, I am telling you. I left him trying to pull it out without breaking the blade." He chuckled.

Sharpe was impressed. "Vishal, I had no idea at all that you had these skills. You're a dangerous man to know."

"Jon is more dangerous, though," Barclay added. "And it sounds as though he has completely lost control of himself. He must be mad if he thinks he can go around knifing people on Tokyo streets. If he has the whole of Tomiko's gang to back him up, this is not good news for anyone he is angry with. I think you ought to know that although I haven't worked with him for very long, I have seen him lose his temper a few times, and it is not a pretty sight. I think you could almost say he goes temporarily insane at these times. He's on a very tight string."

"Excuse me for interrupting," said Kurokawa. "What exactly is going on? Why should Jon be interested in this Katsuyama face business enough to get him waving knives in people's faces? What else is involved?"

"Ah," said Sharpe. "I'm afraid that we never brought you up to date on all of this, did we?" He explained how the Katsuyama device was much more than face recognition technology, and how it had been capable of making an enormous sum of money in the right hands. Kurokawa said almost nothing as he listened, but he asked one or two questions that showed that he understood exactly what the device did, and what the implications were. When Sharpe described the money that had been made while the markets were stable, his eyes grew wider.

"Why didn't you tell us?" he asked Barclay, when Sharpe had finished describing the whole business.

"Because Ken here only had the goodness to tell me

Chapter 16: Seoul, Tokyo

about it an hour or so ago, on the way back from Seoul," Barclay replied. "Ken, I think you should tell us all some more about the more recent developments that have affected you personally."

Sharpe started off. "Yesterday, I found out some very disturbing things about Katsuyama and Kim, and I was attacked by armed North Korean agents." Gasps from Mieko and Meema. He went through the talk that he'd had with Katsuyama, and then started to describe how the North Korean agents had held him up in the lift and how he had slammed the door in their faces.

"Oh my God," from Mieko. "You're all right? Why didn't you tell me earlier?"

"I tried to call from the cell in the police station but I couldn't. And then I thought it was better to let you know directly. I knew that you'd be really worried if I told you before I got back."

"That trick with the key and the door is also being a pretty smooth piece of work, I think," said Vishal. "My compliments to you on that." Sharpe bowed in mock acknowledgement.

"What about that poor waiter?" asked Mieko.

Barclay answered her. "They told me in the police station when I arrived. He was not in a serious condition, but he was badly shocked by the whole incident, as you can imagine. Ken, I think you should just continue with what happened after that."

"Well, there isn't that much more to tell. The hotel security called the police, and I had a fairly uncomfortable interview with what I guess was their secret political police or intelligence service – am I right about that?" Barclay nodded. "They decided I wasn't working with the North Koreans, but put me up in one of their executive cells and someone contacted Major Barclay here who hopped on a plane and fixed things at a very high level, it seems."

"Not just me. You owe your thanks to Ishihara and Kurokawa here."

"Hang on a minute," Vishal said. "This is all sounding very wonderful, but it is all being very worrying into the bargain. Do you think that the North Korean goons are after Meema and Mieko and me as well as they are for Kenneth here?"

"Almost certainly they will have done their homework, and marked you three down as additional targets," said Barclay. "Sorry to sound so casual about it, but I see no point in sugar-coating the truth for you. You're all mature adults and can handle bad news."

"So what is your opinion on all this?" asked Vishal. "And what is going to happen to us all?"

"You need protection," said Kurokawa. "The sort of protection that top diplomats get. We'll have people looking after you to make sure that nothing happens, wherever you are."

"Why should Japan do this for us? We're not even Japanese citizens," asked Meema.

"Why not? It's the police's job to protect you. And the more danger you are in, the higher the level of protection. Really quite simple. And if you want a reason that's connected with self-interest, the Japanese police have no interest at all in seeing another unsolved murder of a Briton." He was referring to two murders of British girls in recent years, where the Japanese police had appeared spectacularly incompetent, leading to criticism from the British authorities, up to Prime Ministerial level. "So you're getting the best, and I mean that. These people are as good at their job as anyone else in the world, and we're lucky to have them working with us. I promise you that they won't be in your way. They're professionals, and it's part of their job to be unobtrusive."

Chapter 16: Seoul, Tokyo

"It all sounds all right for now," said Meema. "But we can't spend all our lives being followed around by policemen. Even if the Japanese government is willing to do this for us for ever, which I doubt."

"And that brings us to part two of the operation," answered Barclay. "We have to find a way of one, either silencing these people permanently, or two, directing their fire in another direction."

"It sounds as though you want to kill them when you talk about silencing them permanently," said Mieko.

"Not really. Only if they play rough. I meant arresting them and making sure that they won't be a nuisance to society in the future. But I have the beginnings of a plan B in my head that may just stop them bothering you and kill two birds with one stone. I'll tell you all about it later, Ken."

THE DOORBELL RANG, AND SHARPE ANSWERED the entryphone system.

"It's our bodyguards," he announced to the others. "Or so they say."

"I'll check," said Kurokawa. He strode to the door and talked to the men outside. As he looked at each man's ID, he spoke into his mobile phone, and waved in the visitors one at a time.

"I am sorry," he said, when all the visitors had been admitted, "but the men here speak very little English. Some of the officers in the team do speak English, but not the ones on this shift. You will all receive 24-hour coverage, and the shifts will change every eight hours. We will need duplicate keys to this office and to your homes. You are not required to provide food for these officers, though if you do, it will be appreciated, I am sure." He went on at some length about the way in which Sharpe and his friends would be protected.

At the Sharpe End

The procedures were obviously the result of experience, and Sharpe, for one, felt much happier when he understood the attention to detail that had gone into the system.

"One question," asked Meema. "Do our friends have guns?"

"Yes, they do, and they're trained how to use them. More importantly, maybe, they're trained as to when their use would be inappropriate. If you're worried about accidents, you shouldn't be. These are professionals. Any more questions?"

There were none, and the minders paired off with Sharpe and his friends, introducing themselves informally.

Sharpe and Vishal went to the back of the room and started talking quietly.

"Meema's got to get back to India," said Sharpe. "She's the perfect person to look after your sister and make sure that she gets the treatment she needs."

"I suppose so. You'll be finding me coming round to your place an awful lot for meals until I go back to join her, you realise?" Vishal grinned.

"You're going back for good?" Sharpe was surprised.

"Kenneth-san, do you honestly think there will be jobs for all of us here in Tokyo, now that the world is coming to an end?"

"I hadn't really thought too much about it," Sharpe confessed. "I've had my mind on other things over the past few days."

"Well, I am just worrying about how we are going to survive over the next few years until things are returning to normal. And you, of course."

"We have enough money to last, unless Tomiko decides she's going to steal it all."

Their conversation was interrupted by a loud crash as something burst through the window in a shower of splintering glass. The brick bounced on the floor and was closely followed through the window by something that smoked and smelled of gasoline. One of the bodyguards fell on the plastic bottle with a burning rag sticking out of it and smothered the flame with his hand wrapped in his jacket, which he'd managed to remove as he raced across the floor.

"Jesus Christ!" exclaimed Sharpe. "What the hell was that?" He helped the policeman to his feet. "*Domo arigatō gozaimasu* – thank you very much. Are you OK?" The policeman said nothing, but picked up the bottle and edged sideways to the broken window, unholstering his automatic pistol as he did so.

Sharpe moved towards the window, but was waved towards the opposite corner of the room, where he joined the others. Mieko and Meema appeared terrified, and Sharpe couldn't blame them. A series of short commands in Japanese, and two of the remaining three police shot out of the door. Sharpe could hear their feet pounding down the stairs.

There was silence for about a minute, and then suddenly the noise of a shouted argument came from below through the broken window. There appeared to be three voices, one louder, and the other two softer. After a short time, the louder voice stopped, and there was an eerie silence from below. A couple of minutes after that, the two police who had left appeared, with a shabbily dressed man between them. His hands were behind his back, and as he turned round to face the policeman by the window, Sharpe noted that the wrists were joined by some sort of plastic handcuff device. One of his cheeks looked swollen, and a bruise was starting to form.

The policeman by the window, together with Kurokawa, started to shout at him in Japanese which was too fast and too idiomatic for Sharpe to follow, as were the replies. He turned to Mieko.

"He was doing this because he's lost his job. No he wasn't, he lost money with us, so this is his revenge."

"Bullshit. We never had any clients other than Kim."

"He's changing his story with every answer. Wait until they get the truth out of him."

"If they ever do," said Sharpe.

During this exchange, the firebomb thrower had turned to look at Sharpe. There was a click of mutual recognition as their eyes met, and Sharpe found himself on the receiving end of a low respectful bow.

"He's one of Kim's men," Sharpe explained.

"Which means he's one of Tomiko Katsuyama's men now, doesn't it?" replied Kurokawa. He spat some more Japanese out at the man who continued bowing apologetically. "Yes, he is," said Kurokawa. "Mr Sharpe, do you have her telephone number to hand?"

"It should be somewhere in my phone. She called me not so long ago. Wait a moment … Yes, I do."

"Call her now. We can't arrest her or even touch her for this, but I want you to make her understand that this is not in any way acceptable and that we're here to take care of you, and any more tricks like this will make her life very difficult."

"What should I say?"

"I'm sure you'll find the right words," Barclay told him.

"Please set the speakerphone on," Kurokawa told him. He brought a small recorder out of his pocket and flicked a switch. A red light came on. "Recording."

Sharpe dialled, and waited for three rings before the phone was picked up.

"Tomiko Katsuyama?" he said, before she could say anything.

Chapter 16: Seoul, Tokyo

"*Hai.*"

"Can we speak English?"

"Yes." A little grudgingly after some silence.

"This is Kenneth Sharpe here."

"Oh." More silence. "When am I going to get the money that you promised to my father?"

"I really don't want to go over all that again. Please take the trouble to read and understand your newspapers and find out what's going on in the world. More importantly, we have your man here. The one who threw your little present at us."

"My man? What are you talking about?"

Sharpe sighed. "Please, can we stop playing silly games? The police have him here now in handcuffs and he's told us everything."

There was an intake of breath at the other end. "The police? What are you doing with them?"

"I called to let you know that, courtesy of Tokyo's finest, my friends and I now have 24-hour police protection. If you know what is good for you, your recent visitor to us will be the last one you send round."

"Is that a threat?"

"It's a promise. And it's not me making it, either. It's someone who has the power to make that promise come true."

"I'm not going to forget this, you know. And that's a promise, as well."

"Love you too, dear," said Sharpe under his breath, as he cut the connection. "I hope that got the message across," to Kurokawa.

"We might reinforce it with a friendly visit from the local police some time soon. But I think you made it clear enough. Excuse me, I think the refuse collectors have arrived."

He opened the door to two uniformed police who

entered, and after an exchange of paperwork, led Tomiko's goon out of the room.

"Good riddance to bad rubbish," said Barclay. "Nicely done, lads," he said to the bodyguard squad. To Sharpe, "I think you and Kurokawa-san and I need to sit down and talk strategy. Apologies to the rest of you, but this is something where I really only want a few people to start with. Later we'll talk about what we're going to be doing in more detail. I'm off now, and I'll call for you here at 10 tomorrow morning, Ken, and we'll go on together. Kurokawa-san, you know where to find me. Bye for now, all."

Chapter 16: Seoul, Tokyo

Chapter 17: Tokyo

True to his word, Barclay appeared at the office at 10, and he and Sharpe, together with Sharpe's minder, took a taxi to Barclay's lair. They walked in after Sharpe had watched Barclay's fussing with a number of complicated locks, including a fingerprint reader.

"No, that's not what it is," said Barclay, when Sharpe mentioned it. "It actually reads the infrared patterns in the fingertip veins. Almost as distinctive as fingerprints."

"And no-one can lift your fingerprint and make a fake using Photoshop and gummi bears?" suggested Sharpe. "And no-one can cut off your finger and use it to get in, right?"

"Exactly. Which is one reason why Japanese banks are using this and the palm vein readers rather than fingerprint or handprint."

They sat and waited in silence. Barclay looked at his watch which for some reason best known to himself, Sharpe had noticed, he always wore on the inside of his wrist.

"Strange. Ishihara's usually pretty punctual, and he makes a point of calling ahead if he's going to be held up." As he spoke, the phone rang on his desk.

"Yes. He what? Thank you. We'll be right along." He put the phone back, and Sharpe noticed his hands were shaking.

"I need a bloody drink. Doesn't have to be a big one, but by God, it has to be strong."

He opened one of his desk drawers and pulled out a bottle of whisky and two glasses, into each of which he poured a finger's worth of neat spirits. He pushed one over to Sharpe.

"What for? I don't want this."

"You will, laddie, you will. That was Kurokawa. Ishihara's been found dead. Knifed to death in his office. Kurokawa went in there to check on something, thinking Ishihara was with us and found him there just now." He tossed down the whisky and shuddered.

"Dear God!" exclaimed Sharpe. "I suppose it's the usual suspect?" He reached for his own whisky.

"You mean Jonny? Almost certainly. No evidence, of course. No traces, but if it turns out to be anyone else, you can kick my arse all the way up Mount Fuji. And down again."

Sharpe drank his whisky in one gulp. Barclay was right, it had some sort of calming effect. "Why the bloody hell would he do that?"

"I really don't know. I just told Kurokawa we'd be over there. Come on, let's di di mau."

"Let's what?"

"Get the fuck out of here. Come on, lad." The two of them, together with Sharpe's minder, piled out of the room, with Barclay locking up carefully, and once on the street, hailed a taxi.

Barclay gave an address in Kasumigaseki, the government office district, and they sped off, Barclay and Sharpe using their combined Japanese to explain the situation to Sharpe's baffled monolingual bodyguard. Once they arrived, Barclay raced out of the taxi faster than Sharpe had ever seen him move, leaving the other two stumbling in his wake. When they caught up with him, Sharpe saw him talking in very passable Japanese to the security guard at reception, and showing an ID card that was being very carefully scrutinized. There seemed to be an impasse, but this was quickly overcome by the production of a very official-looking piece of plastic by Sharpe's minder, and they took the lift to the fifth floor. Yellow crime scene tape crisscrossed the corridor, and police were already swarming around the place, taking photos, measuring, and generally getting in each other's way.

Kurokawa was standing to one side, and moved towards them as he saw them come out of the lift.

"Want to see him before they move him?" he asked. I warn you, he's far from being nice to look at."

He led them to an office where the police were swarming in greatest numbers, and nodded to one of the policemen, who pulled down a sheet covering something large and lumpy on the floor.

There was a lot of blood. The face was ... "Sorry," said Sharpe and rushed out of the room. His legs turned to rubber, and he half-fell to the floor. His minder and a sympathetic policeman knew exactly what was happening, and where he wanted to go, grabbing an arm each and half-dragging his collapsing body to a toilet, where he vomited copiously and painfully. Barclay followed him into the toilet a little later. He, too, looked more than a little green.

"Don't worry about losing it like that, Ken," he said. His voice was almost gentle, and his usual flippancy had completely vanished. "It's nothing to be ashamed of. Half the police here lost their lunches, and they should be used to it."

"I don't know how you could ever get used to seeing someone with their eyes gouged out and their nose cut off. It's like something out of a really sick horror film."

Barclay nodded. "It *is* sick, isn't it?"

"Why did no-one hear him?"

"You didn't notice the gag? Poor bastard was tied up and gagged before Jon started his filthy work." The veins were actually standing out on Barclay's neck as he spoke. "To think that bastard's British. We'll be lucky to have a fucking embassy in Japan if the truth of all this comes out."

"It won't," said Kurokawa, who had followed them in and shooed out the others. "Don't worry about that. But I do want to see that little bastard of yours safe where he can do no harm, Major."

"He's not *my* little bastard," growled Barclay. There was nothing comic about the little man now. He was very obviously more than simply angry, and looked extremely danger- ous. "Kurokawa. Sharpe. Come back with me." He marched out of the door. Kurokawa and Sharpe looked at each other, shrugged and followed. There wasn't a lot of choice.

ONCE BACK AT BARCLAY'S LAIR, the three of them sat around the desk. Sharpe's minder sat to one side, nursing a cup of coffee.

"Why?" asked Sharpe.

"Oh, for God's sake, Ken. To make him talk, of course. Campbell obviously thought he knew more than he actually did, and this was his way of getting to the knowledge. I was up practically all night following up the leads you gave me. Let me tell you, Ken, the stakes in this are enormous."

"I thought they were pretty high."

"You don't know the half of it, lad. Kim's family was orig- inally pretty high up in the Central Committee and Party hierarchy. This is some time back, you understand – nearly at the start of the Great Leader's reign. And as one of the clique in charge of the country, the family amassed a con- siderable sum of money, which they converted into gold. Remember that North Korea mines gold in relatively large quantities. Quite easy to convert cash into gold if you have the right connections, which of course they did. Some of the filthy lucre may also have been war loot, some might have been bribes, or confiscated from prisoners. Dirty money, blood money, whatever. It's not clean or nice money at all."

"How much?"

"Hold your horses, I'll save the best to last, if you don't mind. Some time ago – at least thirty – our Mr Kim's parents fell foul of the Great Leader, in one of the purges. They died, and the teenaged Kim escaped with his older sister to the South. Not quite sure how he managed to get through the border, but I am sure money played a significant role there. Then to America, as he may have told you. And when things got too hot for him there a few years later, he came to Japan. It was relatively easy to pass himself off here as a Korean whose family had been brought over to Japan in the war, and he could play on guilt feelings and so on. Of course, he had little to do with the North Korean community here, since they could make life very unpleasant for him if they were to find out exactly who he was and where he was coming from. So Kim knows – knew, rather – that he was heir to a goodly number of dollars in gold—"

"How much?"

"Brace yourselves. When I say the sum was considerable, I mean by today's standards, not by those of half a century ago. I did some calculations on the back of an envelope, and I think that we're probably talking about the best part of half a billion dollars' worth of gold at today's prices."

Sharpe rocked in his chair and Kurokawa sat with his mouth wide open. Sharpe had just got used to dealing with millions of dollars through the currency exchange system. Now he had to raise his sights by a few orders of magnitude. Barclay grinned.

"Yes, it is a lot, isn't it?"

"It's a hell of a lot," said Kurokawa.

"How did you find out about all this so quickly?" Sharpe asked.

"I'm not just a pretty face, Ken. Credit me with a little intelligence. I also have lots of interesting friends here in Japan, as well as in London and other places. Shall we simply say that my job may not be all that it says on the nameplate on my door, if such a thing existed?"

"It's all in North Korea?" asked Kurokawa.

"Exactly. Holed up in North Korea, and no obvious way of getting it out. It seems there was no time for the family to move it to Switzerland before the bullet in the back of the neck. It comes to a fair bit over 14 tons of gold – I worked out how much just for the fun of it – and it wouldn't be easy to shift that out of the country, would it?"

"You'd need to bribe a lot of people to look the other way?"

"Indeed you would. I've no idea where it actually is located, but I am sure it's in a remote area, far from prying eyes, which means a lot of people going to a place where people don't usually go. And you'd probably have to buy an Army regiment or two to do the heavy lifting and to fight off anyone along the way who thought they had a right to it. Not to mention hiring some sort of transport – almost certainly by sea – and bribing officials at both ends, not just the Korean one, to turn a blind eye."

"The other end being Japan?" asked Kurokawa. "I'm not saying all Japanese officials are incorruptible, but I don't see them going for that."

Barclay shrugged. "I don't know. Probably not Japan. I would guess Vietnam or even Cambodia. I am sure it would be easier that way than through Japan. In any case, it would be an expensive operation overall."

"About twenty-five million dollars?"

"Depending on what the going rate for bribery and securing the mercenary services of North Korean armed forces is, yes. Probably about that. Could be more, could be less. Don't know, I've never tried moving half a billion in gold out of a Stalinist dictatorship." He smiled.

"This is a rather different story to the one we were told," said Sharpe.

"This is purely private enterprise – admittedly in a Stalinist context. My guess is that he wanted to see his family – and it's still quite a wide-spread clan, it seems – restored to some sort of status. Whether he really wanted any real change from the status quo, other than toppling the Great Leader's dynasty, is another matter."

Sharpe considered what he'd just learned. Assuming that Barclay was right in what he was saying, he and his friends had been taken for a ride by Kim, who had taken advantage of their better natures.

"So where the hell does Katsuyama fit into all of this?"

"Oh, Katsuyama is a genius, no doubt about it. I am sure that Kim found out about this rising young star in the Japanese computer world and set his daughter to seduce him." Sharpe's illusions were being shattered one after the other.

"So Kim knew all about the currency trading system? He said that he only knew about the face-recognition program."

"I'd bet my life that he not only knew about the currency program – he funded Katsuyama's research at Stanford with that very object in mind."

"In order to make money to get the gold out of Korea?"

"Right."

"Dear God in Heaven." Sharpe thought back. Had there ever been any time when Kim had betrayed any knowledge of the trading system other than what Sharpe had told him? Yes, he remembered, there had been at least one occasion when Kim had seemed to know more than he admitted about the basics of the operation. "And you think Jon knows all about this, and that's why he killed Ishihara?"

Barclay nodded.

"It's sick. Jon's sick," said Sharpe. He knew he was repeating himself, but there was no other word he could come up with that met the facts. "Ishihara knew nothing. What sort of person is Jon Campbell, anyway? I really don't want to discuss the results of this psychopath's mind at work. Let's talk about how to nail the bastard."

"That's the way, Ken lad. What the three of us have to do is to put our heads together and come up with a way of stopping him. And if it can stop the North Koreans from going after you and your friends, so much the better."

"I'm beginning to see what you're driving at. Give him the Katsuyama thing so that he can make the money for himself when the market cools down a bit, and set the North Koreans onto Jon and Tomiko's mob?"

"Give the man a Kewpie doll," said Barclay. "Right first time. Set the bastards against each other to do our dirty work for us. Divide and conquer. Works a treat."

"I don't like it," said Kurokawa. "Not at all. You're providing an open invitation to some pretty bloody gang warfare in Japan, and we don't want that to happen. We have a reputation for safe streets and we want to keep it that way."

"But you agree that Ken here has got to get rid of the Katsuyama technology? Quite frankly, Ken, your life is in danger, as you know, and the danger gets more acute the longer you hang onto it."

"I agree with all that," said Kurokawa. "I have a twist on your plan, Major. Mr Sharpe here decides to give the technology to Campbell. They arrange a meeting place, and the handover takes place. Then twenty policemen spring out of the bushes, and arrest Campbell and Mr Sharpe—"

"Hey!"

"—On suspicion of stealing Japanese trade secrets."

"That would work," said Barclay, rubbing his chin.

"Why the hell arrest me?" asked Sharpe. "What have I done to deserve that?"

"It's for appearances only," Kurokawa assured him. "If we only arrest Campbell, it's going to look far too obvious that you're working with us, and the Kim gang and the North Koreans are going to come after you as a traitor, or at least an enemy of their plans. But if they see that you're on the same side as them, and that you're not holding the technology, there's no reason at all for them to come after you. We'll get you off on a technicality. You'll have to stand trial, of course."

"Can't you do it without putting me on trial? It really does seem to be taking things to extremes."

"We can work something out, I suppose. And of course, could make sure that all records of the case would be eliminated so nothing would ever appear on future visa applications or anything like that."

"You can promise that?" asked Sharpe.

"Not right now, I can't. But give me a couple of days at the most to make the phone calls and to talk to the right people at the Ministry of Justice, and I think I can promise you that we can do it."

"I want that in writing when you have it fixed up. I'm not going in there without a guarantee. Sorry. I trust you, but I don't know if I can trust everyone in the whole of the Ministry of Justice sight unseen."

"Wise man," agreed Barclay. "You get that in writing."

"No worries. I'll get you something."

"One other thing. Two other things."

Barclay sighed. "What?"

"You know what? I'm not that keen on going on my own

to meet a psycho who seems to think it's fun to carve up other people. I'll bet it was him who cut off Al Kowalski's head."

"The Major told me about that," said Kurokawa. "We thought it was the work of Kim's gang, but seeing what this lunatic is capable of, I wouldn't be so sure now."

"Kim did know where the head was, though," pointed out Barclay. "He gave you that locker key, Ken."

"Doesn't necessarily mean he put it there himself, though, does it?" said Sharpe. "Jon Campbell might have put it there and then given the key to Tomiko who gave it to her father. But that doesn't alter the fact that I am not keen on meeting him in a situation where it's quite likely that he's in a position to do me an injury that I will regret for the rest of my life, however short that may be. You can bet that he's not going to want my friend," he indicated the police guard, "or any of his colleagues along with me."

"We can take care of that," said Kurokawa. "We can get a sniper team in place to cover the area at an hour's notice if it's in Tokyo, and two hours' notice if it's a bit further out."

"Not the SWAT teams, please," said Sharpe. He'd watched the Japanese SWAT teams on TV news reports, and they looked incompetent compared to their European or US counterparts.

"Not the SWAT teams," Kurokawa agreed. "This is going to take surgical skill and not brute force."

"Glad you have your head screwed on," said Barclay. "Unlike Al Kowalski." He grinned at Sharpe, who had started to retch at the memory of the contents of the bag at Tokyo station. "All right, sorry. Not that funny, really. I keep forgetting sometimes that this isn't your usual line of business. Me, I've seen far too much of this kind of thing in my time. Doesn't stop me feeling angry about it, though. You said you had two things. What's the other?"

"I'm wondering just who Ishihara was and Kurokawa is, and all the rest of you. I mean, being able to pull in a sniper team at a moment's notice, arrange diplomatic-level protection, and fix the results of trials means that you have a good deal of authority working outside the normal system, doesn't it?"

"Ken lad," said Barclay. "You really don't need to know exactly who's looking after you. Just be thankful that they exist. You're really lucky, even though it may not seem like it right now."

"One more thing, sorry. If I give Jon the gizmo and the CD-ROM, do you think he will think that's enough?"

"Almost certainly not, now you come to mention it. It took you people some time to set up your operation, didn't it? I think you are going to have to deliver either a working system or a full set of documentation. Or both."

"That's going to take time."

"Better still," said Kurokawa. "It means that while he's waiting, he and the gang won't do anything, because they know they're going to get the goodies from you soon. And that allows us to focus on one enemy – the North Korean agents – and with luck we can eliminate the threat from them before you meet up with Campbell."

"Good point," said Barclay. "Excellent point, in fact."

"So can we wait a couple of days while you get your guarantees in place, Kurokawa-san? I don't think I should be making any moves until I see those."

"Couldn't you start things rolling now?" asked Kurokawa.

"No, he couldn't," replied Barclay. "Ken's right. If you're going to start playing silly games involving British subjects, I think the innocent parties need some sort of insurance against a massive foul-up. I don't want to see Ken end up in prison for something he didn't do. I'm sure we could get him out in the end, but I don't want to have to do that at all. But Ken, I suggest you talk to Vishal about how to get the system onto some sort of disk or something that can be handed over easily. And start writing some sort of instruction manual for the bloody thing."

"That's my job, I suppose. All right, I'll proceed on the assumption that you're going to give me my Get Out Of Jail Free card. But there's no way I'm going to start talking to Jon Campbell until I have that in my hands. Oh," as a thought struck him. "Extend that advance pardon to Mieko, Vishal and Meema. I don't want them to be caught up in all of this and arrested in revenge for my getting out from under the court's nose."

"Not too shabby, Ken. I'm sure Kurokawa here would never do anything like you're suggesting, but the final decisions may not be his."

"I'll make sure that it's taken care of," confirmed Kurokawa, writing in his notebook.

"All right, Ken," said Barclay. "Your next job is to get back to the office and make sure that you get your people on your side about getting the technology over to Jon Campbell, God rot his soul. Then, as soon as Kurokawa-san gets you these assurances we've been talking about, you call him, or you might think about calling Tomiko – my guess is that it comes to much the same thing right now – and tell them that the whole lot is coming their way soon. Be vague about the delivery time."

"Not hard to do. Being vague, I mean. Most computer projects take longer than they're meant to."

"Right. And then get on with it and make sure that you do it bloody fast."

"What's the point of actually doing it if he's going to be arrested as soon as I hand it over?"

"That's a good point, Major," said Kurokawa.

"It's got to be convincing bait, at least for a superficial

look by the victim, but the main point is that it's got to be convincing enough to convince the prosecutors when you're both arrested," pointed out Barclay. "Otherwise it's never even going to come to court, and they're not going to bother investigating Jonny-boy any further than they have to. And being a lazy bunch of sods, that's not very far."

"So you're saying that we really have to get down and produce the real thing?"

"That's exactly what I'm saying. Don't you agree?"

"I see your point, Major. Yes, I think there's no time to waste, Mr Sharpe. Don't worry about things – I'll get my end of the matter sorted out in a day or two at the most."

Chapter 17: Tokyo

Chapter 18: Tokyo

"Vishal," said Sharpe when he returned from Barclay's. "How would you package our system if we wanted to move it to another computer?"

"Easy enough. Since we're running Ubuntu Linux, I can get the whole thing, operating system and all, onto a memory stick. The 16 gigabyte ones now will do it with lots of room to spare. But you know we are needing the Katsuyama hardware to be installed in the PC, and there's no way we can duplicate that. Why?"

"We're going to hand the thing over to Jon Campbell. Lock, stock and barrel."

Vishal stared at him. "Why the bloody hell are you going to be doing that?" he asked.

"Because," Sharpe said. He went over the arguments that he'd just been through with Barclay and Kurokawa.

"I see. As long as you're happy with it. We have enough money for my sister."

"And that was the main thing, after all."

"Well, you should come out ahead as well. Nothing would have happened if it hadn't been for you."

"Not convinced that it's been a 100% success."

"Come off it, Kenneth, thanks to you, my sister is probably going to have a new life. And Meema and I are a bit better off than we were, and so are you and Mieko."

Sharpe sighed. "I suppose you're right, but I really don't feel like exposing everyone to these risks, and I don't fancy being exposed to them myself."

"It seems a shame, but you're the boss. Do we tell the girls?"

"Of course. We know that Meema's had enough of all this, and I am sure that Mieko will be relieved."

"What are you going to be doing while I'm doing all this work of packaging the system?" asked Vishal.

"Doing what I do best. Writing sodding documentation, that's what. And I don't understand half of what you've been up to, so you're going to have to explain it in words of one syllable."

"It's not as bad as that. Most of the hard work was the testing, and now we know what the answers should be, I think you're going to find it quite easy to write about those procedures."

"Hope so," said Sharpe.

As he had predicted, both Meema and Mieko took the news with a sense of relief once he had explained the reasons, and reassured them that there was enough money to pay for Vishal's sister's treatment in the worst possible scenario, and still leave a little over.

He and Vishal worked together on making the Katsuyama technology into a product that could be easily transferred and operated by anyone with relatively little computer knowledge.

"We should be selling this," grumbled Vishal. "Think how much it's worth to someone."

"There are two good reasons why not," said Sharpe, glad of the chance to take a break from the business of writing about market data feed installation. "One, it's not our technology to sell."

"You think Katsuyama's going to object? He's a bloody psycho from what you say, and the police will have him in jail PDQ if he comes to Japan."

"Even so, it's not ours, and we couldn't run the risk. And, more importantly, the way it makes profits depends on only one of these systems being around. If everyone has the same technology, it's not going to work. No-one has the advantage over the others. Come on, Vishal, this is why Meema was developing all those trading strategies at the bank. To give your bank an edge over the others. There's no advantage if we're all on the same playing field. The free market's a myth – always has been – someone is always the leader with an unfair advantage."

"I suppose that's true. Seems to me that we're throwing this all away for no good reason that I can see. I'm going to make a copy to keep for myself, in any case."

AFTER ONLY A DAY, Kurokawa called Sharpe. "Everything is sorted out," he smiled. "Here's the piece of paper."

Sharpe read it through. He assumed that the English and the Japanese were the same. In any case, someone had inserted a clause stating that the English was to be used as the official text in cases of disagreement. All the clauses seemed to be in order, and promised that any arrests made of him, Vishal, Meema or Mieko in connection with that was termed "the Katsuyama technology" would be mere formalities, and that they would never be brought to trial. Furthermore, all record of such arrests would be removed from the records, leaving a clean sheet.

"Who is this?" asked Sharpe, pointing to the name and seal at the bottom of the document.

"A very senior civil servant in the Ministry of Justice. You're all very well covered, believe me. All you have to do is sign. All of you. There's a copy for each of you and two more for the government."

Sharpe went round collecting the signatures, and passed two copies back to Kurokawa.

"Thanks. Now, if you don't mind, Mr Sharpe, I'd like you to call Campbell and arrange a handover."

"How long till you're ready, Vishal?"

"About another three days, if the testing goes well."

"And if it doesn't?"

"Five."

"And I reckon I've got at least five days' writing to do, so let's tell him this time next week. You happy with that, Vishal? There's no pushing this deadline back, you know."

"Go with it, man. I'm with you all the way."

"You want to record this call?" Sharpe asked Kurokawa.

"Yes. Don't put it on speaker this time, though. Can you do it from your office phone?"

"Sure."

Kurokawa brought out some cables that connected the phone to his pocket recorder. "When you're ready," he invited Sharpe.

Sharpe took a deep breath and started dialling Jon Campbell's mobile number. It was answered after about six rings.

"Hello?" came Jon's voice. "Who's this?" Obviously the number displayed by the office Internet phone system had confused him.

"Kenneth Sharpe here."

"Ah, Kenny." Sharpe gritted his teeth. "How nice to hear from you. I heard from Tomiko that you have some special friends looking after you who don't really want me to meet you. Is that still the case?"

"It is indeed, Jonny," said Sharpe, returning the compliment. "Where are you? And who's giving you that information?"

"Both of those are my business, not yours, I think."

"Please yourself."

"So what can I be doing for you, then?"

"Actually, it's what I can be doing for you," Sharpe corrected. He tried to make his voice sound a little more submissive. It wasn't that hard to feel frightened when he remembered what he had seen of Ishihara's face.

"Go on."

"We're not in a position to give Tomiko the money she wants. You know as well as I do how fucked up the markets are right now."

"I can accept that. I've tried to explain all this to the crazy bitch but I think it's a case of the deliberate dumbs. So? You're not calling me just to say you can't pay, are you?"

"No. I'm going to make you a present of the whole of the Katsuyama technology. The hardware, which as you know, is the only one of its kind, the original disc he gave to me, a real live working system – a copy of the one we were using, and the instruction manual. It's going to take a little bit of work for you to set it up and get it working, but I'm busy writing down how you can do that."

"You're not going to do that for us?"

"You wish. No, I'm not. I don't want you or Tomiko breathing down our necks while we do it. There's lots of competent people out there you can use to set it all up and get it working, now the banks are shedding IT staff like dandruff."

"How poetic you are, Kenny. We may call on you for help."

"The way I write manuals, you're not going to need any help. It will all happen nice and smoothly."

"Famous last words. So why this sudden burst of generosity? Has Christmas come early this year?"

"Let's just say that I'm rather fed up with the lifestyle you and your lady friend have imposed on us. I'd like a return to normality, and this seems the best way of going about it."

"Fair enough. And when are you putting on the Santa suit and driving the reindeer over? On second thoughts, no reindeer. Just you."

"The system and the documentation won't be ready for another week."

"An IT contractor's week or a real week?"

"Very funny. A real week."

"OK, I'll call you in a week's time and give you the time and place. And no funny stuff. Any tricks and you're history, mate. Trust me on that, and keep it in mind any time you think about being clever."

"I understand."

"Then you'll have the pleasure of hearing my voice this time next week. I'll pass on the news to Tomiko and I'm sure that she'll send out a hands-off notice, if that makes you feel any better."

"It does, as it happens."

"Then I'll bid you a fond farewell until next week." Jon hung up, and Sharpe looked up at Kurokawa who was grinning.

"Excellent, Mr Sharpe. That's exactly what I expected. So as soon as you get the time and place, send me a message on my mobile, and I'll get the men in position to protect you. Good luck with your work."

Chapter 19: Tokyo, Shonan

Sharpe and Vishal's work went smoothly. Vishal approached the task as if he were making a commercial product for sale, smoothing out any rough edges, and providing what he called a "pretty damn' fine turnkey installation". All his hard work was to fit on one small USB memory stick.

"And all they have to do is to run the configure script and answer questions that even you could answer, Kenneth-san," he said proudly.

Sharpe ignored the implied insult to his computer skills. "Fine, so the installation works. What about maintenance? How can they fine-tune the latency on the Quick feed? I need to write about that."

"They shouldn't need to. I rewrote a routine so that it's self-adjusting."

Sharpe sighed. "If it ain't broke, don't fix it. Have you never heard that saying?"

"Well it *was* broken. That's why I fixed it."

"And tested it?"

"Of course."

Sharpe sighed again. Though he trusted Vishal's ability,

sometimes he leaped ahead of himself and caused problems for other people down the line who couldn't follow his thinking. "So you're saying that I don't need to document that at all? Is that right?"

"That's right, Kenneth-san. You're worrying too much. None of this is going to matter in the end, is it?"

"You never know."

As it happened, Vishal hit no major snags, and Sharpe's writing was surprisingly easy, at least partly because he had spent so much time setting up the system in the first place. As a result, everything went much smoother than Sharpe had expected, and the work was all finished with a few days to spare.

"If I were you, I'd get out of Tokyo with Meema. Get yourselves off to a hot spring in the country or something," Sharpe said to Vishal. "Come to talk of it, why the hell is she still in Tokyo and not on a flight to India?"

"We talked it over, and contacted my sister as well to talk to her. We think that Meema doesn't have to go until you've got all this mess sorted out. A week or so won't make a lot of difference to my sister's condition, the doctors tell her. She told me that she wants to make sure that you're safe. She's very grateful – we're all very grateful to you, if you hadn't guessed."

"I'm touched. So why don't you and Meema go away for a few days and take Mieko with you? This is something I want to do without any of you around. I don't want you too close to this. I have this feeling it is going to get rather messy."

"A man's gotta do what a man's gotta do?"

"Something like that. Really, I've dragged you all into enough of a mess as it is. I really don't want you guys to suffer any more. If anyone ends up in the shit this time, it's going to be me. Anyway, I have to do this on my own – that's what Campbell said. If there's anyone else with me, God knows what's going to happen."

"Well, if you are being really sure about this, I'll do it."

"I'll make sure that you know when it's all over. If I'm still officially arrested, we'll arrange for Kurokawa to contact you when it's safe. Happy?"

"Not the word I would be using, but all right."

Vishal booked himself, together with Meema and Mieko, into a Japanese-style inn in Izu, to the south of Tokyo. Kurokawa made sure that the minders went with them. "It'll be a nice break for them," he said. "Not often that they get this sort of opportunity to get away from Tokyo like this. I think we'll put two watchers on you, all the time, though, since your lady and her watcher aren't going to be with you."

So Sharpe spent a lot of his time at the flat, drinking beer, and losing at *go* to one of his minders, who, he found out, had been his university's champion.

It was late one evening when the call came.

"Why isn't it ready?" was Jon's first question, launched with no warning.

"It *is* ready. Packed up and ready to go."

"Oh. Apologies. That's the first time in my life that I've ever heard of an IT project being ready on time." The surprise sounded genuine, even if the apology didn't. "Then you're ready to meet me tomorrow, then?"

"Sure."

"Alone, you understand. Any funny business, and things will start to go very pear-shaped in your general direction."

"Understood."

"So we're going to meet at Enoshima. Ever been there?"

"Yes, I know what you're talking about."

Chapter 19: Tokyo, Shonan

"Then I'll see you in the middle of the causeway leading to the island. Six fifty-two."

"Isn't it going to be a bit crowded for us?"

"Not going to be crowded at six fifty-two in the morning, is it? Tomorrow morning, six fifty-two. AM, that is. Middle of Enoshima causeway. Got it?"

"Got it," replied Sharpe.

"Good. Don't be late. I fucking hate hanging around in the cold early mornings. And remember, I want just the one of you. Not a crowd."

As Jon hung up, Sharpe was already calling Kurokawa. Damn it, answer your bloody mobile, man. A recorded voice came on the line telling him in Japanese that Kurokawa's phone couldn't be contacted, and inviting him to leave a message. He pressed the appropriate key on his phone and started to speak, but a hideous electronic squeal interrupted him about five seconds into the message and a voice thanked him for recording his message. He hung up and tried again several times, but every time he was unable even to connect to the voicemail system, which seemed to be out of action.

He tried Kurokawa's office number, but he very much doubted if this would be any use, since the mobile appeared to be out of range, and it was therefore unlikely that Kurokawa was in his office. Sure enough, he heard at least twenty rings at the other end before he disconnected in disgust, cursing the fact that there was no voicemail system in Kurokawa's office. The problem now was that he really didn't have much time to make contact. Less than twelve hours from now. He decided that at the very least he could text Kurokawa's phone and send an e-mail message to his office. Surely he'd see one of those, or possibly both.

He pulled out Kurokawa's business card, and sent an urgent message to the office e-mail address that had been handwritten on it, outlining the situation. Now for the text message. Probably easier to do it in Japanese than fight the phone's English input system – he reckoned his language skills were just about up to the job. He wrestled with the phone's overly convoluted interface and eventually managed to get his message giving the time and place into what he hoped was tolerable Japanese, and sent it off. All he could do now was wait.

He packed up his folder of documentation, Vishal's memory stick, and Katsuyama's original disc into a small day rucksack, and added a box containing Katsuyama's gadget wrapped in anti-static plastic. He left the rucksack by the door, and checked the train times on the Internet. Ouch! He'd have to leave at about 4:30 the next morning.

Time to let Mieko know what was happening. He called the country inn where she was staying with Vishal and Meema.

"Good luck," she said when he'd explained what the arrangements were. "Wrap up warmly as well."

Sharpe laughed. "I think that's the least of my worries."

"No it's not," she said, seemingly quite seriously. "I have every confidence in you, Kenneth, that you can beat this man's nasty tricks and come out of it alive. I'm just not sure that I trust you to put on a warm pair of socks and wear an undershirt."

Sharpe found himself laughing and crying at the same time. "I love you, Mieko," he managed to say. "Who else would ever say anything like that to me?"

"I love you, Ken-chan," she replied. There was a harmonious silence between them which said more than any words could express.

"So," he said after a minute had passed.

"So. We'll see you soon. I miss you, Ken-chan."

"And I miss you," he replied. "Bye, love."

He hung up. His minders had discreetly turned their backs during the conversation. Even if they didn't understand the English, they could understand his tears.

He explained to them that he had to go early the next day, and he had to go alone, but that he had tried to contact Kurokawa, so that he would be safe.

"We'll come with you to the Enoshima monorail station," one of them said.

"I don't think that would be a good idea," said Sharpe. "If Campbell is working for Tomiko, they'll almost certainly be watching all the possible trains I could come on, and … It just wouldn't be a good idea. Let me go on my own." His mobile phone beeped, and he read the text message from Kurokawa, thoughtfully in English. "Look," showing them the phone. "It's OK. He says he's got my message and that his men are going to be there to look after me. Please, this really is something I have to do on my own."

The two shook their heads dubiously, but eventually agreed, given the message from Kurokawa confirming Sharpe's protection.

The message relieved Sharpe's mind more than he wanted to admit. Ever since Jon Campbell's phone call he realized that the butterflies in his stomach had been multiplying and that he was living on adrenaline. Booze now would be a bad idea, he thought to himself. Maybe something to eat would help.

Did they fancy sushi? he asked the two police minders. Fine, they told him, and about thirty minutes later, they were all sitting round the table demolishing a tray of sushi that had been ordered by phone.

"Early morning tomorrow," said Sharpe afterwards, with a grin that he didn't feel. "I'm off to bed. Goodnight."

THE ALARM CLOCK JOLTED SHARPE AWAKE only a minute or so after he'd finally got off to sleep, or so it seemed. He blearily killed the sound, and debated with himself whether to put the clock on snooze for another five minutes. Lethargy fought the fear of what would happen if he didn't keep the appointment, and fear won. His wake-up ritual didn't include a cold shower, but he took the trouble to shave properly, which helped to wake him up a little. He put on a clean undershirt and a thick pair of socks, remembering the previous evening's conversation with Mieko, and smiling as he did so.

Time for a ... He looked at his watch. Damn! There really wasn't time for coffee or breakfast. The condemned man got up late and missed his hearty breakfast, he thought. Famous last words. His two minders, who'd obviously changed with the previous evening's shift some time when he was asleep, bowed to him deeply as he left the flat, picking up the rucksack he had left there the night before. He returned the bow, and made his way through the surprisingly cold dark streets to the station. He'd worked it out that he only had to change trains once to catch the slow train down to Ōfuna, from where he could catch a monorail down to Enoshima, the seaside resort near Kamakura, south of Yokohama.

Usually, he could doze on trains and wake up automatically at his destination, but as the train rattled through Tokyo, through the grey industrial suburbs of Kawasaki, and through the endless enormous blocks of flats of southern Yokohama, he found himself too wound up to even consider closing his eyes. After what seemed like a whole day's journey, he arrived at Ōfuna. He only vaguely remembered the monorail from a day spent there the previous summer, but happily it was signposted, and he bought his ticket and found a seat in the three-car futuristic monorail that ran to the coast about four miles away, suspended beneath its track, and running up and down hills and through tunnels.

After the monorail had reached its final destination, he made his way down the concrete steps and started to walk towards the shore, and the causeway where he was to meet Jon. A cold wind blew in from the sea, and he wished he was wearing something more than the fleece jacket he had snatched up as he left the house. As he passed a vending machine, he bought a can of hot coffee. Disgustingly sweet, and he didn't think that whatever made it white had ever been near a cow, but at least it warmed him up.

He went through the underpass that led to the causeway, noticing some types who looked more than a little out of place. Heavy-set middle-aged men in dark suits and permed dyed hair didn't really seem like what you would expect to see in Enoshima before seven o'clock on a weekday morning. He hoped to God that the police snipers had been a little more subtle in their attempts to be inconspicuous.

As he climbed the steps from the underpass to the causeway, he could see a lone figure waiting halfway along, wearing a long leather coat, and what appeared to be a strange shiny hat. He walked closer, and realised that Jon wasn't wearing a hat, but had shaved his head, probably in imitation of something like The Matrix. Prat, thought Sharpe to himself.

He got to within five yards of Jon and stopped, obeying the upraised hand.

"Thank you," said Jon. "Now stay where you are, just put that bag down, turn round and put your hands in the air. Have to make sure you're not wired."

With rivers of cold sweat running down his spine, Sharpe did as he was asked. He felt Jon's hands running over him, and emptying his pockets, turning the contents out onto the ground, and thanked God that he and Kurokawa had decided against his wearing a bug, or recording the conversation.

"It wouldn't be admissible in court, anyway," Kurokawa had explained. "Laws for the protection of personal information and so on. I trust you and your memory to give an accurate account of the conversation."

"OK, turn round," came the order. "Now pick up that bag and hand it to me."

Once again, Sharpe did as he was told, seeing no point in arguing. He watched as Jon went through the contents, searching through all the zipped compartments and pockets.

"What's this?" Jon asked, holding up the USB memory stick.

"It's the whole of the currency trading system. The looseleaf binder there tells you how to get it onto a PC and how to get it working."

Jon flipped through the pages of the binder. "Impressive, I'll give you that." He put the USB stick into his coat pocket. "And this?" holding up Katsuyama's original CD that had formed part of the contents of the Hello Kitty box so long ago.

Sharpe explained. "It's encrypted," he added. "But we broke the encryption. That's also documented."

"OK. And this?" holding up the box containing the circuit board.

"That's the real goodies," said Sharpe. "Without that, you're stuffed. Take good care of it, because that's Katsuyama's masterpiece."

Jon opened the box to look inside. "So that's what it looks like," he said. "Hardly seems worth all the people, does it? That poor sod at Shinjuku station, and then Al Kowalski and Ishihara, Kim, and you."

Chapter 19: Tokyo, Shonan

"Me?" said Sharpe. "That's not part of the agreement, is it?"

"I lied. You hardly thought I was going to let you walk away from all this, did you?"

"Don't you have any sense of honour? Or even any common-sense? How the hell do you think you can walk away from this?" Sharpe asked. This was going to be tricky. He couldn't see for the life of him where the snipers were going to be stationed. It would be a bloody long shot, wherever they were, and there was a strong wind blowing in from the sea. Not good odds.

"Not a lot of honour, no. Al Kowalski trusted me right up to the end, and look where it got him." He grinned.

"That was you?"

"That was me. I got away with that. What makes you think I can't repeat the process? I am a diplomat of sorts, after all."

"I see." A pause. "A question. Why did Katsuyama have those pictures on him? The ones that Al Kowalski had?"

"Because he took them off Tomiko. Or she gave them to him. Not sure which."

"And just what was she doing with them?" Sharpe looked around him desperately. There was no-one in sight whose attention he could possibly attract to save himself. Just a fishing boat some way off. He hoped to God that Kurokawa's snipers were in position.

"Don't bother looking. There's no-one there to help you. We'll just carry on talking for a bit if you want. Why did Tomiko have the photos? Oh, Al Kowalski gave them to her. This was after he cocked up that burglary round your place. He wanted her to get Katsuyama's gadget off you. Seduce you or something. Or send her dad's boys round."

"And who told him that I had it in the first place?"

Jon just grinned at him.

"So he was working for you?"

"Yep. He just thought he was working for Ishihara, through me."

"But?"

"He was working for Kim and Tomiko, through me."

"Why didn't he get all the stuff directly off Katsuyama? Or why didn't you? If you were so close to Tomiko, why couldn't you have done it?"

"There was no way in hell that anyone could have got into his lab and taken the gadget. Too much security. And we had no idea, quite honestly, what to take in terms of the software. We had to wait until Katsuyama was ready to take it out of the lab and give it away to someone – you – before we could start making a move."

"I suppose it was too risky just to knock him over the head and take it?"

Jon nodded. "Exactly. All the time he was carrying the thing, he was watching his back. No way could we get to him."

"And how the hell did Kowalski know to go straight to the Hello Kitty box when he turned over my flat?"

"Remember the day you met Katsuyama? It was the same day I met you and fed you that bullshit about mantises, right?" Sharpe nodded. "You don't think all of that, meeting me and him on the same day, was a coincidence?"

"But you never saw the box. You couldn't have done. You were never close enough, were you?"

"Didn't need to. Remember that little tyke on the trike shouting that she wanted the box?" Sharpe nodded. "Thought you might. All I had to do was to get Al to look for anything with Hello Kitty all over it."

"Why the hell did you use Kowalski to do your dirty work? Why didn't you try to get it yourself?"

"I did try to get it myself, after Al had fucked things up. Why the hell do you think I took you to see Tim Barclay?"

"I was wondering that myself. You never told him what it was all about, though, did you? He thought it was all to do with image recognition."

"Do you think I'm completely daft? Of course I didn't tell him. I took you there because I wanted you to be under some sort of control instead of running round Tokyo sitting on a bloody fortune without knowing about it. Tim Barclay can pull weight where I can't. Didn't work, though, did it?"

Sharpe thought for a moment. "The timing's wrong. Katsuyama skipped the country the day I met him, or the next day. The burglary happened the evening after I met him. There's no way that Kowalski could have got the photos to Katsuyama via Tomiko."

"Shows how little you know about all that, doesn't it?"

"And how did Al Kowalski die?"

"More painfully and slowly than you will. He'd fucked up and let me down, after all. You've come through with the goods. You deserve something for that." Jon reached inside the leather coat, and came out with a long wicked-looking knife.

"Why the hell did you put the head in the locker?" Sharpe wanted the answers. Anything rather than find out what it was that Jon thought he deserved.

"I didn't. That must have been Kim's idea of a joke. Or maybe it was Tomiko's. She has a strange sense of humour sometimes, that one."

"How did Kim get hold of the body, then?"

"I left it with him to dispose of. He has more practice than me at these things, after all. You talk too much, Sharpe. You've been asking too many questions, and wasting my time giving you answers that won't do you any good in the long run. Time for you to say bye-bye to the world."

He advanced towards Sharpe, the knife held in an underhand grip. It looked like a reasonably experienced move, as though he knew how to use the knife, and Sharpe instinctively edged backward, towards the railing by the side of the causeway.

"Thanks," Jon said, with his teeth bared in a snarl. "It's going to be easier to get rid of you with you standing there. Just stay where you are and don't move. There's a good boy." He lashed out with the knife in a slashing movement, and Sharpe instinctively raised a hand to guard his face. The tip of the knife grazed the back of his hand, and Sharpe felt a searing pain.

Jon chuckled and took a step further, thrusting with the knife this time.

"One more question," said Sharpe. He really didn't expect any answers at this stage, but he was desperately trying to buy time before his *deus ex machina* in the form of Kurokawa and his men arrived to save him.

"All right," said Jon. "I suppose I'm feeling in a generous mood today, I suppose. Ask away."

"How did Kim die?"

Jon shook his head. "Not guilty there, either. Crazy bitch," he added.

"Tomiko? Why?"

"I suppose you know by now that there's a whole shitload of money out there which the Kims stashed away some time back?" Sharpe nodded. "She didn't want to share what she saw as her wealth with a whole load of North Korean apparatchiks. She wanted to pay the money and get as much out for herself as possible. He really did want to do something about changing the country, you know, silly sod, even if it wasn't the exact story he might have told you. A lot of that money that he wanted to retrieve would have stayed in Korea, lining the pockets of some senior army officers, and some would have gone to grease some palms in China. She didn't want that. They argued. She picked up a knife. She was fast. He was too slow. End of story. RIP. Happy now?"

Hardly the word Sharpe would have chosen to describe his feelings at that moment, but he nodded, and Jon suddenly lunged forward, leading with his knife hand.

Sharpe wasn't going to try to block the knife, but he thought he might be able to catch Jon's wrist and twist the weapon out of his hand. Faint hope. Jon's hand shot out and back far too fast for Sharpe to have any chance to even think about catching it. He was quick enough to avoid the thrust, though, as he stepped sidewise and back.

Jon lunged again, using only his arm, and Sharpe took one more step back, stumbling over a pile of garbage that had probably been swept up the previous evening, waiting to be picked up that morning. His shaky legs gave way under him, and he fell to his knees. He put his hands down on the ground to push himself up to his feet again.

"Don't bother, it's a waste of time and effort," came the mocking voice. Jon crouched down so his face was only slightly above Sharpe's eye level, and the knife was at about throat level. Throat-cutting level, Sharpe corrected himself in his thoughts. His left hand, behind his back, came into contact with something in the pile of garbage that felt long and hard and round, and gripped it tightly. Bringing his hand forward, he discovered that he was holding a toy wooden sword, of the type often sold as a souvenir at Japanese tourist spots. About three inches had broken off the tip – presumably the reason why it had been thrown away. As a weapon against a knife, it was pretty pathetic. Still, it felt better than nothing, even if it was only as a psychological prop.

Sharpe had studied kendo, but that didn't seem to be any use in the present situation. Kendo is a martial art that depends on movement for most of its effect, and kneeling isn't a recognized kendo stance. However, a kendo friend had introduced him to the basics of *iaidō* – the art of drawing a sword, often from a sitting or kneeling position, and killing one's enemy swiftly –and if ever there was an occasion for this obsolete and somewhat unusual martial art, this was it. Sharpe straightened up his kneeling position, and held the wooden sword by his side. Jon laughed. "Never give up, do you?" The knife waved hypnotically from side to side in front of Sharpe's face. Sharpe went through the movements of the first and easiest *iaidō* exercise, which was the only one he could bring to mind. Happily, that was the one which actually seemed most appropriate for the current situation.

He used his right hand to grab the sword and slash it in a horizontal arc in front of him, missing Jon's face by a matter of inches, making him draw back in surprise as Sharpe rose to one knee.

"What the—?" but Sharpe had already raised the sword above his head and, sliding forward while kneeling, brought it down two-handed with a loud crack on Jon's shaved head. The sharp splintered tip gouged a deep gash in Jon's skull as it slid off, and landed hard on his collarbone with another crack. The knife dropped out of Jon's hand as his left arm clutched his right shoulder.

"You fucking bastard, Sharpe. What the hell did you want to go and do that for?" Sharpe noticed that Jon's eyes appeared to be unfocused, staring into space. The blood from the cut on his scalp was pouring down his face, giving him a truly ghastly appearance, like something out of a cheap horror film.

As Sharpe scrambled to his feet, Jon appeared to notice him, and made a lunge in his general direction, but Sharpe managed to avoid the blind rush easily. He felt like a bull-fighter, but the bull appeared to be on its last legs.

"Where the hell are you?" Jon's face was now a mask of the blood which was welling from his lacerated scalp, and Sharpe could hardly see his eyes. "Why has it gone dark?" He seemed to focus on Sharpe and made another charge. Sharpe stepped aside in another matador-like move, dropping the wooden sword, and Jon careered past him to the railing, which caught him at about the level of his waist. He doubled over, seemingly staring at the heaving sea below.

"I can't see a fucking thing. Jesus. I spend over two fucking years setting up this whole bloody thing, and I end up getting hit on the head with a fucking stick. Christ, Sharpe, where are you, you bastard?"

"I'm here," said Sharpe behind him. "Get away from that rail or you'll fall in."

"What the fuck do you care about it?" asked Jon. "I'm fucked anyway. Hell, I can see those fucking mantises again. Been seeing them every night for months now. Oh, shit. There's no way I'm going to get out of this, is there?" He leaned further over the rail and then, suddenly, he was in the water below. The long leather coat floated obscenely behind him like some sort of weird sea creature, impeding his movements.

"Fucking cold in here. Don't bother coming in after me," he called up to Sharpe, before his nose and mouth went under the waves. Sharpe could hear noises now. The sputter of the motor of the fishing boat he had noticed earlier got louder, and the fishermen in it were shouting to Jon, calling to him to swim towards them. Waste of time, thought Sharpe, he can't hear you with most of his head underwater.

He'd half-noticed some of Tomiko's thugs running towards him from the mainland side of the causeway as he started his attack on Jon with the wooden sword. Now he heard the sound of a siren, and saw that the gang members had slowed their pace. A police car was coming up the causeway towards him. About time, he thought, and continued watching the fishing boat, which had reached the place where Jon's body had sunk and had throttled back the engine. Two men in the bow of the boat were fishing with poles and nets, and as he watched, he saw Jon's limp body brought to the surface.

He was hardly aware of the siren's noise getting louder, and the car screeching to a halt behind him until he felt hands gripping his shoulders.

"Oh, it's a foreigner," he heard a voice say. In slow, careful Japanese, the voice added, "Turn round slowly, and put your hands in the air." Sharpe did so, with a feeling of déjà vu.

"Where is Kurokawa-san?" he asked the more senior-looking policeman.

"Who is that?" came the reply. "I don't know any Kurokawa-san."

"Then why are you here?" Sharpe asked, astonished.

"Those fishermen saw a fight and called the emergency number on their mobile phones. Our car was nearby, so we came. Now please get in the car."

Sharpe did as he was told. There was little point in arguing.

Chapter 20: Shōnan

AT THE FUJISAWA POLICE STATION, Sharpe was pushed into a small room with a table and two chairs, and told to sit on the chair facing the door and wait. He was left alone, listening to the sounds of the police station coming to life. He looked at his watch. Not even eight o'clock yet.

The door opened, and a senior-looking uniformed officer entered. Sharpe stood up and bowed deeply. It seemed like a sensible thing to do, and from the reaction, was the right thing to do under the circumstances. The officer grunted in surprise and bowed back.

"Sit down," he said. "Your name and address, please."

Sharpe provided these details, together with one or two other pieces of general information. There was no move on the other's part to introduce himself. He might have been an automaton playing an assigned role and used few words except to ask the routine questions. He did, however, seem to possess a fairly wide vocabulary, in the form of grunts, which he used to respond to Sharpe's answers as he wrote them down.

"Now, who is this Kurokawa you were talking about? And what has been going on?"

Sharpe decided to ignore the second question for the

moment. "He's someone I know in Tokyo who works with a special police department. I think it would help if you were to speak with him."

A grunt from the repertoire. "Do you have his number?"

"Of course. Here you are." Sharpe passed over Kurokawa's card, which, like "Sugita's" card that he had been given what now seemed like years ago, contained little except the two characters for Kurokawa's name and a mobile phone number. Kurokawa had added his e-mail address, though.

"Thank you." He picked up the phone on the desk and started to dial. Pray God that he's awake and his phone's in range, thought Sharpe to himself. His prayers were answered – the phone was obviously picked up on the second ring. Sharpe's interrogator introduced himself, and then suddenly reacted to what was being said on the other end. He sat up straight in his chair (Sharpe wasn't sure if there was such a thing as "sitting at attention", but the phrase certainly seemed to fit here) and started answering in short sharp monosyllables. After a few minutes of this, he passed the phone to Sharpe.

"He wants to talk to you," and bowed as the phone changed hands.

"What the hell are you doing in Fujisawa police station? You're not meant to be there until this evening."

"What do you mean? I sent you a message yesterday and you replied, saying that you understood and you and your people would be here today."

"Yes, and it said 6 o'clock. You also said evening. If you don't believe me, check the sent messages folder on your phone."

Sharpe pulled out his mobile and pushed buttons. Holy shit, Kurokawa was right. He'd messed up his message and written the Japanese characters for PM instead of AM. What an idiot.

"I see," he said, chastened. "Can you come here now? I think there's a lot of explaining that needs to be done."

"I'm on my way. I've called for a car on the other line, and we'll be here as soon as we can. I'll find out the answers to my questions when I see you. In the meantime, hand the phone back to the gentleman who's taking care of you, and sit tight."

Sharpe did as he was requested, and watched with amusement as Kurokawa barked orders down the phone.

As the police officer returned the phone to its cradle, he bowed deeply and then turned to face Sharpe.

"Coffee?" he asked with an ingratiating smile.

"Yes, please. That's very kind of you."

A shout down the corridor through the opened door for the coffee. "I am sorry that we might have been a little rough with you. We had no idea ..."

"Not your fault," replied Sharpe. "Of course you couldn't be expected to know these things."

The other relaxed a little. Down the corridor, Sharpe could hear the tinkle of crockery and the sound of coffee being made.

Sharpe's would-be interrogator was obviously aching to find out what was going on, but Sharpe guessed that Kurokawa had told him to keep his mouth shut and not to ask too many questions.

Along with the kitchen sounds, Sharpe could hear other noises, which sounded as though a group of men was being brought in against their will, shouting and cursing. Tomiko's gangsters? Sharpe wondered to himself. He strained his ears, but it seemed as though the Japanese had an impenetrable accent.

The policeman noticed Sharpe's attention and also cocked an ear to listen. "Koreans," he said.

Well that explained why Sharpe couldn't understand

them, and it pretty much confirmed that these were Tomiko's men.

There was a welcome jingle of cups, and a young policeman arrived with two cups and saucers on a tray, together with some of the ubiquitous coffee whitener in tiny plastic containers and a couple of sachets of sugar. He carefully placed the coffee in front of Sharpe as if he were performing some part of the tea ceremony. He placed the other cup in front of Sharpe's interrogator. Sharpe noticed that it contained Japanese green tea, not coffee.

"After you," said the senior policeman when Sharpe had thanked the youngster, who looked as though he was just out of high school.

Sharpe sipped the lukewarm instant coffee. "Delicious coffee," he said, taking another sip of the vile brew. The youngster smiled and withdrew, bowing.

"May I leave you until the Tokyo people get here?" the senior police officer asked Sharpe. "You'll be comfortable?"

"This is fine," Sharpe assured him. Actually, it was fine. It certainly didn't appear that he was being treated as a prisoner, and that was OK by him.

"Feel free to use the phone," he was invited.

"Thank you," privately vowing not to use it at all. The odds were that all conversations were recorded, and he wasn't going to leave anything behind that might conceivably be turned into evidence against him at some time in the future. He trusted Kurokawa's good intentions, but only so far. They could easily be overruled by those above him.

The door closed, and he was left alone in the room. Time to catch up on some sleep – it seemed as though he'd been awake for hours, and hadn't gone to bed at all the previous night. Idly he wondered how he'd managed all-night music and drinking sessions when he was younger. It wasn't just lack of sleep that made him tired, he guessed. The emotional strain of the confrontation with Jon had probably had its effect, he reasoned. On that note, he dozed off, to be rudely awakened what seemed like hours later by someone shaking his shoulder.

"**Mr Sharpe**," said **Kurokawa**. "Time to wake up and face the world."

Sharpe rubbed his eyes and struggled to focus. He looked at his watch and realised that he'd been asleep for less than an hour.

"What the hell was the point of sending me that message in Japanese?" asked Kurokawa. "What a cockup. You're a lucky bastard, you know."

"Don't tell me. I can't believe I was that stupid. Why the hell wasn't your phone answering? I tried several times and I couldn't even leave a message on the voicemail."

"The battery had run flat on my phone," Kurokawa confessed. "I was charging the phone but hadn't turned it on to connect to the network. I really don't know about the voicemail, though. Not sure what end the problem was at – maybe my end, maybe yours. I got your text message as soon as I turned the phone on, and made all the arrangements for this evening."

"All right, sorry. I really was lucky that there was a police car nearby. I was sure you'd sent it there, though. Lucky that the fishermen were there as well, I suppose. It gives me the creeps to realise I was facing that lunatic without your people in place to back me up. All the time I was coming down here to Enoshima, and while I was talking with Jon, the thing that stopped me from running away was the thought that you and your people were nearby."

"The snipers were meant to start moving in about

midday. I would never have expected a meeting at this time of the morning. I'd have expected him to prefer the dark."

"Maybe he wanted to be able to see clearly if anyone was following him, or to give a clear view to Tomiko's thugs? If anything happened to him, they'd have been able to come running. Which they did, of course."

"Yes, it sounds from the little that I have heard that you were very lucky indeed that the car reached you before the gang members did."

"Did the police arrest any of them?"

"For what? They hadn't done anything wrong. There's no way that they could have been arrested or held on any charges."

"Anyway, thank you for coming down so quickly," said Sharpe. "I really freaked out when the police car came by and they'd never heard of you." He shivered.

"I really need to know exactly what happened," said Kurokawa. "We have a dead man on our hands, and he is, or rather he was, a member of the British Embassy staff, which means that there are some diplomatic issues involved. I think we can rely on Barclay to sort out most of the unpleasant aspects of this matter connected with the embassy, but it's vitally important that we know everything. I don't want any comeback on this from anywhere. My government, the British government, Campbell's relatives, whoever. I want this completely closed as soon as possible before there's any chance at all of the thing escalating."

"He's dead, then?" There hadn't really been any doubt in his mind that Jon Campbell would ever survive, but he had to ask.

"He was in shock when the fishermen pulled him out of the water. He died in their boat. Apparently he was bleeding like a stuck pig. He must have hit his head on the way down when you pushed him over the side."

"Actually, that's not at all what happened," Sharpe said. He proceeded to start an account of the way that he and Jon had met and talked.

"Leave out what he told you for now," said Kurokawa. "Right now, I'm much more interested in what actually happened. Then we'll take the back-bearings on the whys and wherefores." Sharpe went into some detail on how Jon had pulled the knife and how he'd found the wooden sword and used it. "So where's this wooden sword now?" asked Kurokawa.

"I've no idea," replied Sharpe. It was the honest truth. He had absolutely no idea of having left the stick anywhere – he supposed he must have dropped it at some time, but had no idea when.

"If that's the murder weapon, we have to have it available."

Sharpe looked at him in horror. "Did you just say 'murder'? I'm a bloody murderer now, am I?"

"Calm down, it's a figure of speech. *If* you were ever to be brought to trial on this, which I can pretty much assure you isn't going to happen, the charge almost certainly wouldn't be murder. The police probably wouldn't even hold you on the charge of abandoning a body if the facts are made clear."

"Some sort of comfort," Sharpe agreed. He was never quite sure how this crime of abandoning a body ever came to be on the Japanese books. He assumed it was used as a catch-all if the police were reasonably sure that the suspect had killed the victim, but hadn't enough evidence to convict or indict on the murder charge.

"Calm down. I'm sure we can make sure that there is absolutely no fallout on this. It was self-defence, and there's no way that anyone's going to call it any differently by the time I've finished. But they are going to need the stick, if only for form's sake." He opened the door and called for the policeman who'd been with Sharpe earlier, Shimamura.

Chapter 20: Shōnan

"Where's the weapon?" he asked. "Mr Sharpe here has just told me that he used a wooden sword against the dead man," (Sharpe was relieved to note that Kurokawa didn't use the word "murdered" and had used the honorific *-san* to refer to him, implying that he wasn't a suspect) "and didn't push him over the edge as the fishermen reported."

"We didn't pick it up, sir," confessed Shimamura. "No-one mentioned it, so we thought it wasn't necessary."

Kurokawa shook his head. "Mr Sharpe was probably holding it or had just dropped it, at any rate, when your people turned up. Did no-one really notice it?"

Shimamura bowed in apology. "Please allow me," he said, and picked up the phone. Sharpe couldn't make out exactly who he was talking to at first, but he worked out it was the driver of the patrol car which had picked him up. He was glad he wasn't that driver. Shimamura, having had his backside kicked by Kurokawa, was now taking it out on his underlings. And, Sharpe had no doubt, the driver would now take it out on his partner.

"There really seems to be no need to bother yourself with the death of the other man any further." Kurokawa, having established a tactical advantage with the non-discovery of Sharpe's weapon, was moving in for the kill. "I think it's fairly clear to me what happened, and there's no need to take it any further on your side." Sharpe noticed how Kurokawa had avoided any mention of Jon Campbell's name.

"The dead man was a foreigner. I think we should at least fill in the proper forms and so on. Sir," replied Shimamura, trying to regain some sort of standing.

"Not necessary," said Kurokawa. "These things are better handled by Tokyo, rather than the provinces, don't you agree?"

Sharpe actually felt a little sorry for Shimamura, but he

had to admire Kurokawa's handling of the situation, which definitely seemed to be moving to his advantage, if body language was anything to go by.

"So that's all out of the way," Kurokawa said, dusting his hands as if he'd just finished a strenuous job. Shimamura seemed to be slightly less than convinced by this conclusion, but he kept any doubts to himself.

"Thank you, Shimamura," said Kurokawa. It was a clear dismissal of the provincial by the city slicker, and Shimamura obviously took it as such, bowing out (literally) with a bad grace.

"So, where is the wonderful gadget now?" asked Kurokawa, when he and Sharpe were alone together.

"What do you mean? Jon's got it … had it, rather."

"How do you mean?"

"I packed everything up in a rucksack, and passed it to Jon."

"Everything?"

"The original disc that Katsuyama gave to me, a USB stick that Vishal prepared to make it into a turnkey system, a binder with all the instructions that Vishal and I could think of to make it work, and the hardware – the DSP array that Katsuyama made up."

"Yes, I saw the rucksack. Those idiots in the patrol car picked it up, but left the stick or sword or whatever it was. Typical. Couldn't find their own backside with both hands and a flashlight. But the rucksack was empty."

"Yes, I was going to explain that. Jon searched me and the rucksack for recording devices before he took the things out of the rucksack and stuffed them in his coat pockets."

"Ah." Kurokawa called out for Shimamura, who entered, looking more than a little browbeaten.

"Did you find anything in the dead man's pockets?" he asked.

"Please wait a moment." He shouted down the corridor. Couldn't they install some sort of system for summoning people? Sharpe asked himself. Mind you, Japanese people seemed to do a lot of shouting at any time. And when you got to the police or the military, it was probably obligatory at all times. Anyway, it seemed to work on this occasion. A few minutes later, the same young policeman who had brought Sharpe's coffee earlier now entered with another tray. This time, instead of coffee, it held a miscellaneous collection of objects – keys, a handkerchief, a knife sheath, and other things, all neatly labelled. Sharpe examined the selection a little more closely.

"Here you are," pointing to something on the tray. "This is the USB stick I gave him.

Kurokawa looked at the label. "Left hand outer coat pocket. Was he left-handed?"

Sharpe closed his eyes, trying to remember. "No, but he had his knife in his right pocket. He must have stuffed these things into the pocket on the other side."

"All of them?"

"Yes, I'm sure of that. The disc and the hardware in a separate box went into the same pocket. Long loose leather coat." He closed his eyes again. "There was a flap over the pocket, but the pocket was too small to hold the box, so the box was sticking out of the pocket a bit. The flap didn't cover it." He re-opened his eyes.

"Well, it's not there now. Or rather, the things weren't there when they searched his pockets, which means they weren't in his pockets when they found the body."

"Maybe they fell out into the boat when they pulled him out of the water?"

"It's a thought," Kurokawa admitted. "Shimamura, get that boat searched." More of the same shouting down the hall procedure. "Thank you. That will be all for now." No love was lost as Shimamura made his way out of the room, pointedly closing the door behind him.

"So, what else did Campbell tell you?" Kurokawa settled himself into the chair.

"Not an awful lot, I'm afraid. Well, not a lot that made a lot of sense." He explained how Jon had told him that the photos he had found in Katsuyama's wallet had been passed by Kowalski to Tomiko Katsuyama.

"But that doesn't explain how they found their way to Katsuyama," Kurokawa pointed out. "We had him pegged as leaving the country the evening that the body was found at Shinjuku station."

Sharpe looked at him curiously. "You know that for a fact?"

"Yes. Don't ask. And we are also pretty certain that he went back home to say good-bye to her before he took off for Vietnam." Sharpe didn't ask, but still marvelled at the exact extent of Kurokawa's powers. They seemed to be extensive.

"Did anyone else leave Japan at that time? Someone connected with all this, I mean?"

"That is something we will have to work on. I am pretty sure that's not the case, though."

"Or they could simply have been posted to him? But that seems a little silly when the original digital files could have been e-mailed."

"Assuming the original digital files were still in existence, or at least available for transmission, that is. We have to assume that Kowalski died the day after the burglary. You told me Kim gave you the key to the station locker that evening. That means he must have been killed and disposed of before then."

"The night he did the burglary, then? Some time early in the morning?"

"Probably. That's the 'when' part of it all. What about the 'who' and the 'why'? Any ideas?" asked Kurokawa.

"I was told Kowalski was working for someone and wasn't doing this as a freelance job. If he came back and reported empty-handed, the person who'd hired him to do the job would be pissed-off enough to dispose of him, if he was that sort of person. And then send the photos to Katsuyama just to let him know that whoever we're talking about had you under observation. Just a friendly warning."

"Agreed – sounds reasonable at any rate."

"By the way, I was told that your late boss ordered the burglary."

Kurokawa stared at him. "Are you serious?"

"I'm serious that I was told that, yes. It's a load of crap, quite frankly. There would be much easier ways for you people to get hold of the Katsuyama technology than getting Al to burgle my flat, surely?"

"I can guess who told you that fairy story. And I can also guess that it was the same person who hired Al to do the job on your flat."

"And the same person who killed him when he failed to deliver the goods. He as good as admitted all of these things."

"Oh, did he? Surprising how many of these psychos seem to want to show off when they feel the end is in sight. And who was responsible for the head in the locker? The same person?"

"He said not. He said that he was responsible for the killing, but not for the garbage disposal. That seems like one of Tomiko's little jokes. He passed Kowalski's body to the Kims, and that was the result."

Kurokawa nodded thoughtfully. "Can't have British diplomats scurrying round the place at night disposing of dead bodies. Wouldn't be cricket, would it?" There was a knock on the door. "Come in," yelled Kurokawa. Sharpe mentally massaged his eardrums. Did they all have to shout all the time?

"There's a foreigner who wants to see you, sir," a young police officer said to Kurokawa.

"Show him in, then."

Sharpe was puzzled. Who on earth was going to be coming to see Kurokawa at this time in the morning?

"**Sorry to take so long**," said Tim Barclay to Kurokawa as he entered the room, stripping off his trench coat. "I started as soon as I got your message, but it took me *hours* to get down here. Bloody trains had stopped. Some silly bugger had thrown himself under a train at the next station. *Selfish* bastard. Good morning, Ken," turning to Sharpe. "I hear things have been happening."

"That's one way of describing it."

"So we are permanently deprived of the charming company of Mr Jonathan Campbell, may the Devil bugger his immortal soul? Good riddance to bad rubbish, is what *I* say."

"I'm not going to comment on that. Will you make the official identification for the record as soon as we finish up here?" Kurokawa asked him. "I think it will make things easier if you do it, rather than anyone else from the embassy."

"Fine. I don't see Consular wanting to touch it, anyway. I can always bring in the Official Secrets Act or some such bullshit. What's the inquest going to conclude as the official cause of death?"

"Death by misadventure," replied Kurokawa.

"Can you really fix the result of an inquest just like that?" Sharpe asked.

Kurokawa and Barclay looked at each other and laughed.

"We can do a bloody sight more than that, Ken lad," replied Barclay. "So what really happened?"

Sharpe gave him a brief summary of events, and Barclay chuckled appreciatively. "Hit on the head with a stick and fell into the water? You have to admit that 'death by misadventure' sounds a bit more respectable, don't you think? So the little shit killed Big Al, you think?"

Sharpe and Kurokawa both nodded. "I know so," Sharpe said. "He as good as told me all the gory details."

"And who did for Kim?" asked Barclay. He and Kurokawa looked at Sharpe, who answered.

"He claimed that wasn't him. A family squabble over the money."

Barclay sighed theatrically. "Aren't they always? Over money, I mean."

"Apparently, despite what you told me, Tim, Kim actually did seem to have some sincere interest in reforming North Korea. Quite a lot of the gold would have gone to doing that. Tomiko wanted it all, and there was an argument."

"Pull her in?" Barclay asked Kurokawa.

"We've no proof, and she might even have done Japan a public service by getting rid of him. I don't care what she thinks, but our boys in the organised crime side of things don't seem to think that she's going to last very long, and that the gang's going to fall apart anyway. Let her go. With looks like that, and the proof and evidence we don't have, she'd walk anyway." He shrugged. "Some things are better left untouched, and I think this is one of them."

"I'm truly sorry about your boss, though," Barclay said to Kurokawa. "I liked him and respected him. We were friends at Cambridge, you know, and I feel a bit ashamed of myself for not having done more to get Jon out of the way. Truth to tell, I really didn't think he would go as far round the bend as he did. But I really had hoped to have got him out of the country before he could do any damage to anyone." Sharpe looked up. "No, I never told you, did I? I knew he was up to no good right from before the first time that you and I talked. I had pretty good evidence that he was using some kind of drugs – cocaine or amphetamines or something – maybe not enough evidence for conviction, but suspicious enough to get him sent home. Problem was that the little bastard then went ahead and muddied the waters with all that crap about my alleged insider trading, and the stupid idiots in London would have thought this was just a revenge hatchet job. Which it would have been, I suppose," he reflected, "but I really wanted him out of the way before he did something stupid. I have no wish to be accused of harbouring druggies in my organisation. I have enough problems as it is without that sort of thing."

"I'd say that killing Ishihara in that way was worse than stupid," Sharpe said.

"Please, Ken, like Humpty Dumpty, when I say 'stupid', it encompasses a whole multitude of sins. It doesn't just refer to intellectual incapacity." He turned to Kurokawa. "I really am so sorry about this," he repeated. "I feel that it was my responsibility to have made sure that he was never in a position where this could have happened."

Kurokawa was saved the embarrassment of replying by yet another knock on the door. Shimamura let himself in.

"No sign of anything in the boat. Sorry."

"OK." Kurokawa sighed. "Have you instructed the fishermen what they should say about all this?"

"Yes, sir. They've been told to say nothing at all."

"And if they forget and do start talking?"

"We found two empty *shōchū* liquor bottles in the boat. They were drunk and didn't know what they were talking about."

"Good, good," said Kurokawa. "I don't think we're

going to have any problems in that direction. So," turning to Sharpe. "Where is the original disc and the hardware?"

"My guess is that they're at the bottom of the sea."

"Which I see no point in dragging, with the tides and currents being what they are in that area. Even if we did discover it by some miracle, almost certainly the electronics would be damaged, and probably unusable. And that was the only example?"

"As far as I know, yes."

Barclay swore. At least, that's what it sounded like, as it was somewhat under his breath.

"May I ask," said Sharpe to Kurokawa, "if you do— did find it, what would you do with it?" He had a feeling that he wasn't going to like the answer. He didn't.

"It would belong to the Japanese government, of course," replied Kurokawa.

"Why 'of course'?"

"Invented by a Japanese citizen—"

"A self-confessed murderer, living outside Japan, who did most, if not all, of the work in the USA." This from Barclay.

Kurokawa waved a hand. "Details. You didn't really think we were going to let Sharpe keep it, or hand it to you British, did you?"

"I suppose not. I might have expected some compensation, though, don't you think?" said Sharpe.

"It's a dead issue," replied Kurokawa.

"Damn it, that thing's worth billions, if it's worth half as much as you say it is," complained Barclay. "Even if you spent two weeks – two months – dragging the ocean floor, and a year reconstructing things from what you discovered, you'd still come out ahead."

"You've missed the point," said Kurokawa. "We'd want to bury this thing so deep that you'd never see it again. Something like this in professional hands – no offence to you," turning to Sharpe, "wouldn't just feed off the market. It would influence the market to such an extent that it would become a disruptive force. I'm guessing there would be non-linear equations involved, and the whole global economy would be completely disrupted."

Barclay shrugged. "That's hard to believe."

"Not at all," said Sharpe. "I'm beginning to see what you mean. If we were hedging not just the delta, but the theta by shorting through a third currency … I haven't worked it all out in my head yet, but I have a gut feeling about what you mean. There'd be an awful lot of stuff feeding back on itself, wouldn't there?"

"I'm very happy to say, dear boy, that I haven't the faintest bloody clue what you're talking about." Barclay grinned.

"I'm not convinced I do, really, either," said Sharpe. "But I have a glimmering of what Kurokawa-san's talking about. I'm not sure if I can think of an analogy off the top of my head, but for now, forget any idea that the markets are efficient. They're not. It's all herd mentality and mob psychology, and the market's not much more than a positive feedback loop, whose next set of parameters are driven by the results of the previous event, meaning that we're really talking chaos theory, and …"

Barclay covered his ears with his hands. "Please don't," said. "I'm just a simple soldier boy."

"And I am Marie of Romania," retorted Sharpe. "You don't have to understand every little last thing. I think you get the drift. I had a feeling that this might be the case and I actually raised this very point when we started out. Meema is pretty damn smart, after all, but she's not a whole research department. If we'd been trading in any kind of real volume, and using some fairly smart trading algorithms, it's conceivable we could have done some real damage there."

"I'm glad you see it that way," said Kurokawa. "It really could be a dangerous toy if the wrong person got hold of it."

"Like North Korea?" suggested Sharpe.

"Exactly. Maybe they don't have the financial wizards that exist in other countries, but they could certainly make a mess of the world's economies by being only a little more sophisticated than your trading operations. Of course, they'd need a lot more money to start with than you were using, but they could always use their gold reserves."

"Are you seriously telling me that this thing could fuck up the global economy worse than the current gang of Wall Street morons have done?" asked Barclay.

"Almost certainly," replied Kurokawa. "Want to see the dollar drop down to 50 yen? I have little doubt it could be done."

Sharpe considered an objection. "If we're talking chaos theory, which we are, aren't we, surely the Katsuyama gadget would also be a factor in the market, and it would fail to predict its own effects?"

"Want to try and prove that?" asked Kurokawa.

"I'm assuming that's a rhetorical question? Maybe it could predict itself if it was a large enough factor to affect the market on its own. I don't know. You'd probably have to be a genius along the lines of Katsuyama to know for sure."

"So you're saying that, to use my phrase earlier about Jon Campbell, we're saying good riddance to bad rubbish? The wonder gizmo is in fact the destroyer of worlds?" Barclay sighed.

"A bit poetical, but not at all wrong. Now, we have things to do. Our colleagues here in Fujisawa must be appeased, and I am going to have to smooth some ruffled feathers, not just here, but at the Kanagawa prefectural headquarters. Mr Sharpe, you are going to have to stay here for a day or so. Sorry. I'll make sure you get good treatment."

"No more coffee from these people, please." Sharpe smiled.

"Seriously, I'll make sure you're looked after OK. And I'll make sure your lady and your friends are informed."

"Thanks, I appreciate it."

"Major, I am going to need an official note from the British Embassy demanding Mr Sharpe's release. I leave the how and who to you. Also, I can trust you to sweep things under the carpet when it comes to the untimely demise of your colleague?"

"I think so. He went swimming early in the morning, got cramp and got into difficulties. His head hit the causeway as he struggled to get out of the water, causing him to lose consciousness and drown."

"Perfect," said Kurokawa. "So let us get on with our appointed tasks, Major, and leave Mr Sharpe to enjoy the hospitality of Fujisawa's finest."

They left. As they did so, Sharpe could almost have sworn that he heard Barclay singing an old hymn to himself: "The trivial round, the common task ..." Sharpe grinned to himself. For all his faults, Barclay could be amusing at times.

Chapter 21: Tokyo, Narita

It was two weeks after Sharpe's final encounter with Jon Campbell. Despite Kurokawa's breezy assurances, he had spent over a week in police custody before being released. However, while his accommodation fell short of the "luxury cell" he had experienced in Seoul, it was far from being as unpleasant as he had feared. Obviously Kurokawa did have some influence. He'd even managed to get decent coffee sent in from a coffee shop for Sharpe's benefit.

At the end of his stay, Kurokawa had come in person to release him.

"I am sorry that you had to stay in there so long. It took a little more time than I had hoped to get it all sorted out."

"So what's the situation? Officially, I mean."

"As we agreed, Jon Campbell died while swimming in water that was far too cold for him. He got cramp and died after hitting his head on a rock."

"Did anyone believe it?"

Kurokawa shrugged. "Who knows? They accepted the story, anyway. Major Barclay informs me that there are several in the British Embassy who aren't shedding too many tears about his loss. He was cremated here in Japan, of course, and the ashes have been flown back to the UK. The likelihood of your facing any charges based on exhumation are slim, to say the least."

"Where have I been?"

"Well, of course I told your friends, as we agreed. Sorry they couldn't come to see you, by the way, but we decided that this would attract too much attention. Hope the phone and Internet connection allowed you to keep in contact, anyway."

"Yes, they did. Thank you for that."

"Anyway, it's taken this long, I'm afraid, for us to create all the official documents, and then lose them."

"Why did you have to create them in the first place?"

"Bureaucracy. Someone would probably have felt it was their duty to create them at some time. But since there's a record that it's been done, there's no need. And if the same nosy-parker should start looking for them," he shrugged, "they're nowhere to be found. But that, as you can probably guess, is hardly an uncommon state of affairs in the Japanese civil service."

"So nothing's happened?"

"Officially, nothing's happened," Kurokawa confirmed. "So let's go. I have a car waiting outside for you."

"**AND SO HE DROVE ME BACK TO TOKYO** and dropped me back home."

Sharpe was sitting in a café in the departure area of Narita Airport, explaining to Vishal and Meema, who were flying back to India in a few hours, what had happened to him.

Because of all the problems that Sharpe had encountered over the past week, and because Vishal and Meema had been busy packing up to go back to India, he'd hardly had a chance to fill them in on all the details.

"And so here you are back with us," said Vishal.

"But only for another," he checked his watch, "fifty minutes at the most before you start boarding."

"Weren't you scared?" asked Meema. She was looking more relaxed than Sharpe had seen her for a long time, and happy, leaning comfortably against Vishal.

"Scared? When? When I was facing Jon Campbell? I certainly was. I defy anyone not to be scared if they have a maniac like that waving a bloody great knife in their face."

"I am wishing I could have seen his face when you hit him, though." Vishal smiled.

Sharpe shook his head. "You wouldn't want that, believe me. I killed someone—"

"You didn't kill him, Ken-chan," Mieko told him. "From what you told me, he dived into the sea of his own accord. We've been through this so many times over the past few days," she explained to the others.

"He wouldn't have done it if I hadn't hit him. I've been waking up seeing that bloody face in my dreams every night."

"He attacked you, though. It was self-defence."

"Even so. I know he was a psycho and out to kill me, but it makes it no easier to live with the memory."

"Poor Ken," said Meema. She reached out and held his hand, squeezing it a little before letting go.

"So what are they going to be doing about Tomiko?" asked Vishal. "It seems to me that she is the most guilty person left in Japan. You say she killed her father, and she is partly responsible for this Jon fellow being what he is. Are they not going to do anything about her?"

"And what about Katsuyama?" asked Meema.

Sharpe held up his hands. "One at a time, and keep your

voices down. I don't want to be telling the whole of the airport about what's been going on." Meema and Vishal apologised. "They've let Katsuyama know exactly how much they know and what sort of prison sentence he'll be facing if he comes back here. They seem to be seeing him as a kind of mad genius, with the emphasis on the 'mad'. I don't think it's going to bother him too much if he never sees Tomiko or any of that family again. And according to the police, without the money, Tomiko's not going to be able to hold the gang together. They don't see how they could ever get any kind of conviction, anyway."

"So do you think Katsuyama's just going to stay in Vietnam?"

"Why not? Goodness knows what his business is going to end up doing, and who's going to be in charge, but he's smart enough to get by, whatever happens."

"And what are you going to be doing, Ken-san?" asked Meema. "No bank's are going to be hiring contractors like you for a while."

"I know. But you did save enough money for me to be able to take stock of the situation for a few months at least. I'm not completely helpless, you know. Still," he stretched, "it was strange being a millionaire for a few weeks."

"And you will be again," said Vishal. "When you are joining us later."

"What's this?" said Sharpe. Meema and Vishal burst into giggles, and Mieko seemed amused. "What on earth has got into you?"

"Kenneth-san," said Vishal. "While you were enjoying your holiday in Fujisawa, we were thinking. The market's going to settle down. We can use Katsuyama's technology from Mumbai. As soon as my sister's had her operation, and she's feeling well enough to come home, I am thinking that will be the time that we should be starting up the business again."

"What are you talking about?" said Sharpe. "All of Katsuyama's great ideas are at the bottom of the sea. Do you want me to take up scuba diving or something?"

"Remember, my friend, I have the safety copy of Katsuyama's disc that I made so long ago. And a copy of the USB memory." He fished in his pockets, and a look of sheer horror spread over his face. Eventually, after much frantic searching, he came up with a USB stick. He gave a gale-force sigh of relief. "Here you are. And it even contains all the documentation you wrote."

"One little thing," Sharpe reminded him. "We need the DSP array that Katsuyama put together. Without that, there's no way you'll be able to make real-time calculations."

"Kenneth-san." Vishal was grinning widely. "Remember what Meema has her Ph.D. in?"

"I did get quite a good look at the board several times. I know what chips are being used. I honestly think I could put something similar together. Vishal knows all about how the code talks to the hardware and so it's just a question of working backwards." She smiled sweetly.

"And," Vishal added, "even if we cannot be doing this entirely by ourselves, there are many people in Mumbai who can be helping us. I think there will be no problem with making money to pay these people."

"So when are you coming to Mumbai, Kenneth-san?" Meema batted her eyelashes at him, and Sharpe burst out laughing.

"Let me think. It's a big move."

"Look," said Mieko, "You two should be going through security and everything. The board's changed."

The four friends stood up.

"Bye, Meema." He hugged her carefully, and they kissed

each other on the cheek, bringing back memories he would sooner have forgotten.

"I won't kiss you, Vishal." But they hugged. There were tears in their eyes as Vishal and Meema picked up their bags and walked towards the security gates.

"Bye," they called.

Sharpe and Mieko stood holding hands, and waving with their free hands until their friends were out of sight.

"So," said Mieko, as they turned away and walked back to the airport station. "When *are* we going to Mumbai?"

"Soon, dear. Soon." And he meant it.

At the Sharpe End

First draft sections

THE SECTIONS BELOW WERE ORIGINALLY WRITTEN in 2007. Even then it was obvious to me that a major earthquake could have repercussions as regards Japan's nuclear power. It doesn't make me a prophet or prove that I am endowed with great wisdom, obviously, but it is interesting to see how much of what I wrote back then actually happened (and what didn't happen!) after March 11, 2011.

By the time I came to publish the novel, the 2008 Wall Street bank meltdown had occurred, and the earthquake had not happened. I therefore changed the story considerably to reflect the real-life event, which I could use as part of the story and add realism. This involved many changes to the plot, so there are a few references here to an older version of the story. The original used different names for some of the characters, so I have changed these to match the final published version, otherwise it would be too confusing.

Tuesday, Tokyo

THE NEXT DAY, SHARPE WAS ON THE TELEPHONE talking to Kim about Barclay again, when things started to happen.

"Please don't have your man follow me today. I'm sure that Barclay will foul up the deal if he feels that he's being watched," he began, when a familiar sickening feeling started. "Uh-oh, earthquake," he said to Kim.

"Yes, I felt it too, a few seconds ago," said Kim. "I'm down in Yokohama at the moment. I think we're getting it down here first." There were loud crashes and banging noises from the other end of the line.

"Are you all right?" asked Sharpe.

"Yes. Hang on. Big one coming your way," said Kim briefly. As he finished speaking to Sharpe, the floor shook violently up and down, which Sharpe had been told was the sign of a really serious earthquake, as opposed to the usual side-to-side shaking. He actually felt himself being thrown a couple of centimetres off the floor as the lights in the room went out, and the shaking continued what seemed like hours, but was only thirty seconds, as Sharpe found out later from the reports in the media.

Shrieks from Meema's room, where Mieko was also sitting at the moment

"Hello? Hello?" Sharpe called into the phone, but there was no answer. The line seemed to have gone dead, He dropped the phone and rushed into the trading room. Meema was sitting, transfixed and rigid, staring blankly at the black computer screen.

"I knew we should have put in a UPS," said Vishal, pointing to the blank screens.

"And what good would an uninterruptible power supply do in a situation like this, then?" snapped Sharpe. "The whole bloody city's probably dead in the water." He crossed over to Mieko, who was shivering with fear, and put his arms round her. Vishal did the same for Meema, who seemed the most frightened of all of them.

"It's all right, that's the worst of it over," calmed Sharpe. He had no way of knowing whether that was true or not, but Mieko relaxed a little in his arms.

"That was a bad one," said Meema, still shaking.

"It was the worst I've ever been in," Mieko said. "I guess that was about a five or six." The Japanese scale of reporting earthquake intensity focuses on the perception of the earthquake at the point where it is experienced, rather than the intensity of the earthquake itself at the source. It's an open-ended scale, but the earthquake that destroyed Kobe in 1995 was regarded as a 7+. Any earthquakes above a three are instantly reported on TV.

"Scared the shit out of me," admitted Sharpe. "Fucking hell!" His sudden obscenity was caused by the floor heaving once again. More things started to fall off shelves, jumping off as if they were alive—big things that Sharpe would never have believed could fall. There was a crash in the next room as something large and heavy fell over, and one of Meema's large computer screens toppled to the floor next to Sharpe.

"Bloody hell!" said Vishal. "Those things are expensive and tricky to get hold of." Despite himself, Sharpe was quietly amused at Vishal's sense of priorities.

"Get me out of here," Meema whimpered.

"You're right, Meema," said Sharpe. "We shouldn't be here. To the toilet."

"What?" said Vishal, who hadn't heard this piece of Japanese earthquake folklore.

"The corners of the small room will form a rigid box. Even if the rest of the building collapses, we'll be safe." The building was creaking ominously now. The vertical jolting had finished, but there were still aftershocks, which were themselves as strong as many earthquakes that Sharpe had experienced in the past. The four of them crammed into the toilet. Meema and Mieko sat on the toilet itself with their arms around each other, and Vishal and Sharpe stood beside them, grinning a little shamefacedly.

They listened to the creaking of the building around them in silence.

Suddenly Meema spoke. "I think I just wet myself," she confessed.

"Don't worry," said Mieko, taking her hand and holding it firmly. "I did that a long time ago. I just hoped no-one would notice."

"Hey!" said Vishal. "I think things are getting a bit quieter." They listened carefully. There were sirens in the distance, and the noise of someone speaking over the ubiquitous public announcement system in the streets. Sharpe strained his ears, but his Japanese wasn't up to catching the words.

"There's been an earthquake," Mieko translated for them. (Meema started to giggle hysterically. "Tell us something we didn't know," she said. "Quiet," hissed Vishal.) "Its centre was near Shizuoka, and it was over a seven in strength." ("Bloody

Tuesday, Tokyo (first draft sections)

hell," said Sharpe.) "No danger of tsunami, but aftershocks are expected. If your building is damaged, go to the nearest emergency centre which is the number 2 elementary school. More information available later."

"I wonder what's on TV?" asked Sharpe.

"No electricity," Vishal reminded him.

"I know," Sharpe said, pulling out his mobile phone. "I changed phones recently. This has a TV tuner in it."

They watched in silence, but NHK had little more concrete news to give, except that a lot of damage seemed to be centred around a place called Omaezaki in Shizuoka prefecture and that Yokohama and the surrounding areas had reported suffering extensive damage.

"That's almost certainly going to block the all main roads, and the expressway and the railway lines between Tokyo and Osaka," pointed out Sharpe. "It'll bugger up the whole country for some time to come."

"There's a back way through the mountains," Mieko pointed out.

"Yes, of course, but the bulk of all the traffic goes along the coast past the earthquake site. The bullet trains won't be running for at least a month, I bet you, and I'm sure at least some of the tunnels on the expressway are going to be unsafe as well, if they're not actually blocked." The four of them stood in silence for a while as the aftershocks continued, and further crashes and bangs were heard in the other rooms.

"I'm calling my parents," Mieko announced, and pulled out her mobile phone, covering her mouth with her hand as she spoke softly into the mouthpiece. A few minutes later, she put the phone back into her bag. "They're all right," she informed Sharpe. "Dad says that all his bonsai have fallen over, but he and Mum are all right."

Sharpe suddenly remembered a magazine article he had written some time previously. "Holy shit!" he swore.

"What?" asked Mieko.

"The stupid bastards have put a nuclear power station at Hamaoka near Omaezaki—right over an earthquake fault line. This is going to make Chernobyl look trivial."

"You're joking?" asked Vishal.

"I wish I was. This could be truly terrible, depending on which way the wind's blowing."

"They always claim that the power stations are totally safe," ventured Mieko.

"They said that about the *Titanic*, too," countered Sharpe. "More to the point, they said that about the Kobe expressways that collapsed." The silence returned, with an added chill.

"They'll let us know if anything's wrong, won't they?" said Mieko.

"I doubt it, I'm afraid," said Sharpe. "If you remember that accident in Tokaimura some time ago, when those workers nearly caused a nuclear meltdown through their incompetence and ignorance, the government was really quiet about the danger. They don't give a damn except about their own pockets."

"You're always criticising Japan," complained Mieko.

"With good reason," retorted Sharpe. "The politicians here are a bunch of crooked no-good incompetents."

"And how is that any different from America?" shot back Mieko.

"I never claimed America was perfect. If you hadn't noticed, I'm British in any case."

"Will you two be quiet?" said Vishal. "It's not helping anything, you know."

Sharpe and Mieko both apologised to the other two and to each other, and went quiet. After about ten minutes,

Tuesday, Tokyo (first draft sections)

when no further shocks had occurred, Vishal suggested that they leave the cramped safety of the toilet.

The place, to put it mildly, was a mess. Everything which had been on a shelf seemed to have fallen from its place. Meema's workstation screens had all toppled over, and her kitchen area was a mess. Turmeric seemed to have spilled everywhere, turning everything yellow. One windowpane seemed to have fallen from its frame, and two others were cracked.

Sharpe clicked the light switches. Nothing.

"I don't think we can expect any power for a few days," said Vishal. "Listen, though."

They listened. The usually bustling city of Tokyo seemed like a ghost town—there was almost no sound in the streets outside. In the distance, sirens wailed. The loudspeakers started up again.

"They're telling us to drink only bottled water," said Mieko.

"That would be a good idea, if we had some," said Vishal.

"I'll get some, and some other stuff," said Sharpe. "I'm betting that the convenience stores will be open again soon, if they're not already."

"I'm coming with you," said Vishal. "I know this is Tokyo and we're probably safe, but I think two are safer than one here. We don't know what's going to happen in an emergency, or how people will react."

"Thanks," said Sharpe. He turned to Mieko and Meema. "Lock the door behind us, and don't open it up to anyone, unless you know it's us."

Sharpe and Vishal went out, taking some plastic carrier bags with them in anticipation, and expecting the worst. They were pleasantly surprised. The streets were nearly empty, and the few people they met greeted them with expressions of solicitude, even apology that foreigners as guests to Japan should have been exposed to such a terrible thing. Despite the damage within the office space, the streets showed remarkably few signs of the recent upheaval. Here and there glass had fallen from windows above, covering the street wish shiny glittering particles. In one place, there was a crack across the width of the road, from which water was spurting as the result of a burst main. There was, of course, no electricity, and very few cars were moving. The train crossing at the end of the road was closed, with the barriers down.

"Why?" Vishal asked, as they squeezed under the barriers and walked across the deserted tracks.

"To stop ambulances and fire engines and hinder rescue efforts?" suggested Sharpe sarcastically.

"That's a mercy, anyway," remarked Vishal. "There are no fires, anyway. Not in this part of Tokyo that I can see."

"I suppose we should be thankful that this didn't happen at a time when everyone was cooking and the gas stoves were lit," commented Sharpe. "Though it does seem as though we've come through it fairly well here." Just then his mobile phone rang.

"Are you safe?" said Barclay.

"You're not asking for your money after all this, are you?" asked Sharpe incredulously.

"*Au contraire*, dear boy, that's just what I was calling about. Let us postpone our little arrangement until things have quietened down a bit, shall we? I doubt if I could get over and meet you in any case, and it's not very nice to see everyone else in the same sort of temporary boat as myself was, to be honest. I'd feel a bit of a bastard, you know, taking toys from a blind baby, or whatever the phrase is."

"What are things like on your side of town?" asked Sharpe.

"Bloody grim, to be frank. Some of the older buildings have collapsed, and I'm trying to organise some of the local lads to dig out some of the old folks trapped there. We'd welcome another pair of hands, but I'm sure you have your own worries." He rang off.

"What the hell was that?" asked Vishal.

"Someone I'd written off completely as a selfish bastard, who's spending his time digging old folk out of the rubble." Sharpe shook his head. The complexities of human nature left him sadly perplexed at times.

When they reached the convenience store, an orderly line had already formed. The staff were calmly dispensing rice balls and bottles of water, and not charging for them, though they were accepting money for other items. Since the area was primarily a business area, most of the customers were dressed for business, and were obviously some way from their homes. There were very few families or children in the store. "They always say that disasters bring out the best in people. I never really believed it," said Sharpe.

He and Vishal returned to the office, laden with bottled water, some of the rice-balls, and a collection of assorted foods which would last a few days and which didn't need cooking. Sharpe had insisted on handing over money for all of these, over the protests of the shop staff, and they had compromised by taking the money for the water and rice balls separately and stuffing it into a Red Cross collecting box.

Meema and Mieko let them in. "Quiet?" asked Sharpe.

"Not a soul," replied Mieko. "I'm really surprised how quiet everything is. Is it bad out there?"

"Not nearly as bad as we feared," replied Sharpe. "I wonder how Kim is getting on? He was down in Yokohama. I was talking to him when the earthquake hit." He dialled Kim's mobile number. He had to try several times, as all the circuits seemed to be jammed, but on the fourth try he made a connection. After about ten rings, a strange voice answered in Japanese.

"Mr. Kim, please," Sharpe requested in Japanese.

"Sorry, he died in the earthquake," said the voice. "A falling tile from the roof hit him on the head as he went outside to look at the house, and he was killed almost instantly. You are Mr. Sharpe?"

They must know from the caller ID on the mobile phone, Sharpe thought. "Yes, I am."

"You and your friends are all right?"

"We are, thank you for asking. And you?"

"It's terrible here in Yokohama, but apart from Mr. Kim, we are all unhurt."

"I'm really sorry to hear about Mr. Kim. My sincere condolences to you all," Sharpe replied.

"Thank you. Good-bye."

Sharpe slumped into one of the chairs. "Kim's dead," he told the others.

"What?" said Meema, astonished.

"Died in the earthquake. That was one of his goons I was talking to. It seems he went outside to look at the house and got hit on the head by falling masonry."

"Dear God," said Vishal reverently. "He may have been a gangster, but I liked him."

"So did we all, Vishal," said Mieko.

"Had he given us his money to invest?" asked Meema.

"It was going to be today. He might well have started the transfer when the earthquake struck, but God alone knows what the Japanese bank computer systems are like when it comes to disaster recovery."

"Did he have anyone else who he was working with on this?"

"He never mentioned them if he did. I suppose he might have done, but he struck me as the sort of person who kept the details very much to himself. His daughter, maybe, and possibly his son-in-law, Katsuyama, but I think they weren't on very good terms."

"So unless we reinvest the money I made the other day, we're finished as M&M Trading?"

"You're not risking that money!" said Vishal firmly. "That's my sister's life."

"Only some of it is for your sister," Meema pointed out.

"We can always get investments from other people," Sharpe added. "We have the license to do it, after all. If we charge them a commission, then we'll make money off it, if that's really what you want to be doing with your life."

"Can we talk about something else?" said Mieko. "Like the toilet won't flush, and we're going to have to work out what to do about that. Let's face it, we're not going to be able to go back home for some time, and we're going to have to live here for a day or so. We have food, thanks to you, but we do have other needs, and you boys are going to have to fix them."

"Oh God," groaned Sharpe. "I wish that you'd let us know before we set off, and then we could have bought some large garbage bags or something."

Suddenly the lights came on, and Meema's computer hummed back to life. "That was faster than I expected," commented Vishal, but as he spoke, the lights went off again.

"Better unplug all the computer equipment if they're going to start playing silly buggers like that," suggested Sharpe. He and Vishal went through the office putting things straight, and unplugging all the IT equipment as they came to it. As they worked, they experienced a few minor tremors, but nothing like the powerful initial earthquakes or the immediate aftershocks.

"I wonder how the rest of the country's getting on," Sharpe remarked to Vishal. He turned on his phone's TV function and saw pictures of devastation in Yokohama. There were reports that the Landmark Tower there, Japan's tallest building, had partially collapsed, and that the world-famous statue of the Buddha in Kamakura a little to the south of Yokohama had toppled to the ground, but no pictures were shown to confirm either of these reports. There was, as Sharpe had expected, no news about the nuclear power plant that had given him so much cause for concern.

"Wonder what all this is going to do to the markets?" Vishal wondered aloud.

Funnily enough, Sharpe hadn't really thought about this angle to any extent up until this time.

"Everyone's going to be dumping JGBs," he guessed, referring to Japanese government bonds.

"So buy them," retorted Vishal. "They're not going to stay down for long and the market will be flooded with a new short-term low-interest issue which will push up the value of the long-terms. But I think the currency market's going to be crazy for a long time to come. People are going to be buying and selling yen like there's no tomorrow. I wonder what's going to be happening to the US dollar?"

"Why?" Vishal had a lurid imagination when it came to financial matters, but in many cases he was more accurate than the self-styled experts when his predictions were matched to the reality of events.

"Because the Japanese government will be starting to sell all their T-bills they've been buying to keep the American economy afloat up to now. They will be needing the ready cash for emergency relief and rebuilding. And once they start unloading, you can bet all your bottom dollars that the Chinese will be starting to do the same. You'll be able to buy US Treasury bonds for toilet paper."

"Why the hell aren't you an analyst or a trader, Vishal?" Sharpe asked. As far as he knew, Vishal had never used his financial analytical powers to make money for himself, or for his bank.

"Boring, man. Computers are being many times more interesting."

Wednesday, Tokyo

They slept the night on the floor of the office. It was cold but, as Sharpe pointed out to the others, at least they had a roof over their heads.

They were awakened at two in the morning by the lights coming on, and the air-conditioner roaring and clattering loudly. Sharpe got up and inspected the air-conditioner before turning it and the lights off. "Earthquake's damaged the air-conditioner," he remarked. "I don't want to run it until we have had a chance to look at it properly."

"I'm cold," complained Meema, who was wrapped in her coat, as well as Vishal's, who had gallantly given it up earlier that night.

"Sorry," said Sharpe. "But you can have my coat, if you like."

"Thank you," replied Meema, snuggling down in her pile of coats. Sharpe slept fitfully, huddled against Mieko for warmth, but still dreaming of penguins and Antarctic expeditions as the draught from the door seemed destined to hit him in the small of the back, no matter which way he turned in his sleep.

They all woke up to the repetitive clanging of the bell on the level crossing of the local railway line as dawn was breaking.

"Does that mean that the trains are running already?" asked Mieko wonderingly.

"Maybe it's just a repair train, rather than the regular service," said Sharpe. "But it's an encouraging noise, isn't it?"

"I want to go home," said Mieko.

"Don't we all?" replied Sharpe, wondering to himself what "home" really meant to them all: their parents, their home countries, or the place in Tokyo where they were living? For now, he'd be content with his Japanese flat being "home".

"I'm going out to see what's happening with the railway," said Vishal.

"I'll go with you," said Mieko.

As the two left, Meema rolled over in her nest of coats and turned to Sharpe.

"I want to look at what's going on in the markets. Please get the computer ready for me," she said.

"Well, there's a lot to do to get it all set up," replied Sharpe. "I'm not sure if I can manage it all. Vishal's the expert there."

"Oh, please," pleaded Meema. She got up on all fours and looked directly at Sharpe. Whether by accident or design, he found himself looking down the front of her loose-fitting top, with a perfect view of her smooth brown bra-less breasts, and discovered he was staring at them, fascinated.

She followed his gaze coolly, but made no attempt to cover herself up. "Please, Kenneth?" she importuned.

Sharpe turned away from the enticing view with mixed feelings. "All right," he grunted. "But don't forget that you're going to need an Internet connection as well as a Bloomberg and a Quick feed, and if they're not all working, you won't be able to do a thing."

He went round the computer equipment, reconnecting power cables, and setting up the links to the market data services as best he could.

"Looks like the Quick feed's down," he called to Meema, who was lying on her back again, pouting.

He tried to start up the Katsuyama program, but it told him what he had already guessed—the Quick feed was unavailable.

Just to make sure, he called the Quick support line. Somewhat to his surprise, it was answered on the third ring. It was no surprise to hear that there was no time and date scheduled for the resumption of service. As far as Quick were concerned, the Tokyo Stock Exchange had suspended trading indefinitely, and the bond markets were likewise in suspense. They confirmed that although foreign exchange trading was taking place outside Japan, they were unable to provide a feed for these markets "at the moment".

Sharpe reported this all back to Meema, who seemed to be sulking. "Well, if that's the way it is, I suppose," she said, crawling out of the pile of coats. "Pass me my bra over there on the chair," she said to Sharpe.

"Get it yourself," he nearly said, tired of her brattish attitude. However, he went over to the chair and picked up the flimsy undergarment. When he turned back, Meema was standing stark naked in the middle of the room, breasts and hips thrust deliberately and provocatively in his direction. He noticed that the cold had made her nipples stand out and that her otherwise perfect skin was covered in goose pimples. Even so, the overall effect was even more attractive than his fantasies had imagined, but he managed to turn his head away as he passed the bra to her. He'd decided some time ago that the money or the pregnancy or something he didn't know about had affected Meema for the worse, and though part of him (most noticeably, the part below his

Wednesday, Tokyo (first draft sections)

waist) urgently felt the desire to accept the unspoken invitation, common-sense told him to keep well away. He didn't want to replay the Vishal-Mieko thing in reverse.

"And my panties over there," demanded Meema.

"No way!" retorted Sharpe, more amused than angry. "Get yourself dressed and stop playing around like a fool." He began to realise the absurdity of the situation, and burst out laughing uncontrollably. Much to his discomfiture, Meema burst into a flood of tears. "Oh, for God's sake shut up!" exclaimed Sharpe, leaving the room and slamming the door behind him, suddenly furious with both Meema and himself.

[Part omitted–it dealt with a previous part of the plot which was cut from the final version.]

"**Anyway**," remembering, "**what did you and Mieko** find out about the trains?"

"Oh yes, of course. The private line is going to start running a limited service this morning. That will take us into Shinjuku, and it looks as though the JR lines will start again today as well. I think we're going to be able to go home today."

"I really think we should get away from here as soon as possible," said Sharpe. "I'm getting bad vibes about this place today."

"I didn't know you believed in that sort of thing," retorted Vishal.

"I don't, usually, but this is a bit different. Maybe the earthquake has affected more than one of us."

It turned out to be relatively easy to make their way back to their respective dwellings once the trains had started running again.

As Sharpe had feared, the flat was a mess. The floor was covered with books and ornaments that had leapt from their shelves, and the crockery cabinet displayed an archaeological mass of potsherds together with a few unbroken plates and bowls. It didn't seem as though the flat had suffered any serious structural damage, though, and, unlike the district in which the office building stood, the water seemed to be running in this part of Tokyo.

Sharpe switched on the television as the news was just starting. He caught the characters for "Hamaoka" in the subtitles, and called for Mieko to come and help translate.

"Oh my God," she said, listening to the news-reader. "You were right, Ken-chan. The earthquake badly damaged the atomic reactor at Hamaoka. It started leaking radiation really badly, they are saying. And then..." She listened a little more, "three workers took cement mixer trucks from a construction site nearby. And they used the cement to fill and seal the room where the radiation was leaking." More from the newscaster. "And now they are all dead from radiation. They died within an hour or so. No more danger for now from radiation, but a lot escaped in the first thirty minutes. We are being told not to go to that area, or to eat fish caught near there."

"Those guys were real heroes," said Sharpe. "We'll never know how many lives they saved."

"Hang on," said Mieko. "They're talking about Yokohama now. It looks like Yokohama got hit really badly." A picture of the Landmark Tower, the top jagged, and the bottom standing in a mass of rubble, flashed on the screen.

"Not good," said Sharpe. He saw the estimated death toll as a caption at the bottom of the screen. "Three hundred and sixty-seven dead in Yokohama alone. I'll be willing to bet that the final death toll's higher than that."

"And that's just Yokohama," said Mieko, wonderingly. "I wonder what happened in the Shizuoka area."

"I can't help remembering that Kim is one of those three hundred and sixty-seven in Yokohama," said Sharpe. "I really am sorry about him."

"Me too," said Mieko.

They sat in silence, absorbing the grim news from the TV. As Sharpe had predicted, all of the southern coastal routes linking Tokyo to the south-western parts of the country were blocked—all railways, including the bullet trains, the expressway and the ordinary roads. Landslips and tunnel cave-ins made it unlikely that they would be working again in the near future. However, Sharpe admitted to Mieko that it did seem as though the Japanese government was a little better organised than it had been at the time of the Kobe earthquake, and was definitely more inclined to accept offers of support from non-Japanese sources. The giant American aircraft carrier usually based at Yokosuka was moving to Yokohama, and was to be used as a combination of floating hospital and airstrip to allow emergency supplies to reach the stricken city easily. Other US Navy vessels and resources were being dispatched. A British cruise ship visiting Yokohama had immediately offered its facilities and was providing emergency shelter for those left homeless. Even China, with whom Japan had had several territorial disputes recently, was offering assistance. Significantly, maybe, there was no word from Pyongyang, although every other nation seemed to have sent messages of sympathy, or more practical forms of assistance.

"It's terrible," said Mieko.

"We were very lucky, I think," said Sharpe. "But this has been overdue for some time. I really don't know how they could have been so stupid as to build that atomic power station there."

The doorbell rang. "Who could that be?" asked Mieko. "Shall I get it?" She rose and went out into the hallway. Sharpe could hear her welcoming the unknown visitor, so presumably it was someone already known to her. Probably Mrs. Miyata from the neighbourhood association.

But no. Mieko was returning with the visitor, and she never invited the neighbours into the flat.

"Good evening," said the visitor as she entered the room.

Sharpe got to his feet. "Good evening, Mrs. Katsuyama," he replied. "We were very sorry indeed to hear of your father's death."

"Thank you," she replied. "I really couldn't believe that he had been so stupid. Usually he was very sensible and cautious." This time she was wearing jeans and a sweatshirt, presumably since they were more practical garments for the aftermath of an earthquake than formal mourning clothes, but they did nothing to disguise her looks, which Sharpe found just as stunning as before. "We're holding the wake tomorrow evening at this funeral home," passing over a card, "and the funeral the day after that."

"Thank you. We'll be there and I'll tell my colleagues who were working with him," replied Sharpe, accepting the card with both hands, and bowing slightly.

"I'm sure that he'll appreciate it."

"Please sit down," said Mieko. "Would you like anything to eat or drink?"

"Can you make tea?" she asked. "Please."

Mieko disappeared off into the kitchen to start the tea, and Tomiko Katsuyama turned to Sharpe.

"My father told me that he had taken you and your friends into his confidence about his plans. Yesterday morning, just before the earthquake, he transferred a large sum of money to your company for investment. I will want you to continue with the investment as if nothing had happened to my father. I will take over his work."

Sharpe was somewhat taken aback by the demand. "Do you really think the bank computers will be working? If you want my honest opinion, there's no way that any of the bank transactions yesterday are going to be properly recorded."

She looked at him in horror. "Do you think the money is lost, then? I mean, money can't just vanish like that, can it?"

"I'm afraid it can. At a time like this, with the bank systems in chaos, and large investors clamouring for their money, anything is possible. Japanese banks are not exactly renowned for wonderful customer service, after all."

She grudgingly admitted the fact.

"How much money are we talking about, anyway?" asked Sharpe.

"A lot." She named the equivalent of about two million dollars.

"Oh," said Sharpe, more than a little surprised. "That's a lot. I certainly wasn't expecting that much money at once. May I ask what proportion of his money that represents?"

"Almost all of it, except for the money invested in my husband's company, and a little bit he kept to live on. This is what he'd been saving for his life's work."

"You do have the proof that he paid it into the account, don't you?"

"Yes, I do. I have the receipt slip. It was in his pocket when they carried him inside after the tile hit him." She pulled out a handkerchief and started sniffing. At that moment, Mieko came back in with the tea. With a 'what have you done now?' look directed at Sharpe, who shrugged, she put down the tray and put her arm around Tomiko, attempting to comfort her. The sniffles subsided.

"Sorry," said Tomiko. "I'm going to miss him a lot. He was very good to me, despite everything."

And what was that last phrase meant to mean? Sharpe asked himself. Aloud, "Listen. You have the piece of paper, and we can go and check with his bank and my bank tomorrow if they're open. With such a large amount of money, I'm fairly certain that there will be some sort of pressure we can apply to them." She looked grateful for his suggestion.

The phone rang.

"Hello, there," came a familiar voice. "This is the British Embassy, checking on the welfare of its distinguished citizens."

"How the hell did you get my new number, Jon?" asked Sharpe angrily. "I changed it specifically so that I wouldn't get annoying phone calls from random members of Her Majesty's Government."

"From Consular," replied Jon smoothly. "You gave them your new mobile number as an emergency contact number and I managed to get myself on the team checking through the part of our list with the people whose names begin with S." Sharpe swore to himself. He'd done exactly that—the British Embassy requested British citizens to register with the Embassy for that very purpose and he hadn't considered the implications.

"So what do you want?" he snapped. "If you hadn't noticed, everyone in Tokyo is extremely busy at the moment clearing up. Or haven't you noticed inside the Embassy?"

"Oh we've noticed," replied Jon urbanely. "We have Second Secretaries flapping around the corridors with their heads up their arses wondering what is going on."

"Well do your bloody job and tell them what's going on, then," replied Sharpe.

"Temper, temper," admonished Jon. "Glad to see you're still your old cheerful self."

"Oh, piss off," said Sharpe, and hung up.

"Who was that?" asked Mieko.

"Someone I didn't want to talk to," said Sharpe briefly, and turned back to Tomiko. "Where can I meet you tomorrow? Where are you staying? Or more to the point, where's your father's bank?"

"We'll meet at Shinagawa station," she answered. "It's an easy walk from there. I'll see you at the north exit at half past ten." Leaving no room for discussion. She finished her tea and set the cup on the table. "Thank you," to Mieko, and got up. " Here's how to get hold of me," she said to Sharpe, passing him a name card with phone numbers and an e-mail address. Mieko and Sharpe escorted her to the front door where she put on her shoes and walked out without saying another word.

"Weird," said Sharpe, closing the door behind her. "Coming round like that. Was she alone, do you think? I didn't notice any of Kim's people waiting for her."

"There wasn't anyone with her that I could see when I opened the door. And I don't think it's that weird if there's a lot of money involved. It's natural to want to see your money back."

"I suppose so," said Sharpe. "It just seems rather strange, when all's said and done. I definitely get the feeling that she's hiding something. And she didn't even mention her husband, did you notice?"

"She had no reason to mention him," Mieko pointed out. "Like I told you before, she seemed very close to her father. I'm sure her thoughts are with him rather than her husband. Anyway, the earthquake seems to have sent everyone a little crazy. I don't think that anyone's thinking straight right now. Including you, dear," and kissed him on his forehead.

"I suppose you're right," he said. "Maybe I'm just seeing ghosts."

At the Sharpe End

"Don't say that," shivered Mieko. "Not when so many people have just died so suddenly."

"A figure of speech. It just means that I'm imagining things," explained Sharpe. "But you're right—it's a bad choice of words."

They turned back to the television. Despite many things appearing to be back to normal in the centre of Tokyo, it did seem that severe problems were continuing outside the capital and it would be a long time before the country as a whole would recover.

Wednesday, Tokyo (first draft sections)

Thursday, Tokyo

SHARPE ARRIVED AT THE APPOINTED PLACE in Shina-gawa station five minutes early, and was surprised to find Tomiko Katsuyama already waiting for him, dressed in funeral black. Without saying a word, she nodded briefly to him in recognition, turned on her heel and started walking, obviously expecting him to follow. Annoyed at being treated in this way, Sharpe followed.

After trailing her for about ten minutes through the streets, he arrived at a branch of one of the major Japanese banks. It was open, and the interior was a mass of customers milling around, trying to get to the cash machines and to the teller windows. People trying to ensure the safety of their money, thought Sharpe. Despite a widespread and tolerably efficient banking system, Japanese customers often preferred cash to banks. The amount of money locked up as cash in cupboards and hidden away in Japanese homes was probably larger than the value of retail customer bank accounts, he'd read once. He knew that when a friend's mother-in-law had died, a search of her papers revealed that she'd kept small amounts of savings in ten different bank accounts, and still had several million yen in cash hidden at the back of drawers and in the bottom of wardrobes, etc. It was small wonder that the crowds were attempting to get their money out of the banks, or at least make sure that it was safe.

At length, he and Tomiko found themselves at the head of the line. Tomiko produced her receipt, explained the situation, and asked if there were any records.

"Sorry to hear about your father," said the teller, shaking her head. "Our computer records are completely out of order, and there's no way that we can verify that transaction."

"Have you any idea when the computer system will be available again?" asked Sharpe.

"No, sorry," she replied.

"Can we see a manager, please?" asked Tomiko, rather curtly. "As you can see, this is a large sum of money, and we are naturally worried about where it is right now."

"All our managers are busy," explained the teller. "You may have to wait."

Sharpe was familiar with this Japanese tactic of declining a request. "Yes, we're prepared to wait," he added. "Just let someone who can make decisions know that there are two customers enquiring about a considerable sum of money that seems to have been lost by your bank's incompetence. About 230 million yen." Usually, Sharpe avoided direct confrontation with Japanese institutions as being counter-productive, but he had discovered in the past that a frosty angry attitude sometimes worked wonders in cases like this.

The teller scuttled off to the back of the bank.

"I really don't know why I bother using Japanese banks," sighed Sharpe. "Except that the past few times I've been back to the UK the situation's not been a lot better."

The teller returned, a little red in the face. "Sorry to have kept you waiting. The branch manager will see you now."

A smartly-dressed senior manager was approaching behind her, and waved Sharpe and Tomiko into a private office to the side of the main customer area where he exchanged business cards with them, and waved them into chairs, seating himself facing them across a table. Sharpe couldn't be sure, but he was reasonably certain that at least one button of Tomiko's top had come undone since they had entered the bank, leaving a tempting expanse of flesh visible. Her skirt was also hiked a little higher than was strictly necessary. He looked to see if the manager had noticed. He had.

"As our teller explained," the manager started, nervously, "our computer systems are unable to find any trace of this money."

"When do you expect them to be available again?" asked Sharpe.

"Well, that may be rather difficult. You see, our main computer centre was located in Yokohama, just in case the main earthquake struck Tokyo. It seems to have been rather a bad decision."

"And the backup system?"

"That was due to come on line in Osaka in a few months," he admitted, coughing, obviously more than a little embarrassed. He examined the transfer receipt slip that Tomiko passed to him. "Well, this certainly looks genuine," he admitted.

"What do you mean, it 'looks' genuine?" Tomiko replied angrily. "It *is* genuine!"

"Well, the time on this is approximately one hour and thirty-seven minutes before the earthquake struck," (Sharpe was quietly amused at the 'approximately') "and of course, the data on the central computers would not have been backed up in that time."

"So?"

"So it's perfectly possible that we cannot prove that the alleged transaction was ever recorded on the central computers, which would mean that we would not be bound to honour it."

Sharpe considered the meaning of these words, which seemed to indicate that the bank (or at least this manager) had already decided that the money was not going to be paid, and that the bank was going to walk away with about two million dollars of Kim's money, washing its hands of any responsibility.

"All right, let's assume that you can't prove that it went through the computers," pointed out Sharpe, "don't you have a paper copy of this receipt in your files?"

The manager looked slightly taken aback, as though he'd never considered an alternative to expensive high technology. "I suppose it's possible," he stammered. "Of course, we haven't had time to file and organise the papers we collected that day. I'm sure you can understand that we've been very busy since then." He smiled nervously.

"Then may I suggest that you collect all the papers that you dealt with that morning," Tomiko pointed out to him, "and get one of your staff to go through them?" suggested Tomiko.

"Yes, that's a good idea," agreed the manager nervously.

"Tell me," asked Sharpe curiously, "are we really the first people to have suggested this to you? Has everyone else in this position just accepted your explanation about the computers and just left your bank holding the money you collected from them and will never pass on?"

"Well," admitted the manager, "yes, that is the case. But then not many people were in your position. Most had bank books which showed that the money had left their account. In your case, the receipt shows it was a cash transaction." He picked up a telephone and summoned an underling to whom he issued the appropriate instructions. "Thank you for your patience," he said, turning and bowing to Tomiko and Sharpe. "We'll have an answer for you tomorrow morning."

"Oh no you won't," said Tomiko. "You'll have an answer for us within thirty minutes, starting now," looking significantly at her watch.

"But that's impossible," protested the manager.

"I doubt it," replied Tomiko. Sharpe admired her coolness. He'd hardly ever seen a Japanese customer standing up for her rights in this way. Usually he found Japanese to be very passive and willing to accept atrocious service from restaurants, stores, and banks, which was all too prevalent, despite the traditional Japanese reputation for excellent customer relations, and the proverb that "the customer is king". "I'd suggest," she added, "that if you don't have enough staff. that you start doing it yourself, personally. Otherwise I will recommend to my husband that his company's corporate account, which currently holds considerably more than the amount we're discussing right now, is moved to another bank. And I shall make sure that the reasons for moving the account are forwarded to your head office, together with your name. Twenty-nine minutes now," looking at her watch again.

"I'll get onto it right away," the manager stuttered. "Excuse me." He got to his feet and, bowing deeply, backed out of the office.

Tomiko turned to Sharpe. "I think that showed him that I was serious," she smiled.

"You scare me," replied Sharpe.

"Good," she replied. "I've got to get used to being in charge of my father's business, and that kind of thing needs someone tough at the top."

"You're going to take over his businesses?" asked Sharpe. "Is that usual? For a woman, I mean?" There was probably no doubt about her inheritance—amazingly, over 95% of

Thursday, Tokyo (first draft sections)

Japanese people don't make wills, as the law automatically disposes of the estates of those who die intestate to surviving relations, while exacting a price for this security in the form of steep inheritance taxes.

"I don't care if it's usual or not. I'm going to do it. Mind you, I'm not going to carry on with his illegal businesses—believe it or not, most of his money came from legitimate sources like truck delivery services and so on. He liked to play at being the big bad gangster, but that was partly an act. He did play rough, though, and it was a bad idea to cross him."

"I found that out for myself," said Sharpe, fingering his cheek. There was still a small scar left from where Kim had attacked him with the gun.

"Yes," continued Tomiko, "he could be a very violent man, and that's why Masashi went off to Hanoi."

"Oh?" said Sharpe. He had no time to receive an answer, as the bank manager, looking slightly chastened, knocked and bowed his way into the office.

"Very sorry," he said, bowing deeply, "but you were right after all. We did indeed have the copy of the transfer slip."

Sharpe decided to let the unspoken accusation pass, but Tomiko had other ideas. "What do you mean, 'you were right after all'?", she almost screamed at the hapless manager. "Did you mean you suspected us of lying all the time."

"Er, no. Nothing like that. I mean, we had to confirm," he mumbled. Sharpe decided it was time to let him off the hook a little.

"Never mind," he interjected. "The main point is that we have proof that the money was paid, in cash, to this bank, with instructions to transfer it to my company's account." Tomiko, although it appeared that she wanted to take matters further, nodded agreement. "So when," Sharpe went on, "can we expect to see this money in my company's account? Tomorrow?"

"I'll do my best to make it happen as soon as possible," the manager promised. "But you do understand that as soon as I start the transfer, it's out of my hands?"

"As long as you make everyone involved understand that this is urgent," Tomiko reminded him as she and Sharpe rose to leave.

"I won't forget," the manager assured them. More ostentatiously low bows as he escorted them out, echoed by the rest of the bank staff who were obviously taking their cues from him.

"So you'll let me know as soon as the money arrives in your account?" Tomiko asked Sharpe. "Here's my mobile number."

Thursday, Tokyo (first draft sections)

Other books from Hugh Ashton

SHERLOCK HOLMES TITLES
Tales from the Deed Box of John H. Watson M.D.
More from the Deed Box of John H. Watson M.D.
Secrets from the Deed Box of John H. Watson M.D.
The Darlington Substitution (novel)
Notes from the Dispatch-Box of John H. Watson M.D.
Further Notes from the Dispatch-Box of John H. Watson M.D.
The Death of Cardinal Tosca (novel)
The Last Notes from the Dispatch-Box of John H. Watson, M.D.
The Trepoff Murder (ebook only)
Without My Boswell
1894
Some Singular Cases of Mr. Sherlock Holmes
The Lichfield Murder
The Adventure of Vanaprastha (ebook only)

CHILDREN'S BOOKS (WITH ANDY BOERGER)
Sherlock Ferret and the Missing Necklace
Sherlock Ferret and The Multiplying Masterpieces
Sherlock Ferret and The Poisoned Pond
Sherlock Ferret and the Phantom Photographer
The Adventures of Sherlock Ferret

OTHER BOOKS
Tales of Old Japanese
Beneath Gray Skies
Red Wheels Turning
The Untime & The Untime Revisited
Angels Unawares
Leo's Luck

Full details of all of these and many more at :
https://HughAshtonBooks.com